UNDONE IN THE BILLIONAIRE'S CASTLE

LOUISE FULLER

CONTRACTED AND CLAIMED BY THE BOSS

CLARE CONNELLY

MILLS & BOON

First published in Great Britain 2024
by Mills & Boon, an imprint of HarperCollins*Publishers* Ltd,
1 London Bridge Street, London, SE1 9GF

www.harpercollins.co.uk

HarperCollins*Publishers*, Macken House, 39/40 Mayor Street Upper,
Dublin 1, D01 C9W8, Ireland

ISBN: 978-0-263-31999-6

03/24

This book contains FSC™ certified paper
and other controlled sources to ensure responsible forest management.

For more information visit www.harpercollins.co.uk/green.

Printed and Bound in the UK using 100% Renewable Electricity
at CPI Group (UK) Ltd, Croydon, CR0 4YY

UNDONE IN THE BILLIONAIRE'S CASTLE

LOUISE FULLER

MILLS & BOON

CHAPTER ONE

'I CAN'T BELIEVE you're actually here in England. In fact, I won't believe it until I see you.' Cassie's voice was high and shaky with excitement.

'Honestly, babe. You do not want to see me right now,' Joan said, yanking open the door of the hire car and tossing her suitcase onto the back seat. 'After eight hours on a plane, I am not looking my best.'

As she got in the car, she heard her friend laugh. 'I've seen you before and after weights sessions, remember? I know how bad you can look.'

That was true. She had met Cassie on the first day of term, when she had arrived in Florida from Bermuda as a nervous international student with too much luggage and an athletics scholarship. They were roommates first and best friends soon, and for the whole of that first year at university Cassie had put up with her alarm going off at five forty-five every Tuesday and Thursday, when nobody looked their best.

Cassie had seen her at her worst. Been there for her when all her hopes and dreams had turned to ashes. And it had been the cruellest timing to lose everything in the same week she had finally been shortlisted for a place on the Bermuda national squad. She'd also been approached with not one but two sponsorship deals that would have meant she could finally give something back to the family who had supported her so selflessly.

Maybe it might have been easier if she had consistently been posting slower times, but she'd had her best season ever, and had been placed first in every race that year. It was hard to accept that one infinitesimal error could change her whole life.

If it hadn't been for this woman talking to her now, she would never have finished her degree. Never have got out of bed or dressed at all.

But now was not the time to think about those long, joyless days.

'I know you do. But you also know how well I scrub up.'

Cassie laughed. 'Too well. I'm just glad Jonathan is so short-sighted.'

'Jonathan is completely crazy about you and you know it.'

'I know he is…' Cassie hesitated. 'I love him so much, Joanie. I never thought this would happen to me. That I'd find someone who could love me. Someone who actually wants me in their life.'

Joan felt her throat tighten. Cassie's parents had divorced when she was a child, and after remarrying her father had moved on with his new family. Left behind, her mother had struggled to cope, and Cassie had ended up being raised by her reluctant and disapproving grandparents.

'He's lucky to have found you, Cass,' Joan said truthfully. 'I am too.' Without her friend she would still be wallowing in misery and despair. 'You're the best friend anyone could have.'

Her fingers reached for the bracelet tucked beneath the cuff of her jumper.

'It's lapis lazuli. The stone of friendship and healing,' Cassie had said as she gave it to her.

It had been two months after the accident. Cassie had taken her away to Vegas for the weekend.

'And apparently it can help you confront and speak your truth. So I might need to borrow it next time my mum taps me for some money.'

She'd smiled weakly, as Cassie had hoped she would. Because it was her friend, not the bracelet, who had healing properties.

As for speaking the truth…

She knew Cassie suspected that she hadn't completely given up on a career in athletics. She also knew that her friend thought it was time for her to move on.

But Cassie didn't know about the surgery. Nobody did. She had only just found out about it herself, and there was no point in mentioning it because everyone would worry that she was clinging on to a future that didn't exist.

She would just have to keep it to herself until she heard back from the clinic. Then, when it was there in black and white, she would be able to get her life back on track.

Cassie's laugh down the phone snapped her back into real time.

'That's because I know what's best for you,' she said.

Even though she was busy adjusting the seat, Joan felt her ears prick up. There was a different note in her friend's voice. Teasing. A little guilty, but excited, like a child hiding something behind her back.

'What have you done, Cassidy Marshall? Please tell me you haven't set me up with someone at your wedding.'

'Actually, it wasn't me. It was Jonathan.'

'What?' Joan's chin jerked up in surprise. 'That is a big, fat lie.' Jonathan was an academic who rode a pushbike round his college campus. He was sweetly smitten with Cassie, but he was the last person she could imagine playing matchmaker.

Cassie sighed. 'Obviously he doesn't know he did it. This

is Jonathan we're talking about. But Ivo is his best man, and I know for a fact that he's single.'

Joan groaned. 'You're like a woman possessed. I am *not* hooking up with the best man at your wedding.'

'Well, I look forward to watching you eat your words—because he is a total hottie. Best man doesn't do him justice. Girl, he is *fine*. Honestly, if this wasn't my wedding, and I wasn't totally in love with my husband-to-be, I would be hunting him down with a net and a spear.'

'I don't want a hottie,' Joan protested, leaning forward to turn up the heater.

She knew Cassie meant well, but relationships required a level of reciprocity she didn't have right now. That was why, on her return to Bermuda after graduation, she had offered to help look after her sister Gia's children while she set up her business. Children, especially young ones like Ramon and Reggie, were like little animals. It was all about getting the basics right, and that she could manage.

But the thought of trying to form a relationship with an actual adult was beyond her. How could she? She had nothing to give in return. No hopes. No dreams. No future. She was basically a stand-in in somebody else's life.

But not for much longer.

'I know you want me to find my own Jonathan,' she said carefully. 'But I can't handle a relationship right now.'

'So don't,' Cassie said briskly. 'Just have fun. Flirt a little. Maybe have some mind-blowing meaningless sex with a stranger. Isn't that what's supposed to happen at weddings?'

'No. What's supposed to happen is the happy couple stand in front of everyone and exchange vows of undying love. Besides, casual sex at weddings is just an urban myth. Like losing your virginity at prom.'

Cassie laughed. 'I *did* lose my virginity at prom.'

Joan groaned. 'Wedding sex is just something that happens in the movies.'

'It's not, Joanie. Apparently, twenty percent of wedding guests hook up with one another.'

'Says who?' Joan protested. 'It's not like they hand out surveys afterwards.'

'You don't need a survey to know that weddings are basically as close to a frat party as you're going to get outside of college. Everyone's been drinking. They all have something in common. And they don't have to worry about driving home.'

Joan laughed. 'You make it sound so romantic.'

'Oh, so now you want romance?'

'No,' she said firmly. 'I want to hang out with my best friend for one whole evening and then I want to get up the next day and watch her marry the man she loves. What I don't want is some tweedy professor mate of Jonathan's.'

'Ivo Faulkner is *so* not tweedy and he's not a professor. He's the CEO of Raptor.'

'The tech company?'

Joan frowned. Raptor was a cool brand—the one that almost caused the internet to break whenever it released a new product.

'Which means,' Cassie continued, as if she hadn't spoken, 'that he's very rich as well as very handsome.'

'Are you suggesting that I charge him for my time?'

'You're funny… I'm just giving you some facts, so that when you meet him you'll know what you're dealing with.'

'Is that right?' Joan glanced in her rear-view mirror. 'So if he's so rich and hot, why is he still single?'

'For the same reason Jonathan was single. He hasn't met the right woman.'

'Well, I can tell you now I'm not her.'

Right now she wasn't ready to hook up with anyone—especially someone who would be immortalised in all Cassie's wedding photos.

'Babe, you are a woman with needs.'

'I know, but right now a man isn't one of them. Particularly some rich oddball.'

'He's not odd. He's just a bit of an acquired taste.'

Joan screwed up her face. 'You mean like oysters?'

'No. I just mean he's not like Algee or Jonathan. He's difficult to read and he has boundaries.'

Joan scowled. Her ex, Algee, had been transparent in wanting to date someone with the body of a track star. She just hadn't wanted to see it. Just as she hadn't wanted to admit that he'd been jealous of the time she'd spent hurdling.

'But he's Jonathan's best friend. And—get this—he's flying over for the wedding from New York on his *private jet*. He has a penthouse there. But you'll never guess what he also owns.'

'I'm not listening.'

'You are so stubborn.'

Joan felt her mouth twitch at the corners. Cassie was right. She *was* stubborn. Look at how she had kept on thinking she could hurdle even when she had lost her scholarship and it had become obvious she was never getting back on the team. But her stubbornness had paid off, hadn't it? If the surgery went well, she could be back training in less than a year.

'Does that mean you're going to stop meddling in my love-life?'

'What love-life? You haven't been on a date in, like, for *ever*.'

She meant since Algee. And dating someone who'd wanted to have his cake and eat it had done more than break her heart.

Trying to keep Algee sweet while sticking to her training schedule had pulled her in too many directions. The night before the accident he had engineered another one of those rows about love and loyalty. It had gone on and on, and she had got hardly any sleep, and her head had been all over the place the morning of the race.

She shook her head. 'I'm happy riding solo, okay? Promise me you won't say anything.'

'Fine—I promise. But I'm not giving up on you, Joan Santos.'

Catching sight of her reflection in the rear-view mirror, Joan shook her head. 'I'm hanging up now.'

The two-and-a-half-hour drive to reach Edale was going to be a bit of a challenge—particularly as she had only driven abroad a handful of times, each time in the States. On the plus side, it would be a chance to enjoy a playlist that wasn't nursery rhymes sung by chipmunks…

Two hours later, the worst of the journey was over.

And it had been worth it, she thought, gazing at the graceful green hills with their criss-crossing grey stone walls.

She had always wanted to come to England—well, London, really. Who didn't want to see the Houses of Parliament and Buckingham Palace and those guys in the red uniforms with the tall furry hats?

But Cassie's wedding was the real reason she was here in England.

And she was so looking forward to seeing her friend get married.

Cassie deserved to be loved and cherished, and being her best friend's maid of honour was one small thing to do by way of recompense for everything Cassie had done for her.

After she fell at the competition, everyone had been incredibly kind. Athletes were at the top of their game for such a short time, they said. And her experience of missing out would be a great help when she graduated as a sports psychologist.

Her Auntie Winnie had said that to her.

As if being forced to give up her dreams was a positive.

Joan gripped the steering wheel more tightly. She knew her aunt was trying to be supportive, but only Cassie had understood that being a sports psychologist was just supposed to be a back-up for when Joan could no longer compete as a hurdler professionally. Only Cassie hadn't pushed her to move on with her life, and that simple fact had made her final year at college bearable.

But then they had graduated, and she had gone back to Bermuda and her family, and Cassie had met Jonathan.

Joan fixed her eyes on the pale sun in the soft grey sky.

She could have got a job that made use of her degree, but even now, nearly eighteen months after the accident, she was too angry to do that. Too bitter. Too stubborn, like Cassie said. Her shoulders stiffened against the seat. It was easier to look after Ramon and Reggie than to try and explain to her family that she wasn't ready to put aside her dreams—not least because she knew how mad she would sound. Better to help Gia out. That way she could put her life on hold without drawing attention to what she was doing.

And she had been right not to give up.

The article on Dr Sara Webster and her pioneering tendon surgery on a heptathlete had been brief, but she had instantly known that it was what she had been waiting for all those months. She hadn't told anyone back home, but for now it was enough just to know that somewhere in Los Angeles Dr Webster would be reading through her medical notes. Well, maybe not today, but Monday for sure.

She glanced over at her phone, her forehead creased into a frown. The avatar car was hovering above the onscreen road as if it was debating which way to go.

She gritted her teeth. Why did she have to lose signal now, when there were literally no road signs? Jemima had warned her this might happen, and suggested getting a map, but she hadn't quite believed that anywhere in England would be really off grid.

Oh, thank goodness—it was back.

Pressing her foot down on the accelerator, she changed up a gear and thought back to her conversation with Jemima Friday, the woman whose cottage she was going to be living in for the next ten days.

They had only spoken once, but Jemima seemed nice—if a little nervous about letting a stranger into her home. Although at this rate she might not need to worry. According to the satnav, she was now further away than she had been five minutes ago.

There must be something nearby messing with the signal. Or maybe it was because she was at the bottom of this hill. Perhaps if she got to higher ground she would be able to see where she was and do the rest of the journey from memory, given that she was so close now.

Of course that would mean turning round. Only the road here was so narrow, and there was a low bank that she would have to negotiate as well.

Then again, she hadn't seen another car for at least fifteen minutes…

Spotting an opening into a field, she slowed down, reversed between the hedges, and then swung back onto the road. It would be tight, she thought. And, panicking slightly, she accelerated harder than she intended.

Which wouldn't have mattered at all if only another car hadn't appeared around the corner at exactly that moment.

Huge, black, as wide as the road, its headlights filled the grey air between them and for a few frozen seconds she simply watched, body stiff with panic and fear, as they swept towards her. And then she was pressing down on the brake pedal and tugging the steering wheel to the side sharply. The tyres slid across the road and she gave a small scream as the car mounted the bank with a soft shudder, the momentum of the back wheels pushing it up and over the grassy verge.

Breathing out shakily, she loosened her hands from around the wheel and switched off the engine. She wasn't hurt, just shocked. But her car was still nose-down in the ditch, as if it was trying to drink the water at the bottom.

Her heart was beating so loudly she could only just hear the heavy throb of the other's car's engine, but it was a near-miss not an accident, she told herself quickly, pulling up the handbrake. It had felt dramatic in the moment. But it had been nothing like tripping over that hurdle.

She felt her hamstring tense. The scar was six inches long, but the real damage was beneath her skin. Sometimes it was stiff and tight, and even after months of rehab and water therapy it still felt as if there was a thread beneath the skin that someone was pulling.

She reached down to rub her calf, her breathing harsh in the silence.

It had all happened in the time it took to lift her leg over the crossbar. One moment she was in the air, soaring, the next she was tangled in the hurdle and hitting the livid red asphalt. She had cleared hurdles of exactly the same height with a gap to spare, but that day she had been distracted and tired from Algee's meltdown the night before…

A rush of cold air filled the car as the door was abruptly yanked open. 'Are you hurt? Did you bang your head?' The voice was deep and male and urgent, but beneath its urgency she could hear a flicker of anger.

But he didn't have the right to be so angry. It wasn't his car that had been run off the road.

'I'm fine.'

'Are you sure?'

She glared up at him then. Or maybe she wasn't glaring, she thought a moment later. Maybe she was just staring. He was older than her—in his thirties, maybe—and some people might think he was good-looking, even beautiful, when… *if…*he smiled.

But he wasn't smiling now.

He was just standing there, his face expressionless, his eyes resting steadily on her face, and she couldn't remember anyone ever looking at her like that—so intently, almost fiercely.

Nor could she remember ever having this feeling of not being able to look away. But she couldn't because, yes, he was beautiful—undeniably so, with those blue, blue eyes and that curving mouth. If anything, his beauty was more shocking, more unexpected, here on this quiet, country road than the sudden appearance of his outsized car. And it wasn't just his eyes. He had high cheekbones, and in the soft winter light, he was all dangerous contours and dirty blond hair, lifting in the breeze like the grasses that edged the sand dunes back on Bermuda.

Her heartbeat was fluttering against her ribs like a trapped butterfly and, confused, almost affronted by her baffling and unsettling reaction to this stranger, she said crisply, 'I told you, I'm fine. I just need to get out of this ditch.'

He frowned. 'Ordinarily that would be my first thought too, but I'm not sure you'll be any more competent at returning to the road than you were at staying on it.'

What the—? Her gaze skimming the jacket that seemed moulded to his chest, she felt her jaw tighten. Just because he wore bespoke suits and drove a fancy car, it didn't mean he could tell her what she could and couldn't do!

'Then it's lucky I didn't ask for your opinion,' she said coolly, cutting him off mid-sentence.

His forehead furrowed, expression hardening. 'It's not an opinion. It's a fact.'

She glared at him. 'There are no facts—only interpretations.'

That mouth of his curved into something that could only be described as mocking. 'Do you have that on a fridge magnet? Or is it something you read on social media?'

'I don't think Nietzsche posts very often.' She gave him a small, cool smile. 'He's a philosopher, not an influencer.'

And that was all she knew about Nietzsche—and she only knew that because Cassie had dated some guy who was taking a philosophy class at the time.

'I know who Nietzsche is.' His eyes narrowed between ludicrously long lashes as he leaned into the wedge of space between her and the door. 'And, from memory, he wasn't an expert at vehicle recovery.'

'And you are? Then perhaps you'd like to help me.'

He treated her to something between a smile and a scowl, and she found herself torn between wanting to see him smile properly and slamming the door in his face.

'What I'd *like* is to be able to carry on with the rest of my journey. I have somewhere to be.' He twisted his arm, jerking back the sleeve of his suit to reveal an expensive-looking watch. 'Right about now.'

'Aren't you the perfect gentleman?' She gave him a disparaging glance. 'Well, don't let me stop you. It's not like I need your help,' she added as he started to interrupt. 'I don't need rescuing.'

That was a lie. Truthfully, she had no idea how you got cars out of ditches—but how hard could it be? And being here with this man was making her body prickle with a kind of panic and excitement that she didn't understand.

Probably it was just some kind of reaction to the accident. Adrenaline was a powerful hormone that did all kinds of crazy things to your brain and body. Look at how she used to feel before a race.

But she didn't have time to be sitting here ogling this stranger. Tonight was the night before the wedding, and she and Cassie were going to have a hen-do just for two, with face masks, rom coms and rum and raisin ice-cream.

Focusing on that thought, she pushed the gear stick into reverse. But before she had a chance to put her foot down on the accelerator pedal the man reached past her and pulled the key out of the ignition.

'What the hell do you think you're doing?' she demanded, turning to face him and instantly wishing she hadn't. He was too close. Too everything, she thought as he looked down at her, his hand wrapping over the top of the door as if it was his car, not hers, reducing her view of the world to his chest and shoulders.

'The ground isn't dry enough for you to get any traction.' His voice was cool and clear like spring rain. 'You'll just end up spinning the wheels, and if that happens you'll dig yourself in further. So, to answer your question, I'm stopping you from making a bad situation worse. You're welcome,' he added as she stared up at him in silence.

The scathing note in his voice scraped against her skin but it was easy to ignore. Unlike the way he was looking at her. Her throat tightened. With another man she might have been scared or annoyed, but she didn't feel either of those things. Instead, her body felt hot and taut and achy.

'Well, if you'd been looking where you were going we wouldn't be in this situation in the first place,' she snapped when she could speak again.

Yes, it had been a risky manoeuvre, but he was partly to blame for driving so fast, and she wasn't going to let him browbeat her into taking responsibility for his actions as well as hers.

'Are you seriously trying to imply that this was my fault?'

He spoke softly, but there was a hard undercurrent that made her feel lightheaded. 'Because I can assure you that the fault is entirely on your side. Unlike your car, which was on *my* side of the road.'

She stared up at him in outrage.

'What are you talking about? There are no *sides* on this road. Which is why you shouldn't be driving that tank down here. It's far too big, and you were going way too fast.'

Her heart started beating very fast too as his lip curled.

'*You* came round that corner like a bat out of hell!'

'Actually, I'd just reversed into that field down there—' she gestured over her shoulder '—and I was pulling back out onto the road so there's no way— What?'

He was staring at her incredulously. 'Are you seriously saying you couldn't have been speeding because you'd just done something even more dangerous?' There was a barely sheathed edge to his voice.

Now she officially hated him. 'It wasn't dangerous because there was nobody else on the road.'

The air around him seemed to tremble slightly. 'Apart from me. I was on the road.'

She felt as if she'd missed a step in the conversation and his cleverness enraged her. 'Look, my satnav stopped working and I realised I'd gone the wrong way.'

'So it's the satnav's fault you nearly ran me off the road?'

She glared at him. 'You ran *me* off the road. And it's your fault because you were going downhill, and vehicles going uphill have the right of way.'

Obviously she wasn't completely without blame, but he was being so belligerent and bloody-minded.

His eyes narrowed, two shards of sharp blue disbelief in a face made up of clean lines interspersed with blond stubble. 'I'm not going to be lectured by an American on how to drive my car in England.'

'I'm not an American. I'm from Bermuda.'

He stared down at her, his forehead creasing into two vertical lines above his straight nose, as if the idea of such a thing was just too random to be believed.

'You need to put your hazard lights on,' he said at last. 'And you'll need help getting out of that ditch. Professional help,' he continued when she didn't react. 'You do have breakdown cover, don't you?'

She had looked into getting it. But she would have had to pay an additional charge. An expensive additional charge for what had felt like an unnecessary extra cost when she had filled out the car rental agreement.

Now, though, she wished she had just paid the extra. Except she wasn't paying. Not for any of it. Her sisters had given her the money for her flight and her bridesmaid's dress. She couldn't have asked them to pay for anything else.

'Actually, I don't,' she said quickly.

The man's silence was accompanied by the barest flicker of an eye-roll that made her want to get her suitcase from the car and beat him to death with it. Instead, she glowered at him, and tried to stop her limbs from shaking. Now that the sun was edging downwards there was a definite chill in the air, and all the heat from the car seemed to have evaporated.

'You're a long way from home, Ms…' The man let the silence fill the space between them as he waited for her to provide her name.

'Santos,' she said finally, reluctantly, as she flicked on the hazard lights.

She didn't ask for his name. There was no need. In fact, she needed *not* to know his name. Knowing his name might allow him to linger in her head for longer than he should. She was shocked that that was even a thing, and yet it was—undeniably, incomprehensibly. She could feel her body growing tenser and achier by the second…as if he was a virus, a fever in her blood.

'And I'm not that far from my holiday let,' she added.

'Before I lost the satnav it was saying I was only about five minutes away.'

'You're on holiday here?'

There was a note of surprise in his voice, but then she was a long way from Bermuda, and most tourists went to England to see London, not some tiny village in the Peak District.

'I'm visiting a friend. I flew in this morning.'

She held his gaze and her breath as his eyes bored into hers.

'Then perhaps you could call him to help you.'

There was nothing in his voice to explain the sudden prickling across her skin, but she felt it all the same and momentarily she wished she actually had a boyfriend to throw back in his face.

'I can't. She's busy.'

Not just busy. Cassie was getting married in less than twenty-four hours. There was no way she was going to drag her all the way out here.

'I see,' he said, still not taking her eyes off her face.

Now he straightened up, and as he did so she abandoned the idea that it was his nearness making her feel so unlike herself. Even with more space between them, his penetrating blue gaze made every single nerve inside her quiver almost painfully.

'That's unfortunate. Because your car isn't going to get out of that ditch by itself.'

Without warning, he turned and walked back towards his car. She stared after him and then, yanking off her seatbelt, she got out of the car and stalked after him. Her pulse was jerking in her throat with shock and disbelief, and something else that she couldn't quite put her finger on. But it made her feel naked and exposed and hot and hungry all at the same time. And it was so unwelcome and overwhelming that something snapped inside her.

'Is that it? Are you just going to drive off and leave me here?' she demanded, focusing her panic and anger on his broad back.

He spun round then, and there was a tense, electric moment as his gaze narrowed in on her face.

'It's tempting, but no,' he said softly, staring down at her, that mouth of his curling slightly at the corners. 'I'm not going to do that, Ms Santos.' He pointed his key fob at the rear of the huge black car that was hunkering in the middle of the road. 'I was getting these.' As the boot swung open he reached inside and pulled out two reflective triangles. 'Cars coming up the hill will see the hazard lights, but anyone coming round that bend won't spot them until it's too late.'

That made sense. Unlike the singed feeling inside her, she thought, watching him turn and stride away. *He* was causing it. This stranger was making her feel like this. She knew that. She just didn't know how or why.

She scowled at his departing back and then turned back towards her car to check for damage. Aside from being liberally spattered with mud, there didn't seem to be any, which was a relief. Turning, she saw that he was coming back down the road and that he was talking to someone on the phone. As he stopped in front of her, he hung up.

'Right, I've arranged for someone to come and sort this out.'

So he was helping her. She frowned, caught off guard, and a little embarrassed at having misjudged him. But, really, what was there to judge? He gave so little away, and what he did reveal was hard to read. Like now. His voice was cool and dispassionate, but the blue of his gaze seemed to slide right through her.

'You didn't have to do that. It was kind of you…thank you.' Still frowning, she fumbled in her jacket pocket. 'How much is the call-out charge? I have some cash, or I can send you the money.'

'I don't need your money and there is no call-out charge. It's just someone from the farm.' He gestured vaguely towards the khaki-coloured fields. 'His name's Paul, and he's bringing his son Ben to help him. They're going to tow the car out with their tractor and drop it back to you later tonight. I'll leave the keys for them on the front tyre. As for you…'

He paused, and she blinked as his blue gaze hovered on her face.

'I can give you a lift.'

CHAPTER TWO

A TENTATIVE RAIN had started to fall, and the light was changing colour.

Glancing up at the darkening sky, Ivo turned and trudged over to her car and decanted the luggage from the back seat. He couldn't quite believe that he had just offered to give her a lift, but then again, he could hardly leave her on her own out here. It would be dark soon, and he had no idea how long it would be before Paul turned up.

And, in reality, it would be a small diversion. He would still have time to get home and change and then get to the pub.

Tucking the bags under his arms, he swung round to find the woman still standing there.

'Chop-chop,' he said curtly, as if she was a child dawdling on her way to school. 'You're not the only one with plans for tonight. Ms Santos.'

To emphasise his point, he clicked his fingers, and he could sense from the way her eyes narrowed that it was on the tip of her tongue to tell him that she would wait with her car.

Finally, she moved, stalking past him like an angry little cat.

He stared after her, his teeth on edge. At the best of times he had no patience for theatrics of any kind, and this was not the best of times. He was tired, and tense. Unsurprisingly. The Clean Green Battery deal flatlining like that had been a shock, and then he'd read that email from Steve Farmer about his brother Caleb's transfer…

At first he'd thought there was turbulence on the flight, but then he'd realised that it was inside him. He was making the walls of the cabin shake. And he'd just sat there, clutching the armrests, while everything shuddered and broke apart around him.

But he would think about that later. Now, he just needed to get this stroppy, stubborn woman out of his life and out of his car.

Dumping her bags in the boot, he made his way round to the driver's side.

'Where are you trying to get to?' he asked, dropping into the seat beside her.

'Snowdrop Cottage. It's on Burnt Oak Lane—'

He cut her off. 'I think I drove past it.' Leaning forward, he pressed a button and the car purred into life.

It took just under five minutes to reach their destination, and he spent most of those minutes wondering why he had this sense of déjà vu… this feeling of having already met the woman in his car. He hadn't, but he couldn't shift the feeling that he knew her.

'I'll see you in,' he said as he pulled up alongside Snowdrop Cottage.

He half expected her to argue, but she just nodded and he realised that she probably wasn't even listening to him. She was too busy staring at the cottage.

It was a pretty little house. Too small for him. But he could see why she was so taken. It was perfectly proportioned and neat-looking, with its newly painted front door and small, square windows.

'Do you have a key?'

She nodded. 'It's under the flowerpot. The white one.'

He unlocked the door, stepping back automatically to let

her pass, and then wished he hadn't. It was an oddly intimate action. Almost as if they were a couple on holiday together.

'Oh…'

He heard her soft intake of breath and his eyes flicked to her face, but she was already moving through the little house, her eyes bright with excitement and pleasure.

It was as small as it looked from the outside. Smaller, because of all the furniture. But it had a nice feel to it, he thought. Shabby, but clean and loved. Some of his foster homes had felt like this. Not where he'd lived with his mother and brothers. But then you couldn't call a flat with boarded-up windows a home.

As she disappeared upstairs, he frowned. It seemed churlish just to dump her luggage and leave, so after a moment he followed her. The bedroom was tiny too, and the bed took up most of the space, so he put the bags down in the doorway. Ms Santos was standing with her back to him, gazing out of the window, humming softly.

His pulse twitched as he took a step closer. Her view was pretty special, but his was better.

She had taken off her coat, and without it he could see that she was slim. But there was also a hint of muscle in those long, endless legs and the sculpted curves of her bottom.

What the—?

He winced as she took a step backwards and trod on his foot. She spun round, too fast—so fast that she lost her balance. Her eyes widened with panic, her mouth opening into an O of shock as she tipped sideways, and then she was grabbing for him.

He caught her elbow, steadying her, and he felt the ripple of his reflexes move through her body, and with it a heat that seemed to melt everything in its path so that it felt as though his legs might give way.

And she felt it too; he could see it by the way his eyes

locked onto hers. Feel it in the sudden tightening of her fingers around her arm.

He felt his throat tighten. For a second the room blurred. He could feel the blood pulsing in her body, and he had a sudden crazy urge to pull her close and kiss her until she lost her balance again.

'Sorry,' she said quickly. 'I didn't hear you come upstairs.'

'No problem,' he said, shifting his gaze past her shoulder. He let go of her arm. 'Do you want it on the bed?'

Her pupils flared. 'What?'

He held up the suitcase. 'The floor? The bed?'

She pressed her lips together as if she was trying to stop herself saying something she'd regret. 'On the bed's fine,' she said finally.

He put the case on top of the quilt.

'Thank you.'

For a second they both stared at each other.

'Enjoy your trip,' he said abruptly.

And then, before she could respond, he turned and walked swiftly out of the room and down the stairs. He shut the door behind him and stared across the empty landscape, surprised to see that it was still there. That it hadn't been swept aside, swallowed up by that flash of white heat.

He ran a hand over his face and forced his legs to move. The cool rain made his head clear a little. It was probably exhaustion and stress. He glanced up at the window but there was nobody there. Feeling both relieved and inexplicably bereft at the same time, he yanked open the car door. Before he'd even slammed it shut, he had started up the engine and begun to drive.

'Just tell me the truth.' Cassie gripped Joan by the arm, her grey eyes wide with panic. 'Do you think my dress is too much?'

Taking both her friend's hands, Joan shook her head slowly. 'It's not too much. It's beautiful, and you're beautiful.'

It was more than the dress. Cassie's skin was glowing, like someone who'd just woken from a restful dream.

Joan felt her stomach flip over. She'd had dreams too, but they hadn't been restful. Over and over she'd dreamt that she was warming up by the track when she'd heard the starter pistol go. Only instead of running she'd taken a step backwards and collided with someone. Even before she spun round, she knew it was the man from the car accident, and just like at the cottage he had reached out and grabbed her arm. Only instead of helping her regain her balance he pulled her closer and kissed her until her head was spinning and she was falling into the deep, endless blue of his eyes…

Blanking her mind, she cleared her throat. 'Honestly, Cass, you look like a princess.'

Cassie glanced down at her cream satin dress, her lips trembling. 'Really? I'm scared that when the vicar asks if anyone knows if there's any lawful impediment to the marriage someone's going to stand up and say that they do. That I'm not good enough. And they'd be right, wouldn't they? Otherwise my parents would be here.'

Joan felt her throat constrict. Her own mother and father had been at the heart of both her sisters' weddings. But Cassie's mum was drying out in some clinic and her father hadn't even bothered replying to the invitation. She had never met either of them, but right now she hated them both.

Outside, through the window, she could see the wedding cars sitting in the driveway. Jonathan's father, Simon, was standing next to a gleaming vintage Rolls Royce, his kind face rapt with excitement as he chatted to the driver.

She took a breath. 'They're not good people, Cass. But you are and Jonathan is. And he chose you, and he loves you. His parents love you too, and so do I. And you really do look beautiful.'

Cassie squeezed her hands. 'I'm so glad you could be here.'

Joan smiled. 'Where else would I be?'

She felt a sharp nibble of guilt, and briefly she allowed herself to remember that moment at the airport back in Bermuda, when she had almost bottled it. She had wanted to be there for her best friend, but the thought of having to face all those people from university had sent her scurrying to the restroom.

Seeing how everyone was getting on with their lives would be hard—particularly as she didn't want to jinx anything by talking about her plans. But she had to remember that her life was just stalled, and that with Dr Webster's help it would soon be back on track.

She glanced back out of the window at the waiting cars. Jonathan's mother, Diana, was holding hands with her granddaughters, Olivia and Jasmine, who were Cassie's flower girls. Cassie hadn't wanted a dress rehearsal, because she thought repeating the words of the ceremony then would detract from the actual day, but Joan had met the two little girls over video calls, and then in person yesterday, and they were a handful. Jasmine was already tipping petals out of her basket.

'I need to go, babe.' Pulling her friend close, she hugged her. 'Oh, I just remembered. I got you this.' She held out a tiny blue velvet bag.

'Oh, Joanie…' Cassie held up the gold bracelet with its tiny blue heart charm. 'Now we match.'

Joan felt her throat tighten. 'It's your something blue—no, don't hug me again, otherwise I'm going to start crying. And don't you start crying either!'

It took them ten minutes to reach the little church. Like all the other buildings in the village where Jonathan's parents lived, it was made of some kind of grey stone and its walls shone silver-bright in the sunshine.

Joan led the flower girls up the path to the entrance of the church, and as they stepped beneath the arch of pale pink and cream roses the organ began to play. Inside, Joan forced herself to walk slowly up the aisle. She liked her dress, although she rarely wore dresses that fitted her body so snugly. But to someone who lived in trainers and flip-flops her heeled court shoes seemed perilously high, and by the end of the night she knew she would be lucky if she wasn't limping.

The thought made her feel panicky and conspicuous, but she had learned to hide it when her leg hurt, and truthfully everyone was probably looking at the little girls in their pretty pale pink dresses and matching ballet slippers.

Only there were a lot more people than she'd expected. So many that she couldn't take in all the faces…

Her feet stuttered against the tiled floor. Not all of them, no. Just one in particular. She could feel her legs moving automatically, but inside her head she was back in the cottage in that moment of shared pulse and possibility.

The vicar nodded as she came to a stop in front of him, and Jonathan gave her a quick, strained smile, but she barely noticed either of them. She was too busy looking at the man standing next to the groom.

It was the man whose car she had nearly hit yesterday.

Her heart skipped a beat.

It was the stranger who had sneaked into her dreams last night to grip her arm. Only not to stop her from falling, but to anchor her to his body as she moved against him.

She glanced at his buttonhole.

Except he wasn't a stranger. He was Ivo Faulkner. Jonathan's best man.

Heart still pounding, she thought back to her dream. It had felt so real…almost as if he was there in bed with her.

And now he was here in the church.

Suddenly she had to grip her bouquet to stop her hands from trembling. She felt aware of everything and nothing at the same time. The polished wood of the pews. The jewel-coloured stained-glass windows. The upturned faces, all smiles and goodwill.

And Ivo. Tall, unsmiling, wearing another of those expensive dark suits that looked as if it had been crafted with the sole purpose of making every other man look ordinary.

Not that he needed a suit to do that, she thought dazedly. Beneath that polished exterior there was something raw about him…something devastatingly male that commanded attention.

Slowly, reluctantly, she lifted her chin and met his gaze—and instantly wished she hadn't as his blue eyes locked with hers and she felt a tingling kind of shock, as if she'd hit her funny bone. Only she didn't feel like laughing.

If Ivo was as shocked as her, he didn't show it. But even on this, only their second meeting, she understood that showing emotions was not his thing.

For a moment she didn't think she would ever breathe normally again. However self-conscious she felt walking up the aisle, it was nothing compared to this feeling of being skewered. Music swelled around them and the congregation got to their feet. Jerking her gaze away, she saw with relief that Cassie was starting to walk down the aisle with Simon.

But her relief was short-lived.

As maid of honour, she had to stand opposite Ivo until he had handed Jonathan the rings, and although it probably only lasted for five or six minutes at most, it felt like a lifetime. They were sitting in different pews, but she couldn't seem to stop her eyes from darting over to where Ivo was sitting. Other times his eyes flickered towards hers, and at least twice the line of her gaze connected with his. On each occasion she felt like a fish caught on a hook, plucked from the safety of her stream into the air, breathless and twitching.

Finally the ceremony was over, and the moment had come to walk back up the aisle. Only this time, to her horror, she had to walk with *him*.

'Small world.'

Her head jerked sideways. Ivo Faulkner was staring down at her, his face expressionless, the blue of his eyes steady on her face, that mouth of his in a curl of disapproval.

'So Cassidy is your friend. The one you're visiting.'

'Yes.'

She nodded unnecessarily. He was stating a fact, not asking a question. But there was something about this man that made her say and do and feel unnecessary things.

'She told me that you were at university together in America,' he said, almost accusingly.

'We were. I had—' Her fingers tightened around the bouquet. 'I had to leave Bermuda to do the degree I wanted.'

It was the most neutral response she could think of, but she didn't feel neutral. She felt off balance. And she couldn't tell if it was because he was here at the wedding…because his arm kept brushing against hers in a way that felt like a caress even though she knew it was entirely accidental.

Heart pounding, she tried to remember what Cassie had said about Ivo, but she had been so busy trying to deflect her friend's matchmaking efforts that nothing had sunk in. Except that he was very rich and very handsome.

The skin across her cheeks felt suddenly hot and, hoping that penetrating blue gaze wouldn't allow him to read minds, she said stiffly, 'I thought you were American. Cassie said you were flying in from New York. But you're English.'

'Originally, yes.' His answer sounded as if it had been dragged out of him by wild horses.

'So, did you meet Jonathan at university?'

'No. School.'

And they'd been friends since then? But why?

She glanced ahead to where Jonathan was gazing at Cassie in unfiltered adoration. Jonathan was so good-natured and eager to please. Unlike the man striding beside her. But then men were strange. Both her brothers-in-law had mates who were utterly objectionable, and if you asked them why they were still friends they said bafflingly irrelevant things like, 'Oh, we used to play cricket when we were kids.'

Without thinking, she said, 'Did you play cricket together?'

A slight crease of confusion appeared in the centre of his forehead—unsurprisingly, given that her remark was a total non sequitur—but as he opened his mouth to reply Jasmine, the younger of the flower girls, dropped her basket.

'Sorry…'

Trying to avoid the now crouching child, she made the mistake of sidestepping at the exact movement Ivo did, and for the second time in less than twenty-four hours, she trod on his foot.

He winced as the stiletto heel impaled his shoe. 'Do you ever look where you're going?'

His eyes locked with hers and she felt the jolt of blue like an electric current.

She glowered at him. 'You walked into *me*.'

'And yet it's my foot you're treading on.'

Reaching down, he scooped up the little girl and her basket in a flurry of petals, and then turned to face Joan.

'We'll let you go ahead. Give you more room. Perhaps then you'll manage to get out of the church without causing bodily harm to anyone else.'

'Fine by me,' she muttered under her breath.

But maybe he heard her anyway, because she felt his gaze roll through her as she stalked past him and out of the church.

Outside in the sunshine there was just time to give Cassie

and Jonathan a congratulatory kiss each, and then the photographer began chivvying everyone into position. Thankfully, she wasn't required to stand next to Ivo in any of the shots, but she could sense his presence the whole time…like the princess rubbing up against the pea beneath her pile of mattresses.

'I'm bored.' Jasmine was tugging at her hand. She gave her empty basket an experimental swing, as if she was planning on hurling it at the wedding party. 'And I'm hungry.'

Sensing trouble not that far ahead, Joan led the little girls away from the chattering guests. It was quiet in the churchyard, and the children seemed to quieten too. As they wandered around, picking dandelions, Joan sent some photos to her mum and her sisters, but she was still too unnerved by Ivo's appearance at the church to add more than the most basic of messages.

'Is that the Angel Gabriel?' Olivia asked, pointing at a stone statue on a plinth.

The three of them gazed up at the winged figure.

'I think it's just an angel,' Joan said softly.

Standing on tiptoe, Olivia touched the hem of the angel's robe. 'She's beautiful.'

'I want to touch her.' Joan felt Jasmine pulling at her hand again. 'Lift me up.' She clutched at Joan's dress now, yanking hard, her little face screwed up with the injustice of being too small. 'I want to touch her!'

'And you shall—but not if you scream and shout.'

The deep, male voice made her chin jerk up, and she felt her heart judder sideways like a needle on a scratched record as Ivo peeled Jasmine's hands away from her dress and then lifted the little girl into the air.

'And angels are male, not female,' he added, his face softening as she grabbed the angel's lichen-flecked wing triumphantly.

In the sunlight, his fine gold hair lifted across his forehead, and she watched, mesmerised, as he pushed it aside with a frown. It would be soft to touch, silken…

Fingers twitching, she blinked away that possibility. 'Is that true?'

'I believe so. Although there's also a school of opinion that says they're genderless. But I thought that might throw up some questions I don't feel authorised to answer,' he added, his eyes flickering towards the two little girls' rapt faces.

Remembering his autocratic manner out on that quiet lane, Joan raised an eyebrow. 'And there was me thinking you had the answer to everything.'

She felt his gaze like a lick of flame, and instantly there was that same, strange pull of attraction as before that made it impossible for her to look away.

'I may have been a little officious yesterday.'

It was more of an admission than an apology, but she was still surprised.

'And you came all the way out here to tell me that?'

His mouth curved into an almost-smile that danced along her limbs and made her skin feel too hot and tight for her bones.

'Actually, no. They wanted me to tell you the cars are waiting. Do you want a piggyback?'

'What?' She stared up at him, her eyes resting on his face in confusion.

'I was talking to Jasmine,' he said mildly, but there was a dark gleam in blue eyes that made her breath catch. 'Then again, it might be sensible to carry you. After all, you do seem rather accident-prone.'

She flinched inwardly. She had never been clumsy before the accident, but those few seconds when she had nicked the hurdle with her foot had changed everything. It was as if her body had lost confidence. And consequently she had lost confidence in herself.

She shouldn't have worn heels. Her leg was aching now, and she was terrified that she might inadvertently start limping in front of this perfect man.

'I can walk, thank you. Come on, Livvy,' she said stiffly.

And, taking the older girl's hand, she walked as swiftly as her heels would allow back down the path to where Diana was waiting for them.

Shifting back against his seat, Ivo switched on the engine and felt the big car rumble awake. As he accelerated forward, his eyes flicked to the rear-view mirror, just as Joan walked past the church, and he wondered why she had tensed up like that.

Not that he cared. He just wasn't used to women backing off like that.

As if she had heard his thoughts, Joan turned then, her chin lifting, and even though he could hardly see her features in the small rectangle of mirror he had a sudden, utterly irrational impulse to stop and get out and—

And what?

Nosing past the line of parked cars, he felt his chest tighten. He didn't know. But it was exactly the same feeling he'd had as he drove away from Snowdrop Cottage. He'd wanted to stop and reverse back down the road and finish—

Finish what?

Nothing had even got started in that tiny bedroom.

But what if he had stayed? What would have happened then?

The question—or more correctly the possible answers to it—made the road in front of him shudder.

Seeing her walk into the church, he'd felt as if he was drunk. When Cassie had told him that her friend Joan was going to be her maid of honour, he'd expected another version of Cassie.

Got that wrong.

Cassie was a curvy, glossy blonde, whereas Joan had a mass of dark curls and eyes that managed to be both curious and wary at once.

Thinking back to the moment last night when she had walked into the cottage, he felt his pulse jerk. She had made that soft breathy sound of surprise and her eyes had been flame-bright with an excitement that made his stomach flip almost as if he could feel what she was feeling.

Or maybe it had just been the fortifying anger from earlier out on the road draining away, leaving him disorientated.

Either way, it should have been a red flag. He should have waited in the living room. But instead he'd taken her luggage upstairs and she had stepped back onto his foot and lost her balance.

She wasn't the only one, he thought, flexing his fingers around the memory of her wrist, remembering how her pulsing heartbeat had made his own heart beat faster.

His jaw stiffened. That his heart had been affected at all was a shock. Up until that point he'd assumed it was deficient in some way. Sure, there were women in his life, and in his bed—after all, sex was a primal urge—but none had made his heart race in such a way before.

The opposite, in fact. He'd turned one-night stands into an art form.

In part that was a conscious choice. Loving, caring, needing someone—that made you vulnerable. And he never wanted to feel that kind of dependency again. And it hadn't been a hard choice to make—probably because hardening his heart had stopped him feeling anything beyond the most basic of human responses.

But this thing with Joan wasn't about love or anything close to it.

Okay, she had got under his skin, but he had been reeling from the shock of almost hitting her car. Because, despite his claims to the contrary, the accident had been as much his fault as hers.

His mind had not been on the road. Instead he was replaying that meeting in New York with the board of Clean Green Battery—or rather the moment when their CEO, Andy White, had told him that they were not interested in his more than generous offer for their business. Not interested in being swallowed up by a behemoth like Raptor.

'CGB is a family business. Two of my cousins work for me. My brother and I built our first prototype in his garage.'

'But you're not working in his garage now, are you?' he'd asked. *'You had to move on to develop the business. That's what I'm offering. A chance to move to the next level. To take your designs global. To make them matter.'*

Andy White had shaken his head. *'I've no doubt if we took this deal that's exactly what would happen—because you're a phenomenal businessman, Ivo. But this is personal to us.' He'd pressed his hand flat against his chest. 'And there's no heart to your business. For you, it's just profit.'*

He frowned at his reflection in the rear-view mirror. What else was there?

He'd been disappointed. More than disappointed. He'd felt desolate. It was the first time he'd ever been rejected in business since those early days. He'd started Raptor at university, with two other guys from his course. Alex and Dan's parents had loaned them some money, but Ivo had worked three jobs one summer to pay them back and buy out Alex and Dan. He'd needed to be in control.

After that, things had spiralled. There were setbacks, of course, but nothing so absolute as this in a long time, and the feeling of powerlessness had caught him off guard. That and Andy's use of the F-word.

Family.

Even just thinking it made him want to put his foot down on the accelerator pedal and drive until the ache in his chest was a distant memory. He understood the concept and, thanks to Jonathan, he had experienced at least some of the benefits. Holidays. Trips to London. Christmas dinners and presents under a tree.

But the truth was he had no family of his own. And he'd done just fine without one. Not that he'd had any choice. His father was a blank space on his birth certificate. His mum had stayed around, but had always been either high or coming down from drugs. Ditto her boyfriends—but with fists. As for his brothers… Marcus was dead, killed by an IED in Afghanistan, and Caleb—

His spine stiffened. The last time he had seen or spoken to his brother was twenty-four years ago, when he had been nearly thirteen and Caleb sixteen. It was his third offence for stealing cars, and the judge had wanted to teach him a lesson.

Those six months in custody had been the start of life in and out of young offenders' institutions and then prison. After that first time Caleb had called him and tried to explain, but he had hung up. Later, his brother had written to him, but he'd never replied. He couldn't. He had been too angry and scared. Of what he might feel. What he might say.

Later there had been a gap: the lost years between leaving the children's home and when he had bought his first property.

Then, and only then, had he felt strong enough…emotionally detached enough…to approach the prison service. He hadn't wanted to get in touch with Caleb. That hadn't changed. Caleb had lied to him. Had told him he would always be there. But he'd left him alone and he couldn't bring himself to forgive Caleb for that. Because his brother knew what it had felt like when Marcus had died and their mother left.

But he'd always needed to know that his brother was okay. That he was alive. Safe.

These days he had people to find out that information for him, and he got updates every three months. Steve Farmer was efficient, reliable, and most important of all discreet, and usually his calm, measured voice down the phone acted as a buffer against the emotional impact of hearing news about his brother.

Usually.

Yesterday morning, Steve's call had sent him spinning into the darkness of space.

But then he had lived in the States for so long now. In New York, Caleb was a painful but distant memory, and even after he bought Castle Alwyn as a UK base, to accompany the acquisition of office space in London, his brother had been at the other end of the country, separated by hundreds of miles of land. Now, though, he was less than an hour away. A guest of HMP Lockwood, along with two hundred and fifty-three other Category C prisoners.

He was gripping the steering wheel so hard now that his knuckles were white.

The shock of knowing that his brother was so close had made something splinter apart inside him. Now everything was off-kilter, and he felt horribly wound up and powerless, just like the kid he'd once been. It was as if the past had crept unseen into the present, overlapping it without his permission, so that he felt like he was in one of those dreams where things were familiar and yet not right.

And now suddenly the mysterious Ms Joan Santos from Bermuda had appeared out of nowhere, quoting Nietzsche and teaching him the Highway Code.

He flicked on the indicator and turned into the drive of Seddon Hall, the country house hotel where Jonathan and Cassie were having their wedding reception.

Obviously leaving Joan on that road alone hadn't been an option, but when Paul had offered to send Ben over to take her home he had refused. And he still couldn't put his finger on why he had done that.

Except that something about her had made it impossible to hand her over to another man.

Hand her over?

He gritted his teeth. What the hell was he talking about? She wasn't his to hand to anyone—nor was he some kind of medieval warlord who thought of women as chattels.

But in those few seconds it felt as if they belonged together. He'd even had that sense of déjà vu, as if they had met before.

He felt his body tense as he remembered the moment she'd spun round and the feel of her arm beneath his hand. His reflexes had kicked in before his brain had even known what he was doing. It had been nothing; his grip had been the most simple and impersonal of touches.

And yet it had made him burn. Then and now.

He thought back to that extraordinary burst of heat, the fire that had roared through him as her eyes met his, her pupils huge, a pulse beating wildly in her throat, making him feel taut and needy.

No, it wasn't her, he told himself again.

She had been the consequence—not the cause. His jaw tightened. A stroppy stranger with green eyes. Or were they brown? He tried and failed to decide. If only he could see them again…

And if he did, then what?

Then nothing.

Whatever hadn't happened between them would stay unhappening. Which was fine by him. After all, he had more important things to think about right now—good and bad. And yet, for some reason he didn't understand, Joan Santos kept making him forget each and every one of them.

CHAPTER THREE

GAZING UP AT the beautiful Georgian building with its ivy-covered walks, Joan felt a pang of guilt. After she lost her scholarship, her parents had paid for the final year of her tuition, and Gia and Terri had chipped in too—even though it had meant they both had to have their wedding receptions in the back garden.

'It's what families do,' Terri had said to her, but she knew they had both dreamed of something more glamorous for their big day.

Something more like Seddon Hall.

A shriek of laughter made her turn sharply, and she felt her stomach lurch with panic as she saw a group of people from college hugging one another, their colour high with excitement. Thanks to her role as maid of honour she had managed to avoid having to do much more than smile and wave so far. Obviously she would go and talk to them at some point, but not right now.

Ducking her head, she edged behind one of the beautiful floral arrangements.

So many people had made so many sacrifices to make her dreams of athletic success at the highest level come true—and what did she have to show for it? Her throat tightened. A six-inch scar on her knee, that was what. But it was the invisible damage beneath the skin that was the real problem.

The imperfectly healed tendons and the slight but unchangeable stiffness to her knee.

Finally, though, there was some good news. She glanced over to where Cassie was talking to Jonathan's grandparents. Plus, her best friend was getting the wedding she deserved. Cassie looked, Joan thought, luminous with happiness.

'You know I can't thank you enough for doing this, mate. Cassie is so happy.'

Her chin jerked up. That was Jonathan's voice.

She peeped between the flowers and almost lost her footing again. It was Jonathan—and Ivo Faulkner was standing next to him.

Heart pounding, she held her breath. There were one of two things that could happen right now. She could front it out. Just act casual and step into view, smiling breezily. But then she might end up stuck in another conversation with Ivo, and her body was still humming from the last one. Or there was plan B. Just stay where she was and wait for them to leave.

She inched backwards.

'You don't need to thank me for anything—particularly in your speech, if that's what you're planning.' Ivo's voice sounded curt, but then it softened. 'I wanted to do it, and Lord knows you've done enough for me in the past. This was the least I could do.'

Jonathan was shaking his head. 'The least? What about school? If you hadn't been there I would have been toast on day one, and you know it.'

Ivo shrugged. 'We just have different skill sets.'

Hidden behind a tangle of trailing leaves, Joan felt like one of those wildlife photographers in hiding. Ivo was so close to her she could have reached out and touched him, and the itch to do so made her shrink further back.

'You can say that again. When you stand up you can hold an audience of thousands spellbound. I can't even hail a taxi.

And now I've got to give a speech in front of everyone I know.'

Joan felt her stomach twist in sympathy as Jonathan groaned.

'It's going to be terrible. Cassie will probably ask for a divorce.'

'You'll be fine. Look, the groom's speech is quite straightforward. Just thank your guests for coming, compliment your beautiful wife, thank her for agreeing to marry you and then ask everyone to raise their glasses.'

'Aren't I supposed to thank the bridesmaids too?' Jonathan had taken off his glasses and was rubbing them on the edge of his jacket. 'Or would you rather do that in your speech?' He cleared his throat. 'I noticed you talking to Joan earlier. You seemed to be hitting it off rather well.'

Watching the blush creep up over Jonathan's face, Joan felt as if her own face had caught fire. *Damn you, Cassie Slater nee Marshall.* It was so cringingly obvious that Jonathan had been told to mention her, even though Cassie had agreed not to interfere.

There was a long pause, and she wondered if they had walked away, but then she caught a glimpse of Ivo's profile through the foliage. Her stomach flipped. A moment ago it had felt as if she was watching him in some jungle, but she had been wrong. This wasn't his natural environment. He was more like a lion in a zoo. Detached, incurious, but on edge.

'We did talk,' he said, in that cool, precise way of his. 'And I'm sure Ms Santos has many admirers.'

He didn't finish the sentence—but he didn't need to, Joan thought. To her, at least, it was clear that he wasn't one of them.

'She does. Cassie, for one.'

Joan felt her heart contract as Jonathan glanced over at his wife, his face softening.

'She adores her—and you.'

'And I adore her. But you know who I am, Johnny.'

'I know.' Jonathan nodded. 'But just so you know, she's put you next to Joan at dinner. And I think you'll have a great time. Joan's a great girl,' he finished, with the obvious relief of one who had done what he'd been asked to do. 'Now, how about we go and grab a glass of champagne?'

Joan waited a minute or two and then, face burning, made her way around the edge of the room and through the double doors to where the tables were set for dinner.

No way. Absolutely not.

To think that she had actually allowed Ivo into her dreams.

'You know who I am.'

Cheeks stinging, she replayed Ivo's words. She had no idea what they meant, but it sounded to her as if Mr Big Shot from New York found this whole country wedding schtick and all its very average guests a bit beneath him. It was a pity they didn't know that, she thought, her gaze taking in the various clusters of women who had been glancing over at him furtively, as if he was a particularly exquisite dessert.

What was just as obvious was that she was lumped in with everyone else. He had phrased it carefully, because now Jonathan was married to Cassie, but it was humiliatingly obvious that she must have imagined that strange shimmering tension between them at the cottage.

Which was the exact reason why she wasn't ready to start dating again. Because ever since the accident, her body had been misfiring on so many levels. Including, apparently, her ability to work out if somebody found her attractive or not.

Stopping in front of the table plan, she gritted her teeth as she spotted her name next to Ivo's.

Because of Cassie's parents being a no-show, she and Jonathan had decided to have a sweetheart table, just for the two of them. The rest of the eighty guests were sitting at round tables dotted around the room.

She felt a twitch of irritation. Eighty guests to choose from and she had to be next to Ivo. How could Cassie do this to her? There was no way she was going to sit there and make forced conversation with him for the rest of the afternoon. And she didn't need to. Ivo Faulkner might not find her company stimulating enough to amuse him, but he certainly had his own coterie of admirers, she thought savagely as she wove between the tables. Why not let one of them enjoy his company?

That almost-smile...tugging at the corners of his mouth.

Her body stiffened as she remembered that slight, teasing curve of his lips in the churchyard, and she felt a pang of something a little like jealousy as she imagined him smiling for real at some other woman. But what was it to her if Ivo Faulkner smiled at another woman? She was welcome to him and his snarky remarks.

As she reached their assigned table, her eyes cut across the room. Everyone was still chatting and laughing next door, but in a few minutes they would be asked to take their seats. If she was going to do this, it was now or never. Pulse accelerating, she picked up his place card. She would have to swap it with another man, ideally someone with blond hair, so Cassie might not notice.

But the only other male guest with hair that could remotely be described as blond was Jonathan's jolly cousin Duncan, who had volunteered to entertain all the elderly female relations at dinner.

Her mouth curled into an impish smile. Oh, but that would be perfect. And the best part was that Ivo was far too stiff and proper to make a scene—which meant he would just have to suck it up in silence, she thought, reaching for Duncan's place card.

'I have to say that this is starting to feel a lot like a vendetta.'

Joan spun round, stomach clenching and unclenching in time with her suddenly racing pulse. Ivo was standing there, his blue eyes fixed on her face.

'First you try to run me off the road,' he said softly. 'Then you tread on my foot—*twice*—and now you're apparently exiling me to the great-aunts' table.'

Pulse jumping in her throat, she stared at him coolly. 'Vendettas are personal. Twenty-four hours ago we were perfect strangers, so surely everything between us is impersonal.'

He ignored that 'You do know that Cassie spent the best part of a week agonising over the seating placements,' he said softly.

'Of course I do,' she snapped.

Trying to find an arrangement that would work had been like a particularly exhausting game of Sudoku. Cassie had ended up in tears. And now her parents weren't even here.

Ivo's eyes rested on hers, steady and unblinking. 'Then don't you think you should let who sits where be her choice, not yours?'

The simple truth of that statement made her throat constrict and she stared at him, wrong-footed, hating him for being right, and hating herself more as she saw Cassie hurrying towards her, the smile fading from her face.

'Joanie! What's the matter? Is there a problem?'

She cleared her throat. 'I was—' she began.

'There's no problem,' Ivo interrupted smoothly, snatching the place card from her fingers. 'I wasn't sure where I was sitting and *Joanie* was just showing me—weren't you?'

His level gaze met hers, but she was too distracted by him using that version of her name to do more than nod. Nobody but her family and Cassie called her Joanie.

'I was.' Taking a breath, she pasted a smile onto her face.

'You know what men are like. Can't see what's in front of their noses.'

'Tell me about it.' Cassie rolled her eyes. 'Jonathan couldn't find his glasses the other day. Do you know where they were?'

'On top of his head,' Joan and Ivo said together, and Joan laughed, because it was funny, and it was such a Jonathan thing to do.

Only then Ivo's eyes met hers, and there was a quivering electric moment that she felt everywhere, and suddenly she was fighting a blush that felt like both a confession, and a betrayal.

'That's because he only has eyes for you, babe,' she said and, taking hold of Cassie's shoulders, she turned her around and gave her a little push. 'Now, go and sit down at your ridiculously romantic table for two.'

Everyone was starting to take their seats, but Ivo was standing, waiting politely for her to sit. Still distracted by that sudden flare of heat, she let him push her chair in. As he sat down beside her she stared straight ahead, but it made no difference. She was aware of nothing except his silent presence and the beating of her heart.

Abruptly she turned to face him. 'Why did you do that? Why did you lie to Cassie?'

He shrugged. 'Why would I tell her the truth? It would only upset her,' he said, flipping open his napkin and laying it over his thighs. 'And as it's her wedding day, that seemed like a bad idea.'

'You mean worse than sitting next to me?'

She spoke without thinking, but now, as his eyes met hers, she felt her muscles tense and her face grow hot beneath his scrutiny. She knew he was waiting for her to explain that comment, but she didn't want to admit what she'd overheard in case he guessed—correctly—that she'd minded enough to try and swap his place card with Duncan's.

Then again, it was clear he didn't want to sit next to her anyway.

Beneath her embarrassment, her temper flared. 'You don't need to bother denying it. I heard what you said to Jonathan earlier. I know you're not one of my admirers.'

His gaze never shifted from hers, but a slight flush of colour bled along his cheekbones. 'That was a private conversation.'

Picking up the menu card, she rolled it into the shape of a megaphone and held it to her lips. 'Then maybe don't have it in a public place.'

She felt the air snap to attention as his eyes locked with her. 'That's a fair point. Perhaps I may make one in return.' His voice turned hard. 'If you choose to eavesdrop, maybe listen to what is being said.'

'I did,' she protested. 'You said…' She hesitated. 'Well, it was more what you didn't say,' she finished. 'It was what your face was saying…what you were thinking.'

He shifted back in his seat so that she was forced to tilt her head to maintain eye contact.

'Cassie told me you had hidden talents. If I'd known she meant you could read minds I'd have offered you a job.'

'And I would have turned you down,' she said fiercely.

'I believe you would.'

He stared at her—no, his eyes bored into her—and then suddenly he gave a reluctant laugh.

'You know, I don't think we've been properly introduced.' He held out his hand. 'Ivo Faulkner.'

She stared at him warily, caught off guard by his outstretched hand. But in a way he was right, she thought. They hadn't been introduced formally. It had been more a series of highly charged encounters, like atoms colliding and rebounding off one another.

'Joan Santos,' she said. Her pulse twitched as his thumb

pressed into her skin and, looking up, she almost fell headlong into his blue gaze.

'So, aside from mind-reading, what are these hidden talents of yours?' he asked, his eyes fixing on her face as if it was he, not her, who could read minds.

Throat tightening, she shrugged. 'I don't have any.'

Once upon a time she'd been able to fly through the air like a gazelle, but not anymore. No, not *at the moment*, she corrected herself silently, and the thought fanned that hope she was hiding inside.

'At the moment I'm living at home, looking after my sister's two little boys, which is not exactly rocket science.'

He frowned. 'Making children is easy—raising them is one of the hardest jobs in the world.'

She screwed up her face. 'For which I have no qualifications whatsoever. Except that I love them.'

And they loved her. She felt her heart contract, remembering the feel of Ramon and Reggie's solid little bodies as they hugged her before she left.

'Then you have the most important qualification you need.'

She watched, confused, as his gaze moved past her to the sweetheart table at the front of the room. He was right, in a way, but it wasn't the kind of comment she would have expected him to make. It seemed so generous and sympathetic.

His gaze snapped back to hers. 'About earlier—what you overheard me say to Johnny. I was feeling a little cornered. My smiles can be hard to come by, and I don't always express myself that well, but in this instance I can't deny what I said. How could I? You're a very beautiful woman, Joan. Obviously you have a lot of admirers.'

Watching his pupils pulse against the blue of his irises it was hard for her to catch her breath, much less formulate a response to that remark. That moment in the bedroom at Snowdrop Cottage swelled inside her, hot and sharp and vivid, just as if they were still there.

'Not that many,' she said lightly. 'I find it hard to trust.'

She didn't know when that would change.

After the accident, she had forfeited more than money. Once she lost the shine of success, she'd lost her boyfriend too—and track friends who, after the initial flurry of support, had swivelled towards a different light. Others, like some of the people Cassie had invited to the wedding, had been almost ghoulishly interested in the car crash of her life, peering and standing on tiptoe to look at the wreckage, but assuming she was fine because she wasn't in a body bag.

Worst of all, she'd lost faith in her body and in herself, for believing the lie that if you put in the hard work and the hours your dreams would come true.

Feeling Ivo's gaze on her face, she lifted her chin. 'I'm sorry about Cassie's matchmaking. She means well, but she's a menace.' She bit her lip but, try as she might, she couldn't stop herself from smiling. 'Poor Jonathan. He sounded like he was having a tooth pulled.'

'But without anaesthetic,' he said drily.

She laughed. 'Exactly.'

Their eyes met, and without warning his mouth curved into a smile of such sweetness that she forgot it was Cassie's wedding day, and that they were surrounded by people, and that she found him awkward and autocratic and on occasion rudely abrupt. Instead, she felt as if she was being swept out to sea by a curling blue wave, further and further, until she was out of her depth.

And she couldn't look away.

She didn't want to look away.

She just wanted to keep drowning in that blue, blue gaze the same way she had at the cottage after he'd taken her home.

Dragging her gaze away she picked up her water glass.

'You know, I never thanked you for getting the car back to me. I meant to, only then I forgot.' She grimaced. 'I don't know how… I guess the aunties on my shoulder must have had one too many Dark 'n' Stormys.'

He raised one eyebrow. 'The aunties on your shoulder?'

She laughed. 'It's what me and my sisters call them. We have six aunties and four aunties-in-law and they're basically always in our heads, rolling their eyes and tutting like some Greek chorus. But they wear shorts and drink rum.'

His blue eyes crinkled at the corners minutely. 'I'd like to meet them.'

She gazed up into his sculpted face, the shock of his beauty catching her off-guard again. 'Oh, they'd love you,' she said, without thinking.

Although Ivo standing stiffly in her parents' cluttered, colourful front room, surrounded by her aunties, was impossible to picture.

'For giving me a lift,' she added quickly as his eyes found hers. 'They're big on manners. I am, too, normally, so I'm sorry I didn't say it earlier, but thank you for the lift and for getting the car back to me.'

'It was nothing.' He was shaking his head. 'I made a phone call. Paul and Ben did the hard part. Is it running okay? Paul said he checked it for damage.'

'It's fine. And it was not nothing. It was kind of you. Oh, no, not for me, thank you.' She covered her glass with her hand as a waiter leaned forward to pour the wine. 'I need a clear head.'

Ivo frowned. 'Are you driving back tonight? I thought everyone was staying over until breakfast tomorrow.'

'I am staying. But I said I'd teach Livvy and Jas how to do the Renegade and the Camel and the Woo.'

'The what?' He was staring at her as if she was speaking a foreign language.

'They're dance moves. People make up these really short routines and put them on social media. If they get a lot of views, they start trending, and then before you know it everyone is doing them.' He was still looking at her as if she was speaking Klingon. 'They're fun…if you like dancing.'

'And you do? Like dancing?'

'I love it. Why? Are you asking?'

She had meant it as a joke, but he didn't laugh or smile. He just shook his head. 'I don't dance.'

'Not even at weddings?'

Ivo stared at her in silence, the question echoing unanswered inside his head. He could see her wariness, but there was also a flicker of curiosity in her beautiful eyes.

Body tensing, he thought back to the moment when Jasmine had dropped her basket and Joan had walked into him. He had just about got over the shock of seeing her, and then suddenly she was there, her light curves pressed against him, that kissable mouth turned up to his just as if they were dancing.

For a few feverish seconds everyone else in the church had seemed to fade away, and he had been aware of nothing but her, and the desire tearing through him like wildfire.

But he wasn't going to dance with her. He couldn't. Not because he didn't want to. He did. But…

His chest felt too tight for his ribs. Even shaking her hand just now had made the embers of that fire glow. He didn't want to imagine what it would feel like to dance with her… to have permission to hold her close, to move against her. Or perhaps the problem was he *could* imagine it.

He shifted back in his seat, keeping her just out of his line of sight. Most people thought sex was the most intimate of human interactions—probably because they usually had to get naked. Only for him the nudity made it less, not more personal.

Sex was just bodies and lust and gratification.

Dancing was about holding someone close enough to hear their heart beating.

But as far as he was concerned that particular organ was there simply to push blood through his veins. Caring, loving, feeling—whatever it was other people thought hearts did—all of that was beyond him. For the very obvious reason that everyone he'd ever loved or cared about—the same people who should have loved him and put him first—had all abandoned him.

He didn't do love or romance. He had sex and one-night stands.

He was pretty sure that wasn't what Cassie had had in mind when she'd chivvied Jonathan into setting him up with Joan, and if he upset Cassie that would hurt Johnny, and he would never consciously do anything that might risk that happening.

And yet he could feel his body leaning towards Joan… feel his hand uncurling to do the previously inconceivable.

'Especially at weddings.'

He spoke more curtly than he'd intended. He knew that even before her smile flattened and the light in her eyes dulled.

Say something, he told himself savagely.

But as he opened his mouth, to make an apology of sorts, there was the ringing tremolo of a knife being struck against glass and, looking up, he saw that Simon had got to his feet, a piece of paper clutched in his hands.

It was too late to say anything. It was time for the speeches.

After Simon's speech, it was time for the groom to speak. Everyone could hear the shake in his voice, see his love for his wife overriding his nerves, and the goodwill of the guests swelled up around the room.

Jonathan got a rapturous round of applause. And now it was his turn.

As he moved past Joan's chair his hand brushed against her shoulder, but she didn't so much as blink.

It went well—as he had known it would. A lifetime in foster homes had taught him how to read a room. For him, talking to strangers at arm's length was so much easier than dealing with people at close quarters. And yet as he spoke his gaze kept returning to where Joan sat, stubbornly staring at a point past his shoulder.

By the time he returned to his seat she had already left the table. Helping himself to another glass of wine, he watched the dance floor fill up. Jonathan was holding Cassie close against him, his face flushed with happiness, but he barely glanced at them. Instead, his eyes kept returning to Joan.

She was showing Johnny's sisters and the two little bridesmaids some kind of dance routine and, watching her chin tilt upwards, he felt his body tense. She looked so young and untroubled. She *was* young—Cassie's age or thereabouts, so not much more than twenty-two. But he couldn't remember ever feeling like that even at twenty-two. There was always that sense of waiting for the sky to fall in.

Because it had. It always had.

For a moment he pictured Caleb's face the last time he'd seen him. They were messing around on a swing, twisting the ropes and letting them unravel, and his brother had been laughing as they spun together in the air. He could remember thinking that he never wanted to stop spinning—only then someone had come outside and bawled at them to come in for dinner.

That evening his brother had been arrested for joyriding, and that made it even harder to forgive. Caleb had let him down, left him to fend for himself, for what amounted to a few minutes of hedonistic joy.

He hadn't seen him since. There were times—many over the years—when he had thought about reaching out, when he'd almost picked up the phone or typed an email. But then he would hear that Caleb had been arrested again and all the old anger and misery would swamp him.

So now all he had was memories. Except the boy he was remembering no longer existed, and he probably wouldn't recognise the man he'd become.

He downed his wine in one.

On the dance floor, the little girls had disappeared. Instead, a group of twenty-somethings were throwing shapes self-consciously—including a tall, dark-haired man who was dancing enthusiastically to the music. Ivo stared at him, his shoulders stiffening. He was a college mate of Jonathan's called Phil, and he had seemed pleasant enough at the stag night, but now he hated him for no other reason than that he was dancing with Joan.

'What are you doing, sitting here on your own?'

It was Cassie, hands on hips.

'I was observing.'

In truth, he hadn't even noticed that the rest of the table had moved off either to talk or dance. His gaze had been locked on Joan.

'You look like the Grinch.'

He smiled. 'That's a bit harsh. He lived on his own for fifty-three years. I've only been sitting here for twenty minutes or so.'

'But it's a wedding. You shouldn't be on your own at all.' Her face softened and she bit into lip. 'Particularly not at this wedding. I want you to have fun.'

'And I am. Ask Johnny. I just don't have a talent for small talk—you know that.'

'You do all right.' She glanced over her shoulder. 'Maybe it would help if I introduced you to some people. Come and mingle with me. Everyone's dying to meet you.'

Been there, done that, he thought, remembering how he'd held out his hand to Joan.

And now she was dancing with another man. When she could—*should*—be dancing with him. Although that would have meant crossing a line that he never crossed for any woman. Glancing over at the dance floor, he felt as if his stomach had been scooped out. Joan wasn't dancing now anyway. She was nowhere to be seen.

And neither was Phil.

He clenched his hands, the stretch in his knuckles distracting him momentarily from the pain of that discovery.

'I'll mingle. Just give me a moment,' he said. And, getting to his feet, he headed towards the garden.

Despite the coolness of the evening, people were spilling out through the doors to talk and smoke, but he had no intention of joining them and, keeping his head lowered, he skirted the edge of the lawn.

He felt tired and old and jaded. He wanted to keep walking…start running. But he was the best man. And besides there was breakfast in the morning. He just needed somewhere to lie low…

In the distance, he noticed the outline of a domed roof. It must be some sort of garden building. He felt some of the tension in his body loosen as he made his way towards it across the frost-tipped lawn. He just needed some space… some time on his own.

Except he wasn't on his own, he realised as he stepped beneath the arch. Joan Santos was sitting on the stone bench, her hands clasping her knees, her green-brown eyes wide and wary in the darkness like a fox caught in headlights.

His feet faltered. 'Sorry—I didn't know you were here. I thought you were with Phil.'

She got to her feet, and he watched, his heart in his mouth, as the silk of her dress slid down over her curves without a ripple.

'You mean Jonathan's friend?' She frowned. 'I don't really know him. I think he went to get another drink.'

A shiver ran over her skin and, frowning, he pulled off his jacket. 'Here.' Ignoring her protests, he draped it over her shoulders.

'Thanks.'

She gave him a stiff smile. His jacket made her look like a lost child, and he felt a twinge of protectiveness.

'You know you can't hide for ever,' she told him. 'She'll find you. Cassie, I mean. That's why you're skulking out here in the dark, isn't it? I'm guessing she wants you to dance.'

Her voice carried a tinge of hurt, left over from their previous conversation, and he had to fight the urge to tell her that she was the only woman he wanted to dance with.

'Among other things. What about you? Who are you hiding from?'

Her eyes shifted past his shoulder and she suddenly looked small and still. Not at all like the beautiful woman he had watched dancing with her head tipped back under the strobe lights.

'It's stupid, really. There's this whole bunch of people from college, and I haven't seen them since—' She stopped abruptly. 'Since I left.'

She was holding back, and he knew he shouldn't care, but found that he did.

'Why are you hiding from them?'

'It's not really them. They're perfectly nice…'

He felt his throat tighten as she hesitated again.

'And that's the problem. They're all nice and successful

and whole and happy.' Her voice was scratchy and taut. 'I'm happy too, but…'

Was she? She didn't look happy—or sound it. It was almost as if she was reciting words she'd learned. He wondered what could have happened to make that necessary.

'It's just weird, you know…when your past is suddenly there in your present and you can't do anything about it. It makes me want to run and keep on running—but I can't even do that.' Mouth twisting, she pulled the lapels of his jacket closer. 'Sorry, I'm not really making sense.'

But she was, he thought. He didn't know the specifics of what she was talking about, but if he had to guess it would probably be that she was feeling judged by her peers. And he knew what that felt like. As a child he had been the only one in his class in care, and there had been a thousand ways he'd been made to feel that difference—some pointed, most unconscious. But those two small words meant people he'd never even spoken to thought they knew him. And he'd hated it. Hated them. Hated the system. Hated himself.

So, yeah, he understood exactly what it felt like to want to hide, to run. Pretty much his whole adult life had been spent doing both. Hiding from the truth…running from the past. Except you couldn't escape either of them, because they were like a code stored in your genes. Only instead of adenine, thymine, guanine and cytosine, his DNA was composed of pain and fear and misery and regret.

Staring back at the illuminated hotel, he thought he could hear Caleb's voice, begging him to say something…anything. Instead, he had hung up. The alternative had been to start crying and begging his brother to come home, and they both knew that wasn't possible. And afterwards it had been easier to hate Caleb for taking away his choices…for leaving him like everyone else had done.

Blanking his mind, he turned towards Joan.

'I don't think you're stupid.'

He had wanted to reassure her. To take that guarded expression from her face. But there was still a wariness there, and to his astonishment he found himself trying again.

'Our past is part of who we are, but mostly we can forget that. When we remember, it shakes everything up.'

He hesitated, teetering on the brink of offering Joan a truth of his own. But then he came to his senses. Obviously he wasn't going to tell this woman about his childhood.

'I'm pretty sure that all those people from college are feeling exactly the same way when they look at you.'

She had certainly shaken up *his* world. She hadn't left his head since he'd yanked open her car door and she'd looked up at him, chin jutting combatively even though she was trembling with shock.

'Yeah, they're pea-green with envy.' She sounded sarcastic, and shook her head, but some of the tension in her body had softened.

'I would say so, yes. You have many enviable qualities.' And apparently he'd been compiling a list of them in his head, because he found himself saying, 'You're beautiful. Funny. Interesting. Smart. St—'

'Stubborn?' Her mouth curved into a flickering, teasing smile like the tail of a kite. 'You were going to say stubborn.'

'You certainly know your own mind, but what I was actually going to say was that you're stunning. And sexy,' he said slowly.

She *was* sexy. But there was something in her voice, and in her eyes, that hinted at hidden emotions…a vulnerability beneath that lovely face. Was that why he was having this teasing conversation that felt almost like flirting? Except he had never flirted in his life. It wasn't who he was. Flirting was too relaxed, too intimate, and he always wanted to keep his boundaries clear and high.

He saw her swallow, saw her pupils flare, felt her restlessness and his answering twitch of tension and he forgot all the reasons she wasn't for him. His pulse accelerated. He should be offering to see her back to the wedding party. That would be the proper, rational thing to do. And it would give him time to step back from the intimacy that had somehow flowered between them. But that wasn't what he wanted to do.

He wanted to touch her, to kiss her.

He was vividly conscious of his body…of the heat churning beneath the skin.

'We should probably go back inside…'

'Yes.' She nodded, but she didn't move.

Neither did he.

He cleared his throat. 'I told Cassie I would mingle.'

She tipped back her head, just like she had on the dance floor, and when he caught sight of her smooth throat he had to clamp his hands at his sides to stop himself from pulling her closer and pressing his lips against the curve of smooth skin.

Her eyes found his. 'So you're happy to mingle, but you don't dance?'

He felt his body respond to the huskiness in her voice. Truthfully, the only kind of mingling he wanted to do was with Joan Santos, and it involved getting naked with her in an emperor-size bed.

'No, I don't mingle any more than I dance,' he said.

Her gaze shifted past his shoulder back to the hotel and he felt his chest grow tight. Things were getting complicated. This wasn't who he was. This teasing tug of war in words. There was very little time for conversation on a one-night stand and now he didn't know what to say, what to reveal. But he did know that he couldn't leave like he had at the cottage—or, worse, watch her walk away.

He would regret it. He didn't know why. Just that he would. Because it wasn't only about sex. It was about being with someone who understood the tangle of feelings inside him and the need to run and hide.

Trying to soothe the chaos in his body and his brain, he cleared his throat. 'But I wanted to dance with you. Only I knew that if I touched you then I'd want more than just a dance.'

What he wanted was to pull her closer…close enough that he could feel every curve, every dip of her body pressed against him. He wanted to strip off that sliver of silk she called a dress and lose himself between those endless legs until the moon traded places with the sun.

Blocking the image of a naked Joan from his mind, he cleared his throat again. 'I know that's not an option.'

There was a silence, and he waited, holding his breath, his eyes fixed on the pulse beating frantically in her throat. He felt as if he was in a dream, and he was terrified to move in case he woke up.

'What if it was?'

Something shifted then. The sky quivered. The moonlight dimmed a fraction, and that strange, shimmering thread of need and longing snapped taut between then.

CHAPTER FOUR

NOW SHE LOOKED at him. 'What if I want more than a dance too?'

Her voice was husky, and he could hear her breath scraping against the crisp night air, but it was her eyes that fascinated him. They were no longer green or brown, but black with a hunger that matched his own—a hunger that both scared and excited her.

He reached out and stroked her cheek. The softness of her skin made him want things he'd never allowed himself to want before, and he didn't want to consider why that was or what it could mean.

She was staring at him as she had at the cottage, her eyes wide and clear under the dark curve of her lashes.

He took a slow breath in and then held out his hand. 'Come with me.'

Her face was dappled with shadows. 'Is this real?' she said hoarsely.

It was a strange question, but he knew instantly what she meant. This sense of being spellbound wasn't something that had happened to her before. Like him, she was struggling to believe it was not simply a dream…a waking fantasy.

Waking fantasy?

Tensing, he stared down at Joan, his eyes skimming the sliver of fabric that passed for a dress. No, that wasn't what this was. This was about lust and desire. It was about sex.

His eyes found hers. 'It is for me,' he said.

There was a long moment of silence and then she swayed forward. He felt a jab of triumph as she took his hand. He'd been so wound up all day…stretched taut between emotions he didn't want to feel and a need that he couldn't answer.

But she could. This woman could quiet the chaos beneath his skin. She could release this tension humming in his veins. Once they were in bed it would all feel so much more familiar, and he would feel less like a stranger to himself. Less like this needy, impulsive man he didn't recognise.

Tightening his grip on her hand, he led her back into the hotel.

The dancing was in full flow now, and a heavy bassline was punching through the wood panelling like a giant heartbeat.

'Wait!'

Her fingers tightened around his as a group of wedding guests conga-ed out of the reception room and she pulled him into a doorway. It was hard to see her face. The shadows hid her expression. But he could feel the warmth of her body and his own body tensed painfully at the nearness of her.

He wanted her so badly. His hunger, his need for her, was like a living, pulsing creature howling inside him and, unable to hold back, he moved his hands to cup either side of her face.

And then he was tilting her mouth up to his.

The room swam out of focus, the petal-softness of her lips making his head spin as if he was dancing along with the other guests. She edged closer, and the press of her body against his groin made his stomach clench with such intense desire that, before he even knew he was doing it, he'd slid his hand down over her shoulder, grazing her collarbone, slipping beneath her dress to caress the swell of her breast and the taut bud of her nipple.

She moaned softly against his mouth and he jerked his head back, shocked at this uncharacteristic loss of control. Another second and he would have been pulling that dress off her body.

'Not here,' he said hoarsely.

Her room or mine? Her room or mine? Her room or mine?

The question ping-ponged back and forth inside his head in time with the pulsing dance music. He didn't normally have this problem. For him, a one-night stand meant a night in a hotel. On his tab, of course. There was never any *Your room or mine?* It was not quite anonymous sex, but surnames weren't required and a possessive pronoun wasn't needed for the room.

It was just a room. And sex.

He didn't do relationships or serious.

Both words suggested a permanence that he knew he could never offer.

He didn't know how to. Had never experienced it.

Every single person in his life who should have shown him what it meant, what it required, had left his life in one way or another before he'd had a chance to find out. And even the idea of allowing that to happen again was intolerable—terrifyingly so.

They had reached the baronial hall now, and he put his hand on the small of her back to guide her up the sweeping central staircase.

Her room would give him the option of leaving when he wanted. But his rooms were further away from the bridal suite. The last thing he needed was for the newlyweds to find out that he and Joan had hooked up. They were both so loved up there was a real danger that they might do some sums and come up with a wildly wide-of-the-mark answer.

Because this wasn't love. This was about sex. It was about satisfying a hunger. A coupling of bodies. Nothing more. Certainly not the start of being a couple. And that was a good thing. Better than good. It was ideal.

They were at the top of the stairs now and, turning right, he reached into his pocket, pulled out the large, old-fashioned key and unlocked the door to his room.

As he opened the door she grabbed his hand and pulled him inside. He shut it quickly and reached for her, his hands spanning her waist to hold her against him as he waltzed her backwards across the floor. Her kiss was urgent, hungry and unrestrained, as if she had been holding herself back. And he understood that because he felt the same way. She was everything he wanted. Her mouth. Her throat. That irresistibly soft skin.

A pulse was beating frantically under the line of her jaw and he buried his face against the soft curve of her neck, breathing in shakily, inhaling the scent of her skin. But it wasn't enough. He wanted to touch her, to run his hands over that doe-soft skin, and clothes were simply a barrier to that goal.

Clearly she thought so too, because as he pushed the thin straps of her dress away from her shoulders, her hands began plucking his shirt from the waistband of his trousers, sliding up over the bare skin of his stomach.

Breathing deeply, he leaned forward to lick her now naked breasts, feeling them quiver and stiffen as his tongue curled over the tips—and then he sucked in a breath sharply as he felt her hand press against the hard length of his erection.

He'd never felt like this with any woman. He wanted, wanted, *wanted* her…

Then he remembered contraception.

Shaking away some of the dizzying pleasure of her touch, he took a step back.

Her hands clutched at his shirt. 'What is it?'

'Condom,' he said hoarsely.

Her eyes widened, and he knew that in the moment she had forgotten too.

'Yes…'

They were in the bathroom, but the idea of leaving her even for the short time it would take to get one made his chest cramp almost in panic. He pulled her against him again and together they stumbled towards the bathroom.

The lights came on as they staggered through the door, and as he caught sight of their dishevelled reflection in the mirror his need for her banged through him like a wrecking ball.

Her hands were fumbling with his belt now…working at the button on his trousers.

He grunted. This would be all over before it started if she carried on touching him there.

Batting her hand away, he reached for his toiletries bag and shook the contents impatiently into the sink. His breath caught in his throat as she picked up a condom and handed it to him with fingers that shook slightly.

There was a dark flush to her cheeks and her eyes were dark too, the pupils huge. This was the moment when he could choose to stop this.

But he didn't want to stop. And now she was pulling at his zip, freeing him, and he felt her fingers wrap around the hard length of him. Abruptly he leaned forward, his hand sliding through her hair, and he kissed her hard, a searing, open-mouthed kiss of possession and passion, as he tore open the packet and rolled the condom onto his straining erection.

He pushed up the skirt of her dress, then lifted her onto the bathroom cabinet, waiting as she tilted her hips forward to pull down her panties.

There was a long thin scar beneath her knee and he touched it lightly. Her fingers closed over his and she made a noise he didn't understand—and then he did. He knew that she felt self-conscious… No, it was more than that. Her scar made her feel vulnerable, and he understood that feeling even though his scars were on the inside. He bent over and kissed the line of puckered skin, and this time she let him touch her there.

And then he was chasing her shivers of anticipation with the tip of his tongue, moving up between her thighs, and she was pulling him up, parting her legs, and he thrust into her in one strong movement.

Her fingers gripped his shirt and she moaned against his lips, the sound mingling with his own groan of relief and exhilaration as a tremor of pleasure ran through him.

She felt incredible…hot and slick and tight. Reaching down, he found her breast again, cupping it and then squeezing the nipple until she was almost frantic in her movements.

He could feel his body tightening and loosening all at once, and his mind was nothing but heat and a hunger to satisfy her…satisfy both of them. Pulse quickening, he moved his hand to her clitoris, stroking it rhythmically with his thumb, working in time with his thrusting hips, driven by some deep-rooted imperative he had never experienced before that was so physically intense it drove all conscious thought from his brain.

There was just her body, her heat, and her eyes on his face, bright with desire, connecting with the blaze in his.

'Don't stop,' she whispered, and she clasped his face, kissing him hungrily, her teeth catching his lower lip. 'Please don't stop,' she said again.

Suddenly fierce, she was wrapping her legs around his waist, arching forward, crying out incoherently, her voice hot against his mouth, her nails digging into his shoulders. He felt her muscles grip him as her body shattered around his. And then he was tensing, thrusting up, shuddering helplessly, his hands clamping her neck and waist, anchoring her against him as the wave building inside him snapped back, then swelled again and he surged into her, his orgasm mingling with hers, drawing out the spasms of her pleasure.

He breathed out shakily. Joan was clinging to him limply, her body quivering inside and out, and he held on to her until gradually the ripples faded. Then he eased out of her, stifling her soft intake of breath with his mouth as he peeled himself away from her warm, damp skin.

They kissed for a moment and then she shifted forward, clutching her dress against her body, covering her breasts. Her eyes met his and there was a sudden stillness inside his chest as he realised that they had done what they had come together to do.

Only it wasn't enough.

He knew how her body felt and he wanted it again. Wanted *her*. But did she want him?

'Don't go.'

'Okay.'

Her voice was so quiet, almost tremulous in the silent bathroom, that at first he thought might have imagined it, conjured it up out of need and desperation. But then she let go of her dress and he watched, dry-mouthed, as it slid down her legs and puddled at her feet.

Heartbeat accelerating, he stared at her naked body, feeling his own body respond to the jutting breasts, the indent of her waist. His eyes dropped to the strip of dark curls between her thighs. He could hardly breathe. He definitely couldn't speak.

But he didn't have to. Groin hardening, he reached for her naked body and pulled her against him, swinging her off her feet and into his arms, and then he was carrying her into the bedroom, to the bed.

So this was a one-night stand.

Breathing out unsteadily, Joan pressed her thumb against her mouth. It felt soft, almost tender from a night spent kissing. And not just kissing, she thought, remembering how Ivo had stretched her out beneath him, his hand capturing hers and pinning her to the bed as he pressed the flat of his tongue against her clitoris and licked her until she had begged him to stop, to carry on, never to stop…

Her cheeks felt hot against the cool cotton pillowcase. After Ivo carried her into the bedroom he had stripped off his clothes and they had reached for one another wordlessly, swallowed whole by the white heat of a hunger without reason or precedent.

And very nearly without a condom, she thought, the heat from her cheeks spilling down over her neck and shoulders. It was an additional precaution—she was on the pill—but it was definitely safer to do both.

She glanced down at Ivo. He had fallen asleep with his arms still around her and she had leaned into him, breathing in his scent, resting her face against the hard muscles of his chest, assuming sleep would follow.

But here she was, still awake, her mind quivering like her body before a big race.

It was tempting to blame the moonlight that was now shining through the window because both of them had been too in thrall to the other to notice such mundane details as whether the curtains were open. Only it wasn't the moon keeping her awake.

It was him. It was Ivo.

Because even though she had to get up for breakfast in just over two hours she didn't want to shut her eyes. If she did, it would be over. And she wasn't ready for that just yet.

Wasn't ready for him to become a memory or a dream. It had felt so real, and so right, and she had made it happen. And she knew it was only going to be a one-night thing, but for this night he belonged to her and nobody could take him away.

Pulse twitching, she shifted position, tilting her head

slightly to stare at the man lying beside her. *'Maybe have some mind-blowing meaningless, sex with a stranger,'* Cassie had said, and that was what she'd done—even though it was the last thing she'd been planning to do.

After her first boyfriend she had focused on athletics. After Algee she'd felt too fragile emotionally, and her scar had made her feel as if her body was a faulty garment, like factory seconds with a wonky seam. The scar had faded, but that feeling had taken longer to shift, even though everyone in her life had been subtly, and not so subtly—*I'm looking at you, Auntie Winnie*—been trying to get her to date again.

She had met a couple of men for drinks. They were nice enough. Funny. Respectful. Good-looking. But even if she hadn't been in this weird headspace she couldn't imagine herself hooking up with any of them for a one-night stand.

But then none of them had been like Ivo Faulkner.

Her gaze hovered on his face. In the moonlight he looked too perfect to be real. Except he was. And he was here with her. Breathing out softly, she replayed the evening, trying to work out when it had become inevitable.

Not at dinner, she thought, remembering how he'd snubbed her. After that she'd kept her distance, kept moving until she lost sight of him. Only then Jenna and Siobhan had intercepted her on the dance floor, and in panic at having agreed to join them for a catch-up she'd bolted outside. She'd hated herself for running scared, for hiding. But suddenly there was Ivo, beneath the moonlight, and it seemed like a sign. To loosen up. To break the first rule of hurdling and take a leap before looking.

It was her first time sleeping with a stranger. First time anyone had seen her body since the accident. But she had felt safe with Ivo. Despite what she'd said to him about finding it hard to trust, she had trusted him enough to see and touch her scar.

But was Ivo really a stranger? After all, he was Jonathan's best man, his best friend. Then again, what did she know about him?

Her eyes rested on his face, half hidden in the crook of one muscular arm. The same arm that had taken his weight as he stretched over her, kissing her so deeply that she gasped for air. She felt her pulse shiver.

She knew that he knew how to touch, how to torment, to tantalise and tease her to a point of such abandon that she didn't know herself. And he'd felt so right against her. She'd never known that skin could feel so good, mouths so urgent, hands so teasing.

But what did she really know about sex?

She'd had two boyfriends. The first one, Dennis, was one of the cool kids at school. She had imagined sex would be like in the movies, but it had been awkward, and a little uncomfortable, and she had faked her orgasms because she hadn't known how to tell him what she liked. Hadn't known what she liked.

And then there was Algee.

She gazed down at her flat stomach and long, toned limbs. Other girls on the team had warned her that guys liked the body of a sporty girl, the training regime less so. Some of them had actually dropped out because they had found it so hard to train and date.

She thought she was lucky. That Algee was different. And he had been incredibly supportive at first. But then he started to sulk whenever she'd had to train or compete, and if she tried to talk to him about it he'd made her feel as if she was the problem…as if she was being selfish or oversensitive or irrational. He would be cold, and hurt, but then, when she apologised and promised to try and make it work, he would be so sweet.

And she'd loved him and he'd loved her—or she thought she had.

But after the accident she had known with absolute certainty that he hadn't. He wanted sexy, sporty Joan as his girlfriend—not the shell-shocked woman with a limp who had come home from the hospital. He had ended things. Brutally. Just as that hurdle had ended her athletics career.

Her mouth twisted. More brutally, in fact. Because, unlike humans, hurdles had no intent or malice. They just were objects. Humans were supposed to care. About other humans and their feelings. Algee hadn't cared about her feelings.

But then, could she blame him? She had barely been aware of them herself. She had been numb, sleep-limping through the devastated landscape of her dreams, suspended in limbo between reality and denial. And, despite dutifully attending all her hospital appointments and her mandated therapy sessions, it had been that way ever since. Her feeling as if she was acting, imitating what 'normal' did and said and felt like.

Until tonight, with Ivo, when there had been no faking and everything had been real. Intensely so.

Just like a race.

Her eyes were starting to close.

And, like a race, her night with Ivo was a short, self-contained moment in time, where every second counted and the two of them were simply bodies in effortless, fluid motion right up to the finishing line.

No wonder it had all felt so right.

That was her last conscious thought as finally she fell asleep.

The pounding started in her dream. She was running, mid-race, six seconds in, moving with a speed and height that made her heart sing above the roar of the crowd, her feet hitting the track like a metronome. Three strides between each hurdle.

Bang. Bang. Bang. Bang.

No, that was too many.

Her eyes snapped open.

It wasn't her footsteps.

Someone was knocking on the door.

And instantly she remembered where she was and why she was there.

Beside her, Ivo was rolling out of bed. He stood for a moment, naked, poised like a warrior in the bright winter sunlight blazing through the windows, and she stared at his formidable body, a pulse beating in her throat, her own body reacting to his nudity and nearness with a craving that was almost primeval.

'Who is it?' she whispered.

'Hey, Ivo!'

She froze as Jonathan's voice vibrated through the door. There was another knock.

'Are you up, mate? We're going downstairs for breakfast in a minute.'

Reaching down to snatch up his discarded clothes from the floor, Ivo grimaced. 'Sorry, yes—I forgot to set my alarm. Just give me a moment.'

A moment.

Clutching the sheet around her, Joan sat up and looked with dismay, and then a rising panic, around the room.

'Where are my clothes?'

Ivo held up a hand to quieten her. He was dressing with swift efficiency. But then his clothes were readily to hand.

'They're in the bathroom.'

He sounded irritable and accusing, just as he had on the road, and she felt herself respond as she had then. 'I was only asking.'

His eyes found hers and he frowned. 'Just go and get dressed. I'll deal with Jonathan.'

Even though he was whispering, his voice snapped with authority and power and she could only do as he asked.

Still clutching the sheet, she wriggled to the edge of the bed. It was ridiculous to feel shy, given that Ivo had seen every inch of her naked already, but she still felt oddly self-conscious—and, to her horror, her leg was painfully tight after all those hours in heels, so that she had to walk stiffly across the room, snatching up her shoes en route and hoping that Ivo wouldn't notice.

As she shut the bathroom door, she saw with relief that her dress was still on the floor where she had stepped out of it last night. Her body tensed as she remembered how she had pushed it up over her hips and wrapped her legs around his waist. Remembered, too, the flare of heat in his eyes.

Blinking away the memory, she got dressed and sat down on the toilet. All her elation at having done something real, something that was hers, that nobody could take away from her, had evaporated.

Through the door, she could hear Jonathan and Ivo's voices. She strained to hear their conversation, but the words were mostly unintelligible, and then suddenly they fell silent. Her head jerked up as somebody knocked on the door. She opened it cautiously.

Ivo was standing there, his handsome face still and unsmiling. 'He's gone. But I need to get downstairs.' A muscle pulsed in his cheek. 'We both do. But not together,' he added sharply.

Her face stiffened. So was that it? Were they done? Was that how these things worked?

She wanted to ask him, but the Ivo who had stretched her shuddering body beneath him had disappeared, and she didn't want to reveal her ignorance to this brisk, cool-eyed man.

'Obviously,' she said quickly, her fingers tightening around her shoes. 'But I'll need to get changed before I go downstairs.'

His eyes dropped to the pale gold heels and she felt goosebumps cover her arms as she pictured herself standing there in nothing but those same shoes.

Was he picturing it too?

Or was he remembering what had followed?

'It's okay. Cassie's taking a bath, so you should have time.'

'That's good,' she said stiffly.

They stared at each other in silence. Now what? She had the oddest impulse to shake his hand. Or kiss him. Only one would be weird and the other would be dangerous, she thought, gazing up at his face and then turning her head away, afraid of the flare of heat.

'I should go.'

But she didn't move.

'Yes.' His voice sounded taut.

But he didn't move either. He just stood there, filling the doorway, a muscle jumping in his jaw.

Somewhere in the hotel a clock chimed and they both jerked backwards, as if a spell had been broken.

Ivo recovered first. 'Okay, then,' he said curtly. 'I'll see you downstairs.'

And then, just like at the cottage, he turned and was gone before she had a chance to form a reply.

Heart pounding fiercely, she stared after him. She hadn't been expecting a post-mortem, but surely there should have been some kind of acknowledgement of what had happened between them.

She waited a few seconds and then let herself out of the bedroom, glancing cautiously down the corridor for any stray guests. But no one was around and, still clutching her shoes, she ran back to her room.

There was no time to shower, but she changed her clothes.

As she smoothed her hair into a low ponytail she caught the scent of his aftershave on her wrist, and suddenly she could feel his hands gripping her waist and see the blue of his gaze on her face. Just remembering it sent ripples of pleasure through her, and she felt a throb of hunger that had nothing to do with food.

She stared at her reflection uncertainly.

In the mirror, her face looked just the same as always—and yet she felt different. Not quite a new person, but transformed in some way she couldn't quite put her finger on.

She tilted her chin. Would anyone else notice? Or, worse, wonder why? She glanced at the clock on her phone. Hopefully not, but there was no time to worry about that now. She added a quick swipe of eyeliner and lipstick and then headed downstairs.

Breakfast was already underway.

Her eyes moved of their own accord to where Ivo was already sitting, beside Jonathan, a cup of black coffee on the table in front of him. She felt her body tense as he glanced over to her casually, but he didn't so much as blink.

It felt strange, being so close to him but not being able to touch him when their bodies had been so seamlessly intersected all night. Strange, too, to think that she might never see him again except across a room at some christening or birthday party.

Her throat tightened. This morning she had thought that she would always remember him. Now she was wondering if it might be better if she could forget him completely.

'Hey, you!' Cassie looked up at her and, matching her smile, Joan sat down beside her best friend.

'How's your breakfast?' she asked her. 'Does it feel different now you're a married woman? I hope you didn't take all the sausages— What?' She broke off, frowning.

Cassie was looking at her, her eyes wide, her forehead creased into tiny pleats of incredulity.

'Oh, my goodness,' she hissed, grabbing Joan's hand and pulling her closer. 'I cannot believe you, Joan Santos. After everything you said.'

'What did I say?' Joan felt a flicker of apprehension.

'You said sex at weddings was something that only happened in movies. You were adamant. I should have known you were plotting something. So come on, then—spill the beans. Who did you hook up with?' Cassie squeezed her arm. 'Who's the lucky guy?'

Joan sat rooted to her seat as around her the walls of the room seemed to collapse inwards like a house of cards. She knew her face must be red. How had Cassie found out? Had Jonathan told her? Had Ivo told him?

Her eyes darted furtively past her friend to Ivo's profile.

No, she thought instantly. His face looked as if it had turned to stone, and she knew he had heard Cassie's gleeful words.

'There was no lucky guy,' she said quickly.

Cassie was rolling her eyes. 'Don't give me that Little Miss Innocent look, Santos. I called your room this morning and you didn't pick up. Now you turn up for breakfast late, looking all distracted and dishevelled and glowing.'

No, no, no, no.

Joan felt rather than saw Ivo's shoulders stiffen.

Please kill me now, she thought, as she tried to think of something to say.

She was hopeless at making things up on the spot. And it didn't help that Ivo was sitting so nearby.

She forced herself to laugh. 'I didn't pick up because I was brushing my teeth,' she lied.

Along the table, Ivo was nodding at something Jonathan was saying, but she knew his attention was split and that he was listening to her every word.

'And if I'm glowing and dishevelled it's because I went for a jog. I went too far and I had to run fast to get back.'

She swore silently. Why had she said that? It was bad enough lying to her best friend, but to do so about running… Wincing inside, she felt her conscience protest as her friend's expression altered, softened.

'You didn't tell me you'd started running again.'

'I only just started.'

This time the lie hurt. She hadn't run since the accident. Hadn't been near a gym. And Cassie knew that.

'It's not a big deal,' she added, smiling stiffly. 'I just haven't been sleeping well and it helps,' she added, bringing her total number of lies to four in under a minute.

Give the girl a medal.

'That's great, babe.' Cassie smiled encouragingly. 'You know, for a moment there I really did think you'd got with someone. You just looked different, somehow.'

Joan held her breath as her friend's gaze moved over her face.

'I didn't think about you running…' Cassie bit her lip. 'I was only teasing before. It's just that I so want you to meet that special someone. You know—that person who makes you wonder and yearn…' Now a smile tugged at her mouth. 'And who gives you the best damn sex of your life.'

Ivo had done all those things, Joan thought. And that truth tore through her like a herd of wild mustangs, their hooves a dizzying drumroll, kicking up the dust.

Heart pounding, she batted the thought away and smiled. 'I know you do.' She squeezed her friend's hand. 'And I'll let you know as soon as that happens. But it hasn't happened yet.'

After breakfast everybody gathered in the drive to wave the newlyweds off on their honeymoon. Jonathan's car was liberally decorated with balloons and *Just Married* ribbons, and there was a chain of tin cans trailing from the bumper.

Blinking back tears, Joan hugged Cassie, then Jonathan. 'You have a great time. Both of you. Look after her,' she said softly to Jonathan.

He looked suddenly serious. 'It's all I've ever wanted to do.' Swinging round, he held out his hand to Ivo. 'Thanks, mate. For everything.'

Ivo's expression didn't change, but the blue of his eyes softened a fraction. 'You're most welcome.'

It was time for them to leave.

They hugged again, and then Joan joined the other guests to wave them off. As the sound of the engine faded everyone wandered back into the hotel, but she stayed behind to watch the car clatter down the drive.

Finally it disappeared from view. Feeling oddly fragile, she turned—and every single cell in her body seemed to light up like a power grid. She'd thought she was alone, but Ivo was standing there, tall and silent and ridiculously beautiful in the sunlight.

'Here.' He held out a folded handkerchief.

'Thank you.' She breathed out shakily. 'I don't know why I'm crying. It doesn't make any sense when they're so happy.'

Ivo shrugged. 'Love like theirs is rare. It can be a little overwhelming. But don't worry.' The corner of his mouth lifted but there was no softness or humour in his eyes. 'I'm sure you'll meet that "special someone" who can give you what you want.'

He had heard what Cassie said, and her reply.

And clearly he thought she had been talking about the two of them. Her pulse twitched. Last night had been more than special…it was sublime. Not that she would have told him that, even if Jonathan hadn't hammered on the door and sent them scrambling for their clothes. She certainly wasn't going to say anything now.

'I hope so. Goodbye, Ivo.' She gave him a quick, stiff

smile. 'And thanks for last night. It was…' She hesitated, searching for the right word, and then she remembered what Cassie had said to her. 'It was fun.'

And before he could say anything else she turned and walked quickly up the steps.

Fun? Fun!

Stalking back into his bedroom, Ivo tossed the key on the bedside table, seething with frustration and something a lot like wounded pride. But why? Joan Santos was nothing to him, and last night had been just sex.

There was nothing special about it. Or her.

So why did you sleep with her?

The question buzzed inside his head as he zipped up his suit bag and kept buzzing as he scouted round the room to check he had packed all his belongings.

Not because he didn't have an answer: he did. In fact, he had several. He just didn't like any of them.

Glancing over at the rumpled bed, he felt his belly clench. He'd needed a distraction, needed the release of tension that sex would provide. Which made him feel like a selfish bastard. He had also wanted her, wanted to give her pleasure. But, selfish or not, he had been as eager and unthinking as a teenage boy on his first date.

Only it had been a million miles away from his first awkward encounter with a girl. Joan had been liquid fire in his hands. Hot. Fierce. Hungry. Everything he could have wanted in a woman.

His mouth twisted. That made it sound as if he was looking, but he wasn't. If he needed a partner for some public event there were women he knew. Women who were happy to accompany him on a no-strings basis in exchange for a glimpse into the lifestyle of the top one percent. He wasn't cut out for anything more serious.

But his life was off-limits. That glimpse was the closest anyone would ever get—including Joan Santos.

You need to take a shower and clear your head, he told himself, gazing down at the tangle of sheets. Needing to bring back some order to the chaos he'd created, in and out of the bed, he yanked them back savagely, intending to straighten them.

There was a flash of gold and blue and, anger fading, he stared down at the bracelet. Joan's bracelet.

Reaching down, he picked it up and almost dropped it. The metal links were still warm, and he felt a sharp twist of hunger, remembering the heat of her body against his. Then, mouth fixed into a grim line, he pocketed the bracelet.

They'd had their fun. Whatever his brain and body were telling him, it was over and done. Let housekeeping deal with it. It was not his problem.

CHAPTER FIVE

ADJUSTING THE EARPIECE of his headset, Ivo turned to stare out of his study window. According to Karolina, his PA, it was snowing in New York, and it had snowed here too overnight, the first flakes starting to fall on the twenty-minute drive from the hotel back to the castle. Now the fields were an undulating, alien white landscape that stretched to the horizon, and he let his gaze follow the curve of a distant hill as Karolina talked about his upcoming trip to the new London office.

'So, Frank Winters will be on hand to show you round, but I've made it clear this is not a state visit. That you just want a quick, anonymous walk-through.' She paused, and he heard the click of her mouse as she scanned his diary. 'I left the rest of the day clear, as per your instructions.' Karolina cleared her throat. 'And I've warned the Latimer that you might be staying tonight—'

'I won't be,' he interrupted her. 'I'll sleep on the plane.'

He had come to the Peak District to be best man at his best friend's wedding. Now that Jonathan and Cassie were on their honeymoon, his duties were complete. There was no reason to stay overnight in London. No reason to stay on at the castle. No reason to stay in England.

No reason at all.

His breath caught in his throat as, without warning, he pictured Joan Santos's face gazing up at him beneath the moonlight, her hair spilling over her bare shoulders, those mystical green-brown eyes holding him spellbound.

Jaw tightening, he spun his chair away from the window. It wasn't the first time she had popped into his head in the last twenty-four hours. Uninvited, of course. And on each occasion she appeared he found it bafflingly hard to evict her. Although was that really so surprising, given every interaction he'd had with her so far had involved a battle of words and willpower?

Not quite *every* interaction, he thought, heat rushing through him and his body hardening at the memory of his night with Joan. He could still feel the touch of her hand and the way her fingers had felt both delicate and strong at the same time. Could remember the way the dark sky above them had seemed to pulse like some great, unseen heart, and he could hear her soft, husky voice inside his head.

'Is this real?'

'So, is there anything else I can help you with?'

His chin jerked up. Karolina's voice had that careful note of someone having had to repeat a question to their boss.

'No, thank you, Karolina,' he said quickly. 'That's all.'

It was time to hang up. There was no way he could continue this conversation with his PA if Joan Santos was going to start talking in his head as well.

He pulled his laptop towards him, determined to chase her from his head, but trying not to think about her only made him think about her more. It was maddening as hell—not to say baffling.

Why had she got under his skin? He hardly knew her. And yet last night, when she'd talked about running from her past, he'd had a sudden overwhelming desire to tell her about his childhood.

Johnny knew the basic outline. The childhood spent in care. The shuttling between foster homes. But he had never wanted to go into the details. Who would want to hear about the drunken rages and the sordid squats with the pieces of tin foil scattered across the rotting floorboards?

Until last night, with Joan, when just for a moment it had seemed like the easiest thing in the world to tell her what had happened—to start at the beginning and tell her the story of his life. And there was no explanation for that except she had this *edge* to her. Not the sharp edge that scraped against the steel of his desire. This was tauter—like the feel of her scar beneath his fingers. There was pain there, and determination too, but also a vulnerability that wrenched at something inside him.

He hadn't told her anything, of course. It had been the alcohol and all the other stuff that was going on. His whole body had been jangling with a tension he hadn't been able to release. And then, watching her dance, he had wanted her so badly, and he hadn't wanted any other man to have what he was denying himself.

And then he had found her alone, out in that ridiculous whimsical folly. At first it had been tense and stilted between them. But then she had told him she was hiding from her past. He'd never thought that anyone else felt like that—much less be willing to admit it—and her confession had allowed him to confess his desire for her.

Gritting his teeth, he slammed his laptop shut. But it was just sex. That was the nature of a one-night stand. And in the past, no matter how good the sex, the aftermath had always been the same. It was the moment he switched from hunger to, *We're done here*.

Not this time.

This time, he felt as if everything had been snatched, not savoured.

But then he wasn't himself at the moment. There was obviously the CGB project—an unprecedented and frustrating failure that he was still trying to process. And of course there was the shock of Caleb's proximity.

He got to his feet abruptly. He didn't want Caleb in his head either. Was that the reason he kept letting Joan in? So he didn't have to think about his brother? But he didn't know the answer to that question. Despite building a global business worth billions, he didn't have an answer to any of the questions he was asking himself. Just more questions.

There was only one solution to this feeling of powerlessness and uncertainty and that was work. That was what had got him to this point. Work had taken him out of that world where he'd been helpless and dependent and given him a safe space.

So why not leave now and head down to London?

He just needed to find the key for his car.

It wasn't in the pewter bowl in the kitchen, where he usually left his keys. Nor was it on the chest of drawers in his bedroom. He frowned, baffled momentarily, and then he strode into his dressing room and rifled through the jacket he'd worn to breakfast at the hotel.

There it was.

As he pulled the key fob out of the pocket, something tangled around his fingers. His stomach swooped. It was a slim gold bracelet with a tiny blue heart-shaped charm.

He stared down at it, his own heart pounding, picturing the expression on Joan's face as he clasped her wrists and stretched her arms over her head. Her mouth had been a soft curve of desire but her gaze was fierce, a flame-like flicker of gold in her irises.

Irritated to find her back in his head yet again, he untangled the bracelet. He had put it in his pocket, meaning to give it in at the reception desk, but then he'd bumped into Jonathan's parents and forgotten all about it.

No matter. He would get his housekeeper, Linda, to drop

it back at the hotel for him and they could sort it out. By then he would be in London and it would be business as usual.

'I'm so sorry. There's no sign of it in either of the rooms, but someone may hand it in. It happens—and I have your number.'

Joan pressed the palm of her hand to her forehead. The receptionist had been really helpful, but she was just being polite. She might have lost the bracelet anywhere, and the chances of anyone finding it were slim to none.

'Thank for looking.'

Breathing out shakily, she hung up and rolled onto her back. Cassie would be the first person to tell her that it didn't matter, but she could feel her eyes prickling.

How could she have been so careless?

Pushing back Jemima's quilt, she held up her bare wrist and stared at it, as if by the power of wishing alone she could conjure up her bracelet. She had only noticed it was missing this morning, when Cassie had texted to say that they had arrived in Egypt.

I can see the pyramids, Joanie. The actual pyramids. And they're even bigger than the one we saw in Vegas.

Automatically, she had reached for her bracelet. Only it hadn't been there.

She had looked for it everywhere. More than looked. She had practically upended the little cottage. But it was nowhere to be found so she'd called the hotel. They'd checked her room but it wasn't there either. She'd even swallowed her pride and asked them to check Ivo's room. That same room where they had tasted each other as if they were starving. Clutched one another as if they were drowning, bodies quivering with wonder and yearning.

Her lip curled. There hadn't been much wonder and yearning the morning after. Instead, they were back to how it was before on that quiet, country lane with him snapping out instructions as if she was some slow-to-respond PA rather than the woman he had just spent the night with, and on, and in…

Shying away from the memory, she rolled back onto her side. She couldn't think about Ivo now. Nor did she need to. He had been with her most of the night, sliding into her dreams, trailing caresses, the white heat of his body pressing against her, so that when Cassie's text had woken her she had reached over, expecting to find him there in her bed.

But Ivo wasn't here. Cassie wasn't either.

And that was what this was really about. She wasn't just upset about losing the bracelet. She felt as if she'd lost her best friend too.

A lump swelled in her throat.

Obviously she'd always known Cassie was going to leave after the wedding and go on her honeymoon, but for the night before the wedding it had felt as if she had gone back to a time when they were still roommates. When Cassie hadn't met Jonathan or got her Master's or moved to England. And she was still going to be a professional athlete.

But now it was back to a reality, where that dream now hung in the balance. Except it didn't feel real. It felt as if she was sleepwalking.

'Is this real?'

That was what she'd asked Ivo that night and he'd told her it was. She knew it was just words, and yet being with him had felt so much more real than everything she'd left behind in Bermuda. She had felt more alive, more connected to the world, more authentically herself. It was as if his touch had somehow woken her and released her from a self-imposed spell.

She knew it was stupid to feel that way about a man she

might never see again. But she also knew that he wasn't a man she would ever forget. A night she would never forget.

Her skin was tingling.

She had never been so free and uninhibited with any man before. When she was younger she had been too inexperienced to really relax, and since the accident her body had felt as if it belonged to a stranger. Sometimes she'd look down at her softening muscles and wonder who she was.

Until that night. Until Ivo.

With him, taking it further hadn't been an issue. The opposite was true. There had been no boundaries, no brakes. She had wanted everything from him. And she had wanted to give everything back. She had never imagined, much less experienced such fervour, such fire, such feverish need. But clearly knowing that it was only going to last a night had unlocked something inside her.

Then morning came. Obviously she had known it would end, but then Jonathan had knocked on the door and it had all been so rushed and unsatisfactory and awkward. It was only a one-night stand, so it shouldn't matter, and it probably wouldn't be mattering if Cassie had been there to laugh about it with her.

If she was here, Joan thought, *you wouldn't be lying here feeling sorry for yourself. Cassie would be hauling you out of bed and into the bathroom.*

It was enough of a spur to get her groaning and pushing back the quilt. Shivering in the lukewarm air, she drew back the curtains.

What the—?

She stared down at the garden in astonishment. Yesterday, everything had been a palette of greens and rusty browns, but at some point in the night the world had turned white.

Heart pounding, she gazed down at the snow. Both her sisters and her parents had seen snow in real life, but she had only ever seen it in the movies. It had been one of the things on her list to do in the States, but there had never been any time, what with her training and all the competitions. And then, after the accident, she had struggled just to finish her degree.

Oh, but it was so beautiful, she thought, her enchanted gaze moving slowly across a landscape that looked as if it had been iced by a master pâtissier.

Her stomach rumbled. But breakfast would have to wait. Or was it lunch? Either way, it didn't matter.

Yanking on some clothes, she almost fell down the narrow staircase in her haste to reach the back door, where she pulled on her boots and one of Jemima's jackets. She hesitated a moment, then grabbed a kind of knitted beanie, yanked open the back door and stood teetering on the threshold.

Her breath showed white in the air as she reached down and picked up a handful of snow. It was cold, but light, like soap flakes, and it made a satisfying squeaking sound when she squeezed it. Laughing, she picked up handful after handful of snow and spun in a circle, tossing it in the air. As the flakes floated down she opened her mouth and let the crystals fall on her tongue.

Dizzily, she came to a stop. Now, what was that thing that Gia had done? She'd sent a video of herself and her husband Troy, lying in the snow on their backs, waving their arms and legs from side to side…

On impulse, she lay down and stretched out her limbs in the shape of an X, moving them back and forth in the snow. If only she had someone to film her—or better still lie next to her in the snow.

Somewhere in the distance she could hear the rumble of a car engine. Then it faded and suddenly it was completely silent. Not quiet, but completely silent. As if the snow was a blanket, muffling all sound. The sky had changed colour too, the grey lightening to a thin, faded blue and the sun had mysteriously appeared. Closing her eyes, she held her breath, grateful that she hadn't booked a hotel in London and driven up to the Peak District for only a couple of days.

'Joan?'

Her eyes snapped open and she felt her heart stop beating. Ivo Faulkner was standing looking down at her, his expression unreadable, eyes bluer than the sky above him fixed on her face,

'The gate was open. Are you okay?'

'Yes.'

She sat up, feeling stupid and strangely naked, given that she was wearing several layers of clothing and a pair of boots. She felt even more stupid a moment later, when she realised the beanie was stuck to the side of her head like a woollen pancake.

Hoping he hadn't noticed, she snatched it off. 'I've never seen snow before,' she said quickly, by way of explanation.

Her heart gave a thump as he studied her face.

'So you thought you'd lie down in it,' he said, in that measured, precise way of his.

'Yes. No… Well, sort of. I was just doing that thing…you know…where you…' Her mind was suddenly blank and she waved her arms up and down by her sides.

He raised one eyebrow. 'You mean making snow angels?'

The pale sunlight had decided to linger on his face, no doubt attracted by its flawless symmetry, and she felt something stir inside her as she watched it lick the subtle curves of his cheekbones.

'Yeah, those.'

She could feel herself blushing and, hoping that Ivo thought it was just the chill of the air, she scrambled to her feet.

'When Gia went to Colorado on her honeymoon she sent me a video. I've always wanted to see if it worked, because she was laughing so much it was hard to see anything.'

Great. She was babbling. But then she hadn't expected to see him again. And it was particularly unnerving to meet him in person having spent the night with him in her dreams. Replaying exactly what she'd imagined him doing to her in those dreams.

She felt her face grow hotter.

'And now you have,' he said, in that quiet, precise way of his. 'Take a look for yourself.'

He gestured towards the snow and she gazed down at the imprint. It was definitely an angel.

'You don't have a sand angel equivalent back home?' he asked.

She glanced up at him, startled not just by his question but by how accurately she had imagined him. He looked exactly as he had inside her head. *But better*, she admitted, her eyes pulsing over the hard lines of his shoulders then moving back up to his astonishing face. He looked a lot like an angel. Not one of the cutesy Christmassy ones, with the sticking-up halos. More like that beautiful stern-faced stone statue in the churchyard.

'No.' She frowned. 'I never even thought of doing that.'

There was a pause, and then her heart somersaulted as he reached out and brushed some snow out of her hair.

'Who's Gia?'

Good question. She stared at him, her mind blank again, every single cell in her body straining towards where his hand was moving against her hair, his touch echoing how he had stroked her face that night.

'My sister. She's my sister. My oldest sister. I have two. They're both older than me.' She was babbling again.

'And is it her children you look after?'

She nodded. Ramon and Reggie hadn't seen snow either, and she could imagine their wide-eyed amazement. Not that they would be seeing snow any time soon. Thanks to her losing her scholarship and needing to be bailed out financially, it would be a long time before Gia and Troy got to take them away on holiday.

'So you've never seen snow before?'

His voice, and the wonder in it, made her feel suddenly as if she was in a trance.

'Then this must feel pretty surreal.'

Surreal. The word repeated itself in her head as she stared up at him dazedly. It was absolutely the right word for what she was feeling, and the fact that he could do that—that he could read her mind—made her feel utterly off balance and terrified that he would sense that too.

'It is actually making me feel a bit light-headed,' she admitted. 'Jemima, the woman whose house I'm living in, said it could happen but she didn't make it sound that likely, and now I'm worried it will disappear before I get a chance to do all those snowy things they do in the movies—you know, like snowball fights and sledging…'

Reaching down, Ivo scooped up a handful of snow, as she had done earlier, only instead of throwing it up into the air he rolled it into a ball.

'It's not deep enough for sledging and you can't really have a snowball fight with two people.'

He stood there, poised, snowball in hand, not quite looking at her. 'We could build a snowman,' he said softly.

'Build a snowman?' she repeated slowly, as if he had suggested he pull a rabbit out of her beanie.

'Only if you want to.'

He seemed unsure now, as if he was as surprised as she by his suggestion.

'I do,' she said quickly, already picturing the photos she would send to everyone back home. But, glancing over at his suit and crisply ironed shirt, and what was almost certainly a silk tie, she hesitated. He was dressed for some sleek, sky-high boardroom, not for rolling around in the snow.

'It's sweet of you to offer, but don't feel like you have to.' Her eyes dropped to his black leather brogues and she hesitated. 'You're not exactly dressed for it.'

His eyes narrowed a fraction but he didn't reply. Instead he tossed the snowball onto the lawn, shrugged off his jacket and hooked it onto an overhanging branch. Next he unbuttoned the cuffs of his shirt and rolled up the sleeves, and then he crouched down and began shaping some snow into a ball before pushing it around the lawn.

She watched, enchanted, as with each circuit it grew bigger and bigger.

Finally, he straightened up, and despite his exertions his breathing was inaudible in the still, midday air.

He met her gaze. 'Now it's your turn,' he said.

And the dare in his voice snaked over her skin in that way that made heat bloom inside her.

In the end they made her whole family out of snow—from her dad right down to Reggie.

When she'd told Ivo what she wanted to do she'd thought he would excuse himself, but he hadn't.

'Ramon is going to be so excited when he sees this,' Joan said, turning her phone from portrait to landscape. She could feel the smile stretching across her face.

'Let me take one of you with them.'

Ivo was standing beside her—close enough that she could feel his heat, close enough that if she wanted to she could reach out and touch his hair as he had touched hers.

'Okay.'

She handed him the phone and hunkered down behind the snow versions of Ramon and Reggie, posing as he took some photos.

'Show me.'

He handed her the phone without speaking and she stared at the screen, her heart beating too fast. She had smiled—obviously—for the wedding photos, but this felt different. Unfiltered, personal, intimate. She looked happy. Her stomach clenched, tightening hard. She looked the same as she'd used to when she won a race. As if a flame had been lit inside her.

Sensing his gaze, and feeling flushed and self-conscious, she said quickly, 'You should be in a photo too. You helped make them.'

'But they're your family,'

'So let's build yours.'

'I don't think so.' His voice was the same, but his face had turned opaque, his eyes shuttering. 'I should be going.'

She watched in confusion as he unhooked his jacket from the tree and folded it across his arm, then began to walk back towards the cottage.

'You're going?' Vibrating inside with something like panic, she followed him, trying to make sense of the sudden shift in the mood. And then something else occurred to her. 'But you haven't told me what you came here for.'

He stopped then, spinning round so quickly that she almost walked into him.

'I'm guessing you weren't just passing by and fancied building a snowman.'

The tiny muscles in his jaw flickered and he stared at her in silence, his blue eyes glittering in the sunshine. 'I didn't, no,' he said finally.

'So, are you going to tell me, or am I supposed to guess?'

There was another silence. His whole body was taut, as if he wanted to leave without saying another word only he didn't know how.

'I have something of yours. When I went upstairs to pack…' He reached into his pocket. 'I found it in the b— in the room.'

He was holding her bracelet.

'You found it.' Tears were suddenly stinging in her eyes and she blinked them back. 'I thought it was gone for ever.' She tried to put it on, but her fingers were shaking too much to do up the clasp. 'Cassie gave it to me.'

And she had given her friend an identical chain.

'Let me.'

He turned her wrist and slid the bracelet around it. 'There,' he said softly.

For a moment he kept a hold of her wrist and she stared down at his hand. They were strong hands, but gentle too, and he had a great sense of touch, she thought, her breath catching as she remembered the way he had used his hands to cup her breasts, shape her waist, her hips…

'Joan…'

She looked up as he said her name, her pulse jumping. Ivo was staring down at her, watching her, his eyes a clear, soft blue on hers, and for a few half-seconds they stood there, frozen like the snow family on the lawn. Then they both moved at the same time, her fingers biting into his arms to drag him closer as he captured her face and fitted his mouth to hers.

It was a frantic, desperate kiss. A kiss of relief and an admission of their desire. And the strength and intensity of that desire made her head spin and her skin feel as if it was on fire where his body pressed against hers.

Without releasing her, he drew her backwards, colliding with something solid in his path. She felt him fumbling behind his back and then the door swung open and they stumbled into the cottage.

Her fingers were in his hair, clutching and tugging, and she squirmed against him, frustrated by the barrier of their clothes.

'Where?' His voice was hoarse with need.

'Here,' she said, her fingers fumbling with his zip.

'We can't—' He broke off with a gasp as she freed him.

'Kitchen. Table.'

She was fighting to get the words out but he was already lifting her up, carrying her through the house. She heard something smash as he pushed it to the floor and then she was on the table and he was pulling off her boots and pushing down her jeans, taking her panties with them.

She opened her legs, tilting her hips up.

'What about—?'

'I'm on the pill. I just wanted to be sure before. Please, Ivo…'

His face was tight with concentration, with the effort of holding back, and now she saw his control snap. He gripped her hips and pushed into her and began to move, his breath quickening, one hand seeking out her clitoris, working in time with his thrusts.

She clasped his face and kissed him hungrily. Feeling him swell inside her, she grasped the edge of the table, frantic now in her movements, her body shuddering against his as he tensed, his mouth hot against hers, and surged inside her.

CHAPTER SIX

FOR SEVERAL SHATTERING moments that seemed to exist outside of time neither of them moved, and then, head spinning, heart adrift somewhere in his chest, Ivo placed his palm down against the tabletop and leaned forward to rest his forehead against Joan's shoulder. Her hand was still tangled in his hair and he could hear her jerky breath above his own ragged breathing.

Post-orgasmic relief and a reluctance to leave her body was flooding him in equal measure, and he knew he should say something. But his throat was so tight he couldn't speak. Because that first time at the hotel hadn't been a fluke. His need for her had been the same unthinking, irresistible imperative as before, and being with her was even more exquisite and devastating.

'I need to move,' she said against his chest, and he felt her legs start to shake.

Shifting his weight, he pulled back and out of her, stifling her soft gasp with his mouth as he lowered her onto the table.

'Are you okay?' His eyes scanned her face. 'I didn't hurt you, did I?'

His own shoulder hurt where he had banged it against the back door, and his shin was stinging from when he collided with something en route to the kitchen. But he had been so blinded with passion and need he might have been wading through lava and he probably wouldn't have noticed.

She shook her head, and then her forehead creased. 'But I hurt you.'

Following the direction of her gaze, he glanced at his arm and saw where her fingernails had left crescent-shaped marks on the skin.

'I'm sorry… I didn't mean to.'

Her eyes were wide and worried, like a child's, and if he'd been another man—a man who had been raised with kindness rather than the man he was—he might have pulled her close and smoothed those worry lines away from her face.

Instead he shrugged. 'Don't worry about it. It's nothing, really.'

But it was something, he thought. Those indentations were undeniable proof of the hunger that had rolled through and over them just moments before, and he felt indecently gratified to know that she had been as undone by their encounter as he had.

There was a beat of silence as they took in their own and each other's state of disarray, and then, averting her gaze, Joan slid off the table and began to tug up her jeans.

'I might just go and get cleaned up…' Glancing down, she looked suddenly stricken. 'Did we do that?'

'We can fix it,' he said quickly. 'Or replace it,' he added, his gaze taking in the pieces of shattered china and glass that were scattered across the floor. Remembering how he'd swept everything off the table in his urgency to have her, he took a step forward. 'In the meantime, why don't I clear it up?'

She shook her head. 'You don't know where anything is.'

'And you do?'

One fine brown eyebrow curved into an arch. 'I live here.'

'You've been here for three days.'

'That's three days more than you.'

He laughed then. He couldn't help it. She was so stubborn. And funny. He could imagine her as a little girl, forehead creased in defiance, digging in her heels. Although in his experience children never won those battles.

On the contrary, for him, being a child had been all about minimising the losses. No doubt that was why he was so committed to having the last word. And these days he almost always did, because wealth like his made people very accommodating.

Most people, he thought, jaw tightening, his whole body coiling in on itself as he remembered Andy White's parting words to him.

'There's no heart to your business.'

Because hearts got broken. His own had been broken so often and so casually he'd lost count. There were the countless foster parents who'd come in and out of his life whenever his mother had left him and his brothers unsupervised. And then, after she'd finally left for good, he'd lost Marcus first, then Caleb.

Each time he'd patched it together clumsily, but it was damaged now, too fragile for real life, so he kept it shut away inside his ribs like a museum piece in a glass case.

He felt Joan's gaze on his face. A curl of her hair was falling across one cheekbone and beneath it the skin looked a little flushed. Staring down at her, Andy White's voice faded from his head and he felt better, calmer, as if something had been switched off inside him.

'So where's the dustpan?' he asked, unable to resist stroking that curl away from the curve of smooth skin.

'You're quite annoying,' she said quietly, but she didn't move away from his hand.

'Apparently so. But it was me who smashed everything.'

Her gaze was steady, but something flickered across her eyes as she said softly, 'And it was me who wanted you to smash everything.'

For a moment they just stared at each other, and then she

ducked underneath his hand and tiptoed carefully across the floor.

'The dustpan is in the cupboard under the stairs. Don't forget to recycle the glass. It goes in the brown bin at the side of the cottage.'

Minx, he thought, watching her run lightly out of the room.

Halfway up the stairs, she stopped. 'You know I was kidding, right? You don't have to clean up.'

'I know that. But I want to.'

He needed something to help him walk back from an uncharacteristic loss of control that was now becoming less uncharacteristic, thanks to this woman. More crucially, he needed some distance between them—actual physical distance—so that he could break this strange weave of post-coital intimacy. It was one of the risks…a sidebar to the necessary physical closeness of sex…and normally he was careful not to encourage it. But somehow he had let it happen with Joan.

Only momentarily, he reassured himself, and only because they had broken stuff and so had to have a 'domestic' kind of conversation.

It had been a long time since he had done anything that remotely resembled cleaning. Certainly not the kind involving a dustpan and brush. But it was strangely satisfying. And yet as he washed his hands he could still feel that ache in his chest. It was sharp, like thirst. Taking a glass from the draining board, he filled it with water and drank greedily. There was a milk carton on the side, and he put it back in the fridge, and then, after a second or two, he refilled the glass and made his way upstairs.

Joan was standing by the bedroom window, wearing different jeans and a soft blue cable knit jumper that made him think of summer skies and soft, sandy beaches and the kind of holidays he'd dreamed of taking as a child. She looked up as he tapped lightly on the door, her hand pressing against the windowsill almost as if she was steadying herself.

'I brought you some water.'

'Thank you.'

She came over and took the glass from him, but she didn't drink. Instead, she put it down on the chest of the drawers. The gold bracelet—the one he had returned to her earlier that morning—hung loosely around her wrist, the blue charm glittering in the pale sunlight.

Her lashes flickered up. 'Look, I don't know how this works. I've had a couple of boyfriends, but you're my first one-night stand. Except it's not one night any more, is it?'

'No, it's not,' he agreed.

He could see the pulse at the base of her neck beating wildly. His own seemed to have slowed. That night she'd been so responsive, so uninhibited, he had made assumptions. But now it appeared she was less of an expert than he'd thought. And he shouldn't like that, because it made him feel responsible. And yet, against his own will, he did.

'Why did you come here, Ivo?'

Their eyes clashed and held. It was both a blunter and more refined version of the question she had asked outside, but it still caught him off guard. But then to him any question that veered into the personal was a red flag—as more than one ex-lover had complained.

She held his gaze. 'You could have got somebody else to drop off the bracelet.'

True… But truthfully he hadn't known what he was going to do until he'd found himself driving along the road to Snowdrop Cottage. He had got there on autopilot, his libido in the driver's seat, his common sense bound and gagged in the boot.

It had taken until he'd opened the gate and walked into the garden before he'd got around to asking himself what he thought he was doing. But by then it had been too late. Looking down at Joan in the snow, he had known without equivocation that he wanted her.

Still wanted her even now.

And he would do anything to have her again. Even break the habits of a lifetime by answering a question about himself.

He cleared his throat. 'You're right. I could have done that. And that's what I planned on doing. But I ended up here. I don't know how—'

He broke off, searching for the right words to explain the unexplainable, and briefly wondered what kind of conversation they would have had if Jonathan hadn't come hammering on his door that morning. Back when he'd thought their first night together would be their last because, although he enjoyed sex, enjoyed pleasing his partners, with other women one time was always enough to satisfy his curiosity.

He was simply a man satisfying a basic physical need with a woman. Any woman.

Except Joan. It felt different with her.

The mystery hadn't been solved, it had deepened, and he was *intrigued.* Although that wasn't a relationship status he'd ever had or ever imagined himself having. But there was something about this beautiful, spirited woman that was at odds with the look in her eyes when she talked about running and hiding. And then there was that scar. It was not that old, and whatever had caused it would have hurt—a lot.

It still did, he thought, remembering the tentativeness she had sometimes when she walked. As if she was expecting something to snap.

But wasn't he making this all too complicated? Joan Santos was just a one-night stand plus.

And yet it was daytime now. A different day completely, and a different location too. Everything was different.

Except the hunger. That was the same.

Even now he wanted more. More of her body moving against his…more of her soft mouth and teasing tongue.

'Oh, I see.' Joan tilted her head. 'So it's the satnav's fault you ended up in my garden?'

He heard the echo of his own accusation in her words but he was distracted by her eyes. They looked more green than brown now. Like new shoots of grass pushing through the battered winter earth.

Feeling her nearness go through him, he shook his head. 'The satnav works fine,' he said slowly. 'I just don't normally do this.'

It was such an alien concept to him—but then he honestly couldn't remember sex having such power over him before. And that was what it was, wasn't it?

Even having to ask that question made his heart pound. But it was just sex. There were any number of rational explanations for why it felt different.

He hesitated, on unfamiliar ground now. How much did he say? How much did he give away?

'I don't really do random.' He meant turning up at a woman's house out of the blue with a flimsy excuse and no plan of what to do next.

'And that's what this was?'

His eyes moved over her small, guarded face. *No, it was also reckless and unprecedented.* But right now all that seemed irrelevant in the face of something stronger—something that had knocked him off course metaphorically and geographically, he thought with a jolt, as he realised that, had he stuck to his agenda, he would be reaching the outskirts of London right about now.

But instead he was here, with Joan, because this thing between them felt incomplete, unresolved, unfinished.

So why not finish it, then? Why not let it run its course?

Somewhere inside his head he could hear alarms ringing,

as if a perimeter fence had been breached by an intruder. But why? He wasn't planning on marrying her. He wasn't planning on marrying, full-stop.

He shook his head. 'I wanted to see you again,' he said slowly.

She looked up at him and licked her lips, and he could see that, like him, she was trying to figure out what that meant… how much she should give away.

'I wanted to see you again too,' she said finally.

Her voice was fierce, almost aggressive, but her eyes flashed storm-dark with something that made his whole body turn to stone.

There was silence, and then she reached out and touched his face.

'I'm not—' he said.

'I don't—' she said at the same time, withdrawing her hand.

Her eyes clashed with his and he saw the same wariness there that he had seen at the wedding reception—as if she was expecting the ground to open beneath her feet—and he wondered what had happened to make her feel that way. And why she wanted to keep it secret.

Her gaze narrowed in his direction. 'You first.'

He could see a pulse beating in the base of her throat and was vividly conscious of his desire pulsing beneath his skin. 'How long are you in England?' he asked.

'Six days.'

A rush of heat tightened his muscles. Plenty of time to prove to his body that she was a woman like any other, and to reach the closure he apparently needed.

'I haven't had a holiday in a while…'

An understatement. He worked on weekends, he worked in the car, and on the yacht, and on the jet.

'I've been thinking about taking a few days off and I wondered if you might like some company.'

He saw her hands twitch and then press against her thighs, as if she was trying to control them.

'By "company", you mean sex?'

He wondered if it was the bluntness of her words, or hearing her say them out loud, or if it was just the slight lift to her chin as her met his gaze, but watching her throat work as she picked up the glass, tilted it to her lips and drank, he had never wanted anything as much as he wanted to rip off her clothes and lift her onto the bed and take her again.

Only that felt too out of control. And this idea of seeing her again, sleeping with her again, was supposed to be about taking charge, but to do that he needed to make it feel more transactional—like a business deal.

Trying to quiet the chaos beneath his skin, he nodded. 'Exactly, I'm not looking for anything serious.'

'I'm not either.' She put the glass back down on the chest of drawers. 'Why would I be? I'm on holiday.'

It was the right answer—or it should have been. And yet it stung in the same way that watching Joan dance with Phil had stung.

He stared down at her, remembering the silken smoothness of her skin and how she had fitted so perfectly against him and tasted so sweet. On impulse, he leaned forward and kissed her. Her lips parted and he deepened the kiss. He felt her soft intake of breath and his body hardened instantly.

She made him want so much…

He pulled back a fraction, ending the kiss, and she stared up at him dazedly. But it was she who spoke first.

'There's just one thing.' She cleared her throat. 'I don't want Cassie and Jonathan to know about this. I need it to stay just between the two of us.'

Us. The word sounded strange and unfamiliar to his ears. It had been a long time since he had been part of any version of 'us'. Not since Caleb had been arrested and had disappeared from his life for ever.

His brother was the last to leave him and the hardest to lose. He and Caleb had always been so close. It was why he always needed to know that he was safe. Why he kept hoping his brother would change. But hope was what hurt the most. Hoping that people would come back. Hoping that they would change. They never did.

He thought back to all the times his mother had promised that she would stop using drugs. It had broken him, and he had sworn never again to suffer that pain of betrayal, that ache of loneliness. Better to be alone than to have to go through that again.

'That won't be a problem.'

He frowned as Joan's stomach gave a low, accusing rumble.

'Sorry.' She pressed her hand against the waistband of her jeans. 'I was going to have breakfast and then I saw the snow and I forgot to eat.'

'Then why don't I take you out to lunch?'

The invitation was out of his mouth before he realised what he was going to say, and she looked up at him, a V-shaped crease breaking up the smoothness of her forehead.

'Lunch?'

'Yes, lunch.' He took control. 'The Alwyn Arms does excellent food. You eat lunch, don't you?'

'Yes, of course. I just… I just thought this was only about sex.'

Her voice was scratchy when she answered, and her eyes were light and bright with a heat that seemed to soak through his clothes into his skin.

Holding her gaze, he placed his hand flat against the curve of her back and pulled her towards him. 'I don't think the occasional meal together is going to blur any lines—and besides, I've looked in your fridge. There doesn't seem to be anything in there except yoghurt and some strange-looking spoons.'

She smiled then and he drew her closer—close enough that he could feel her heart beating through her sweater. Or maybe it was his own heart beating.

'They're not spoons. They're Cryo-sticks. You use them on your face to reduce inflammation and puffiness. They need to be cold—that's why they're in the fridge.' Her stomach rumbled again. 'And it's not yoghurt. It's kefir. So, yeah, lunch would be great…'

Shifting back against the plump leather upholstery, Joan gazed out of the window of Ivo's car. It was childish, but she couldn't stop looking at the snow. It was just so beautiful and peaceful. Unlike the inside of her head, where everything was still trembling with the aftershocks of the morning's unexpected turn of events.

Which was one way to describe having sex on a kitchen table, she thought, her skin stinging as she pictured herself spread against the table like a personal banquet for one.

Earlier in the kitchen, surrounded by the wreckage of their encounter and with her legs barely supporting her body, she had thought going upstairs might give her space to clear her head. But, as she'd learned last night, it didn't matter if Ivo wasn't in the room with her. He was there in her head.

And then he had come upstairs anyway.

Her spine tensed, replaying the moment when he had walked into the bedroom, remembering how shocked she'd felt as her body had rippled to life all over again, everything suddenly liquid and hot. She'd never reacted like that before, and she hadn't expected to then, but whatever this was between them was bigger than anything she'd ever known. He made her body melt and her head spin so she could no longer think straight.

Then again, what was there to think about?

It was new and unsettling to admit it, even to himself,

but she wasn't ready to walk away from Ivo yet. She wanted him—wanted this beautiful, tightly wound man sitting beside her. Wanted this…whatever *this* was. Because it felt like the right choice for now.

Back in Bermuda, she had more or less stopped dating. People were complicated. They came with baggage. Needs. Hopes. Failures they'd rather forget. Dreams they were still chasing. And she had more baggage than all of them put together. But here, with Ivo, the 'now' was all that mattered. That was the beauty and simplicity of this relationship.

Except it wasn't a relationship. It was just sex.

And lunch.

Why not live in the 'now' with Ivo for a couple of days? She had been stuck in the past for so long, and as soon as Dr Webster got back to her she would be planning for her future. So why not kick back and enjoy this holiday with him?

Her head jerked round as the sound of a phone ringing filled the car.

Frowning, Ivo glanced at the screen on the dashboard, and Joan saw a name flashing beside a number: *Karolina*.

'Sorry, I need to answer that. It's my PA.'

Seconds later a woman's voice replaced the ringing.

'Good afternoon, Mr Faulkner. I'm sorry to bother you—I know you're out of office. I have a couple of time-contingent documents for you, and I thought you could sign them off this afternoon at the London office.'

In an attempt to at least look as if she was giving him some privacy, Joan had been staring pointedly out of the window, but now she glanced towards Ivo in confusion. He was supposed to be in London this afternoon?

Ivo cut the voice off. 'When's the deadline?'

'Two o'clock your time.'

'That's fine. I can send those over.' Leaning forward slightly, he indicated right.

'Thank you.' There was a tiny pause. 'Oh, just one last thing. I was checking your diary for next week… I thought you had a follow-up meeting with Andy White and his team on Wednesday, but it doesn't seem to be there any more.' She cleared her throat. 'Do I need to call his PA and put another date in the diary?'

It didn't seem like a particularly contentious question to Joan, but she saw a muscle pull at his jaw.

'I called it off,' he said finally. 'And no new date will be required.'

There was finality in his voice even before he hung up. For a while, they drove in silence. Ivo seemed preoccupied and remote again, and she wondered if he had changed his mind about lunch, but then abruptly he turned to her.

'Would you mind if we did a quick detour?' he asked. His voice was flat and hard. 'I just need to sign off these—'

'Documents,' Joan said, nodding. 'I heard. And, yeah, that's fine.'

She half wanted to ask him why he hadn't gone to London, but it wasn't any of her business. 'Where are we going?' she asked instead.

He hesitated, almost as if he was deciding whether or not to tell her—which was completely pointless as she was in the car with him.

'I have a place near here.'

He did? She stared at him in confusion. 'Then why did you stay at the hotel?'

'The same reason you did. I suppose I could have left and come back in the morning for breakfast…' The hair on the back of her neck rose as his blue eyes found hers. 'But when I went outside to get some fresh air I got waylaid.'

She had a quivering, vivid flashback to that moment in the garden when he had held out his hand to her as if he was leading her to safety.

Or claiming her.

Suddenly she couldn't catch her breath. She felt helpless, undone, her need for him snaking through her like quicksilver in a thermometer.

With an effort, she cleared her throat. 'I think you'll find that I was the one who was waylaid.'

There was a long, scratchy silence.

'I suppose you were,' he said at last, in that quiet, dark-edged way of his that danced through her like a flame. 'But you left me no choice.'

She had no answer to that—or not one that was coherent, anyway—and she went back to staring at the snowy landscape. It was already starting to melt in places, but…

She sat up straight. They had just reached the brow of a hill and, gazing down into the valley, she could see a beautiful pale grey castle, its walls dappled rose-pink and silver in the winter sunlight.

'Oh, my days! What is that place?'

As she leaned forward to press her nose against the window Ivo slowed the car fractionally. 'It's Castle Alwyn.' Some of the tension in his voice had eased.

'Like the pub?'

He nodded. 'The Alwyn family used to own many properties in the area, but the male line died out about a hundred years ago. The castle was empty for a long time.'

'So who owns it now?'

He didn't immediately answer and she turned to face him.

The light in his gaze sharpened. 'I do,' he said softly.

Ivo owned a castle.

Joan turned back to the window, fixing her gaze on the distant battlements, her head spinning like a carousel.

Ivo owned a castle. An actual, real-life castle.

During the next ten minutes it disappeared from view periodically, as if it was simply a figment of her imagination.

Her chest would tighten, but then it would reappear again, and she'd feel her pulse accelerate.

Ivo offered nothing by way of explanation, but she would have struggled to form a sentence anyway. She was stunned… speechless with shock.

As they turned into a long driveway a cluster of deer scattered at speed and she stared after them longingly.

'Don't worry. They always come back.'

'Are they yours?'

He met her gaze. 'I wouldn't say they're mine, but they live on my land.'

The driveway seemed to go on for ever, but finally they pulled up in front of the castle. As the large, studded door swung open she half expected a knight to appear, swinging a sword, but instead, a smiling middle-aged woman with a silvery pixie crop stepped forward to greet them.

'Good afternoon, Mr Faulkner.'

'Linda, this is Joan,' Ivo said as he led Joan inside. 'I need you to look after her while I sign a few documents.' He turned to Joan. 'I won't be long. Linda is my housekeeper. She'll take care of you. Whatever you need, just ask her.'

He turned and strode away before she could respond, but she was too distracted by the soaring ceiling of the entrance hall to say anything.

Linda smiled. 'Come with me. I think the best place for you to wait would be the drawing room. It has a wonderful view of the lake and there's a lovely warm fire in there.'

Still lost for words, Joan followed her.

Had she simply seen the castle from a distance, she would have imagined that the interior would be impressive but gloomy, with lots of suits of armour and shields. But there was not a shield in sight and the drawing room was surprisingly light. The walls were a soft, muted grey, but there were splashes of colour from the bright pink and peacock-blue sofas and the huge modern canvases on the walls.

'It's beautiful,' she murmured. 'Oh, and look at that view!'

She stopped in front of one of the large ceiling-height windows and gazed out at a silvery lake. Deer were picking their way through the snow at the edges, and in the distance she could see sheep grazing beneath the frost-tipped trees.

'It is very beautiful,' Linda agreed. 'Now, would you like tea or coffee?'

Joan turned and smiled. 'Tea would be lovely, thank you. Milk, no sugar, please.'

As she waited for the housekeeper to return, she stood at the window and gazed at the view.

'Difficult to read. He has boundaries.'

That was what Cassie had said about Ivo, and she'd been right. You couldn't have a more solid boundary than a castle wall. As for difficult to read—well, she certainly would never have imagined Ivo living somewhere so unapologetically romantic.

There was so much to look at in the room that it was almost two hours before she began to wonder where he was. Surely it couldn't take that long to sign a document? Her mouth twisted and she felt her shoulders tense. Almost certainly it didn't. More likely Ivo had forgotten she was here.

Having finished her tea, she got up and walked slowly back over to the window. Outside, shadows were marbling the surface of the lake with black. This morning the idea of having a holiday fling with Ivo had felt empowering. It would be so different form the way she had lived her life up until now. And yet strangely she'd felt that she would be reclaiming her life, taking a path of her own choosing.

Now, though, she felt like she had one time at school, when she was ten years old. A group of classmates she'd thought were her friends had been playing Blind Man's Bluff. When it was her turn, they'd all run off and she had uncovered her eyes to find herself on her own.

Her eyes narrowed on the slowly sinking sun. Why would he do that? Why would he invite her to lunch and then just disappear?

But never mind him—what was she doing? Why was she standing here, waiting for him to remember she existed? She wasn't his wife, who might love him enough to put up with that kind of behaviour. Nor was she some escort he paid by the hour to be at his beck and call.

Her lip curled. Did he think that owning a castle and having household staff meant that he was not subject to the rules of courtesy like everyone else?

Probably. She'd seen it back home often enough. Rich tourists talking to the locals as if they were children or servants, and people putting up with it because they needed the money.

Maybe that was how he saw her.

But she didn't need or want Ivo's money.

And, okay, this wasn't a serious relationship—but she didn't do second place. And she sure as hell wasn't going to come second to some document.

Turning away from the glorious view, she stalked out of the room and down the corridor in the direction that Ivo had walked. The trouble was she had no idea where he was… But then she heard his voice through one of the doors and she yanked it open and stepped inside.

Ivo was sitting behind his desk, his phone pressed against his ear. He was talking, but as she shut the door behind her his blue eyes narrowed on her face and he hung up.

'I was just on my way to find you.'

The cool, dismissive note in his voice made her see a whole new spectrum of red. 'Well, now you don't need to bother,' she snapped. 'Not that I think you were going to—just so we're clear.'

CHAPTER SEVEN

TOSSING HIS PHONE onto the desk, Ivo stared across the room at Joan, his chest tightening. Bringing her here had not been a good idea, he admitted.

Even before she had thrown open the door and stormed into his office like some small, furious tornado, he had been struggling to explain to himself what had prompted such uncharacteristic behaviour. Not least because it had taken him almost twice as long as usual to read through the documents Karolina had sent through. He couldn't stop thinking about Joan. More specifically, he couldn't stop thinking about the sounds she'd made as thrust inside her. And the heat in her eyes as she'd pulled him closer.

There was heat in her eyes now. But not the heat of passion. And instead of writhing beneath him on the table, she looked as if she wanted to upend his desk with him still sitting at it. And he had nobody to blame but himself.

But he didn't want to want her this much. With every other woman he'd slept with, he'd purposely kept things brief and impersonal. Yes, they'd had sex, but always in some neutral hotel room. He'd never gone back to their place or invited them back to his. There was hunger and satisfaction on both sides, but never any emotion or passion. And he'd never had an impulse to change that.

Only then he'd had to go and break the rules with Joan. It had started when he'd not only offered to drive her home but then had followed her upstairs, as if they were connected by a piece of invisible string.

And since then he had kept on breaking rules—right up to the moment he'd brought her back to the castle. As for emotion and passion… He had lost control in both those areas too, he thought, replaying how he'd swept aside the crockery on her kitchen table this morning. He hadn't cared about the broken china, or the fact that he was supposed to be en route to his newly opened office in London.

All that had mattered was her, and that swirling, maddening heat storming through his body.

His shoulders tensed against his chair. In the past, work had been his safe place. Work had given him control of his life. He had been confident that flipping open his laptop would somehow snap that shimmering thread of hunger between them. But for the first time ever in his life it had failed him. Gazing at the documents, he hadn't even known who he was.

And it was her fault.

Joan was doing this to him.

For some reason she had got past the barriers he'd built against the world and was making him feel things. Emotions he hadn't felt in a long time. Emotions he didn't want to feel.

He needed to get a grip.

'It took longer than I thought it would.' He managed to keep his voice calm, but it was harder than it should have been. He didn't want to think about why that was the case.

She stuck her chin up pugnaciously. 'And it didn't occur to you to come and tell me that?'

It had, but he hadn't been sure he would be able to walk away if he found himself alone with her, so it had seemed safer just to keep his head down.

Now, though, he realised that had been a mistake. One of many, it would appear.

'Look, you knew I was the CEO of a global brand before we got into this, and as CEO I can't always delegate. But I am sorry about lunch. I've finished now, so…'

Her eyes flashed green like an angry cat. 'It's nearly four o'clock, Ivo. They'll have stopped serving lunch now. They probably stopped serving hours ago.'

'I'm sure they'll make an exception for me.'

He wasn't being arrogant. Last year he had personally invested in the Alwyn Arms, to keep it from closing, and he'd kept on investing to the point where it had been able to attract a Michelin starred chef.

'And it's all about you, isn't it? What about me? I've been sitting there waiting for you for nearly two hours.'

He heard the catch in her voice and he didn't like how that made him feel. But the fact that he was feeling anything other than lust made his voice harden. 'And I said I was sorry. I don't see what more I can say.'

'You couldn't say *less*,' she snapped. 'You know, this might be how you treat your girlfriends, and maybe that's okay for them—maybe they're happy to put up with it because they're in a relationship with you and putting up with things is what happens between couples—but I'm not okay with it.'

He stared at her, his jaw tightening, stung by her assumption that he treated women badly. Because he didn't. He always made it absolutely clear to them what was on offer, and he thought he'd made it clear to Joan too. But as to what happened between couples… He had no idea, because he had never come close to what she was talking about.

He sensed from her words that she had, and he felt something twist inside him at the thought of Joan sharing herself with another man.

'Why did you even invite me to lunch if you were just going to relegate me to the bottom of your agenda at the first opportunity? It's so rude.'

Now he got to his feet and stalked round the desk. As he stopped in front of her he saw a flicker of apprehension in her eyes and his chest tightened. He didn't want to frighten her. He would never hurt a woman, no matter what the provocation, but he needed to shut this down now.

'But walking into someone's office without knocking and interrupting them when they're talking on the phone is straight out of Debrett's *Guide to Etiquette & Modern Manners*?'

'Don't make this about my behaviour. I wouldn't have needed to interrupt you if you'd been courteous enough to let me know how long you were going to be.' She glared at him. 'What is wrong with you? Were you raised by wolves or something?'

Not actual wolves, no, he thought, his stomach clenching. *They didn't have fur or fangs. They had hands that slapped you, and that wasn't so bad. Other times they had fists and that was worse.* He'd learned to gauge which version to expect by their footsteps. Heavy meant a slap…light meant a punch or worse.

Until he'd left home at sixteen to join the army, his eldest brother Marcus had borne the brunt of it. Stepping in front of the fists. But then he had left and it was just him and Caleb. Until Caleb got arrested. And then it had been just him.

Sometimes, when the bruises showed or they'd missed school for too many days, social workers would turn up and they would be taken to foster parents. Until his mother decided that she could 'cope' again.

But he wasn't about to reveal the ugliness of his past to this beautiful, angry woman.

'There is nothing wrong with me. You're just hungry. And looking for a fight—just like you always are.'

She took a step towards him, her hands clenching by her

sides. 'Don't talk as if you know who I am. You don't know anything about me.'

'Which is exactly the point of this arrangement,' he said coolly. 'We don't need to know anything about each other to have sex, Joan. We don't even need to like each other.'

She blinked. There was a moment of piercing silence. 'I suppose not,' she said slowly. Her voice sounded thin and fractured. 'You know, I think I'm going to go now. I've lost my appetite anyway.'

'You can't just leave.'

'You can't stop me.'

Her eyes met his briefly, revealing the depth of her hurt and anger, and then she turned towards the door.

He watched her grip the handle. Everything in him was suddenly twisted and snarled up tight. She was right. He had never been able to stop people leaving. It was one of the reasons he had never allowed himself to get into this kind of situation. And yet here he was.

Sidestepping past her, he pressed his hand against the door, holding it shut firmly. 'I don't know why I said that. About not needing to like each other. It wasn't true. I mean, I know it is true for some people—maybe it's even been true for me in the past—but it's not true with you. Quite the opposite, in fact. I do like you.'

She didn't turn around, but her fingers trembled against the handle. 'You know, you're the only person I've ever met who could make that sound like a problem.'

Because it was a problem for him, he thought, his body suddenly so taut it felt as if it would shatter into a million shards. Liking someone, caring about them, was dangerous. Life had taught him that lesson repeatedly. But despite that he did like her, and he did care that he had hurt her.

'It's a challenge, not a problem. *You're* a challenge.'

Now she turned and looked at him with a mixture of incredulity and anger. 'So this is my fault?'

'That's not what I'm saying. I'm the problem here. I don't know what I'm doing. This isn't what I do…who I am. With women, I don't ever get this far. One night's always enough. But it wasn't with you. I can't get you out of my head. That's why I took so long signing those damn documents. I couldn't concentrate. I couldn't stop thinking about you.'

Her green-brown eyes lifted to his face.

'Look, I know you must think I'm a jerk. But if you'd just let me show you who I am…'

He felt his whole body grow taut. That was normally the last thing he wanted to do with any woman—but Joan wasn't like any other woman, and he didn't behave as he normally did when he was with her.

He heard her inhale. 'I thought you said we didn't need to know anything about each other?'

His jaw tightened. 'I said a lot of stupid things. I know you owe me nothing, but if you could just let me make this right. Please, Joanie…'

Joanie.

Joan stared at him, her pulse beating in her throat. Her name sounded different when he said it, and she liked the way his mouth shaped the syllables. Only it wasn't fair for him to use her own name against her. Wasn't fair that she should respond…that her pulse should lose speed or her blood thicken and slow like this.

And it would be so easy to say yes. Because she wanted to believe him…because she still wanted him.But…

'You made me feel horrible,' she said, her hands balling at her sides.

'I'm sorry.'

And she could hear in his voice that he was.

'For missing lunch, for all those stupid things I said to you.'

She bit her lip. 'Was that true? Have you really not got this far with anyone before?'

It didn't seem likely. A man as good-looking and rich as Ivo would have no trouble attracting the opposite sex, and yet he had none of the hallmarks of a womaniser. He was certainly not flirtatious. He didn't try to seduce or charm. On the contrary, he was so tightly wound and intense, being with him felt like teetering on the edge of an active volcano.

He nodded. 'I'm not good at letting people get close.'

There was a complicated expression on his handsome face, but she thought that she understood it. Every person he met would know what he was worth, and someone as intelligent as Ivo would know that. And once you knew something you couldn't unknow it. You had to find a way to live with it.

Like her, pretending to everyone that she hadn't got a 'proper' job because she wanted to help out Gia, when in reality she needed to believe she was just taking a short sabbatical from her athletic career.

'My life is not normal in some ways,' he said after a moment. 'That's not an excuse. It's just a fact. But you made it feel normal…made me feel normal.'

Ivo didn't do big emotional outbursts, and she could hear the surprise in his voice. No, she thought a moment later. Surprise wasn't quite right. It was more that he was incredulous—as if 'normal' was something he hadn't considered possible.

'You are normal,' she lied, her eyes taking in the strong sweep of his jaw and the extraordinarily sculpted bones beneath his lightly tanned skin. 'And annoying and bossy. And you don't dance at weddings, which I personally find unacceptable, but you're not the worst.'

His gaze rose to meet hers. 'Does that mean you'll stay?'

'For lunch? I think that boat has sailed.'

He took a step forward, his eyes resting on her face. 'Dinner, then?'

Yes, she thought, but now that they had cleared one hurdle, it felt like the right time to tackle another. Quick off the ground. Maximum force. Like her coach used to say.

'I guess I could stay—' she batted his hand away as he reached for her '—on two conditions.'

His gaze sharpened. 'Which are…?'

'I get that you're a CEO, and you can't switch off entirely, but you have to be respectful.'

'I can do that. And the second?'

'You let me buy you dinner. You eat dinner, don't you?' she added as he stared at her in silence.

'I do.'

Some of the tension softened around his mouth, and this time when he reached for her she let his hand slide around her waist.

'But I should pay—'

'Why? Because you're rich? Or because I'm a woman?'

'Of course not. I'm not some throwback.'

'So it is about the money?' Without giving him a chance to reply, she said quickly, 'Look, I know you said you didn't do anything the other day, but you did. You called Paul and he got my car out of the ditch. That's why I want to buy you dinner. To say thank you. Just think what it would have cost me to call out a recovery truck. Way more than dinner. Particularly as it's only going to be take-out…' She ran out of breath.

'Are you done?'

She felt the slow burn of his gaze all the way down to her toes. 'Yes.'

He threaded his fingers through her hair and she felt his thumb strum her cheek as he tilted her face up to his. 'Then, yes, I accept your conditions.'

Thirty minutes later they were sitting at the breakfast bar

in the kitchen eating two surprisingly authentic pizzas with their hands.

'How's your margherita?' Ivo asked.

'It's good. Really good,' she said, gazing approvingly at the mozzarella stretching between the pizza on her plate and the slice in her hand. 'The thing about pizza is that it's really just dough with tomato and cheese, so it's easy to make one but much harder than you think to make a great one.'

'You sound like an expert.' Ivo leaned back in his chair, his blue eyes steady on her face.

'I should be after all the pizza I've eaten.' She smiled. 'My mum and dad both come from big families, and most Saturdays everyone comes round to ours for take-out. It's really noisy…and all the kids are running around.'

For a moment she was back in Bermuda, sprawling on the couch with the top button of her jeans undone, laughing with her sisters at something one of her aunts had said.

She glanced at the professional-looking stainless-steel oven that nestled in between the expensive pale wood cabinetry. Her mum and her aunties would kill to have a kitchen like this.

'Sounds fun.'

'Fun?' She looked up at Ivo, his words pulling her back to the now.

'Your family's Saturday nights. They sound like good fun.'

She laughed. 'More like your idea of hell, you mean.'

His mouth pulled at the corners. 'Not at all. I'd love to meet your rum-drinking aunties.'

He was joking, of course. He was never going to meet her family. Although Ivo didn't really do jokes, she thought a moment later.

'What about you?' she asked, curious suddenly about his background. If he'd gone to school with Jonathan he couldn't have come from money, so what had turned him into this business titan?

'Tell me about your family. I'm guessing it's not as big as mine. Or do you have a whole bunch of crazy relations too?'

He shook his head. 'Sadly not. No rum-drinking aunties at all.'

'What about siblings? Do you have any brothers or sisters?'

'No. No siblings. But I'll tell you something.' Abruptly he reached over and took her plate and stacked it on top of his. 'I'm still hungry. Can I tempt you with dessert? Linda usually has a selection in the fridge.'

He held out his hand and, sliding off her stool, she followed him into a cavernous larder.

'Let's see what we've got,' he murmured, stopping in front of a huge glass-fronted refrigerator.

He hadn't been wrong about the selection, she thought. There was salted caramel cheesecake. A chocolate and amaretto custard. Pannacotta.

'See anything you like?' he said softly.

Joan glanced up at him. He was still wearing his suit trousers and shirt from the morning, but he had undone the top button and rolled up his shirtsleeves, and his hair was rumpled, as if he'd run his hands through it one too many times.

Her throat felt tight and scratchy. He looked better than any dessert.

'Yes.' She nodded superfluously. 'Do you?'

Staring into her eyes, he nodded too. And then, taking his time, he drew her forward and his head dipped, mouth covering hers. He kissed her and kissed her, until she was melting on the inside and she was so desperate for him that it hurt.

She woke up the next morning, naked, alone and disorientated.

Ivo was gone.

For a moment that was all the information she could process—the only information that mattered. But soon she sat up, clutching the sheet around her body.

It had been dark when they'd come upstairs and there had been no time or need to switch the lights on. But now there was enough sunlight creeping around the edges of the blinds to let her gaze appreciatively around the room. She liked how the ceiling was painted silver. It made her feel as if she had floated up to the sky.

Or maybe that was the aftermath of a night with Ivo.

They had both reached greedily for the other, each of them scraped raw by the same seething hunger that swirled inside them. They'd barely made it upstairs. And they hadn't made it to the bed that first time. But they had made up for that later.

Her body twitched against the mattress as she remembered how he had licked the moan from her mouth as she'd arched against him over and over again. Nobody had ever touched her like he did, or made her feel so helpless and hungry all at once.

And afterwards he had curved his body around hers and held her close until she fell asleep.

'Good morning.'

She turned, her heart skipping a beat. Ivo was standing in the doorway. He was holding two mugs of something hot, and he must have been working out somewhere in the castle, because he was wearing shorts and a snug-fitting tank that showed off his beautifully muscled shoulders and arms.

'Is that tea?'

He nodded. 'Linda said milk, no sugar?'

Turning, he pressed a switch on the wall, and she blinked as the blinds opened with a faint mechanical hiss.

'Perfect.'

As she sat up, the sheet fell away from her body, and she felt her nipples harden as his gaze flickered to her breasts.

He handed her a mug and then he leaned forward and kissed her—a light, teasing kiss that made her belly clench. She leaned into him, quivering inside, because that was all it took. One kiss and she was hot and aching and damp.

She was desperate for him to kiss her again, but she had to have some self-control. She couldn't just take, take, take—otherwise it would be so much harder when she had to go back to Bermuda.

But she wasn't going to think about that now.

Reaching for her phone, she nearly dropped it when she saw that it was almost eleven o'clock.

'I didn't realise it was that late. Why didn't you wake me?'

'I thought you needed to sleep. It's not as if you got much rest last night.'

Their eyes met and she was suddenly breathless, from his nearness and the memory of his touch. 'I hope I didn't mess up your plans.'

'How could you? All my plans include you.'

He held his hand out to her, palm upward and after a second she took it. He meant, of course, his plans for this time they had together, but it made her chest feel tight anyway, as if it was too full.

She squeezed his hand. 'So, what do you have in mind?'

'I thought I could show you around the estate. It's mostly moorland, but it's very much part of the Dark Peak.'

Her eyes widened. 'That sounds like something out of a fantasy novel. But won't it be hard to get to? With the snow, I mean? Oh…' She frowned. Through the window, she saw the world was no longer white. 'It's gone.'

'It rained in the night. And now the sun's shining. That's what happens here. You get four seasons in a day. We could stay in if you'd rather—'

'No, I want to visit the Dark Peak, but do I have the right clothes?'

'Jeans will be fine—oh, and can you ride?'

'You mean a horse? Yeah, I can ride.'

'Good. Then why don't you get dressed? I'll let Linda know what we're doing and I'll meet you downstairs.'

* * *

The castle had left her wordless, but she didn't think she would ever see anything as beautiful as the moors that morning. As they reached the brow of the escarpment she dismounted and ran to the edge. Gazing down, she felt her breath not just taken—it was seized.

It was a wild, brooding kind of beauty that reminded her of the man who had now followed her and wrapped his arms around her waist. And, like Ivo, its remoteness was worth the effort it took to get there. But there was too much to take in…so much that felt unknowable.

'Do you like it?'

Gazing at the endless, uninterrupted landscape, she nodded. 'I think I could stand here for ever and not get tired of it.'

'For ever?'

He loosened his grip and there was a tension in his voice that hadn't been there before. She felt her heartbeat accelerate. For ever was a long time, and this fling would be over in a couple of days. She needed to remember that. Although it was hard not to get swept away by the immutable beauty of this place.

'Well, maybe not for ever.' She gave him an easy smile. 'I'm actually feeling quite hungry.'

He smiled then, and it didn't matter that the sun had disappeared behind a cloud.

'Then it's lucky I remembered lunch. This time.'

He took her hand and led her further along the plateau to where some rugs and cushions had been temptingly arranged on a huge millstone. And laid out on top of the millstone was…

'I asked Linda to make us a picnic, and Bruce, my driver, dropped it off.'

He lifted his hand and she saw a mud-spattered SUV parked a discreet distance away.

She felt a slight ache in her chest, and another behind her eyes. 'I love picnics.'

'I really did mean to take you out to lunch yesterday,' he said slowly.

'I know.'

Her chest felt as if it was going to burst open. She was so confused by what she was feeling right now.

That first time with Ivo had been about embracing the moment. Taking his hand, she had felt as if she was waking from some long hibernation. And then later, when he'd come to the cottage and it had all started up again, they had agreed to this fling in the most pragmatic way possible, signing up for a no-strings sexual affair in the same way that Ivo had signed those documents yesterday.

And yet this felt like the most wonderful fantasy.

But this wasn't real life for either of them, and she had to remember that.

'Come on.' She turned and gave him a dazzling, careless smile. 'Let's eat.'

The picnic was delicious. A lightly spiced carrot and coconut soup followed by warm asparagus quiches with flaky, buttery pastry, and tiny coffee and white chocolate eclairs to finish.

'I'm just going to snap some pictures.'

She wanted to ask him if she could take his photo, but that had *bad idea* written all over it. This was about living in the moment. When finally she left England behind she didn't want to be holding on to the past again.

When she sat back down, Ivo was staring out over the moorland, his blue eyes fixed on the horizon. He seemed preoccupied, just like he had yesterday, after his PA had called. At the time she'd thought it was because he didn't want to have to make a detour, but now she wasn't so sure.

'Did you really sign those documents yesterday or were you just saying that?'

'No, I signed them off.'

Looking up, she met his eyes, saw that he was trying to figure out what she was thinking.

'Why do you ask?' he said.

'You look like someone with a lot on his mind.'

There was a long pause. 'There's a lot going on at the moment,' he said finally.

She frowned, remembering that sudden tension in the car. 'Is it to do with Andy White?'

Ivo felt his jaw stiffen. He'd thought he'd hidden his reaction to Karolina's ill-timed question. But it was better that Joan thought he was distracted by work rather than thinking about his brother. The brother who was in prison less than an hour away and whose existence he'd denied to her face.

'Is it about industrial secrets?' She gave him a small, flickering smile. 'Because you don't have to worry. I spend most of my days with two people. One of them can't talk. The other is only interested in dinosaurs. You're not making a dinosaur, are you?'

Shaking his head, he smiled stiffly. 'Andy White runs a business called CGB. They've created this solid-state battery. It's more stable, greener, has a longer life. He and his brother Jamie started the business at college. They're smart guys, but they're cash strapped. Andy approached me for investment, and I met him and his brother a couple of times. I thought it was going well, but last week he walked away.'

She searched his face. 'Was it a negotiating tactic?'

He shook his head. 'They're not greedy. They're not even very good businessmen. But they have an outstanding product.'

'Did he give you a reason for walking?'

Yes. But not one he could admit to this woman, who had *family* stamped through her like a stick of rock. Telling her what Andy White had really said would mean revealing the ugliness of his life, and she didn't need to know about that.

'He didn't want CGB to lose its identity inside Raptor.'

That was true, although it was only a part of the truth.

'Does it have to?'

There were two small creases above her nose and, fighting the urge to reach out and smooth them, he shrugged.

'Obviously we'd keep the CGB brand name separate, but the money stream would come from Raptor, and I am Raptor.'

'But you're not just Raptor. You have a life.'

He nodded.

Except he didn't. This was the first day in about ten, twelve years he could remember not waking up and reaching for his laptop.

'Maybe he needs to know that.' Joan ran her hand back and forth over the thick-bladed grass. 'I mean, this isn't about money, because you have money. A lot of money. And he's not interested. But he reached out to you. So what made him do that? It must be something about you.'

Some of the disappointment and frustration he'd been carrying with him since the abortive meeting last week seemed to drain away.

'You just need to work out what it is. What? Why are you looking at me like that?'

Her beautiful green-brown eyes rested on his face. But she was more than beautiful.

'You know...you're very smart...'

Her eyebrow arched. 'I do hope the end of that sentence isn't *much smarter than you look*, because I have a knife close to hand.'

She gave him one of those flickering smiles that made his own mouth pull at the corners.

'Actually, I was trying to remember what degree you did at university.' He held her gaze. 'Or maybe you didn't tell me.'

Her smile stiffened ever so slightly. Not enough that anyone would notice unless they had spent the last few days becoming intimately acquainted with the enigma that was Joan Santos. He wondered again what she was holding back.

'I don't think you asked. It was sports psychology.'

Interesting, he thought. But why hadn't she wanted to tell him that?

'It's a good business to be in.'

She nodded. 'People used to be sceptical about it, but it's more mainstream now.'

She was right. He knew quite a few companies who used sports psychologists to motivate staff and set goals. Personally, he found them jargon-heavy, but even without the full facts Joan had read this situation intuitively.

'You're good,' he said slowly. 'Why didn't you take it up professionally?'

'I thought about it, but then Gia bought her business, and she's always helping me out, so I wanted to do something for her.' She looked up at the sky, frowning. 'It looks like there might be some rain heading this way. Do you think we should head back?'

She was right. It did look as if it was going to rain. But as they rode back he barely noticed when it started to drizzle. He was too busy replaying what she'd said about helping her sister. As an answer it was plausible enough to be true, but he knew instinctively that it was only part of the truth. He wondered what she was holding back. And what it would take to get her to tell him.

CHAPTER EIGHT

'SO, WHAT WOULD you like to do today?'

Stretching slightly, Joan tilted her head back from its position in the crook of Ivo's shoulder. He was staring down at her, and today his blue eyes were edging towards the greyer spectrum. But then the sky today was the same colour as the escarpment that stretched across his land, and she wondered, not for the first time, if the one reflected the other and vice versa.

There was certainly something elemental about him.

In bed, particularly, he was like a force of nature. Not rough. It was just that there was an intensity to him that seemed to move through her like a storm at sea, so that it was hard to catch her breath.

'Anything I like?' she asked.

His eyes narrowed and he shifted onto his back, taking her with him so that his gorgeous body was stretched out beneath hers. He was so irresistibly hard and male that it hurt. Needing space from her need for him, she pressed her hands against his chest and sat up, straddling him with her legs as he liked her to do,

She liked to do it too, she thought as his hands cupped her breasts, his thumbs stroking her already taut nipples.

'Absolutely anything,' he said softly, his hands moving to her waist, then down to grip her hips.

Dizzily, she braced herself, her head spinning. She could see a stripe of colour on his cheekbones and his eyes were darkening. Like the sky?

She glanced at the window.

'Oh, isn't it beautiful?'

A huge, shimmering rainbow was arched above the fields. Sensing her need to get closer, Ivo loosened his grip on her hips and she slid off the bed and walked unhurriedly across the room. In the past, she had often found it hard to look at her scar, but even though she could feel his gaze on her back she no longer felt self-conscious in the way she had after the accident. Knowing that he wanted her so much, seeing how turned on he got, made her feel proud of her body and its power to arouse him.

And astonished by it too.

Lying in Ivo's arms, it was quite possible, she'd discovered, to be two seemingly contradictory things at one time. To feel both drowsy, but alive, or taut with anticipation and yet also soft and yielding.

It was all very confusing—but nowhere near as complicated as what was going inside her head.

Sometimes at home she would take the boys down to the harbour. One day there had been a storm heading in, and the boats had all come back early. Ramon had been beside himself with excitement, but she had been looking up at the sky and watching the gulls as they were buffeted by the crosswinds. She felt like one of those gulls now. It was all she could do to stay steady.

Especially when Ivo was there.

And he was there most of the time.

She stared at the window, meeting her reflected gaze in the glass head-on.

He'd kept his word about work. He was CEO of Raptor, so

there were things he had to address, but he dealt with them swiftly and he hadn't disappeared into his study again.

Her body felt warm, just as it had out on the escarpment, when Ivo had wrapped his arms around her and they watched the grass turn gold in the sunlight. He hadn't left her side. Almost as if he couldn't bear to be apart from her.

Only there was no point in thinking like that. This time next week she would be back in Bermuda, and this and Ivo would all feel like a dream.

'Joanie?'

Ivo was standing beside her, frowning slightly, completely oblivious of his nudity. Unlike her, she thought, her breath fluttering in her throat as she followed the trail of fine golden hairs bisecting his stomach muscles to where the hair was thicker.

'I lost you there for a moment.' His blue gaze rested on her face. 'Where'd you go?'

'I was just thinking about what I most wanted to do.'

'And what did you decide?'

She knew from the infinitesimal thickening of his voice that their nakedness was now front and foremost in his mind, and she felt something deep inside her start to pulse, as if just by looking at her he could flip a switch.

She cleared her throat.

'That I'd like you to show me around the castle properly. You said you would. I want a proper tour—with all the history.'

She almost burst out laughing at the tortured expression on his face, and for a moment she was tempted to torture him a little longer.

'But first I want…'

'What?' he said hoarsely. 'What do you want?'

'You,' she said softly.

His face stilled, and his undisguised need for her made

her heart leap high in her chest. Standing on her tiptoes, she leaned in and kissed him. And then she was pulling him back towards the bed.

Kissing was good. Sex was even better. Both were so much simpler than thinking and overthinking. She just needed to distract herself—which was what she'd spent the last six months doing anyway.

Was it really that long? Her ribs tightened. She loved the boys, but as soon as she got the green light from Dr Webster she would have to let Gia know that she couldn't help out any more. When she started to race again she would go back to having those sponsors who'd dropped her, and then she would pay her sister back. Pay everyone back.

Thinking about that made her shake inside, but thankfully Ivo was pressing his warm, hard body against hers, and she let him distract her with his mouth and his tongue and his hands.

It was mid-morning before they finally began their tour of the castle.

'It was built in 1841 for the Duke of Alwyn, Henry Wootton,' Ivo said, pointing to the portrait of a proud-looking man wearing a military uniform. 'He was only the second Duke, and I think he was looking to prove that he was worthy of the title.'

She rolled her eyes. 'So he built a massive castle.'

Ivo shrugged. 'It's what wealthy men who were touchy about their status did in those days. Castles are architecturally masculine—and of course size matters if you're feeling inadequate.'

Her eyes found his. 'But that wouldn't be a motivation for someone buying a castle now, would it?'

There was a pulsing pause, and then she gave a shriek as Ivo pulled her towards him.

She slipped free of his grip. 'No more kissing until after the tour, thank you, Mr Faulkner. Otherwise, I might not leave a tip.'

'Fine. No kissing until after. But I get to choose the tip.'

Joan insisted that they look in all fifty of the rooms. It had clearly been a passion project for Ivo. She could hear it in his voice when he spoke.

'I didn't want it to look like a theme park, but I tried to keep the original spirit of the property in mind. That was really my only input. That and wanting to do it well. You know...not cut corners.'

And he hadn't, she thought, as they went from one stunning room to the next. There was a care and attention to detail that was remarkable.

And there were suits of armour. They were in the state-of-the-art gym, looking nowhere near as out of place next to the sleek lap pool as she might have imagined. But her favourite part of the castle was actually an extension of the main building.

The orangery was like something out of a film set for a lost world. It was still raining outside, but the warm, sticky air inside made it feel like summer. Made it feel like home.

'Why is this called an orangery if you grow all these other plants?' she asked as Ivo led her past exotic palms and trailing hibiscus into the centre of the building, where koi were breaking the surface of a huge octagonal pond.

'I think historically oranges were the first fruit they managed to grow here. But now we have figs, grapes, peaches, even pineapples.'

That was what she was smelling, Joan thought, her chest tightening.

Breathing in the scent, she smiled at Ivo. 'If I shut my eyes I could be back at Snapper Bay. All I need now is some sand.'

She caught sight of Ivo's face. There was an expression on

it she didn't recognise—almost a softness that momentarily stopped her speaking, stopped her breath. And there was a strange ache in her chest.

He reached out and pushed a curl away from her face. 'And some sun?'

No, that wasn't necessary, she thought, gazing up at him. He was more dazzling than the sun. Just looking at him set her alight.

She blinked, then glanced up to where the rain was hitting the glass panes of the orangery roof. 'Actually, I love rain. You see, you may not know this, but it's the best cure for when you're feeling blue about something. It just seems to wash everything away.'

Which was handy when you needed to cry but didn't want anyone to see your tears.

It turned out that lying to her family was harder than she'd thought it would be. But she knew how it would sound if she told them the truth, because she knew how it sounded to herself.

And it had worked. Nobody thought she was still hung up on hurdling. Everybody believed she was only postponing her career as a sports psychologist to help out her sister. Her father had even told her that he was proud of her for trying to do the right thing. She'd hated herself then, but knew the alternative would only make him worry. But now she was in touch with Dr Webster she wouldn't have to lie for much longer.

'What makes you blue?'

Joan felt her body still. She knew Ivo was looking at her in that intensely focused, almost ferocious way of his. She could feel his gaze pulling her in, and it was so tempting to tell him the whole sorry tale, but instead she smiled. 'Not enough ice cream—and, strangely, too much ice-cream.'

It was too glib, too quick an answer, but she let her gaze move past him to the just visible battlements.

'I have a question…' As he raised an eyebrow, she nudged his leg with her knee. 'Okay, I have another question. How did you end up buying this place? I mean, how did you even know it was for sale?'

As they left the orangery she wondered if Ivo was fooled by the sudden change of subject. It seemed unlikely that someone as successful in business as he was would fail to notice such an obvious swerve but, tilting back his head, he said quietly, 'I was looking for a property in the UK, and my agents brought this to my attention. It was near to Johnny, and I thought it would be a good investment.'

'Really?' She screwed up her face. 'I thought you were going to say that you fell in love with it and you were so smitten you couldn't live without it.'

'You mean the falling in love where you drop everything, lose your appetite and find it impossible to concentrate?' He gave her a small, tight smile. 'That's not who I am…who I'll ever be.'

A shiver ran down her spine. There was a warning in those words but she didn't need to hear it. Yes, Ivo was astonishing in bed, and she had discovered there was a sweet side to him that she hadn't anticipated. But there was no need to worry about any heartbreak later because her heart wasn't at risk.

Only it was hard not to get swept away by the romance of the castle. Hard not to think that this was how it was meant to be with someone. This heat, those kisses, that constant need to touch one another. And there was more than heat between them. They had talked, and argued, and resolved their arguments—which was a whole lot more than she'd ever done with any of her previous boyfriends.

Then again, this was all so intense. At times—like out on the moors, with the clouds scudding overhead—it felt like one of those time lapse films, where a seed grew into a tree in a matter of minutes. In a matter of days, she would be flying home to Hamilton.

Maybe one day she would find someone who would make her feel the same way.

It just wouldn't be Ivo.

'It must have been pretty incredible, though, seeing it for the first time,' she said, remembering her own first tantalising glimpse of the castle.

For a moment he didn't reply, but then he nodded, and she sensed that it had been a slightly less pragmatic decision than he was willing to admit.

'It was. I was…intrigued.'

He seemed surprised by the word, as if he hadn't been expecting to use it.

'There you go.' She gave him a swift, teasing smile. 'Now, doesn't that sound so much better than saying *It was in the right area and I thought it would be a good investment*?' she said, putting on an English accent.

He laughed reluctantly, and as he pulled her closer she found herself desperate to make him laugh again.

'I suppose it does,' he said.

She smiled up at him. 'You weren't tempted to buy somewhere in London?'

There was a stillness between them suddenly, as if someone had pressed *pause*.

'No, not really. You see, I know this area,' he added after a moment. 'From when I was younger. Johnny and his sisters used to come up here and stay at his grandparents' house during the school holidays. One year Johnny asked if I could go too, and after that I went every year. We'd camp and go fishing. Just regular kid stuff.'

Regular kid stuff? As if his life had ever been regular, Ivo thought as they made their way back through the castle.

Which was why those few weeks away had stayed with him for the rest of the school year. Even now he could remember the novelty of eating breakfast at a table.

Remembering Joan's light, curious gaze, he swore silently. He hadn't needed to tell her about any of that. But whenever he was with her she seemed to prise him open a little, so that the truth just slipped out.

A fragment. Not the whole truth. He would never share that with anyone.

Before acquiring the London office he had stayed in the city twice, but on each occasion knowing that Caleb was in prison nearby he had found it impossible to relax enough to sleep.

When Johnny had got the job at Sheffield University he'd decided to buy somewhere in the Peak District himself. And then the agents had got in touch about Castle Alwyn and it had seemed like fate. What could be a safer refuge from the past you needed to escape than a remote, high-walled fortress?

Only now Caleb was even closer.

He could see that Joan was confused by his story—but then all stories were confusing if you were only given the odd chapter. No doubt she thought his reticence was due to the necessary caution required by the ultra-rich, but he didn't feel like that with her at all. She spoke about his wealth quite naturally, not skirting round it.

'I can't wait to go to London,' she was saying. 'I know I went to the airport, but I want to see Buckingham Palace and the Houses of Parliament—you know, all the touristy stuff.'

She could hear the excitement in her voice, and it reminded him again of just how young she was.

A jaunty but muffled ringtone made her glance down. 'Sorry…'

Reaching into her pocket, she pulled out her phone and

he watched her face change, light up in a way that made him want to rip it from her hands.

'I have to take this—do you mind?'

'Go ahead.'

The morning's newspaper was sitting on the coffee table and he picked it up and flipped it open to the financial pages. He wasn't consciously listening to Joan's conversation, but he couldn't not hear it either—and besides, she was difficult to look away from.

Make that impossible, he thought, as she walked over to stand in front of one of the windows.

'Thank you for getting back to me so quickly,' she said, and her voice had an unfiltered excitement that matched the light in her eyes as she'd recognised the name of her caller.

She was standing with her back to him now, so he couldn't see her expression—which was why it took him a few seconds to realise that something had changed. He couldn't hear what she was saying, but the excitement had leached out of her voice and there was an odd, taut set to the way she was standing.

As she hung up, he forced his gaze back to the list of companies in the Dow Jones index. Joan's private life was just that. It wasn't any of his business. And yet right now it seemed to matter just as much, if not more, than the global position on oil.

He put the newspaper down. 'Joan?'

She stiffened, but when she turned there was that smile. Except it wasn't quite right. It was as if she was doing an impression of her smile.

'Is everything okay?'

'Of course. Why wouldn't it be?'

She pressed the palm of her hand against her stomach, as if it was hurting, and suddenly he knew that it was. He just didn't know why. With any other woman he wouldn't have wanted to know. But Joan's distress and her attempt to hide it pressed against a bruise inside him that had never fully healed.

'No reason,' he said.

'Everything's fine,' she said. Only there was a shake in her voice.

'Good.'

'You don't think so?'

'That's not what I said.'

She took a step towards him, her phone still in her hand, her eyes darting to the window and then back to his face.

'It wasn't what you said…it was how you said it.'

There was a complicated expression on her face that looked like anger—except it wasn't. He knew that, because he saw that same expression on his face reflected in his laptop screen if he ever allowed himself to think about Caleb and the past.

'Look, just because you're some bigshot tycoon, it doesn't mean to say you get to second-guess me.'

He tried to stay calm. Or at least to sound calm. Because she wasn't angry. She was frightened.

'I wasn't… I don't want to fight with you, Joan.'

She was shaking her head. 'Oh, yeah—sorry, I forgot. This is just about sex, isn't it?' She stopped, and her eyes widened as if she'd seen a ghost.

Turning, he saw his housekeeper standing in the doorway, her face revealing none of the astonishment she must surely be feeling. Without batting an eyelid she melted away, and he turned back to Joan. But she was already halfway across the room, running lightly, running so fast that she made it all the way out into the gardens and past the ha-ha before he caught up with her, catching her elbow and using her momentum to spin her round to face him.

'You can't be out here.'

It was raining so hard he was having to shout, but his

voice sounded faint. Or maybe he couldn't hear it above the pounding of his heart.

'Let me go.'

She pulled at his arm, slipping and sliding on the sodden lawn, and he had to tighten his grip to stop her falling as she struggled to break free.

'I can't do that.'

'I don't want you here.'

But she was crying now, trying to hide her face, and he knew that was the reason she had gone outside and he pulled her closer, kissing her cheeks and her forehead until he felt her body soften and lean into him. He scooped her into arms, and then he was carrying her back inside and up the stairs to his bedroom.

She was shivering—they both were—and he stripped off her clothes, then his, and led her into a hot shower. Afterwards, he wrapped her in his bathrobe and pulled on some dry clothes.

'You need food…something warm. Could you eat some soup? Linda usually has some. I can go and ask.'

'Do you have to go?'

He felt his chest tighten. He'd lost count of the number of times he'd said that in his life. He'd never thought anyone would say it to him.

'No.' Shaking his head, he sat down beside her on the sofa. 'I can stay as long as you need me to.'

She looked shocked and small, and yet also beautiful, with her dark curls framing her face.

'I'm sorry about before.' She bit her lip. 'I didn't want to get upset…that's why I got angry. I do that sometimes.'

He nodded as if he understood—and he did. Historically at least. Thanks to their anger and defiance, he and his brothers had all been deemed 'difficult'. But he couldn't remember the last time he'd had a conversation like this. Probably because he'd spent most of his adult life avoiding any situation which might trigger one. And part of him wanted to avoid this one. Wanted to just pull Joan into his arms and kiss her better. Only he needed to make sure that he wasn't the reason she was upset.

'I don't know what I said, but I didn't mean to upset you.'

'It wasn't you.'

That was all he'd wanted to know. Except it wasn't, he realised. He needed to know what was upsetting Joan so that he could ride off on his white charger and hunt it down.

'How do you normally make yourself feel better?' he asked.

She breathed out shakily. 'I talk to my parents or my sisters.'

That made sense. She was close to her family. He glanced at his watch. 'If that's what you want we can take the jet. Get you back home.'

We? This wasn't a 'we' situation. This wasn't prom. He didn't need to accompany her.

'You'd do that for me?'

With their sheen of tears, her wide green-brown eyes looked misty, like the hills outside on an early spring morning.

'Of course. Is that what you want?'

He waited, his stomach twisting with something like anxiety. For her, not himself—obviously. This relationship would end in a few days anyway, so what difference would a day make?

But she was shaking her head. 'I can't talk to them about this.'

'Then talk to me,' he said quietly.

He was surprised at how easy it was to say those words and he wondered briefly why that was. But he had no ready answer and he needed to focus on Joan.

'Is it something to do with the phone call?' he prompted.

He knew it was, but he knew instinctively that she needed a starting point for this story she needed to tell and he wanted to hear.

She nodded slowly.

'Who were you talking to?' he asked softly.

'It was Dr Webster.'

He stared at her, blindsided with shock, drowning in panic.

'Are you ill?'

Fresh tears slid down her face and she swiped them away angrily. 'Not ill. Broken. Useless. A might-have-been.'

'Slow down, Joan.' He caught her wrists. 'What do you mean, you're broken?'

But she wasn't listening. 'I thought she'd be able to help. She helped Chrissie Atkins.'

Who the hell was Chrissie Atkins?

He tightened his grip, gentled his voice. 'What did you want her to help you with?'

But he already knew the answer. Or at least he knew it had something to do with that thin six-inch scar below her knee.

'My leg. My tendons. The ones I damaged in the accident.'

Letting go of her wrists, he reached out and stroked her small, trembling face. He barely knew where to start, but logically it made sense to start at the beginning.

'When was the accident?' he said quietly.

She didn't reply immediately, and he waited, heart speeding.

'My second year in Florida,' she said eventually. 'You know, I was the first person in my family to go to college.' Her mouth twisted into a small, trembling smile. 'My parents were so excited about me going and getting a degree. But I just wanted to hurdle—and I was good. I was really good. I got a scholarship…'

The fingers of one hand were pleating the hem of the bathrobe.

'For two years I was first in all my races. I broke state records. I was on the shortlist for the Bermuda National Athletics squad. I had all these sponsorship deals.'

She drew a deep breath.

'And then I was at a competition in Alabama and I clipped a hurdle and fell.'

Her fingers were twisting the bathrobe tighter and tighter.

'I bashed up my knee and tore a ligament.'

He reached out and caught her hand in his, stilling it. 'That must have been devastating.'

'I don't really remember it. I banged my head too.' Her eyes were bright again. 'The hospital did a really good job, and I thought it would be fine. I'd do the rehab and then just start hurdling again. Only it wasn't that simple There was all this other damage beneath the surface…'

And that was the damage that mattered most, he thought. The hidden scars and the trauma beneath the skin that never faded. He felt a rush of self-loathing, remembering how he had scoffed at her lack of balance.

'My coach came to my room one day and told me that they couldn't keep my place on the squad.' She turned away sharply, shielding her face with her other hand. 'I lost my scholarship and all the sponsors dropped me. If it hadn't been for Cass I would have given up.'

Her voice was a whisper now, but the pain of her loss echoed round the silent room like a scream in a canyon. And he understood how she felt. Her world—the world she'd trusted to be solid and strong—had imploded, leaving her to pick her way through the wreckage.

'My parents had to pay for my final year, and they were so good about it. They were going to go on a big cruise when my dad retired and they just gave it up.'

Her head drooped, her wet lashes fanning her cheekbones.

'Gia helped out too, and so did Terri, even though it meant neither of them got the wedding they wanted because of me.'

'It was an accident.'

'I was tired. I'd stayed up late, having a stupid argument with Algee, my ex. The one we always had whenever I had a race.'

Ivo felt his jaw clench at her words. Emotions he hardly recognised were churning inside his chest.'

'I had about two hours of sleep. That's why I fell. And then my whole family had to make so many sacrifices for me. And I let them. Because I'm selfish.'

'You're looking after your sister's children. That's not selfish. Does she pay you?'

'I'm not going to take money from her,' she said, snatching her hand from his, eyes blazing. 'She helped pay for my tuition.'

He caught her hand. 'Exactly. You're trying to make it up to her.'

Her mouth quivered. 'It's only temporary. As soon as she can she's going to put the boys in day-care, so that I can go off and have my big career as a sports psychologist. That's her first thought. And what do I think? That I don't want to do that. Like some spoilt child.'

She was raging against herself again.

'In my experience parents don't tend to let other children look after their own precious children,' he said calmly.

By that he meant normal, loving parents. His own had had no qualms whatsoever in leaving him and his brothers alone for days.

He watched the shivers chasing across her skin.

'You don't understand. I wasn't being noble. I never wanted to be a sports psychologist. I wanted to hurdle. Even after the accident. But I couldn't tell my family that, so I offered to help look after the boys. Because it meant I didn't have to face up to the fact that wasn't ever going to be possible. Only then I read an article on the internet about Dr Sara Webster and this heptathlete…'

'Chrissie Atkins?' he said quietly.

She nodded. 'I thought she could help me. Fix me. But she can't. She's looked at all my medical records and she says that surgery might even make things worse.'

Her face crumpled and she started crying. Ivo pulled her into his arms.

'I'd kept on telling myself that something would come along, and then it did, and I thought it would work.'

Ivo nodded. He knew that feeling. Of thinking something would work. Like when his mother had said she wanted to stop taking drugs, or when a foster family had talked about things in the future that included him. The realness of that possibility was so tantalising, so irresistible. But the more you invested in it, the more painful it was when—inevitably—it failed.

'I know I'm stupid. I held on to this for so long. But I wanted it so badly, and I worked so hard, and now I don't know what else I can do. I'm not good at anything. I don't have anything.'

You have me, he wanted to say.

But that would be ridiculous and untrue. He didn't do relationships. He was here now because only a monster would have walked away from Joan in this state.

'You have your family.'

'I lied to them, and I'm still lying to them, and I hate it.'

'You only lied because you wanted to protect them. That's not lying—that's love.'

Letting go of her hand, he reached out and smoothed the tears from her cheeks with his thumbs.

'You also have a degree. I know that doesn't feel like much when you look around and see other people living their best lives and yours feels broken. But I also know that you have to work with what you've got. So start at the most broken part of your life and build from there. Make those feelings of anger and frustration and regret work for you. For other people. That's something you are good at. Look at how you tuned into the Andy White situation. You got it like *that*.'

He snapped his fingers.

'That's rare, Joanie. Rarer than you think. And, yeah, you could use those skills in business. And you could work with athletes at the top of their game who are struggling. But what about helping people like yourself? You know how it feels to have those dreams disappear in one shattering second. So work with that.'

He kissed her lightly on the forehead.

'And grieve for what you've lost. Just don't hide away from me in the rain to do it.'

She burst into tears again then, and he pulled her into his arms and let her cry.

Finally, she shuddered against his chest. 'You're a nice man…nicer than I thought you were.'

He frowned. 'Thank you—I think.'

Now she laughed. It was a shaky, tired laugh, but he could see that she was feeling better. He wished that his own problems could be soothed by tears. The trouble was, he wasn't sure he even knew how to cry any more or if he ever had.

She touched his face. 'You're a good man.'

'I'm not the worst,' he said softly.

But as she curved her body around his he wondered whether Joan would still think he was a good man if she knew that he had deliberately turned his back on his own brother, even though it had been an act of self-preservation.

CHAPTER NINE

IVO WOKE EARLY. There was no light outside and not even a tentative note of birdsong. But it had stopped raining, finally, and Joan had stopped crying too.

He glanced down at where she lay, sleeping beside him. She had got upset a couple more times, so he had led her back to the beginning and they had talked it through. Each time she'd got angry at herself, and sometimes with him, and then she would cry again—until quite suddenly she had fallen asleep while he was still talking to her, like children always did in movies, when their parents were reading them a bedtime story.

And possibly in real life too. Not that he would know. The idea of anyone reading him a bedtime story was an exotic concept. The only thing to read in their flat had been the menu from the Chinese takeaway that the last tenant had glued to the fridge door. The menu was out of date, and frayed at the edges, but he could still remember spelling out the names of the dishes to himself.

Joan shifted in her sleep, murmuring something incomprehensible, her face creasing as if she was having a nightmare. He rested his hand on her stomach, letting it rise and fall with her breath.

Had his mother ever done that? He honestly couldn't say. Maybe on a good day, when she was in that sweet spot between fixes, when the lines stamped into her face by alcohol and drugs and cheap food would momentarily soften, so that he could see the woman she had once been.

It was Caleb who had rubbed his stomach when he was hungry. Caleb who had eaten less so that he could eat more. Caleb who had given him his jacket when the bailiffs had locked them out of the flat and they'd had to sleep outside all night.

He had loved Caleb then, but after his brother had got arrested it had been easier, and so much less painful, to be angry with him than to allow himself to care. And by the time he had calmed down and grown up enough to realise that Caleb was as much a victim as he was, it was too late.

Too much time had passed. They were both men now. Strangers whose lives had followed very different paths. And yet they were both trapped by their pasts. Caleb was in a cell, two metres by three metres, and he was here, in his beautiful fortified castle, too scared even to acknowledge the only living person on the planet who had cared for him when everyone else had walked or stumbled away.

But there was no solution. You couldn't change the past.

And the future…?

Caleb's face—still young, always young—slid into his head. A part of him wanted to reach out to his brother, but he pushed the thought away. He had spent so long being hurt and angry with Caleb, and who was to say his brother wouldn't feel the same way?

He couldn't face yet another rejection.

And there was no need to. You had to live in the present.

He glanced down at the sleeping woman.

Like he was doing with Joan.

You had to keep moving forward. It was the only way to survive. But to do that you had to have a goal. And right now Joan didn't—which was why she was in this unbearable limbo. She needed to tell her family what she'd told him and then it would all be fine. Because they loved her and she was tough and smart and talented.

His chest tightened as he remembered the offer he'd made to fly her back to Bermuda. Joan had refused, but what if when she woke up she'd changed her mind?

He felt that same tugging sensation as before—as if something was being twisted inside his chest.

If only he could make her feel as if she was back home without her having to leave…

Maybe there was something that might work.

He glanced across the room. There was still no light under the window, but Raptor was a global business and over the years he'd got used to making things happen at all times of the day and night.

He lifted his hand from Joan's stomach, and waited to see if his movement might cause her to wake. But she didn't stir, and he shifted his weight to the edge of the bed and got to his feet. Snatching up his phone, he made his way silently across the floor and into the bathroom.

It was three o'clock in the morning, but he had a rolling roster of assistants, so that whatever time it was there was always someone ready at the end of a phone to do his bidding.

'Good morning, Nina.'

'Good morning, Mr Faulkner. How may I help you?'

He shifted the phone to his other ear. 'I have a rather unusual request. Let me tell you what I need…'

Fingers tightening around Ivo's arms, Joan took another tentative step forward.

'You know this isn't fun for me,' she said, trying to squint through the makeshift blindfold that Ivo had used to cover her eyes. But she couldn't see a thing.

He was leading her though the castle, and maybe it was because she couldn't see, so all her other senses seemed heightened, but whenever he moved her or turned her his touch felt like flames licking at her body.

When she had woken up this morning she had been nervous about facing him. She hadn't cried in so long, and it was as if she'd stockpiled all those tears. But he had been so sweet about it.

She had been lying in his arms, with the curve of her back and bottom pressed against his chest and stomach, so that she'd had to roll over to look at him. Her fingers had already been curling into fists in anticipation of what he might say to her, and he had taken her hands and gently unclenched them.

'Are you still upset?' he'd asked.

'Only with myself, for making such an enormous fuss.'

He'd smiled then. 'So you thought you'd come out fighting?'

And then they had reached for each other at the same time, and it had been unlike any sex she'd ever experienced. Maybe it was opening up to him like that, or perhaps it was just the release of that pent-up tension, but she felt as if something had shifted inside her. It hadn't just been about sex any more. There was a sweetness there, but also a sadness. Because she hadn't been able to stop herself from thinking that this was how it was supposed to feel. That this was what real, true intimacy looked like. Passion, of course, but also conflict and misunderstandings and working things out together.

Perhaps if the timing had been different they might have fallen in love.

'You mean the falling in love where you drop everything, lose your appetite and find it impossible to concentrate?'

Ivo's words echoed inside her head. That wasn't who he was…who he would ever be. And just because this wasn't only about sex any more, it didn't mean that it could exist outside of this bubble they'd created.

She suddenly felt close to tears again.

'Stop a minute.' Ivo's voice pulled her back into real time

and she shuffled to a stop, putting out her free hand defensively.

'You're not going to spin me around, are you? Because if people do that to me I don't like it.'

'I'm not going to spin you around—and which people are you talking about? It's just me.'

She felt his hands catch her wrists and knew he was standing in front of her. She felt a shiver run down her spine at his nearness and her near-nakedness. It felt like warm honey dripping from a spoon.

When Ivo had told her that he had a surprise for her earlier, she had assumed that maybe he was going to take her out to lunch. But she'd quickly realised she was on the wrong path when he'd asked her if she had a swimsuit And then he'd held up one of his black T-shirts and told her that he needed to blindfold her.

Not asked...told.

She hadn't been able to breathe. And when he'd wrapped his T-shirt around her head, her heart had actually stopped beating.

'Are you ready?'

This time he asked, but her voice was still a squeak when she said yes. There was the click of a door, and as he guided her forward she felt the change in air temperature. It was warmer, sultry, and she knew that they must be in the orangery. But why?

'Okay, I'm going to help you take your bathrobe off.'

She felt his hands pull the belt loose, and suddenly she was standing there in nothing but a bikini, a blindfold and a pair of flip-flops. Obviously she couldn't see Ivo's eyes, but she could almost feel the sudden narrowing of his gaze. It made the air shiver, made her shiver, and her skin felt flushed with the heat of it.

'Now, take off your shoes,' he said, and the soft edge to

his voice stole through her, snagging and snarling around her pulse.

Toeing off her right flip-flop, she stepped back and gasped. 'What is that?'

But she knew what it was. It was sand…

'Why don't you take a look and see?'

She felt Ivo move closer, felt his fingers brush her hair, and then she was blinking into the light as the blindfold fell away from her eyes. She stared, open-mouthed. They were standing in the orangery but instead of the stone floor there was sand. Soft, pale gold sand. The same soft, pale gold sand she had left behind in Bermuda.

Ivo was watching her…watching her react.

'It's not quite Snapper Bay,' he said after a moment. 'And I couldn't bring you the sea. But I thought it might be a passable stand-in until you go home.'

'How did you…? Where did this…? I don't understand,' she stammered.

He shifted his feet, oddly formal against the sand in their black brogues. 'Raptor does quite a bit of work with the film industry, and I got my office to tap someone at one of the studios. They couldn't help, but they knew a man who could. Apparently he was asked to recreate Mars last week, so he wasn't fazed at all.'

She pressed her hand against her mouth. There were no words for how she felt. And she didn't need the sea. Just looking into the blue of his eyes made it feel as it was pouring straight into her.

'I don't know what to say…it's perfect. Thank you.' She swiped at her cheeks. 'Oh, no, now I'm crying again—but I'm not upset,' she added as his forehead started to crease. She caught his arms and pulled him closer. 'These are happy tears.'

And she *was* happy—happier than she'd ever been in her

life. How could she not be? She had the best of both worlds: a taste of home and Ivo holding her close.

They had lunch on 'the beach', as Joan insisted on calling it. With the sun beating through the glass the orangery was blissfully warm, and when she closed her eyes it really was like being back in Bermuda.

'Why does wiggling your toes in the sand feel so nice?' she asked him, scrunching up her feet as if to prove her point.

'Probably because you associate having bare feet with freedom and relaxing,' Ivo said quietly.

He was lying on his back beside her with his eyes closed, his arm crooked behind his head like Ramon did when he had his afternoon nap.

She liked it when he closed his eyes. It meant that she had the freedom to just stare at him without feeling self-conscious. He looked relaxed. She licked her lips. Actually, he looked gorgeous. In another era he might have been mistaken for a god—a sun god. Maybe because the sunlight loved him, she thought, watching it play across his face, turning him into a living flame.

She frowned as the low but unmistakable sound of a phone broke the silence.

Ivo shifted onto his elbow, blinking.

'No, don't answer it…it's your holiday,' she protested as he pulled his phone from his pocket. 'I'll get it.'

She plucked it from his fingers.

'Joan—'

'It's fine. I know how to answer the phone—and it's not Karolina…it's some guy called Peter Grieves.'

His face altered, and before she'd even realised what he was doing the phone was back in his hand.

She stared at him, shocked, too stunned to move, or to speak. The phone had stopped ringing, as if it too was stunned by his behaviour.

'I'm sorry.'

He looked it—but he looked a lot of other things too. Angry. Confused. And something she couldn't name.

'I didn't hurt you, did I?'

Yes, he had—but not in the way he meant. It was always there…his wealth, his power…but he hadn't thrown it in her face before. Not since their first meeting.

'I'm fine,' she said stiffly, reaching for the bathrobe. 'It's obviously an important call. I'll give you some space.'

'Joan, please don't go.'

His hand caught the edge of the robe and her head jerked up.

'You want that too?' she demanded. 'Have it.'

She let go of the robe as if it was on fire and turned in one swift movement. But he was swifter.

'I'm sorry,' he said again.

'I wasn't going to say anything dumb.'

'I know.' He ran a hand through his hair. 'It's complicated,' he said at last.

'If you say so,' she said, putting her chin up.

There was a long, twitching silence. Then, 'He's the manager of Seddon Hall.'

Joan stared at him in confusion. 'You mean the wedding venue?'

Why would he be calling Ivo? More importantly…

'Why would it matter if I spoke to him?'

There was another longer silence. 'Because he might say something.'

He looked trapped, and uncomfortable, and she could feel him reaching for anger—just as she would when cornered.

Without thinking, she reached out and took his hand. 'About what?'

'I was worried he might let slip that I paid for the wedding,' he said at last.

He had?

She frowned. 'I thought Jonathan and Cassie paid for it...'

Although now she thought about it she had been a little surprised that they could afford such a lavish event.

'That's what we wanted Simon and Diana to think. They were planning on paying, but then one of Simon's investments lost a load of money, so I offered to cover the wedding costs. It was an easy thing for me to do, and I wanted to do it. I told Johnny to tell them that he'd got an advance for that book he's writing.'

So that was what she'd overheard. She'd thought Jonathan had been thanking Ivo for putting aside his dislike of crowds to be his best man.

His face was taut. 'I'm sorry I overreacted.'

She shook her head vigorously. 'If anyone overreacted it was me. I'm sorry...really, truly.' She squeezed his hand. 'You're full of beautiful surprises, Ivo Faulkner.'

And some ugly ones too, he thought, gazing down into Joan's beautiful eyes. Which was why he'd panicked when she'd taken his phone.

Because that was the trouble with truths. One led to another and not necessarily to the ones you wanted to share. But Joan had simply taken it at face value that he was a good person, and her unconditional acceptance of that fact blew his mind.

He shrugged. 'It's not a big deal. Johnny's my best friend and I'm very fond of Cassie.' His voice faded and he stared at the two tiny creases on Joan's forehead. 'What are you plotting?' he asked softly, grateful for the distraction her reply might give him.

She bit her lip. 'I was just thinking about your London office.'

Whatever he'd imagined she might say, it hadn't been that. 'And you say *I'm* full of surprises.'

That smile, the one that was brighter than any sun, lit up

her face. 'Look, I know you were supposed to go there the other day to sign those documents.'

'Actually, I was going to take a tour of the office. The last time I came over it wasn't fully finished.'

'And now it is. So why don't we go down to London and see it? Not me,' she added quickly. 'I can go and see all the sights, and then we can meet up, and I can take you for afternoon tea at one of those fancy hotels.'

'I could do both.'

'Really? I didn't think you'd want to do all the cheesy touristy stuff.' Her green-brown eyes were almost gold in the sunlight. 'I'd love that,' she said softly, and he was surprised again at how easy it was with Joan to just do these things that had always seemed so hard before.

They flew down to London in the helicopter.

Joan sat beside him, her face flushed with excitement, her body wrapped up snugly in a peacoat and a pair of jeans that made him feel as if he was coming down with a fever every time he looked at her.

And he looked at her a lot.

Had to force himself to look away, in fact.

But it was harder still not to touch. Too hard. So that even though he knew he should show some restraint he kept finding himself reaching out to smooth a curl away from her face, or stroking her palm with his thumb when they held hands.

The last two or three times he'd visited London it had rained in that cold, depressing way that rain fell on cities. New York was the same. It was hard to believe that it was even the same substance as the rain that hammered and ricocheted off the roof of the castle. But today the sun was a brilliant white orb above the capital.

They did all the 'cheesy touristy' stuff on her list. She was wide-eyed at the size of Buckingham Palace, thrilled by the London Eye, and underwhelmed by the Tower of London.

'It's not even a tower—and it's nowhere near as beautiful as your castle,' she protested, to the astonishment of a nearby group of American tourists.

She spent a preposterous amount of time choosing postcards, and then nearly as long picking gifts for her family.

'Do you think this one with the crown?' She held up two teddy bears. 'Or this one with the Union Jack jumper? For the boys.'

'Why not get both?'

'Because they'll each want what the other has. Honestly, you only children have no idea.' She rolled her eyes.

'So get two of each,' he said, ignoring the prickle of guilt her remark produced.

'But I won't be able to fit them in my suitcase—and don't say buy another suitcase, because I can't take another one on the plane.'

Taking both bears from her hands, he handed them to the man running the kiosk.

'Yes, you can—if you take my jet.'

What?

His own words raced through his head, tripping over one another as he played them back. Obviously it was madness to suggest such a thing—and yet he didn't want to retract his offer. On the contrary, every nerve was painfully taut as he waited for her reply.

She stared at him in silence. 'How does that work?'

'It's called jet propulsion.'

'No, how does that work for us?'

And it was then, looking down into Joan's small, stunned face, trying to make sense of the ache in his chest when she talked about packing her suitcase, that he realised he had fallen in love with her.

He stared at her, mute and undone with shock.

Later, he would wonder how he managed to stay standing as the blast of that bombshell revelation exploded inside him. Or how all around him, people went on rushing to and from the shops as if nothing had happened.

But how could he be in love? He didn't know how to love. And yet he knew that it had to be love, because whenever he thought of Joan it was as if the world was laid out for him, brand-new and beautiful, without any of the darkness in his life. He felt light, and no longer broken, and he wondered if he would recognise himself in the mirror the next time he looked.

'It's okay…you didn't mean it,' Joan said quietly, tugging his attention back to her. 'I get it. You wanted to do a nice thing, but I'm not going to hold you to it.'

'I did mean it.' His voice was calm. Not at all the voice of someone whose entire life had been turned on its head seconds earlier. 'Look, I'm still on holiday, and it's more or less en route to the States—and it would mean you could buy as many souvenirs as you want.'

She was still doubtful, he saw, but then she stood on tiptoe and kissed him softly, and he had to stop himself from telling her that he loved her right there on Oxford Street.

It wasn't the right time or the right place.

'Buy whatever else you want,' he said quietly. 'And then we should get something to eat.'

He had agreed to let her buy him tea, on condition that she let him buy her lunch. He was also going to take her to the Opera House, to see *Giselle*, but he wanted to surprise her. He knew he was in danger of becoming addicted to watching her eyes light up and seeing that flickering smile pull her mouth into a mesmerising curve.

Symbel was on the twentieth floor of Haskett Tower. It wasn't the newest or the highest restaurant in London, but to his mind that was an advantage. People liked superlatives. The biggest, the tallest, the fastest… But often something got lost in the chase for the title. Symbel knocked out plate after plate of robust food, just the right side of exquisite, the service was good, and they were flexible about timings.

'Do you think I look smart enough?' Joan asked him as they rode up in the lift. 'I don't want everyone chewing on their yuzu kosho salmon and wondering what you're doing with me.'

'Firstly, you look beautiful.' He pulled her closer, pressing the flat of his hand against her back. 'And second, where did you come across yuzu kosho?'

She slid her arms around his neck. 'My family love food, and I scoped out the menu earlier.'

He let go of her reluctantly as the doors opened.

'Good afternoon, Mr Faulkner.' A smiling waitress stepped forward to greet them. 'Would you like to follow me?'

Their table was on the east side of the building. He watched her face as they got closer.

'The Eye was fun, but you can see more of the river here,' she said, her eyes moving, assessing.

He liked it that she'd noticed the difference. Liked, too, how she walked into the restaurant with her head held high even though she was nervous. That he even noticed was nothing short of astonishing—but then she was changing him, undoing him, opening him up to new ways of being.

What he didn't like was the slight wince she made when she sat down. He didn't like thinking about her being in pain. Or trying to hide it. And he knew now that was what she did. No wonder her family had been so worried about her.

'Don't,' she said softly, looking up from her lobster risotto.

He frowned. 'Don't what?'

'You're wondering about my leg. My mum looks at me in the same way.' She touched his hand lightly and he let his hand rest against hers. 'But I really am fine.'

'Are you sure? Because I thought we might go and see a show, but if you're too tired we could go another night.'

'A show?'

'A ballet.'

This was so easy, he thought, watching her face do that miraculous thing that made the diners and the waiters, even the London skyline, topple like dominos. It was no effort at all to eat and talk and listen to Joan. And to smile. That was the easiest thing of all. Aside from loving her.

'Ivo!'

He felt a hand on his shoulder and turned to find Andy White and his brother Jamie, staring down at him.

'Andy… Jamie…' He hesitated before getting to his feet and holding out his hand. 'Good to see you. This is Joan Santos. Joan, this is Andy and Jamie White.'

She smiled. 'Nice to meet you both. I've heard all about you two. Smart guys. Solid-state batteries… Started the business in a garage…'

Andy White laughed. 'That just about sums us up.'

'So what are you doing in London?' Joan lowered her voice. 'Or are we not allowed to know?'

Jamie ginned. 'We're here to see the soccer. Our dad is a big West Ham fan, and we picked up the habit. We try to come over to see a couple of games a season. What about you? I hear you have a new office out at Shaft's Point, Ivo.'

Ivo nodded. 'We went and saw it this morning, and then we went sightseeing.'

'And shopping.'

Joan gave Ivo a small, private smile that made him feel as if the floor was tilting.

'A lot of shopping. Which is why this lunch is my treat. No, it is,' she said as he frowned. 'I know you two gentlemen probably find this hard to believe, but Ivo's been so patient and kind. But then we all have sides to ourselves that other people don't get to see.'

Andy White smiled. 'That's very true.' He glanced at his

brother. 'Look, we need to be heading off now, but how about catching up later for a drink? Maybe we could revisit our last conversation.'

Ivo shifted in his seat. A week ago he would simply have said yes. Business was business, and acquiring a stake in CGB would make him very rich. But now he said, 'Actually, we were thinking about going to a show later.'

Joan leaned forward. 'But we could go another night.'

Her eyes were soft, and dancing with hope and excitement about his deal, and the fact that she cared made him want to get up and leave. Because he didn't know what to do with the emotions that knowledge provoked.

'We could,' he agreed.

White seemed pleased. 'I'll text you when and where.'

'They seem nice,' Joan said as the waitress brought their passionfruit soufflé and two spoons.

'They liked you.'

She met his gaze. 'They like you too. And enough to want to talk to you again,' she said, taking a mouthful of soufflé.

Joan was right. There was no other reason for Andy White to have suggested drinks. He should be pleased, he thought, remembering his anger and frustration when the brothers had walked away from the deal. He tried to enjoy his dessert, but each time he took a mouthful he would think about White's comment about CGB being a family business—and then he would picture Caleb's face.

Don't lie, he told himself dully. *You can't picture your brother's face because you've chosen not to see him for more than two decades.*

And the thought of Joan finding that out made him feel sick to his stomach.

CHAPTER TEN

THERE WAS SOMETHING WRONG.

Joan didn't know what, but it had something to do with the Whites.

Maybe it was just the shock of seeing them when he was out with her. Ivo was the kind of man who liked to keep his life in compartments.

But it felt weird being on the outside when they had been so close for days now. And she was definitely on the outside, she thought as their driver inched the car past a red double-decker bus. Going on a bus had been one of the things she'd wanted to do. Now, though, she was too worried about Ivo to mind that she hadn't.

She glanced over to see he was staring at a different bus—except she was pretty sure he wasn't seeing anything.

Just then his phone buzzed.

She watched him pull it from his jacket and glance at the screen.

'Is that Andy White?'

He nodded.

'So where are we meeting them?'

There was a silence. Ivo shifted against the leather upholstery 'We're not,' he said slowly.

What?

She frowned. 'Why not? I thought you wanted this deal.'

'I've changed my mind.'

'But why?'

'We want different things.'

She searched his face. Was that true? 'Different, but compatible. I mean, he wants money and you want to give it to him.'

Ivo shook his head. 'It's not that simple.'

'You mean don't worry my pretty little head about it?'

His shuttered eyes met hers. 'That's not what I said, or meant, and I don't need you to analyse me. This isn't one of those *I talk, you listen* situations.'

She held his gaze. 'So don't talk to me. Talk to whoever you normally talk to when you need a sounding board. You know…your parents, your friends…'

His face hardened. 'I don't need to talk to anyone and I'm not going to meet Andy White and his brother.' He glanced at his watch. 'Besides, we need to get changed.'

'For the ballet? I thought we were doing that another night.'

He didn't respond. That fierce attention of his seemed to not even be in the car, and she wondered where he was.

'Why don't we stay in?' she said. 'Or we could go back to the castle.'

'If that's what you want.'

Without attempting to discuss the matter, he leaned forward and tapped the glass behind the driver's head.

'Change of plan.'

Ivo didn't say one word on the flight back to Edale. It reminded her of when he had driven her to Snowdrop Cottage. Only then they had been strangers—angry strangers. Now they were lovers. But this didn't feel like a lovers' tiff. Weirdly, it felt as if he was fighting himself and she was simply watching.

As they walked into his bedroom—*their* bedroom, as she had started to think of it—he tossed his jacket on the sofa.

'I'm sorry about the ballet,' she said softly. 'It was a lovely idea. I just thought we should talk.'

'And yet I have nothing to say.'

He was already edging towards the door, not even looking at her.

'I'm going to check my emails. Don't wait up for me.'

She stared after him, her chest aching as if he had punched her in the solar plexus. It was the first time he had shut down like that in days. Maybe that was why it felt so horrible.

Shivering, needing to move, she stood up and walked towards the windows.

Normally when she felt like this, she reached for anger—but she couldn't get angry with Ivo. Probably because all that heat, all that fire, was being mainlined into the searing, incomparable passion they shared. Besides, she wasn't angry—she was worried. And even though he'd stalked off like that, she knew Ivo wasn't angry either. He was scared.

Her heart was a heavy thud against her ribs and then she was moving, taking the stairs swiftly and with the same sense of purpose that she'd once used to propel her over hurdles.

The door to his study was open, but he wasn't at his desk. Panic seized her chest, and she was just turning and walking out of the room when she saw him. She felt her feet stutter and slow, like they'd used to when she passed the finishing line. He was sitting on the window seat, legs slack against the cushions, gaze fixed on the darkened landscape.

As she walked towards him he looked up at her, but he didn't speak, and she didn't speak either. She just kept walking until she was beside him.

'I know you don't want to talk, and that's fine. It's just that the other day when I was scared you were there for me,' she said slowly, ignoring the ache in her chest. 'I didn't want you to feel like you were alone.'

Because he was, she realised with a jolt. At the wedding, at the castle… There was a separateness to him, this man who divided his time between a fortress and an unbreachable tower in New York.

'I'm sorry I snapped at you.'

Joan blinked. Ivo's voice was so quiet that she almost thought she'd imagined it. 'That's okay. I did go on a bit.'

He smiled, or rather his mouth made the shape of a smile, but his expression was bleak. 'I just couldn't accept it before, but White was right about me.'

She frowned. 'Right in what way?'

'He told me there was no heart to my business and that all I care about is profit.'

'But that's not true,' she protested.

His smile twisted. 'You don't make a lot of money by being nice.'

'Maybe, but plenty of people who don't make money aren't nice either.'

He glanced back to the window, although she knew that he wasn't seeing the wild moorland, but somewhere far away.

'I know that,' he said slowly, and there was a heaviness to his voice—a weight there that he had been carrying for a long time.

Heart hammering in her chest, she sat on the edge of the window seat, and then, after a moment, she took his hand. 'Is that why you used to go and stay with Johnny's grandparents? Because people at home weren't nice to you?' she said gently.

It took a long time, but finally he nodded. 'My mum was young…thirteen when she had my older brother Marcus. Then she had Caleb—' his voice tensed around the name '—and then me. She couldn't cope. A lot of the time she'd be off her head on something. So we'd go to foster parents. But we were pretty challenging… And then one day the social workers were waiting for us after school and we were taken into care. I never saw her again.'

'I'm so sorry.' They were the only words she could push past the lump in her throat.

He shrugged. 'Just one of those things.'

She cleared her throat. 'I thought you were an only child.'

His hand tensed against hers. 'In a way, I am. Marcus is dead. He was in the army, and his truck drove over an IED. And Caleb—' He took a breath. 'He's in prison. He's what they call a career criminal. He's been in and out of prison for most of his life. Just stupid stuff…bad decisions over and over again. That morning when we first met I'd had a phone call.' He glanced away, into the darkness beyond the glass. 'That's why I wasn't concentrating. Because I'd just found out that he'd been transferred to a prison an hour away from Edale.'

'So it'll be easier for you to see him.' No wonder he had been distracted, she thought.

His eyes were distant, his mouth tight, as if he was trying to hold something in. 'I won't be seeing him. I haven't seen him in over twenty years. I pay someone—his name's Steve—to tell me what's happening. I just need to know he's all right,' he said, in a bruised-sounding voice.

Joan was mute with shock. She talked to or texted her sisters most days. She couldn't imagine not seeing them. But her shock was forgotten as she glanced at Ivo's rigid profile. It held the rigidity of someone who was managing pain. Not damaged tendons, but the pain of loss and neglect and abandonment.

'I know you must think I'm a monster. But he left me alone. He knew what it felt like when people left, and he still went out and stole that car—even though he knew he could go to prison…even though I needed him. But I don't need him now. I don't need anyone.'

Her stomach twisted. She could hear the echo of the panic he'd felt then pulsing through the defiance in his voice now, and the ache in her chest was spreading. She couldn't begin to imagine Ivo's childhood, or his estrangement from his family. But she could understand the mix of motivations that had made him lie to her. And why he kept people at arm's length.

'I don't think you're a monster.'

She heard him swallow. 'He called me and wrote to me. But I didn't reply.'

'You were a child.'

He was shaking his head. 'I don't think I was ever a child.'

But, gazing into his face, she got a flash of what he had been like as a little boy: wary, solitary, waiting for his world to crumble again.

'You were a child,' she said again. 'And you were scared. But things are different now. If you wanted, you could go and see him.'

'And say what? We're strangers now.'

His jaw tightened and the ache in her chest swelled again. Leaning forward, she captured his face in her hands. And, gazing into his eyes, she realised why it hurt so much to see him hurting—why she cared so much about this complicated, compelling, captivating man.

It was because she had fallen in love with him.

Her head was spinning. Was that possible?

But it was a question that needed no asking, much less answering. She knew that she loved him. Helplessly, impossibly. He had become everything to her. But did he love her?

She took a breath. She didn't know, and she was too stunned by her own private revelation to ask. But he needed her, and that was enough for now.

'It's not too late,' she said gently, but he was shaking his head.

'You know what's crazy? I don't even know what he looks like, but I still miss him.' His eyes glittered with unshed tears. 'Like I said, Andy White was right about me.'

'No, he wasn't.' She stared up at him, suddenly furious

with the White brothers. 'You've built a company that employs thousands of people around the world who rely on you to keep that business running. That means you can't always be nice. But look how you take care of Johnny, and Cassie—and even me, someone who doesn't even matter to you. So maybe you don't have a regular Andy-White-style family. But that's the thing about families: they come in all shapes and sizes. And if that's what's stopping you from going after CBT…'

Breathing out shakily, he pulled her onto his lap. 'It's CGB—and you do matter to me.'

'And you matter to me. So when you want to talk—or, more importantly, when you don't—don't hide away from me.'

He leaned into her, resting his forehead against hers, and they stayed like that for a long time, until she got to her feet and held out her hand.

Upstairs, they made love. And maybe it was his confiding in her, or the fact that she had privately acknowledged her love for him, but there was a sweetness, a kind of innocence to their lovemaking, as if it was the first time for both of them.

It took her breath away. But not the love in her heart. Even though for now that would have to stay private.

'Are you absolutely sure about me taking all of this?'

Glancing across the room to where Joan was wedging a stuffed corgi toy into a suitcase, Ivo nodded. 'There is a limit, I think, but you're well within it. And I travel light.'

Her face softened with relief. 'I didn't realise how much I'd bought.'

She gave him one of those dazzling smiles that played havoc with his breathing and sat back on her haunches. She was wearing one of his shirts over a pair of very small panties and, catching sight of her scar, he felt a rush of love.

He thought back to the previous night, and how she had come to find him. Even then he'd wanted to stay hidden, to keep on hiding the guilt and pain of a childhood that had marked him as a reject and a failure. Someone else—someone less intelligent and kind and intuitive—might have stuck in a knife and tried to force him to open up, but Joan had simply teased the past out of him as if it was a particularly stubborn thorn and the world hadn't ended.

On the contrary, it felt as if it had been reborn—as if *he* was reborn—and that all those things that had previously been off limits were now within his reach. And as he gazed down at this new world, with her hand in his, everything felt possible.

'So what does "light" look like?'

She was walking towards him without a trace of a limp, moving with the smooth grace that made him wish he had seen her hurdling.

'Just the essentials. A change of clothes… My laptop…' he said, his body snapping to attention as she pushed him back against the pillow and straddled his hips. 'And you.'

'I'm an essential, am I?' She raised an eyebrow.

He moved his hands to her hips, pulling her against him. 'For what I have in mind.'

'You have a one-track mind,' she said.

He felt his body harden as her fingers moved lightly over the bare skin of his stomach. But he needed her for way more than sex, and he was ashamed not to be able to admit, that but feeling like this was all so new. Anyway, now that he was going back to Bermuda with her there would be time for him to practise the words in his head until finally he could say them out loud.

Across the room, her phone pinged and he felt her body tense. 'Do you want to get that?'

'Maybe…' She bit her lip. 'Earlier, while you were asleep, I did something. I don't know if it's a good idea, but I thought about what you said about working with people like me and I contacted my old coach. It's probably not even him…'

'You won't know unless you look.' Gently he tipped her off his lap.

He watched her pick up the phone and scroll down the screen. Even before she turned to him he could see it was good news. Her whole body seemed to be lifting a little off the ground. He realised that he was watching her hurdle—but instead of being in a stadium she was leaping over the disappointment and setbacks of the past into a new, exciting future.

'He thinks it's a good idea. He's going to run it past some board or other, and he says he's going to call me next week.'

He got off the bed and walked towards her swiftly. He pulled her into his arms. 'That's fantastic news, Joanie.'

Her arms tightened around his waist. 'Oh, I can't wait to tell everyone at home. Whatever happens, I need them to be a part of it.'

'Of course.'

He kept his gaze steady, but seeing her love for her family made something stir inside him…a shadow he forced himself to ignore.

Leaning into him, Joan kissed him on the lips. 'You know, if it was down to me, I'd still be moping about my lost athletics career.'

'Shh…' He pressed his finger against her lips. 'You would have got there. I just gave you a nudge.'

Her forehead creased and she wriggled free of his grip. 'Talking of nudges… I did something else this morning.' She turned and walked back to her suitcase and picked up a sheet of paper. 'I've found this charity, which helps people who are estranged from family members in prison. I printed this off for you. You can call them. It's all anonymous, and they have loads of advice online about how to get back in touch. Not right now,' she said quickly. 'Or maybe ever. But I thought it might be helpful...'

He stared down at the piece of paper in her hand. That she was worried about him and cared enough to do something to try and help blew his mind.

'Thank you,' he said softly, and the anxious look on her face faded, as he'd hoped it would, and he pulled her against him, his mouth finding hers. 'I'll take a look at it.'

He folded the paper and slid it into the pocket of his jeans. Could he do that? Unravelling the past with Joan last night had been exhausting and painful, but with her by his side, anything felt possible, so why not that? Maybe together they could create new truths, a new future, be that family she'd talked about...the one that didn't fit the mould.

Joan had finally managed to fit everything into her suitcase just as Linda called them for lunch. She still had to pack what was left at Snowdrop Cottage, but they were going to head back there this afternoon.

As she put down her glass Ivo reached for his, and momentarily their hands brushed against each other. His touch made her shiver inside. She loved him so much, and more than anything she wanted him to be happy, but even though he had joked about travelling light, she knew now that Ivo had baggage of a different, darker kind.

She hated it that he had been so hurt and abandoned. Thank goodness Jonathan had been there for part of his childhood.

He had fallen asleep almost immediately last night, and she had watched the light and shadows play across his face, almost as if they were fighting for control of him. But the darkness had lost—she knew that from the way he was holding his body now. And he had taken that piece of paper she'd printed out.

He just needed time.

Look at how long it had taken *her* to move on. But she had, and she felt good about a future helping young people see that there was more than one dream if you let yourself keep dreaming.

Her gaze rested on Ivo's beautiful face.

'Everyone is so excited about you coming over,' she said, reaching over to pinch a piece of asparagus off his plate. 'They're planning some huge beach barbecue, and I'm warning you now… In my family, food is love, so…'

'Love?'

She had spoken unthinkingly, swept along by her excitement about going home with Ivo, but now, glancing over at him, she felt her stomach clench tight. He was staring at her in silence. His face hadn't altered, but there was something different about him—a kind of tension in his spine that hadn't been there before.

'I just meant they like cooking nice food for the people they care about.'

Ivo stared at her across the breakfast bar. Joan had shown him photos of her family and he tried to picture her parents, her sisters, her nephews and aunties. But he could feel that shadow stirring inside him again—only this time it had a face.

Caleb's face.

His chest felt as if it was in a vice. How could he meet her entire family when he couldn't face his own brother? Oh, he could pretend to himself that talking to Joan about Caleb was enough. Joan could pretend that too. But he didn't want her to. He didn't want her living yet another lie for him.

'And they care about me?' he said.

He knew is voice sounded different, stiff, distant. And that Joan would hear the difference too.

'Of course! I mean, they will as soon as they meet you,' she said quickly. 'I haven't told them that much.'

Because it was supposed to be a holiday fling, he thought dully. Earlier, when she'd handed him that printout, he'd been lulled into believing otherwise. But the holiday was over. For both of them.

Joan touched his arm lightly. 'We don't have to go to the barbecue. We can just hang out together. They won't mind.'

Her lips looked soft and inviting, and he wanted to taste her, to kiss that look of uncertainty from her beautiful eyes, but instead he frowned. 'And how would that work? I mean, you can't go home and not see your family.'

Was that what she was suggesting? The thought appalled him. The fact that she was even considering doing that for him made him feel sick.

'I will see them, but the barbecue was a stupid idea.' He heard her swallow. 'I know you're not ready for that right now.'

Ivo knew he had a pulse, but he couldn't feel it. Because there was something else happening—something seismic, a turbulence inside his chest that he couldn't seem to control. And the worst part was that he should have expected it. Because it had always been going to come to this.

If he'd been honest with himself—with her—he would have stopped it before it got this far, this complicated. But he hadn't wanted to because he had fallen in love with her.

But if he loved her—and he did, so much more than he had imagined he could love anyone—he couldn't keep pretending that he could be what she needed.

He gritted his teeth, biting down hard against the softness in her eyes. 'I think we both know that I'm never going to be ready to meet your family, Joan. You and I…we've had fun, haven't we? But that's all this was. Just a bit of fun.'

He could feel her confusion and he wanted to tell her that it was for the best. That he was doing this because he loved her. But it would be perverse to offer his love as a reason for him to leave her.

She was shaking her head. 'It was…in the beginning. But then we talked and it changed for both of us.'

'Maybe in the moment it felt like that to you, but nothing's changed.'

'But it has.' She looked up at him, blinking furiously. 'I love you.'

'But I don't love you,' he lied.

And nothing could have prepared him for how it felt to watch the light in those beautiful eyes fade. It broke him. Broke him into a thousand pieces.

He'd thought it was done. That all his pain and guilt had been exorcised. But the past was no ghost; it lived and breathed. Because it was a part of him. He could never outrun it—and hadn't he always known that? It was why he'd kept people at arm's length.

Until Joan.

And then he had fallen in love. Exactly as he had claimed he never would. And she loved him. And that should have made for the perfect happy-ever-after, but who was he trying to kid? He didn't know how to love or be loved. He had an estranged brother in prison as living proof.

The printout she had given him felt as if it was burning through his pocket into his skin. What did he have to offer aside from money? And Joan didn't care about that. What mattered to her was her family, Cassie, and him. She loved him—incredibly, miraculously.

But how long would she stay loving him? How could she keep loving a man who wouldn't, *couldn't* reach out to his own brother? A man who had rid himself of all feelings, including love?

Because that was the whole truth—the one he had tried to deny for so long.

He still loved his brother, but loving someone wasn't enough to make them stay, to make them choose you, to make them love you back. He knew that because nobody had ever stayed. Nobody had ever chosen him or wanted him or loved him. And he'd wanted to believe that Caleb was different, because he'd tried to get in touch all those years ago, but he knew he couldn't take that risk, couldn't face his brother rejecting him too.

He knew if he told Joan that she would try and persuade him to have faith. Because she was so loved, so sure of love, that she wouldn't understand that what had been broken all those years ago couldn't be fixed.

Whatever way he looked at it, she deserved better than a broken man with a backstory that would become her burden as well as his.

He could feel Joan's gaze on his face. But he couldn't look at her and do what he had to do.

'I'm sorry, but I don't love you.'

The woman still wearing his shirt stared at him, her mouth trembling. 'I don't believe you,' she said finally. 'I know this is new, and I know it's hard, but it will get easier. And I will be there with you.'

The softness in her voice made him feel as if the floor was made of sand. Not the kind of sand he'd had delivered to remind her of home, but quicksand. Because he wanted to believe her, but how many times had he believed before that things would be all right? He couldn't take that risk. Not with Joan.

'I'm sorry,' he said again. 'But I'm not going to go back with you to Bermuda. I have some business in Edinburgh,' he lied.

Joan felt a sharp pain in her leg, and then the room seemed to tilt sideways, as if she was falling.

'You don't need to worry about the luggage. I won't be needing the jet for a couple of days, so I want you to use it.'

Her stomach twisted. She could take his jet? And it was that detail—that tiny throwaway remark—that made it suddenly real.

He was dismissing her. Sending her home with a consolation prize for taking part in the race.

'You think I'm worried about my luggage?' she said slowly.

His face…his beautiful angel's face…looked hard and remote. 'It's my responsibility. I encouraged you to get more souvenirs.'

And to love him.

She wanted to howl as everything inside her lurched and rolled like a foundering ship in a storm.

'Fine, you can take the luggage, but I'm not wasting my ticket just so you get to feel like the good guy.'

He stared at her, his blue eyes flat. 'I should never have let things go this far. I just wasn't thinking clearly.'

'And now you are?' She wanted to curl up and die.

He nodded. 'Look, we had a wonderful time together, and you're a wonderful woman, but it was always going to end.'

'But it hasn't ended for me. And it won't. Because I love you.'

She had to try. She had no choice. Because now she needed to believe in the magic of those words.

As his eyes locked with hers she felt a rush of hope.

'It'll pass,' he said hoarsely. 'I'll get someone to drive you back to the cottage.'

There was a short, stinging silence.

'Don't bother. I can call a taxi.'

'Don't be ridiculous.'

'I'm not.' Blinking furiously, she lifted her chin. 'You know what is ridiculous, though? Living a lie. And you helped me see that. You showed me that I needed to move on. That

I could find a new dream and make it real. Yes, I'll always have this scar, and when I'm tired I'll probably have a limp sometimes, but I'm okay with that now. Thanks to you, Ivo.'

His name stuck in her throat, and for a moment she couldn't speak.

She slid off the chair. The same chair she had sat on when they'd eaten pizza together and then chosen each other for dessert. But it hurt too much to remember that now.

'Run your race.' She forced herself to meet his gaze, to look at his beautiful face one last time. 'That's what my coach always used to say, and that's what I'm going to do. I just hope you find someone who helps you run your race. Because you deserve to. Whatever happened in the past, you deserve to be happy now.'

Breathing in shakily, she walked past him, buffeted on either side by the silence that followed her outburst. She was willing him to grab her arm and spin her round. Tell her that he couldn't let her go. That he loved her as she loved him.

But he didn't. And so, not bothering to hide her limp, she kept walking.

CHAPTER ELEVEN

It was seven o'clock in the morning. The light was starting to filter into Ivo's study but it didn't matter, he thought, glancing through the window at the soft-edged sun creeping up from behind the distant hills. He would always be in darkness now—now that Joan was no longer in his life.

The castle felt huge and echoingly empty without her, and yet everywhere he went he could sense the ghost of her presence.

Maybe that was his destiny. To live with the ghosts of people he'd loved and lost. No, not lost. He hadn't lost Joan. He'd let her go. Pushed her away even though she'd been offering him everything he wanted. Pushed her away out of fear of losing her, even though she had offered him love freely and unconditionally and had kept on offering it until he had offered to have her driven back to the cottage.

It had felt like sunlight in his heart, but her love had broken him because he knew deep down that he wasn't lovable, and he couldn't bear for her to find that out.

And now she was gone.

Except she wasn't. She was branded on his bones and he could smell her scent on his shirt.

He got to his feet abruptly, needing to move, to try and stem the terrible shaking inside him.

His phone vibrated on the desk and he reached for it, his

heart punching against his ribs. But of course it wasn't Joan. She didn't have his number.

It was a message from Johnny. He clicked on it. No, it was from Cassie. He stared down at the photo. She and Johnny were standing in front of the pyramids. They were squinting into the sunlight, smiling. Underneath Cassie had written something.

Thank you.

Beside it there was a row of tiny red hearts. And then:

Your turn next. Love C & J

He rubbed his eyes with the heel of his hand. Cassie was so brave. It was one of the many reasons he was so pleased she was with Johnny. She had parents who were on a par with his own, but she wasn't like him. She was not just seizing the day, but seizing life—with both hands.

His throat tightened as he remembered how grateful she had been to him for paying for the wedding, but she was the generous one. Look at how she had invited her parents to the wedding. She had taken the risk. Okay, they hadn't come, and probably she'd known they never would, but it hadn't stopped her from reaching out.

Because she was brave.

Like Joan.

He thought back to the moment when she had limped out of the kitchen with her chin held high and he heard her voice then...soft like a spring breeze riffling through the heather on the moors.

'Run your race.'

His heart skipped a beat. It was what she wanted him to do—what he wanted to do. If only he could face his fears.

* * *

Staring slowly round the little cottage, Joan felt her throat tighten. Everything was packed and in the car. All she had to do now was put the key under the flowerpot. And yet she still couldn't walk out through the door.

Because then it really would be over.

Last night had been the worst night of her life—worse even than after the accident. Then she'd had a local anaesthetic to numb the pain and misery. But with Ivo there was nothing to soften the agony of his rejection. No hope. No words. She had given him her heart and he didn't want it.

She pressed her hand against the wall to steady herself. She had stubbornly refused to let Ivo arrange for someone to drive her back to the cottage, and after her taxi driver had left she had thought she would rage and cry. But her body had refused to do either of those things. Instead she had curled up on the sofa and let the darkness outside the window pull her down into the depths, where blue was black and love didn't matter.

Waking, she had been cold and stiff, but the daylight had revived her a little. And then she had thought about her family. She knew that they would take care of her if she asked them to, and even if she didn't. That was what families did.

And she had a wonderful, loving family waiting for her. A family and a future that wasn't a compromise but was something she really wanted to do. Soon she would be back with them all, and then she would rage and cry, but now it was time to drive to the airport.

Pulling out her phone, she unlocked the screen—and stiffened as she stared down at her search history. Reach-Out, the charity she had found for Ivo, was at the top of the list and, remembering her hope as he'd taken the printout, she felt as if someone had punched her in the stomach.

She hated it that he was hurting, and that she couldn't help him, but she understood that for him it was too big a risk. He had been left so many times…abandoned so many times. How could he believe that love would surmount all the years between him and Caleb?

She let herself out of the cottage, locked the door and put the key under the flowerpot. It was early, and the roads were empty, but she drove carefully, refusing even to glance at the beauty of the landscape.

Oh, but there in the distance was the castle.

She couldn't help herself. Her eyes moved of their own accord.

And it wouldn't have mattered. Wouldn't have mattered at all if a car hadn't appeared around the corner at exactly that moment.

Huge, black, as wide as the road, its headlights filled the air between them, and for a few frozen seconds she simply watched, her body stiff with shock, as they swept towards her. And then she was pressing down on the brake pedal and the car skidded to a stop.

For a long, shuddering moment, nothing happened. And then the door of the other car opened and Ivo stepped onto the road. Heart pounding, she yanked open her own car door and had a sudden vivid flashback to that first time she saw him.

It was a different road. But Ivo's expression hadn't changed. He looked tense and urgent. His blue eyes were fixed on her face, his body taut like an archer's bow.

'I might not be from around here, but I think there must be something wrong with your satnav,' she said hoarsely. 'Because Edinburgh is in the other direction.'

'There's nothing wrong with the satnav,' he said, slamming the car door and moving towards her with the beautiful masculine grace that made the edges of her vision blur. 'And I'm not going to Edinburgh.' He stopped in front of her. 'I was coming to find you.'

* * *

Ivo stared at Joan, his heart beating in his throat.

If pushing her away had been agonisingly painful, deciding to go after her had been torture. With every half-mile he'd grown less and less sure that Joan would still be at the cottage.

And she hadn't been, he realised, his stomach clenching at the thought that he would have been too late to stop her leaving.

He still might be.

'I don't have anything left to say,' she said slowly.

'Then please would you listen to me? Because I do. I have a lot to say, and the first thing is that I love you.' He took a step closer. 'I love you, Joan.'

Joan stared at him across the stretch of road, her breath catching in her throat. His gaze was so intensely blue it felt as if it was part of her, and it wasn't fair that he could do that. She wanted to tell him so, but her voice was a sob, the words lost in the tangle of emotion that was choking her.

'So why did you send me away?'

She was raging and crying at the same time.

'Because I know how much your family means to you.' His blue gaze held her still. 'I can't even talk to my own brother, and it's bad enough that I'm that man, but then you told me about the barbecue and I tried to imagine myself with your family. I couldn't.'

'Of course, you couldn't. This is all so new,' she protested. 'Not just you and me, but you talking about Caleb. I just wanted you to have a bit of time.'

'I've had twenty-odd years.' His eyes found hers. 'And it wasn't just being part of your family. If we stayed together you'd have to live another lie...be someone you're not. I didn't want you to have to do that again—and for me.'

'So you sent me away?'

'I didn't want to, but I was scared.' His mouth twisted. 'You made me want things I'd never let myself want, and I was scared that once you got to know me you'd see the real me—the one who's not worth loving, not worth keeping.'

'I *do* know you,' she said fiercely.

And she felt strong and certain, in the same way that she'd used to feel before the accident. Stronger and more certain, in fact. Because her love for him had surmounted unthinkable hurdles.

'I know you're as stubborn as you are smart. I know you like to have the last word. But I also know you're kind and generous and you gave my best friend her dream wedding. I know you like to sleep on your right side and that you always let your coffee go cold. I know you, Ivo, because I've spent every hour we've been together watching you. Because that's what happens when you love someone. You can't look away. And you can't stop loving them even when you want to, and I love Ivo.'

There was a sheen of tears in his eyes.

'And I love *you*. But nothing good has ever come out of my loving someone, Joan.'

The rawness in his voice made her tears fall freely.

'And I can't *not* love you. I just can't. I called that charity this morning. Because I want us to be together and that means I have to face my fears…face my brother.'

Joan could hardly breathe. Her heart fluttered like a fledgling testing its wings. 'You called them? What did they say?'

'They were really helpful. I spoke to a counsellor for about an hour, and I'm going to keep talking to her.' He breathed out unsteadily. 'She contacted the prison and spoke to the family liaison officer. Apparently Caleb wants to talk to me.'

She could hear the fear in his voice, and the hope—but then so often they were one and the same thing.

Stepping forward, she took his hands. 'Oh, Ivo. That's amazing.'

A muscle flickered in his jaw and she knew that he was struggling to stay in control.

'He might just want to tell me how much he hates me.' His face was taut. 'Will you come with me?'

'I'd like to…if you want me there,' she said softly.

'I wouldn't even be meeting him without you. I want you there. I need you there.'

Gazing up into his face, Joan could see the love she felt for him reflected in his eyes. It was a love without lies or conditions. A love that could endure pain and doubt and fear because they had already tested it. It was a love that had healed them both.

'That's lucky, because I'm not going anywhere.' Her hands gripped his shirt, tightening in the fabric. 'I can't. You're my breath. You're my heartbeat. You're the race of my life.'

He couldn't breathe past her words, past the relief that he hadn't lost the only woman he'd ever loved. The only woman he would ever love. It was real and miraculous and beautiful, and it was for ever.

And he clasped her face and fitted his mouth to hers and kissed her.

* * * * *

CONTRACTED AND CLAIMED BY THE BOSS

CLARE CONNELLY

MILLS & BOON

PROLOGUE

AT NIGHT, when she slept, Max always checked on his daughter, then flicked out the neon-pink and purple lava lamp that adorned her bedside table, but not before he'd lingered a moment and studied her restful features. Lately, it had brought him a strange clutch of pain, because in sleep it was easy to believe she was the same little girl—gentle and funny—that she'd always been, until the last few months. Now, her temper was so quick to flare, her moods so unpredictable, there were times in the day when he barely recognised his Amanda.

But at night, he stood at her bedside and focused everything he had on her, willing her to return to a state of happiness, to be settled and content. Most of all, he hoped she understood how much he loved her.

His own childhood had made it difficult to express that love, but God knew he'd tried. Showing affection of any kind didn't come easily to the reclusive billionaire, but that didn't mean he didn't feel it.

He wanted, most of all, to be better. Different. A far more active and involved father than his own had been, and his own mother, too. When it came to parenting, he used them as examples of what *not* to do, and until recently that approach had served him well.

But just as the seasons sometimes shifted without being

noticed, so too had Amanda changed without Max's being fully cognisant of it, at first. Little tantrums had been easily ignored—he'd even found them amusing initially. But the storm had kept building, and shifted from the horizon to the homestead, so he could barely remember the last time he'd had a conversation with his daughter that hadn't ended in raised voices—usually hers but, to his shame, sometimes his.

Max had always been a success.

As a boy, he'd been the fastest, the smartest, the best and brightest, his natural competitive instincts stoked to a fever pitch by parents who always withheld their praise even when it was the thing he most badly wanted. While his motivations had changed—he no longer cared for anyone's approval nor praise—he was no less determined to succeed in all aspects of his life.

Under Max's guidance, the family's luxury holdings business, which included his personal project—the pearl farms here in Australia—had gone from a respected yet boutique business to a global powerhouse, their various brands, be that jewellery or handbags or clothing, recognised the world over. That success was gratifying, but his primary focus was always Amanda. Succeeding at being a good parent was what mattered above everything else to him.

If the proof of the pudding was in the eating, then at the moment he was failing abysmally. Though it went against every grain in Max's body to admit it, and he absolutely hated the necessity of what he was compelled to do, there was nothing for it. For the first time in Max's life he needed help, and for Amanda's sake he would damn well make sure he got it.

CHAPTER ONE

IT WAS UNLIKE anything she'd ever seen. Still stiff from the long journey halfway across the world, and a little air sick from the shorter flight to the top end of Australia in a small, private aeroplane, Paige Cooper felt her eyes fill with red dust, but even through that orange haze she could still see, and she was mesmerised. A long way from the airstrip, the road was just a track cut through the desert, lined with sparse trees populated with about a million cockatoos, majestic against the afternoon sunlight. But as she went, the sleek black four-wheel drive bumping across unseen potholes and rocks, the trees thickened, grew greener, the air became darker as the canopy formed overhead, lustrous and sweet-smelling—mangoes, and something else, something indefinably tropical.

The road, which had been straight for miles and miles, began to weave, to twist and turn, each bend revealing more thick forest and tiny patches of blue sky, until there came a final bend and the ocean of Wattle Bay hit her in the face, glittering like a blanket of diamonds, turquoise, so beautiful, better than a postcard, and quite unlike anything she could have conceived of existing in real life. She thought of everything she'd left behind all those years ago in LA, the beach she'd come to associate with a life she would rather forget and parental mistreatment that had permanently shaped and sculptured Paige's outlook on life, but this beach was different. It was more elemental, somehow. There were no high-rises here, no tourist shops. It was just white sand, crystal-clear water, so many trees it took her breath away.

The house itself was also completely different from what she'd expected. After all, the Stones were, Paige knew, one of the wealthiest families in the world, their high-end jewellery stores synonymous with luxury and wealth. Paige had even worn one of their diamond necklaces to the first glamorous awards ceremony she'd attended. Paige had been only twelve, but her mother had insisted she 'look older' and had chosen a revealing dress, sky-high heels and expensive jewellery—despite her success that night, Paige couldn't think of it without a sinking feeling in the pit of her stomach, just like any of the times she'd been pushed by her parents into situations that had made her skin crawl.

What Paige hadn't realised until accepting this job was that the Stone family empire had all started with pearl harvesting, that way back in the early twentieth century, they'd begun to cultivate south sea pearls, and that this property in the far north of Australia was their biggest operation.

So it wasn't unreasonable for Paige to have expected some sort of modern, LA-esque testament to wealth, a showpiece home with miles of glass and visible ostentation dripping from every surface, but what she saw was, in many ways, the complete opposite. Her eyes, a shade of green almost identical to the tropical trees growing rampant overhead, skimmed the house and something like pleasure tugged at her heart—a pleasure she hadn't expected to feel here in the wilderness of the world.

Or was it perhaps relief? She'd been running on instinct

for the last month, since the announcement had been made about her parents' tell-all book and Paige had broken out in a clammy sweat. Would she never be free of them? Despite having legally divorced them in her teens, the ghosts of her manipulative mother and father still haunted her. All Paige had wanted was to pretend the book wasn't happening, but, sure enough, interview requests had found their way to her, paparazzi had even showed up near the school of one of her charges. With her cover blown, Paige had known she needed to flee to a new assignment, ideally as far from civilisation as possible.

Staring at the house, she took in the details without allowing her heart to respond, even when it was difficult to ignore the charms of this property. But Paige was resolutely unaffected: she was always hired for short-term roles—at her own insistence—and an essential part of what she did was provide help without getting emotionally attached to people or property.

There was a large area of neatly manicured lawn, signalling a small claim of man's dominance over the abandon of this forested area, but the house seemed determined to surrender itself back to nature. It was made all of timber, except for the windows, of which there were many, and Paige's first thought was that it was a tree house for grown-ups. It stood three stories high, but it was charming rather than grandiose, from the outside at least, with weatherboard painted a pale cream, a large wrap-around balcony on which, from her vantage point, Paige could just make out a day bed and table. She immediately pictured how nice it would be to sit on one of the cane chairs with a cup of iced tea and stare out at the view.

But she wasn't here to relax. This was work—and she understood she'd have her hands full.

The agency who'd recruited Paige had warned her that the house was quite isolated, and so she'd expected silence—a silence her soul desperately needed after the din in her personal life over the last four weeks—only this was anything but! The birdsong was incredible, a true orchestra of nature, humming, buzzing, carolling all around her, so she had no choice but to stop and simply listen, to pay respect to the beauty of this land and its animal inhabitants, to allow herself to be enchanted by the wonder of it all.

And that was how he found her: Paige Cooper—pale, pearl-like skin luminescent in the afternoon sun, her large eyes transfixed, red lips parted, auburn hair pulled over one shoulder in a concession to the stifling humidity, unconsciously seeking a hint of ocean breeze against the skin of her neck, small, slender frame, in that moment of unguardedness, projecting a hint of the fragility she'd worked so hard to conquer over the years.

Max Stone stopped, mid-step, took one look at the woman the agency had sent and had to stifle a groan. Because while he knew he needed help, he'd fought against that necessity ever since placing the call to arrange a nanny.

Max hated the idea of having someone else living under his roof, taking ownership, in a strange kind of way, of his daughter. It made him feel like a failure. Worse, it made him feel like his own father, who'd outsourced whatever parts of Max's life he possibly could, only taking an interest when it became clear Max had a head for business that would make Carrick Stone's life easier.

He hadn't given much thought to the nanny as a person, certainly not as a woman, but as he stared at the slim person in the middle of the lawn, something inside Max ignited that brought his body to a grinding halt. He stood perfectly still and stared at her, inexplicably angry to find that she was beautiful and attractive—for he'd known many women who were the former without being the latter—and he didn't need the complication of desiring the woman he'd hired to care for his daughter.

He should send her away immediately, ask for someone else.

Only, he was truly desperate, and she was reported to be the best. Besides, this was only a three-month assignment, she was here temporarily. Besides, Max hadn't been with a woman in a long time, and he had no intention of giving into temptation now, just because she'd be living under his roof. He formed one hand into a fist at his side, forced himself to focus.

'Paige Cooper?' His voice was gruff, and her eyes flared a little at the roughness to his words. The churning in his gut intensified. He ground his teeth, squared his shoulders then channelled every last inch of his legendary determination into each long stride that brought him across the dappled light on the lawn, towards the fragile-looking American.

The house was intriguing, filled, Paige was sure, with secrets and mysteries, a history that she was quite fascinated to learn, but even more intriguing was the man who stepped from the shadows and onto the grass, walking towards her with what could only be described as a brooding countenance. Paige was an actress by training; she'd landed her first advertisement as a toddler, gone on to star in feature films from a young age, and had grown up surrounded by actors and actresses. She was fluent in body language and the meaning of facial expressions, and yet this man was difficult to read. That he was irritated was obvious, but by what? She wasn't late, and she'd barely spoken. What could it be?

Besides irritation, there was something else. A heaviness in his features, a look of stress, fatigue, weariness? But that was completely at odds with the sheer strength of him, the way he walked—as though he were some kind of wild animal in human form, each step like a lightning rod striking the ground so she almost felt a spark travel over the grass and into her own feet.

'Miss Cooper?' His accent was Australian, like an actor she'd once worked with, deep and relaxed, broad vowel sounds more compelling than they should have been.

'Paige,' she said with a nod, clearing her throat and forcing a smile. She was so thirsty. Having spent the last few years of her life in Dubai, she should have known better than to have left her water on the plane, but so it was, and Paige hadn't had a sip of anything for almost two hours. In this heat, that was no mean feat.

'I'm Max Stone.'

This she already knew. Not only was he very well known—the billionaire son, one half of the siblings who'd inherited the Stone family empire a few years ago—his details had been included in the file she'd been given upon accepting this assignment.

'Thanks for coming.' His voice was deep and earthy, like the red dust that straddled the road to this tropical paradise—he sounded anything but grateful. His voice was hyper-masculine, leaving her in little doubt he was a man cast from this land, grown from the earth and tropical weather. His jaw was square, strong like cut granite—somehow, it was nothing less than the voice deserved—with a cleft in the centre of his chin that she imagined, quite unhelpfully, to be the perfect size for a thumbprint. His hair was dark, like a raven's, though there was the faintest hint of silver at the temples, and his eyes were a piercing blue, quite hypnotically fascinating. If they were still in LA, she'd have suspected he wore contact lenses, but that was a vanity she somehow knew to be beyond Max Stone. This man was rough, hewn from the elements: he was not interested in his own appearance.

He was looking at her as though waiting for her to speak, but what else could Paige say? That it was her pleasure? That wasn't strictly true. This job was her bolt-hole. She'd desperately wanted—needed—to drop right off the edge of the earth, so she'd accepted the most remote, out-of-the-way assignment she possibly could. Being buried in the Australian tropics felt a galaxy away from the rest of the world, and particularly from the media storm that was building like a hurricane smack bang on top of her old life.

'Thanks for having me,' she said, eventually, then cursed herself for admitting as much. She didn't want her new employer to know that she was on the run. It was hardly a good recommendation for the job.

But if he thought the sentiment a strange one, he didn't show it. 'Amanda will be home in…' he regarded his wristwatch, an old-fashioned Rolex '…just under an hour. Come inside, I'll show you around.'

Behind her, Paige was aware of movement, as the man who'd driven her—Reg, he'd introduced himself as—carried her suitcase across the lawn, towards the wide steps that led to the veranda. There were potted plants on the edges of the steps, terracotta with a shrub she didn't recognise but liked instantly for its wildness and the cheery, bright flowers. As they drew closer, she saw the petals were quite waxy, and there were pods attached that looked a little like peas. She couldn't resist reaching out and feeling one. At the merest touch, the pod burst open and, as if it were some kind of party-popper, tiny little seeds flung themselves like confetti, wide into the air.

She stared at it with a small frown then lifted her eyes to Max. He wasn't watching. In fact, he was four paces ahead, about to reach the wide, old-fashioned doors to the home. She dusted off her fingers and hurriedly climbed the last few steps, until she was level with him. He smelled like the ocean, salty and tangy.

When he opened the door into his home, she went to move inside, but Reg, distracted, stepped out, so Paige had to quickly shuttle out of the way, and the only direction she could move, at last minute, was practically on top of Max Stone.

She'd thought of him as a wild animal and now that their bodies connected she *felt* that, deep inside her, a certainty that he vibrated with a rhythm quite outside the ordinary human lexicon. On a deeply subconscious level, her body was aware of his body and the way it buzzed and radiated an energy that was all his own. She quickly stepped away, her breathing rushed, her fingers tingling.

'Sorry, boss. Didn't see ya there.' Reg grinned, tipped his discoloured hat, then moved down the steps, two at a time. He conveyed an air of relaxation despite the spring in his step.

Paige didn't dare look at Max again—she couldn't. Not while she was fighting her body's completely unwelcome response to him. Instead, she sought refuge inside the house.

Compared to outside, the hallway was dark and cool, with wide timber floors and walls. Everything about the house seemed original, though Paige was no expert in architecture, and particularly not Australian architecture. She only knew that she liked this place a great deal.

'The house was originally a hotel,' Max practically grunted, from right behind her, so Paige realised she had just been standing square in the middle of the hallway. 'My grandfather converted it into a house about forty years ago, took out a lot of the walls to make larger rooms. I improved the kitchens, bathrooms, brought the plumbing into the twenty-first century,' he said with something that might have even been an attempt at humour? At least at civility. So she did her best imitation of a smile, moving deeper into the house.

'Downstairs is all living. Lounge room's over there.' He nodded to the left, and Paige ducked her head through the wide entrance way to a very lovely, comfortable space—enormous sofas around a big rug, a wall-mounted television, and shelves lined with books. A large bay window framed a spectacular view over the ocean, which all the rooms on this side of the house would share. She crossed her fingers, hoping her own bedroom would have this same aspect. A board game was set up on the coffee table—Scrabble—but it looked to have been abandoned partway through, perhaps because Amanda had needed to go to bed or get to school.

In the middle of her chest, she felt a familiar emptiness—a sensation she'd grown used to over the last five years, since leaving LA and working as a nanny. She'd been surrounded daily by dozens of little signs of family love and togetherness and she'd never quite been able to stop contrasting that easy affection and parental kindness she observed in her work with her own upbringing—which had been sadly lacking in both.

Max had kept walking so Paige quickened her step once more. 'Study.' He nodded to the right. The door was shut and Paige didn't look in. 'Amanda's room,' he said, indicating the left. With a curious expression, Paige pushed this door inwards—after all, Amanda was her charge and therefore any room of hers was Paige's responsibility. The room had no bed, but was rather a kids' haven. A rocking chair by the window so she could sit and stare out at the stunning vista, another television, and a shelf with every games machine one could imagine, and some books scattered over the floor—titles she recognised because they were beloved by all children the world over, it seemed.

'That's where she likes to spend time.' His voice was *almost* normal, yet there was a slight tightening in the words. Amanda choosing to be in this room bothered him. 'Dining room. We don't eat in there.' He pushed open the door anyway and, out of sheer interest, Paige took a couple of steps inside. This room had a view of the lawn and, beyond it, the rainforest that surrounded this part of the house. Thick, ancient trunks with strange vines wrapping around them and constantly singing birds made Paige sigh. 'It's lovely.'

'We don't like it.' *We.* Paige's heart gave another little clutch. She'd never been part of a 'we'. She likely never would be. How could someone who'd lived through what she had, who'd been betrayed by the two people who were meant to be your staunchest, most loyal defenders, ever trust anyone enough to be a 'we'?

'You don't? What's not to like?' she asked breathily, covering her heartache with an overbright smile.

His eyes narrowed. 'Amanda says it's too stuffy.'

'I suppose it is a little formal,' Paige agreed, moving towards the enormous, dark oak table, running a finger over the heavily polished top. There were no signs in here of family life. No photographs, no books, no scratches on the table to indicate happy, shared meals. There was a fireplace, which she suspected rarely got used, and enormous floor-to-ceiling windows with burgundy drapes, and, against the far wall, two small doors. 'What's over there?'

His lips twisted in something between a grimace and a smile. 'That would be the servants' entrance. For dinner parties.'

'Ah.'

'There's a corridor connecting the dining room to the kitchen,' he continued to explain. 'From when it was a hotel.'

'Clever.'

'Normal, for the time. Come on, we don't have all day.'

She startled a little at his switch of tone, at the sound in his voice of—something she couldn't analyse, but it was clear he wasn't happy.

She stepped back into the corridor, moving quickly because it seemed imperative to be ahead of Max, and then continued onwards. And let out all her breath in one big whoosh, because the kitchen at the back of the house was absolutely stunning. He said he'd upgraded it, but she couldn't have known how perfect it would be. While retaining all the historic charm of the house, it was also new and spacious. Large, open-plan, with a central island bench and windows that ran three sides of the room, so here she had a panoramic view of the ocean as well as glimpses of the ancient, fascinating rainforest. The floorboards were the original timber and the dining table in here was the complete opposite to the shiny, formal table in the other room. This table looked well used. She moved to it on autopilot, resting a hand on the back of one of the two chairs. That there were only two chairs told Paige a lot—they didn't entertain often, and they weren't in the habit of admitting a third to their table.

It conjured images of a loving father and daughter duo,

of a pair who would be truly in lockstep. She bit back a sigh, focusing her attention on Max and wondering at the slight speeding up of her heart.

'Please, take a seat.' He gestured to the table. She wondered which seat was his and which was Amanda's. It made sense to choose the chair she was already touching, so she pulled it back, sat down and rested her elbows on the table.

Max moved to the fridge. 'Water?'

'Thank you.' Her parched throat practically leapt for joy.

He withdrew two tall glasses from a cupboard and pressed them against a button in the fridge. Ice-cold water made the fine glass frost immediately. Her throat quivered with anticipation.

He carried the glasses to the table, scowling. There was no other word for his expression. He placed a drink in front of Paige and the moment he released his hand she reached out and gripped the glass, almost finishing it before lifting her gaze to his face to find his eyes resting on her with an expression that made her spine tingle in a not remotely unpleasant way. But it was a warning. She felt it and heeded it: Paige had learned to follow her instincts, especially when they were urging caution.

His hands were planted on his hips, his jaw clenched, his body radiating tension, so Paige leaned forward, and couldn't help asking, 'Mr Stone? What is it?'

His thick, dark brows knitted together and her heart began to beat faster. He was so handsome, but in a very rugged way—nothing like the men she'd grown up around. There was nothing contrived about his beauty. It was quite the opposite, raw and uncultivated and all the more overpowering for that.

'My daughter—' His deep, gruff voice tightened. 'Amanda is—'

Paige listened with patience. The agency had given her a brief background on the little girl: eleven years old, first five years of her life spent in Sydney until her mother's sudden death in a car accident. She was now in grade five at school in a small town called Mamili, in the heart of Wattle Bay. Paige had also been required to sign a watertight confidentiality agreement, which suited her just fine. She had a natural aversion to the spotlight these days and naturally respected anyone else's right to protect their own privacy.

'I've done my best,' he grunted, defensive, as though Amanda had laid some charge of failure at his feet. 'But she's changed. She's…unrecognisable.' He dragged a hand through his hair, his crystal-blue eyes pinning Paige to her seat, so a funny heat began to fill her belly. 'I want you to bring my daughter back to me. The agency said you're the best—is it true?'

CHAPTER TWO

PAIGE KNEW HER references had been glowing, and from prominent, wealthy families with deep connections across the world, of course that carried weight, but modesty had her naturally wanting to demur.

'That's high praise,' she murmured, thinking of all the children she'd cared for. Dozens of little faces filled her mind, and she hardened her heart to the familiar feeling of loss. 'I enjoy my work, Mr Stone, and yes, I believe I'm good at it.' Paige had worked hard to flourish in this career. Mostly, she'd wanted to make a difference to the lives of children, having experienced a childhood that was so far from the norm herself. She would never allow herself to love and yet she poured a sense of love into each and every child she cared for, treating them all as she wished she'd been treated.

Max Stone regarded her with a look that set Paige's nerves on edge. A look of appraisal, as though he was only just seeing her now for the first time. She deliberately held herself very still, not showing a hint of nervousness or awareness or any concern whatsoever. His piercing eyes raked her face until she felt her skin warm and she was desperate to look away, to angle her face towards the rainforest and lose herself in those trunks, but she didn't.

'You don't look old enough,' he said after a long silence

had stretched and made the air between them crackle, 'to have enough experience.'

She straightened her spine.

'I'm twenty-four,' she bit out, the words clipped. 'More than old enough to care for a child.'

His expression showed scepticism. 'You're little more than a child yourself.'

'I beg your pardon, but I can't be that much younger than you,' she pointed out, then frowned, because he had an eleven-year-old daughter so that wasn't completely accurate. 'And twenty-four is a long, long way from childhood.'

'My daughter is a handful,' he said with a grimace, and she pitied him then, wondering if there was a sense of disloyalty in the back of his mind, making the words a little halting. 'I need someone who can manage her…emotions.'

Paige's lips twisted into a smile before she could stop them, as she remembered what one of her charges—Carrie—had been like at first. 'I have experience with children and their emotions.'

'That's what I hoped. It's what I need. I—when Amanda's mother died, I thought I could handle this. But as Amanda grows up, I'm starting to wonder if she doesn't need more. If she doesn't need—' He shook his head.

'A woman's perspective,' Paige offered gently, pitying him even more, because she could see how hard it was for someone like Max Stone to face the reality that he wasn't able to single-handedly manage his domestic situation.

'Yes.' He closed his eyes, inhaling sharply so his nostrils flared. 'So let's go over the ground rules.'

Paige snapped out of her pity and felt something else instead. Surprise and then—attraction. Really? In response to what? She *hated* being told what to do. Her independence had been too hard fought to surrender it to anyone and yet his natural sense of control was so intensely powerful and masculine that it couldn't help but speak to a part of her that Paige had long ignored.

She hated being told what to do and yet the tone of Max's voice, his easy authority, didn't feel bossy, so much as…protective. She felt as though he might be the kind of person, and parent, who would have been very good at scaring away all the bogeymen under the bed when Amanda was younger. She wondered if he knew how important that was. How important that safety net was for children, to know that their parents were there, protecting them, making their world a predictable and supportive space.

'Amanda was devastated when her mother died—she cannot come to view you as a replacement for Lauren. You're here for three months, and when you leave, I want it to be no harder for Amanda than farewelling an acquaintance. Quite frankly, I can't pick up the pieces for her a second time.'

Sympathy softened Paige's features. 'I'm a professional, Mr Stone. I have no intention of creating a dependency within your daughter.' She paused a moment, then strengthened her voice. 'However, it's my experience that these situations work best when a genuine bond develops.'

'This is a three-month job,' he said quietly, with a steel underpinning those words, as though his very life depended on this. 'There will be no extension of your contract at the end of the three months. This is our home: Amanda's and mine. We don't need long-term help.'

Surprise showed in her features at the abrupt tone to his voice. 'I understand the terms of my contract,' she murmured, a hint defensively. 'But you must understand when it comes to children—'

He lifted a hand in the air, palm facing Paige.

'This isn't about children, it's about Amanda.'

His love for Amanda was abundantly clear. Something like envy stirred in Paige; she ignored it. 'You asked me here, Mr Stone.'

A rush of electricity, of vitality and life caught her completely off guard. Eventually, he nodded once, his lips compressing with an emotion she couldn't decipher.

'I am simply pointing out that without having met Amanda you can hardly know what is best for her, nor what she needs.'

Paige tried to go gently. 'Do *you* know what she needs?'

That floored him. His eyes, ice blue, bored deep into hers. It was a war of attrition; one Paige had no intention of surrendering.

'No,' he admitted, finally, angrily, but the anger was directed at himself. Paige was torn between pity and irritation.

'Precisely,' she said, standing, because he hadn't sat down and she was beginning to feel the difference in their power dynamic too keenly. 'I was hired—by you—to do a job. Now, I have no intention of getting out there—' she pointed generally towards the ocean '—and telling you how to find big, shiny pearls, but by the same token you shouldn't interfere.'

'She's my *daughter*,' he said darkly.

'And you have asked for help with her. So let me help you.'

'I don't want her to be hurt.'

'You don't want her to feel like you're giving up,' Paige intuited, using the same tone of voice she employed when one of her charges was in need of placating. Calm, reasonable, without emotion. 'She won't.'

He grimaced.

'And I'll be up front with her from the beginning,' she conceded quietly. 'This is a three-month contract. I'm not here to stay. I'm not here to replace her mother. I'm here to help right now, when you need it, and then I'll leave.' She tilted her chin with a hint of defiance. 'And by the same token, Mr Stone, you should be warned: if at the end of the three months you would like me to stay, I won't consider it. I have other obligations beyond this,' she said. Even though that wasn't yet true, she was in demand and knew another booking would eventuate when she wanted it.

And by then, the dust would have settled on the tell-all book, and with any luck she'd be done with licking her wounds, and she wouldn't stay here a moment longer than was necessary. She wouldn't stay anywhere ever again, wouldn't get comfortable, wouldn't let herself relax, because it was just too risky. She had a heart of iron but she wasn't a complete automaton—living with children for any true period of time meant investing her heart and she simply couldn't do that.

'I won't ask you to stay.'

She didn't need to wonder why his rushed agreement made her stomach twist uncomfortably. Being rejected and disposed of with ease was one of Paige's biggest fears in life. With her training as a nanny, she now understood the psychology behind that: she'd never known security as a child. Love had always been conditional for Paige. Conditional on her landing whatever role her parents—managers—had decided was right for her. Conditional on her losing weight to fit the clothes of the brands they'd signed her up to be an ambassador for. Conditional on her agreeing to go on television and do live interviews, even though as a child she was fundamentally ill-equipped for that kind of spotlight.

Paige had never felt loved just as she was, and she probably never would—that sort of conditioning was hard to shake.

And while she wasn't looking for Max Stone—of all people—to 'love' her, she didn't like the ease with which he agreed that she was temporary.

But that was their agreement, plain and simple.

'I work in the study,' he said quietly. 'If I'm not there, I'll be down on the docks.'

'Okay.' She nodded once, ignoring the spark of curiosity ignited in her mind by reference to the docks. The idea of pearl farming had captured her imagination as soon as she'd accepted this assignment. What a strange, unusual and glamorous occupation.

'Amanda's schedule is on the fridge. Reg drives her around, but if you'd prefer—'

Paige bit down on her lip. 'I think it's better for me not to drive her for a while.'

His eyes narrowed and she felt pressured to add, 'I do have a licence. Technically.'

'Technically?'

Now, Paige felt as though she were in the principal's office—not that she'd ever attended a normal school.

'Well, I learned to drive in the States, so there's the whole right-side, left-side thing to contend with. And on top of that, I've been in Dubai for five years. I didn't drive there, either. In the interest of safety—'

'Fine. Reg will continue to drive her.' Then, with a furrowed brow and a concession to civility she hadn't expected, 'And he can take you anywhere throughout the day, if you need anything. There's a town—Mamili—about twenty minutes away, near the school.'

'Are there any tasks I can do, while she's at school? Usually I help out around the house…'

'No.' His flat refusal was another immediate rejection. 'We don't need that. We're fine. Just keep yourself busy…'

'And stay out of your way?' she couldn't help prompting, surprised to find one corner of her lips lifting in a cynical smile.

His eyes narrowed and his Adam's apple shifted as he swallowed. 'My days are busy.'

But he didn't need to explain anything about his life to her. Paige's interaction with parents was usually kept to a minimum. He had offered her the use of a chauffeur, which was a courtesy that wasn't necessary.

'Thank you,' she said quietly, surprised that her voice trembled slightly, but he didn't seem to notice.

'The bedrooms are upstairs,' he said. 'Amanda's and mine at the top of the stairs. You can choose any other room for yourself.'

It was a dismissal and Paige's nerves were frazzled enough that she was glad for the reprieve. With a small nod of her head, she left Max alone in the stunning kitchen, moving up the beautiful wide staircase as though the devil were at her back.

He was surprisingly grateful when she disappeared quickly, and the moment she left the kitchen he expelled a long, deep sigh. What was it about this woman that unnerved him? Was it simply that she was a nanny, hired to care for his daughter? Of course that was a part of it, but Max wasn't an idiot. There was only one way to explain the surge of adrenalin pounding through his body, the direction his mind kept wandering in, as she spoke and her lips parted breathily and her chest puffed out with indignation, drawing his attention to her gentle curves, to the graceful way she moved, almost like a ballerina. She was attractive and fascinating and he could already tell that it was going to require monumental effort to ignore the way she made him feel.

With a sense that a thundercloud had formed directly above him, he began to walk upstairs, sure he'd given her enough time to have disappeared into a room and keen to grab his pullover for a trip to the farm.

He rounded the corner of the landing and strode to his own room right as Paige stepped out, a guilty flush on her cheeks. 'Oh, Mr Stone!' Her eyes thudded to his. 'I'm sorry. When you said your room and Amanda's were here, I thought you meant those two, I didn't think—'

She waved blithely over her shoulder, in the direction of his bedroom, which she'd evidently just been in.

He realised now how vague his instructions had been; he couldn't really blame her, and yet something like anger fizzed inside him because he didn't want to think of her in his bedroom, while it was just the two of them alone in the house.

'I'm sorry again,' she breathed huskily, so close he could feel her breath, and ancient, long-forgotten, repressed nerves began to fizz and burst beneath his veins. How long had it been since he'd touched a woman?

That was an easy question to answer.

Since Lauren had died.

Since well before Lauren had died, in fact, because their relationship had been messy for some time prior.

Six years? In the back of his mind, he registered the fact with shock, and wondered why it hadn't occurred to him before this.

'I misunderstood,' she responded with a small shake of her head. But the same awareness flooding his veins was apparently making it hard for Paige to focus as well, because her cheeks were flushed and her breathing rushed and, beneath the fine cotton of her shirt, her nipples had hardened to form two perfect shapes, silhouetted by neat, round breasts. He could feel their weight in his palms without touching them, he just knew they'd be satisfying to hold. His jeans strained as the idea of doing exactly that lodged in his brain and refused to go away.

Neither moved.

The air thickened, like at the end of a hot, sultry day when the humidity had reached breaking point and the sauna-like atmosphere meant the sky would need to burst at the seams and flood the earth with rain to stave off spontaneous combustion. But they were inside, there was no rain here, only him, and her, and one of them had to be strong enough to break the spell weaving around them.

'Don't misunderstand again,' he growled, stepping back to let her pass. She startled, looking up at him as though he'd threatened to kill a cat, then quickly moved around him, and down the hallway, spine straight, magnificent auburn hair like flames cascading down her back.

He closed his eyes on a sigh of relief, but when he breathed in to fill his lungs back up, he could taste her in the air. Great. Just great.

Amanda, at eleven, was tracking about three years ahead of what Paige might have expected. She was sullen, moody, had a few spots on her face, and was clearly unimpressed with the idea of a stranger living in her home. Particularly when that stranger's purview was *her*.

'I don't need a babysitter,' Amanda, with eyes as startlingly clear blue as her father's, had snapped, shooting Paige a withering glance. 'I'm old enough to take care of myself.' And with that, she'd slammed the door in Paige's face.

There'd been no chance to form an expectation of how Amanda might behave. Paige had only Max's warning to go off—that she was a handful at the moment. But he hadn't elaborated on what that entailed, nor had he shared any insights into what was making Amanda behave this way. Paige had nothing to go on but her gut feeling, and it told her that something had happened, or was happening, to upset the girl, and she knew it was her job—more than her job, her responsibility—to get to the bottom of it. She owed nothing to Max Stone, but as a woman who'd once been a little girl in distress, who'd been saved by the kindness and interest of a kindly adult, she made it her business to pay that same kindness forward whenever she could.

And it was abundantly clear that Amanda needed kindness.

She also needed patience, something she wondered if Max Stone had any idea how to demonstrate.

But Paige did. She needed answers, and not from Amanda—it was clear that the little girl would need some time to adapt to the new dynamic and Paige knew better than to push it.

Despite the fact having a conversation with Max made her blood do funny things in her veins, she balled her hands into fists and walked back downstairs, along the pleasingly cool corridor, to the room with the closed door. Knocking on it twice, she waited for him to call something out, but when he didn't, she turned the door handle slowly, cautiously, poking her head around the door in time to catch Max evidently lost in thought, standing at the window and staring out.

In those few seconds, her wretched eyes observed details that were none of her business, like how athletic and toned he was, how pleasingly slim his waist was, how his trousers fitted him snugly in all the right places, hugging his bottom and hips, making it impossible not to notice his virility, so she startled, lifting fingers to her lips and blinking away quickly, but not, she suspected, before he caught her in the act of staring at a very personal part of his anatomy. Oh, good heavens. How she wished the earth would open up and swallow her whole.

What was wrong with her?

'What is it now, Paige?'

At least he'd dispensed with the 'Miss Cooper'.

But Paige's mouth had turned to dust, as dry as the desert airstrip she'd flown into, and her tongue was all thick and stagnant in her mouth.

He made a growling noise, then strode towards her, reaching behind Paige and pushing the door closed. 'Let's get one thing straight,' he said, pressing a finger to her chin and lifting her face towards his, so their eyes met and their lips were only inches apart. Her breathing was rushed, her chest moving quickly to allow for the fast pace of her lungs. 'I am not part of what's on offer here. You're here to care for Amanda. If you have any other ideas, then I suggest you forget them.'

Paige was aghast, her lips parting and her eyes flooding with white-hot rage at his disgusting assertion. She wanted to slap the man in front of her for daring to suggest such a disgusting thing, even when the rational part of her brain could see, on some level, why he'd leaped to that conclusion. Finding herself in his bedroom that afternoon had been one thing but, coupled with the way she'd just been ogling him, yes, she could understand how he'd added two and two together and arrived at four. Pride however made her defend herself.

'You are so, so wrong,' she said stonily, when she could trust her voice to emerge without breaking.

'Am I?' His eyes probed hers, a warning in them, but also a surrender, so Paige knew that if she didn't step away from him, something was going to happen. She didn't know what. She couldn't have said, but it felt as if a time bomb were ticking, counting down to an inexorable explosion. 'And so being in my bedroom was really an innocent mistake?'

'Of course it was,' she hissed, wondering why she still wasn't moving away.

He held her chin, and then his other hand lifted, as if drawn by magnetic force, to her hip, his fingers splayed wide.

'You should keep your distance, Paige.'

Her eyes fluttered closed and her senses were filled with him. His smell, his nearness, his strength and warmth. She swallowed, her mouth not working properly. But she thought of Amanda and how much that little girl needed her, needed help, how her behaviour was likely a classic cry for that, and knew she had to push through this.

'I can't do that.'

His nostrils flared. He was so close it was hard to think straight but she forced herself to focus.

'This situation is going to work best if you and I are a team. We have to work together.'

'But we're not talking about work right now.'

No, they hadn't been. They were talking about something distinctly unprofessional, something messy and fraught with difficulties, the kind of complications Paige avoided like the plague. Her personal life was already imploding, she didn't need to throw this kind of dynamite into the mix.

With another deep breath, and a glare for good measure, she stepped quickly away from him, deeper into an office that was clearly a sanctuary for the man. 'Believe me, I'm not interested in that,' she said huskily, waving a hand in the vicinity of the door while her troubled eyes landed on the rainforest.

'That's good, because it's not going to happen.'

Was he trying to convince her? Or himself? After all, he was the one who'd put his hand on her hip, who'd touched her as though he couldn't stop himself. She remembered the way she'd been taken advantage of as a teenager, the unwelcome advances, the pressure to hook up with men just because it was expected of her, or the possibility it could be professionally advantageous. She should have hated being touched. She thought she did, yet there was something about his tanned, broad hand that was so masculine and so—reassuring, even as he was throwing lewd accusations at her. But this wasn't going to work if she allowed this strange energy to take over everything. She had to concentrate.

'We need to discuss Amanda.'

His expression was unreadable, but on his lips she thought she caught a hint of derision and dug her nails into her palms to stop herself from explaining further.

'What would you like to discuss?'

'Her behaviour.'

He stiffened. 'Yes?'

'One of the reasons children lash out like this is that something specific has happened. Something upsetting. A fight with friends, for example. Can you think of anything that's been going on with Amanda?'

His eyes narrowed. 'Nothing out of the ordinary.'

Well, that wasn't saying much. To an eleven-year-old girl, even an ordinary upset could be quite destabilising. 'Has she mentioned *anything*, whether you think it's significant or not?'

'No.' Then, with a deepening frown, 'She hasn't been talking much lately. I've spoken to her teacher. She told me Amanda's generally well liked, though there has been some movement in her social circle. But it's got to be more than that. She's just become so—' He hesitated, and she felt his protective loyalty and something inside her softened. He was a strange beast of a man, with many facets, but she thought she might actually come to like this side of him—the loving, confused father. 'Argumentative,' he added slowly, rubbing a hand over his jaw. 'It's like I'm her least favourite person on earth. I can't say anything right.'

His deep Australian accent drawled over the last few words and Paige's heart ached for him.

'I don't know what's going on, Miss Cooper.' Suddenly, he was in charge again. Confident bordering on arrogant, and slightly disapproving.

Paige nodded once. She believed he was at a loss. He wasn't going to be able to provide any sudden epiphany: if he'd had any useful insights he might not have needed to hire a nanny. And with that in mind, the smart thing to do would be for Paige to leave.

There was certainly no point in staying, in the heart of his office, looking at his furniture, his work desk, the photograph behind it of a jetty with two teenage boys and an older man, and wheelbarrows lined up behind them filled with oysters.

And yet…

'Is that you?' she murmured, moving towards the picture.

He grunted. A confirmation?

With her interest overriding any fear of overstaying her welcome, she moved closer to the picture. ‘This one?’ She pointed to the young man on the left—she’d have guessed he was about seventeen in the photograph, all long limbs and broad shoulders.

She heard the quietest rustle of clothing as he moved across the room, coming to stand right behind her. ‘Yes.’ The word was drawn from him reluctantly. He lifted a finger to point to the other boy, his arm brushing hers as he reached past her. Paige caught her breath in her throat. ‘And my brother, Luca. My father.’ He dropped his hand away, stood there, right behind her, and though she was looking at the photo, she could hear him, feel him, and if she closed her eyes, she could *see* him.

They had to find a way to work together, for Amanda’s sake, which meant clearing the air. Turning slowly, with the very best intentions in the world, Paige blinked up at Max. ‘I meant what I said before,’ she whispered. ‘I’m here to help with your daughter, not for—not because—’

His eyes swept closed and when he exhaled, his breath tingled the hair at Paige’s temples. She stood her ground quite miraculously, given that her knees felt as though they might give way.

‘Good,’ he said after a silence that stretched a beat too long. ‘Let’s make sure we both remember that.’

The way he said it made Paige wonder though: was he finding that hard too?

CHAPTER THREE

BY THE NEXT morning Paige felt as though she'd run a marathon, yet she didn't let anyone see just how drained she was.

Amanda was truly awful.

Or rather, she was behaving in a way that was awful. Sulky, grumpy, temperamental and *mean*. Paige had no benchmark for what the girl had been like before, but from everything Max had said—and the dazed expression on his face—this was coming out of the blue like a freight train off its tracks.

Paige drove into the township of Mamila with Amanda, but purposely didn't make conversation on the trip. She was there to observe. From the back seat of the luxury four-wheel drive, she watched the interactions between Reg and the girl—Reg seemed not to notice any changes in Amanda, and if he did, he wasn't going to let her obvious unwillingness to chat get in the way of the stories he wanted to tell. He deserved a medal for his ability to chatter in the face of such obvious belligerence. He talked about the desert, the trees, where he'd grown up, in a house on the other side of the forest with a hole in the deck you had to jump over to reach the front door.

'Don't know why my old man never got around to fixing it,' he said with an endearing chuckle and shake of his head, before turning off the main road and onto another—equally straight, long and lined with those same remarkable trees. Houses began to appear amongst the trunks, just a few at first and then more and more and then they were on the outskirts of a town, with proper roads and signs, and a couple of overhead lights.

Just a main street, really, with a few shops and cafes on either side. It was historic and charming. Paige couldn't help sighing as they drove past. How she'd have liked to stop and explore! But her first priority was Amanda.

She watched as the girl sat with crossed arms, hunched over, staring out of the window with a scowl every bit as impressive as her father's, eyeing the same little shops Amanda had just been admiring.

They approached the school and Amanda tensed visibly. Paige held her breath, watching with even more care. It was a tiny, telltale reaction, just the stiffening of her shoulders, the tightening of her body, but it confirmed for Paige that school was at least one source of stress for Amanda. Perhaps the only source? If Paige could help Amanda navigate whatever was happening at school, it might help turn her mood around. Could it be so simple?

No, of course not, she chided herself mentally. Nothing was simple with hormonal, prepubescent kids.

'What are you doing?' Amanda demanded fiercely, when Paige stepped out of the car.

Paige kept a neutral expression. 'Walking you in.'

Amanda's jaw dropped. 'Nuh uh. No way. I'm not a baby.' She pulled on her school-bag strap and glanced over her shoulder.

'I know you're not, but my job is to see you through the gate.'

'And you can *see* the gate from here,' Amanda hissed.

Paige counted to five slowly. Amanda was right. She could see the gate, and she knew that schools in Australia didn't require parent or guardian hand-off. Kids were often dropped in a zone and a teacher supervised their entry.

She weighed up her options and decided that placating Amanda was the most important thing for now. 'Okay. I'll stay here.'

'Good.'

'Amanda?'

The girl glared at Paige, defensive and prepared. Paige softened her features into a gentle smile. 'Is there anything in particular you'd like as an after-school snack? A favourite food or drink?'

Amanda's eyes darted to the left, her expression shifted for the briefest moment before it tightened once more into a mask of anger. 'What I *like* after school is *privacy*. Got it?'

Max was just leaving the house when Paige approached it. Dressed in beige shorts and a white polo shirt with aviator sunglasses and a wide-brimmed hat, he was the picture of rugged, outback masculinity. Her feet slowed and her mouth went dry.

'Miss Cooper.' He nodded in her direction, lips compressed in a tight line.

A zing of something ignited in her bloodstream. She ignored it. 'I want to talk to you about Amanda, Max.' She deliberately used his first name, and she couldn't have said why. Only, they were to be living together, and working in some ways as a team when it came to Amanda. It was time to drop the formalities. 'Do you have a minute?'

He hesitated, eyes flicking in her direction, landing on her face first then travelling the length of her body quickly, like the cracking of a whip.

'I'm going to the farm,' was his gruff response. 'If you want to talk, you'll have to come with me.'

Consternation flooded Paige. She was curious to see the farm, and desperate to start working on the problem of Amanda's behaviour, but it would mean being in a car with Max, close to him, being stranded who knew where with him, and each of those considerations lit a strange little fire in Paige's belly.

'I—'

'I don't have all day. Yes or no?'

She shot him a withering look then changed course, moving towards him. 'Fine. I'll come with you.'

He had no idea what had bloody possessed him to issue that invitation. Invitation? Command, more like. He'd backed her into a corner rather than just giving her five minutes to talk—a conversation he actually *wanted* to have because if this woman had any insights on Amanda then he was desperate to hear them. And yet he'd manoeuvred them into this situation, and he couldn't say why.

'Hop in,' he grunted, gesturing to the front passenger seat of his car.

He slid into the driver's seat and started the engine, forcing himself not to focus on Paige Cooper's legs as she climbed into the passenger seat. The morning sun sliced through the tinted windscreen so he noticed for the first time the smattering of freckles across her nose.

Paige turned to face him as she buckled in her seat belt and their eyes met, and the same surge of insanity and desire that had paralysed Max yesterday was back, with a vengeance. He was far too conscious of her physicality. Of her eyes. Her lips. Her ski-jump nose. Her slender, graceful neck. The pulse point in her neck that was undulating visibly. The way the soft fabric of her simple cotton shirt clung to her breasts, the long, silver necklace she wore dangling down low, drawing his attention to the valley of her cleavage. Her sweet fragrance, like vanilla and coconut. His brows drew together, his mind vaguely aware of the strange direction of his thoughts, of the fact he should really be thinking of anything but Paige Cooper, of the fact that, after six years of celibacy, apparently he was like a matchbox flooded with gasoline, just waiting for a single flame to make him explode. And she was the flame.

Paige Cooper, here in his home, and now in the confines of his car, and the intensity between them burned brighter than he'd expected possible.

But it wasn't really her, so much as his natural proclivities. He'd ignored them for too long, prioritising instead all things Amanda. Wanting to be a good dad. A good parent—he had to be *both* parents to her, and he'd been determined not to stuff that up. He would do everything he could to parent differently from his own parents—a father who'd been so intently focused on his business he'd neglected his son and a mother who couldn't bear to see Max after the trauma of her divorce because of how Max reminded her of her husband.

He tore his eyes away from Paige with effort, staring out of the windscreen with a stern expression.

Desiring Paige was inconvenient. Hell, it was about a thousand shades of inconvenient, but it couldn't be helped. He *did* desire her. He was aware of her on every level, and there was no sense pretending it wasn't the case. But no way would he be selfish enough to put his own interests ahead of Amanda's. Paige was here to help his daughter, Paige clearly *wanted* to help Amanda, so Max would just have to control his baser instincts. When this was over and

Paige had left, presuming Amanda was back to normal by then, he'd change his lifestyle. Let himself start living again, just a little. A weekend in Sydney from time to time, the freedom to remember that he was a red-blooded male.

Paige was conscious of him every single inch of the drive. Even when the view was quite incomparable, she was only vaguely capable of appreciating it, because the man beside her took up so much damned space. Not just physically, though there was that too. His size was awe-inspiring enough in the outdoors, or in a large room like the kitchen, but here, in a car, he seemed twice as big as a regular man, his long legs speaking of athleticism and confidence, his fingers curved around the gearstick drawing her gaze far too often, so she couldn't help remembering what it had felt like when those same fingers had curved around her hip and held her there, when he'd gripped her chin, tilting her face towards his.

She cracked the window a little, because the air in the car was so full of buzzing electricity, and she needed ventilation to clear her mind. She breathed in, the fragrance of the forest lush and woody. Out of the corner of her eye, she saw Max shift his hand from the gearstick to the steering wheel, gripping it tightly, until his knuckles turned white. The silence stretched and Paige's skin lifted in goosebumps.

She opened her mouth, needing to speak. But Max beat her to it. 'What made you take on this job?'

She was surprised by the question, because it came close to small talk, but perhaps it was more an addendum to a job interview. He was trusting her to care for his daughter; naturally he had questions.

'I've never been here,' she said simplistically, leaving

out a fair bit of her reasoning—namely, why she wanted to drop off the face of the world.

'Australia?'

Flashes of memories assaulted her. World premieres in Sydney, Melbourne. Camera flashes. Exhaustion from travelling and being so young. Uncomfortable shoes, late nights, interviews. Her face was pale as she shook her head. 'I've been to Australia.' Her voice emerged a little high-pitched; Paige cleared her throat. 'But never somewhere as remote as this. So tropical.' She lifted her shoulders. 'I wanted to see it.'

'I suppose that's fair.'

'I'm glad you approve,' she observed wryly.

'I don't know if I approve or not. I was simply interested in your decision-making process.'

'Why?'

He turned to face her, lifting one of those thick, dark brows, so her heart fluttered.

'I mean, does it matter? I'm here. Anyway, I think I can help you with Amanda. But it will take time,' she said, switching into work mode, her voice gentling. 'I'm pretty sure I'm right, that it's something at school.'

His hands tightened on the wheel.

'Amanda seemed tense when Reg dropped her off this morning. You said her friendship group is changing; maybe she's feeling excluded and that's upsetting her. She hasn't said anything to you?'

His grip on the steering wheel tightened further. 'No. But I'm starting to think I'm the last person she'd open up to.' His jaw moved as he ground his teeth together. 'But there's only me.'

'That's why you decided to hire a nanny?'

He jerked his head once, in silent agreement. 'I need

help and I think Amanda needs…a woman in her life. Some of the stuff she's going through, I've got no idea how to help her. I had a brother, no sisters. My brother's wife is great, but they're busy with their own kids.' He shook his head. 'My mother left when I was twelve. Amanda is literally the female I've spent longest with in the world, so I have no advice or wisdom to give her.'

Paige frowned. 'Where's your mother now?'

Silence stretched between them. 'Hong Kong, last I heard.'

Paige shifted a little in the seat. 'You don't see her much?'

He shook his head.

Paige pleated the fabric of her skirt, not wanting to pry but naturally curious. Fortunately, Max continued without being prompted.

'She decided to live overseas, after the divorce.'

Paige wasn't sure what to say. Her own parents were pathetic enough, but she was still always surprised to encounter other examples of maternal or paternal failure. It seemed so outside the natural order of things. 'But why?' she asked, simply.

'Why not?'

'Because you're here. Amanda…'

He glanced at Paige then returned his attention to the road. 'But also my father.'

'It's a big country,' she pointed out.

'And she hates him just that much.'

'But you're her son.'

'I'm also his son.'

Paige sat back in the seat, mulling that over.

'I'm too much his son,' Max admitted grudgingly, after another moment. 'She looks at me and sees him.'

Heaviness shifted inside Paige and she reflected on how impossible it was to really know what was going on inside a person, because her first impression of Max had been one of sheer arrogance and alpha masculinity and now she couldn't help but wonder at the wounds his mother's rejection must have caused him. And because it was the most natural thing in the world to do, because Paige was someone who gave the sort of comfort she wished she'd received more often when distressed, she reached out and put a hand on his knee, intending it to be a light, reassuring touch, a vote of confidence. But his leg flinched beneath her fingers and the breath that hissed from between his teeth was not friendly. It made her aware of him on a level she didn't want to feel and, worse, it made her realise that he was dangerously aware of her too. She pulled her hand away as though she'd been burned.

'Where are we going?' Her voice was stilted, breathy.

'To the farm.'

He'd told her that, but the word was a misnomer. Far from being anything like any kind of farm Paige had ever seen, this 'farm' was actually the beach. A beautiful cove of white sand and turquoise water, palm trees along the coastline, and white boats bobbing on the water's surface, lines of rope on the top, and a hive of activity—people moving in and out of the water, to a shaded jetty in the middle of it all.

'It's so beautiful,' she murmured, instantly wishing she'd brought bathers. But then, the thought of wearing something skimpy in front of Max did funny things to her body so she pushed that thought right out of her mind. When things improved a little, she'd ask Amanda to go to the beach with her. It would be a bonding experience.

'Yes,' he agreed, without looking, cutting the engine

and reaching across her to pull a book from the glove box. His hand grazed her knee and now it was Paige's turn to flinch. She felt the electric shock travel all the way through her body.

He expelled a sigh, turning to face her. 'Look, Paige.' His voice was deep and raw. His brows drew together, his eyes boring into hers as if trying to read her thoughts. 'About yesterday—'

She blinked up at him.

'I was wrong to say what I did, how I did.'

His statement was totally unexpected.

'Obviously I'm attracted to you.'

Her lips parted, her mouth forming a circle. This, she had not expected. 'That's—I—'

'And I think it's mutual,' he continued, his lips a grim line.

Her cheeks felt as though they were about to go supa nova.

'I believe in honesty,' he drawled. She squeezed her eyes shut on a wave of unwelcome wants. 'There's no sense ignoring the elephant in the room.'

Paige grimaced, then, finally, nodded. 'Fine, okay. Yes.'

'Good.' His approval sent a thousand little arrows darting through her veins. 'But Amanda is my focus. She has been my focus from the day she was born. Earlier, even. From the moment I found out Lauren was pregnant.'

Something shifted in his voice, and a feeling pressed heavily against Paige's emotional wound, like a finger in a bruise. She blinked away, trying not to think about how much she would have loved her own father to express even an iota of that sentiment for Paige.

'So whatever is going on between us, obviously we have to control it. I'm not going to risk Amanda getting caught in the middle of something, just because we couldn't keep our hands to ourselves.' He looked away, features locked into a mask of self-control. 'Because *I* can't keep *my* hands to myself,' he corrected darkly. 'It's important to me that we both keep it professional.'

She appreciated his honesty, and, in some ways, was glad to have him bring their attraction out into the open, but at the same time, something about his words sat uncomfortably in her gut. 'Of course,' she murmured, because what choice did she have? Besides, he was right. The last thing Paige wanted was any complication, and nor could she afford to jeopardise her job, which she was pretty sure having an affair with her boss would do.

So they were attracted to each other. Big deal. Someone like Max Stone probably had a woman he was attracted to in every city of the world. She'd known men like him. Bigshot billionaires, the behind-the-scenes financiers who greased the money wheels of Hollywood and made the magic keep happening. She knew what men were like. Just because Max Stone seemed more comfortable in rugged outback clothes and his big, comfortable, charming, old house, didn't mean he wasn't also capable of being just like those men she'd known before, in her other life.

Except none of that really tallied with a man who was insisting on putting his daughter first.

Paige turned away and opened the door in one movement.

'Thanks for the drive,' she called over her shoulder. 'Tell me when you want to leave.'

He needed to inspect the harvest—which was looking exceptional, even by their exacting standards—but every few seconds his eyes strayed to the shore, where Paige was walking in the shallows, kicking the water a little, head bent, eyes trained on the splashing droplets as they flicked into the air then landed back in the frothy shallows, being swallowed up once more by the sea. She left small, wet footprints that he could just make out as the water receded, and the skirt she wore pulled at her legs in the light coastal breeze, so he couldn't help but register how delicate and feminine her shape was… Desire surged through him and he dropped his head forward, acknowledging to himself that resisting his desire for Paige was going to be one of the hardest things he'd ever done.

Paige had always thought the Mediterranean was the most idyllic, stunning beach in the world. It was certainly famed for the juxtaposition of culture, history and natural beauty. But here, in the very north of Australia, Paige wondered if there'd ever been a more breathtakingly lovely sight. The water was so clear she suspected that if she were to wade out up to her neck she'd still be able to see her feet against the white crystal sand. The water made little diamond shapes as it danced and caught the sunlight, reflecting and refracting it into myriad patterns. She desperately wanted to swim, but the most she allowed herself, having looked over her shoulder to be sure Max wasn't nearby, was to tuck her long skirt up a little, into the elastic of her underpants, and go into the water to her knees. It was so delightfully cool, so refreshing, that she actually moaned out loud. She went a little deeper, reaching her fingertips out and drawing them through the water, lifting it and pressing it to her throat and neck, which were too hot courtesy of the beating mid-morning sun.

How was it possible that somewhere could be so pristine and unpopulated? She turned her back on the ocean, looking instead to the coastline, with its glorious green forest almost the whole way to the beach, so wild and untamed. There were some houses she could just make out and, in fact, her eyes chased west. And there it was—Max's tree house. She smiled, because it really was incredibly beautiful, magical seeming, wise and ancient against the backdrop of resplendent nature.

'Paige.' His voice caught her by surprise. It wasn't his fault. She'd been in her own little daydream world. She turned too quickly, guiltily almost, and lost her footing, slipping in her haste, half stumbling into the water, so she was wet all the way to her breasts on one side. Heat flushing her cheeks, embarrassed at her silly, clumsy body, she stood quickly, glaring at him even when it wasn't his fault, stalking out of the ocean without being able to bring herself to meet his eyes.

But then, she thought better of it, turning to face him and changing direction, walking right up to him so they were toe to toe. 'That was an accident,' she said crankily. 'I slipped. It was not some kind of "wet T-shirt" scenario designed to make my clothes stick to my body.'

'Thank you though for drawing my attention to the fact that your clothes are in fact sticking to your body.'

She bit down on her lower lip and looked away.

'Though yes, in fairness, I had already noticed.'

Her cheeks felt as though they were burning.

She crossed her arms over her chest. 'What did you want?'

'When?'

'Then. You called my name.'

'You said to tell you when I'm ready to go.'

'Oh.' She cast one last, longing glance at the beach. 'And are you?'

He hesitated a moment, eyes raking her face, expression impossible to read. And then, 'Yes. We should go.'

Disappointment unfurled in Paige's chest. What had she been hoping? That he'd suggest they go swimming together? He was working, and she wasn't his houseguest. She was an employee in his home, that was all.

'We should,' she agreed, her voice tinged with glumness. But still, neither moved. The air between them crackled and hummed and Paige's lips parted, warmth spreading through her as she imagined what it would feel like to be kissed by him. Out of nowhere, an image of him doing exactly that assailed her and she trembled all over. What on earth was happening to her?

He wanted to kiss her. He wanted to pull her against his body and taste those sweet pink lips, to feel her curves hard against him. He wanted to know the touch of a woman again, to know the heady rush of intimacy, and he wanted that, particularly, with Paige. She'd stirred something to life inside his chest, something he'd been fighting since the moment she'd arrived. He'd blamed her.

He'd accused her of instigating it but that was wrong.

The moment he had seen her he'd felt re-energised, reborn, a red-blooded man again, fully aware of his needs and desires.

He wanted nothing more than to act on them.

But how could he?

He was going around in circles here, knowing he couldn't take advantage of this situation even when every cell in his body was demanding he do *something* about this desire. She felt it too. He might have been out of practice with women but he understood people and the way her eyes lingered on him, stuck to his lips, or his body, when she thought he wasn't looking… She was as much under siege as he was.

So wouldn't he be doing them both a favour if he acted on this?

And then what?

Frustration whipped the base of his spine. Desire unfurled in his belly.

'Don't you need to go?' she whispered, her voice soft, curling around him like the waves of the ocean.

Didn't he?

Shouldn't they?

'Is that what you want?' His voice was made hoarse by desire.

'Max.' Her word was a sigh and then her hand lifted to his chest, almost as if she couldn't help herself. The second she touched him, sparks exploded in his gut. Heaven help him, he was stirring to life—with a vengeance. Every part of him was energised and hyper-charged, hyper-aware of Paige. 'We can't—'

Her voice trailed off and he closed his eyes, trying to latch onto sanity, to his legendary self-control. He did so, but with monumental effort.

'No.' He took her by the wrist and removed her hand, swallowing hard at the simple, possessive contact. 'We can't.' Now his voice was flint, as if the simple act of asserting dominance over his desires had rendered him stone. 'Let's go, Paige. We both have work to do.'

CHAPTER FOUR

THEY ATE TOGETHER that night, the three of them. It was Paige's suggestion, but the moment they sat down Max wished he'd had an acceptable excuse to leave. He'd become used to the awkward, prickly silences when it was just him and Amanda. He'd learned how to zone out to ignore his own deficiencies, and to drown out the proof that his daughter was starting to hate him. But with Paige in the room, he felt every single one of those thoughts banging into him until he wanted to scream. Worse, the air between him and Paige seemed to hum with all the power of an extremely localised electrical storm, so there was no refuge from tension, no respite. He should have avoided this like the plague.

Amanda sat on one side of the table, opposite Paige, with Max at the head.

And for all Paige had orchestrated this happy little scenario, once they were seated, she made very little attempt at conversation, so he found himself wondering almost obsessively about what she was thinking, what she wanted, noticing all the small details, like how she held her fork and shifted her water glass when she was lost in thought.

Max ground his teeth, forcing himself to focus on his daughter, to ask Amanda the staple round of questions she generally liked to ignore:

How was school?

What did you do at lunch?

Did you learn anything interesting?

What do you have on tomorrow?

Amanda, for her part, had made an artform out of the almost non-existent response.

Good.

Walked around.

Not really.

Nothing.

The whole routine took about forty-seven seconds and then silence returned, except for the scraping of their plates. Once they were finished, Amanda pierced him with her blue eyes then stood. 'May I be excused?' He couldn't tell if it was hostility or something else that was making her voice shake but he nodded curtly.

'Clear the table and then you can go get ready for bed.'

'But I cleared it last night!'

'Amanda.' His voice held a warning, but inside, he felt an unfamiliar emotion—lack of control. The same feeling he'd been grappling with for months as his daughter morphed into a stranger. Worse, transformed into parts of Lauren that Max had thought he'd never see again. It was all made worse by Paige's presence, by how she made Max feel, and by the certainty that he really didn't want her witnessing his abject failure as a parent. 'Now.'

'Fine,' she snapped but with a withering glance at Paige that crossed about ten lines. He glanced at her to see if she'd noticed and of course she had. But unlike his interactions with Paige, which had been defined by emotion, she was now watching with an almost serene expression on her face. Hadn't he thought, when he'd made the decision to hire a nanny, that he needed someone with more patience than he had? Evidently, that was true of Paige.

'Would you like a hand, Amanda?' Paige asked, reasonably.

'No.'

'No, *thank you*,' Max corrected, knowing it wasn't fair or right to be embarrassed by his daughter, even when that was exactly how he felt.

'No, thank you,' she mimicked, rolling her eyes and carrying the plates into the kitchen, dropping them on the bench with enough force to break them—though they didn't.

'Go upstairs,' he ground out, already at breaking point.

'I'm going. Jeez.' Amanda stomped from the room and all the way up the stairs, slamming the door shut behind her.

Max turned to Paige and felt…deflated. Defeated. Emotions he wouldn't have said were in his wheelhouse until recently. But there was something about Paige's expression, even just her *presence*, that offered a hint—just a very small hint—of respite, at least in so much as dealing with Amanda. There were, for the moment, two grown-ups. Two adults. The scales were tipping in his favour, even just by Paige's presence.

He reached for his wine and took a long drink, wished it were something stronger, like a double shot of whisky. Even when he'd been married to Lauren, he'd never felt as though he had another adult in the house. Lauren had been worse than a child, worse than a hormonal adolescent. Her mood swings and unpredictability, always a force to be reckoned with, had grown out of control after Amanda's birth. He'd tried to make her better, encouraged her to get help, halfway dragged her to appointments with the world's best psychologists and psychiatrists, convinced there was a form of postnatal depression at play, but Lauren had refused to give anything a try.

He ground his teeth, turning to Paige, then standing slowly, moving to the kitchen, uncharacteristically lost for words. Ordinarily, he tidied the kitchen after dinner with a sagging sense of relief to have such a boring ritual to lose himself in, but tonight he felt Paige's watchful gaze and the air had taken on the same strange quality it had been exhibiting all day.

'Do you mind if I make an observation?' Her voice was soft and pretty, her accent hard to place. He knew she was American, but perhaps her time in Dubai had softened the edges of it. Learning another language could do that, he'd heard, as if your palate reshaped itself to accommodate a whole new raft of sounds.

'It's what you're here for, isn't it?'

She tilted her head to the side. 'You're different from what I expected.'

It wasn't exactly what he'd thought she'd say. He had been waiting for some indictment of his parenting or some insight into Amanda, and yet the personal observation wasn't unwelcome. 'Am I?'

She gestured to him, standing in the kitchen, sleeves rolled up to the elbows. 'You have way less staff.'

'Staff?'

She made a noise of agreement from low in her throat. It shouldn't have been sexy but, given Max's gasoline situation, he felt that sound reverberate all the way through his body. 'To cook for you. To clean up after you.'

'I have a housekeeper—Reg's wife.' He shrugged. 'She comes in for a few hours a day, cooks a meal, does some cleaning and laundry.'

She tilted her head to the side, regarding him thoughtfully, then changed the subject abruptly. 'Tell me about Amanda's mother.'

The question hit him right in the solar plexus, coming so soon after Amanda's grumpy departure. He hesitated, midway through stacking a plate into the dishwasher.

'Because you're curious, or because you knowing about Lauren will help you with Amanda?'

She was quiet a moment. 'Both.'

He appreciated her honesty. It was only natural that she would have questions. He'd invited her into his domestic sphere. He'd asked for her help. Now that she was here, he had to work with her. He returned to stacking the plates, one after the other, finding it easier to talk when his hands were occupied.

'Lauren died when Amanda was five.'

Paige nodded sympathetically but Max didn't notice. He was sinking back in time, to those memories, those dark days. 'Our life was different then. We lived in Sydney—that was Lauren's idea.'

'Whereas you wanted to be here?'

He braced his palms on the bench, turned towards the windows. The moon shimmered over the ocean and his heart stilled, as it always did when he soaked in that outlook. 'She liked it there.' He didn't answer the question. 'The shops. The nightlife.' He cleared his throat. 'We had a place on the harbour, and a lot of live-in staff. Two nannies,' he said, careful to keep emotion from his voice. 'Lauren…' But he faltered there.

Even this many years later, even with all the evidence of his wife's failings, loyalty made it hard to face her faults head-on. He sought refuge in frustration and anger, rather than letting his own failings, and the abysmal failure of his marriage, resonate too deeply.

'She died in a car accident. She wasn't driving but the driver was drunk. He lost control coming around a corner—too fast—and rammed into a building. The car burst into flames. Lauren died immediately.' His voice was gruff. Regardless of their differences, of the fact their marriage had most likely been heading towards divorce, he couldn't think of the waste of Lauren's life without a searing sense of shock and sadness. She had grown and birthed his daughter.

When he flicked a glance in Paige's direction, she was expressionless, a mask she was doing her best to keep in place, he guessed, because her eyes had the slightest sheen of tears.

'Amanda was so little.'

Silence fell. Max finished stacking the dishwasher, wiped the bench then dried his hands, coming to stand at the table, lost for words and strangely, despite the heaviness of the conversation, not wanting the night to end just yet.

'And they were close?'

'Lauren was her mother and so she was her world,' he said quietly. 'But in the day-to-day sense, Amanda spent considerably more time with her nannies. And I—' He gripped the back of the chair tightly. 'I was busy with work.' He tried to flatten the defensiveness from his tone. 'I didn't realise at first—'

He shook his head. He wasn't going to discuss his failings. Not with Paige.

As if sensing his reticence, she leaned forward slightly. 'It must have been a very hard time for you.'

She meant Lauren's death. But the truth was, it had all been hard. Their marriage had been a disaster zone, almost from the first.

'You can't do it, bro. I know why you want to, but she's not right for you.'

Luca's warning had been accurate, but Max hadn't had a choice. Lauren had been pregnant with his baby, and there had been no way he was going to fail to meet his responsibilities. He wasn't his father.

'Amanda was devastated,' he said, honestly. 'Lauren was—' He tried to find the right words. 'She was larger than life. Everything she felt, she felt to the nth degree, and she *loved* baby Amanda. She doted on her, spoiled her. Even though she didn't spend that much time with her, the time she did spend left a huge impression on Amanda.'

'And her death a huge absence.'

'It's become worse as Amanda's grown older. She's turned Lauren into some kind of god.' He lifted his shoulders, at a loss. 'She idolises her.'

Paige nodded sympathetically, then stood, the slim curves of her body shown by the soft cotton of her shirt and shorts. 'What are her hobbies?'

Something spasmed in his chest. A feeling of failure. 'Hobbies,' he repeated, as though he hadn't heard.

'Sure. Things she likes to do for fun, outside school. Does she swim? Surf? Read?'

'She reads.' He latched onto the last one, though he couldn't think when he'd last seen her actually finish a book. 'She loves Harry Potter.' But did she? She'd watched the films on repeat the year before, but since then? Flashes of his own childhood, his absent father, rammed into him and Max felt the inexorable pull towards defeat. Maybe you couldn't alter genetic predispositions after all. His father had lacked any kind of parenting gene; Max probably did too.

'Okay.' Paige nodded thoughtfully. 'That's a start.' She hesitated a moment, her lips parted, her eyes round, and he had the now familiar desire to reach out and touch her.

To kiss her. To feel those soft lips beneath his. He wanted, more than anything, to kiss her because if he kissed her, maybe he could drown out everything else. Maybe the sheer urgency of their desire would silence the steady drumbeat of the inevitability of his shortcomings as a parent and for a while, a small while, he might even be happy.

'Thank you for dinner,' she said with a smile that had him pausing, because it was somehow familiar. Somehow, and that question jolted him out of his reverie.

'Have we—?' He frowned. It was a stupid question to ask—he knew the answer. And yet… 'Have we met before, Paige?'

Her smile dropped instantly and her eyes darted towards the door. He recognised the emotion: panic. Suspicion took his breath away.

'No, of course not,' she said, the words high-pitched.

Something shifted inside him. A warning. She was lying. His instincts were rarely wrong and she was a *terrible* liar. He wanted to believe her, he realised, but it was so clear that she was hiding something from him.

This woman he'd invited into his house wasn't being honest with him.

And he was trusting her with his child.

Had he been so blinded by desire that he'd missed obvious, earlier signs of this? Anger, entirely directed at himself, made his face tighten.

'I don't believe you.'

She started, eyes wide. 'Well, I'm telling you the truth.' Her voice faltered. 'We've never met.'

But it all made sense. Why else would he have felt this drugging sense of need for her from the first moment they'd met? He'd seen her and wanted her and it had been so blisteringly overwhelming. Besides, now that he'd seen that look of panic in her eyes, he knew she wasn't being honest with him.

'Damn it, Paige, I need to know the truth. You're caring for my daughter. I have to be able to trust you.'

'You can trust me,' she insisted, and when she flinched a little, he realised he'd come around the table and was now standing only inches away from Paige.

'So you're being completely honest with me? You're not lying?'

Her lips compressed and her hesitation was the beginning and end of the confirmation he needed. 'Why are you so sure I'm lying?' she asked, going on the defensive.

Max's hackles rose. But it wasn't just this conversation, so much as the tumult of feelings he'd been putting up with since Paige arrived in his life. Desire was unwelcome and desperate and so too his sense that he was wading deeper and deeper into the ocean.

'I'm a good judge of people. I can tell you're hiding something.'

'I'm not hiding anything relevant to my job,' she responded, and this time it was Paige who moved closer, her eyes locked to his, her expression defiant and angry, so a thousand questions burst through him.

'Aren't you?' With effort, Max made his voice sound as though he were in control, when his insides were rioting, thrown into total chaos by her nearness.

'You have no right to interrogate me like this.'

'I have every right. You are my employee—'

'Yes, but I am still my own person entitled to my own private life and thoughts.'

'Not if that life involves secrets that somehow endanger my child.'

Paige glared at him, her face pale. 'I would *never* do

anything that would put a child in my care at risk. How dare you even suggest it?'

'Because I don't know you,' he hissed. 'You have arrived out of nowhere.'

'I came from an agency. I know you've seen my references.'

'Yes,' he agreed, wishing she didn't smell so good, that he weren't conscious of her warmth and softness and curves. 'But what do they really tell me about you?'

'We are both unknown quantities and I cannot see that it matters. Are you telling me I know all your secrets, Max?'

He flinched. 'That is not the same thing, and you know it.'

'Of course it is,' she disputed quickly, pressing a finger to his chest. 'You know I'm a good nanny, this isn't about that. You want to know more about me because of this.' She gestured from her chest to his. 'Because of whatever is sparking in the air every time we're together.'

'It's insanity,' he muttered, reaching for her hand, but instead of removing it from his chest he held it there, his eyes issuing a challenge she didn't back down from.

'Yes, but it's the truth.' She jutted her chin at him defiantly and Max couldn't help but take the bait. With her face so close to him, her body so near, his hand wrapped around her wrist, he stared at her mouth and before he knew it, before he could understand what he was doing, his lips pressed to hers and it was as if the ground were splitting in two, so earth-shattering was the sense of relief and desire.

She froze against him, completely still, and then she moaned softly, leaning forward so her body was crushed to his, and he deepened the kiss without thought, angry and frustrated and so hungry for her all at once. It had to stop. He had to stop it, but when she whimpered against his mouth, all thoughts of putting an end to this flew from his mind and, instead, he imagined scooping her up and carrying her to his chest, to his bedroom, or anywhere, and making love to her until she was finally out of his mind.

'We can't…' she muttered as her hands crept to his shirt and pushed it up, so her fingertips glanced across his skin and a surge of need exploded. 'Amanda…'

God, Amanda. Hell. It was like being doused with water. He pulled away from Paige with a stricken expression, staring at her as though she were an alien from outer space.

Paige stared back, her lips parted, her fingers trembling in mid-air before she dropped them to her side and looked away.

With sanity returning, Max began to realise what a monumental mistake that was. Paige worked for him. She was his staff member. And he *needed* her help, desperately. He was the one who'd said they couldn't let anything happen, so why hadn't he been strong enough to fight that?

He dropped his head forward, trying to grab his breath, and a moment later lifted his face and found her eyes. She hadn't left the room, which he took as both a good sign and an indication of her strength of character. She was a fighter; he was glad.

'I have to be honest with you,' he said after a pause, realising that for all the admission was the last thing he felt like making, it was important in light of what had just happened.

She crossed her arms over her chest in a clearly defensive gesture but at least she stayed.

'I haven't slept with anyone in a long time. Since my wife died, in fact. I've been single, and you're here, and obviously you're a very beautiful woman, but I refuse to let this go any further when I know it's just because I've been celibate way too long.' He paused, wondering if this was coming out okay. He thought it might all be a bit offensive, but it was important to him that Paige understood: none of this was about her. 'It shouldn't have happened.' He cleared his throat. 'It won't happen again.'

He stared at the trees, silver in the moonlight, with an anger radiating from him that came from so deep in his gut it might as well have been welded to his bones.

He shouldn't have done that.

He shouldn't have kissed her, shouldn't have provoked her, shouldn't have argued with her when things between them were so incendiary, it was obviously going to end in only one way.

He should have fought his feelings harder. Pushed her away better. More fully.

But he hadn't, and they'd kissed, and it was as if something had shifted inside Max so now the idea of not kissing Paige again was like acid burning away at him, the inevitability of his desire for her a tsunami overtaking his entire landscape.

He dropped his head forward, cradled it in his hands, tried to grip hold of who he was. Successful. Driven. Focused. A father. A businessman. Relationships had never been front and centre for Max, even before Lauren. He'd married for Amanda, not because he'd wanted a wife, nor a life of love. He'd tried to be a good husband—in his own way—but as their marriage had continued, he'd felt convinced that he was echoing his father every day, even when he tried so hard to be different.

'You are just like him.'

His mother's sneering words ran around and around in

his mind, sometimes almost suffocating Max. He stood abruptly, strode to the edge of the veranda and wrapped his hands around the timber.

No matter how hard he fought it, Max kept finding himself in these cul-de-sacs that forced him to face the truth of that statement. He tried not to be like Carrick, his father, and yet wasn't that kiss exactly how he would have behaved?

Not quite.

Carrick would have had no compunction in seducing Paige then and there, regardless of who might have seen or been hurt by his decisions. And how close had Max come to that? If Paige hadn't reminded him of Amanda, would he have stopped what they were doing?

He clenched his teeth, the feeling that the earth was slipping beneath him making his stomach dip uncomfortably.

What he needed was to push Paige out of his mind. And even more than that, a cold shower. He did both, or at least tried, but Paige seemed lodged in the parts of his mind over which he had minimal control, so hours later, in the solitude of his bed, he finally gave up on ignoring her and allowed her total access to his thoughts and dreams, so finally he fell asleep with memories of her body invading his dreams, and finally, for the first time in days, he was truly at peace.

CHAPTER FIVE

PAIGE WAS UNSPEAKABLY glad when, the next morning, she realised Max had already left for the day. With just her and Amanda in the house, she was almost able to pretend last night hadn't happened. Except, when she stood in the kitchen, supervising Amanda's lunch-box preparations, she could *feel* Max in the air, the whisper of his breath against her skin, the sound of his voice, the sensations in her body as he kissed her, as she yearned for more. But there was also the terror that his question had evoked.

He'd recognised her, only he didn't realise it yet. They'd never met, but he'd probably spent hours being bombarded by a younger Paige's face in movies, and advertisements and schmaltzy television shows. In the first decade of this century, Paige had been everywhere, and despite how her face and figure had changed with age, despite the superficial alterations she'd made, it was impossible to escape her features. They were simply a part of her—from her dimples to her smile to her wide-set round eyes.

If Max didn't trust her, it was because he'd glimpsed a figment of the girl she'd once been.

Amanda was particularly surly, but Paige was only operating on one cylinder. She did her best to focus, asking questions, ignoring the monosyllabic answers, making sure Amanda had everything she'd need for the day.

While Amanda had been very clear that she didn't want Paige to go onto the school property, Paige had known she needed to introduce herself and form a personal connection, so she'd emailed both the principal and Amanda's teacher. The responses had been interesting. Both said what a valued and positive member of the class Amanda was, and how well she was doing.

It was something for Paige to focus on, because it showed that Amanda was really just letting out her frustrations at home.

At the school, Amanda exited the car without a backwards glance.

Paige quickly opened her own door, stood there watching the young girl, waiting to see if she'd look back, but she didn't. At the gate, Amanda simply dropped her head lower and kept walking, faster, her body language completely defensive.

Paige sighed to herself then took a seat in the car.

The drive home was filled with Reg's chatter, but Paige only half listened. In the back of her mind, all she could think about was Max, and how stupid she'd been to let him kiss her like that. No, to basically beg him to.

His admission of celibacy had stolen all the air out of Paige's lungs.

Had Max been so heartbroken by his wife's death that he couldn't imagine being with another woman? Something twisted inside Paige. Just imagining that kind of love and devotion made her yearn for something she knew to be impossible.

Love.

Real, life-altering *love.* She blinked rapidly, staring out at the country as it passed, the dark asphalt cutting through thick, ancient trunks.

To feel love like that you had to allow yourself to trust without limits, to be vulnerable and exposed, and Paige knew that was beyond her. Just as she couldn't alter her features beyond recognition, she couldn't change the parts of her personality that her childhood had brought to bear.

For a brief moment though, she found herself wishing, really wishing, that she knew how to let go of her self-protective barriers and be open to something more in life. To really connect with someone without the awful fear of betrayal, of being used, and, worst of all, being hurt.

Back at Max's home, Paige walked into the corridor with her breath held, unconsciously looking to his study; it was empty, and it remained empty all day.

Paige, determined not to seem as though she was waiting for him, busied herself around the house. She tidied Amanda's bedroom, then the room downstairs Amanda used for recreation, then made a batch of blueberry muffins for after-school snacks, before being drawn by the beauty of the day and a restlessness in her soul to step out into the garden. She was halfway through the psychology book on teens and she brought it with her, choosing a sunny seat on the edge of the grass and reading until an alarm on her watch told her it was time to go and collect Amanda.

Right on cue, Reg appeared in his four-wheel drive.

Without taking the time to replace the book in the house, she moved to the car, swung into the front passenger seat and offered a smile to Reg that she hoped concealed the turmoil of her thoughts.

'You're burned,' he said with a nod.

'Oh…' She looked at her arms, which were indeed a little pink. 'So I am.'

'The sun's a shocker out this way. You need to wear sleeves.'

Reg's own skin was leathery, turned that way from a distinct lack of sleeve wearing, she suspected. 'Next time,' she said with a nod.

As they were approaching the school, Paige pointed towards a park at the end of the street. 'Would you mind parking down here? I'm going to wait for Amanda over there.'

Reg pulled into the kerb but gave Paige a dubious look.

'I'm not sure she'll like that. She always makes me stay in the car.'

'I know,' she said, with more confidence than she felt. 'But I'd like to take a quick peek.'

She was more nervous than she conveyed but it was imperative to *see* what was happening at school, to observe Amanda's demeanour as she left. However, she kept Amanda's missive in mind and waited just outside the gate, rather than stepping inside. She wanted to respect the girl's boundaries while also doing her job, and so she stood, and she watched as the crowds filled the school yard and began to filter through the gates and, finally, she saw Amanda.

She emerged from an undercover walkway with her head bent, walking completely alone. Her backpack was slung over one shoulder. A small group of girls walked a little way behind her, not making fun of Amanda in any way, but nor was the group including her. Amanda looked incredibly tiny and very solitary.

Paige had once been a young girl herself, and though, to the rest of the world, it might have seemed that she had everything one could ever want, in fact her life had been a constant merry-go-round of needing to keep up. It didn't matter that she'd had stylists at her fingertips, she'd still never felt quite *good enough*, which was, she knew, the prerogative of almost teenagers the world over. It could be an incredibly demoralising time.

Trying to keep up was futile and silly. Happiness and self-confidence had to come from within. At the same time, though, it quickly became clear to Paige that Amanda was an outlier to these girls, that her shoes were different, her bag was different.

There was nothing wrong with different if that was a personal choice, but, looking at Amanda, Paige wasn't clear on exactly how much of this had been Amanda's choosing and how much was circumstance.

Her brow furrowed. It didn't make sense that she wouldn't, materially, have whatever she wanted. Max Stone's personal wealth was famously extraordinary. Though he kept a low profile, the Stone family owned and operated one of the most prestigious groups of jewellery stores in the world, supplied with their stunning pearls, as well as exquisite diamonds. They were synonymous with wealth and luxury. Beyond that, she remembered reading some article before coming to Australia about their investments in real estate and knew that their portfolio was quite incredible.

So if Amanda wanted different shoes, surely that wouldn't have been an issue?

Paige stood a little straighter, stepped forward, and the shift in movement caused Amanda—as well as a couple of the other girls—to look in her direction. Amanda's face fell immediately and then one of the group moved closer to her, said something under her breath, laughed and returned to her friends.

A pang of worry radiated through Paige.

Amanda stomped towards her. 'What are you doing here?' she hissed, arms crossed, sullen expression more perfect than anything Paige could have pulled off back when she was acting.

'Waiting for you. Isn't that obvious?'

'You should have waited in the car. I don't need you to come in to get me. I'm not a baby.'

'I didn't come in,' Paige pointed out.

Amanda rolled her eyes.

Paige couldn't help saying, 'I've never seen an Australian school. Want to give me a tour?'

Amanda shot her a withering glance. 'No. I want to go home.'

'Okay.' Paige shrugged. 'Can I carry your bag?'

Amanda looked as if her head were going to explode. 'No.'

'No, *thank you*,' Paige reminded her gently, then wished she hadn't, because Amanda's mood was volatile and she switched quickly from angry to hurt, tears sheening her eyes.

'Can we just go? *Please?*' she tacked on with a little huff, so Paige's arms stung with the desire to reach out and hug the girl close.

She didn't.

Amanda was nowhere near ready for that.

'Sure. Let's go. You can tell me about your day in the car, if you feel like it.'

Amanda didn't.

She sat quietly the whole way home and once they arrived Amanda jumped out of the car, slung her bag over one shoulder and stomped up the stairs and inside.

Paige sighed heavily.

It was only early on in Paige's assignment—and this was clearly going to take time—but she could recognise the other girl's suffering and wanted, more than anything, to be able to help. She saw the hurt in her eyes, she felt her suffering. Having been on the receiving end of a great kindness in her own life, Paige knew she had to work to find a way through to Amanda.

But she couldn't push it.

The evening passed much as the night before had. Amanda sat in silence, except for the few questions Max asked her, and then demanded to be excused. He agreed, once she'd cleared the table, which Amanda did, albeit with pretty bad grace, and then left the room.

Max looked marginally less shell-shocked tonight.

He moved to the kitchen and Paige found it hard not to stare. Memories of last night throbbed all around them. She was awkward and uncomfortable but also glued to the spot. A glutton for punishment?

He was so…masculine, and somehow even the simple act of rolling up his sleeves and tackling the dishes just made him more so. Growing up with all the trappings of the Hollywood life, Paige had never seen her own dad do much more than put a coffee cup in the dishwasher. They had housekeepers and cleaners and a cook, 'to help keep your calories in check'. Even now, memories of her mother's nagging about weight had the power to make Paige's stomach churn.

'Paige.' Max's voice was deep and something in her gut pulled, like an invisible string, drawing her towards him. She dug her fingernails into her palm as she stood, in an effort to control her movements, to be sure she went only to the other side of the counter and not around into the kitchen and right up to him. It didn't matter that she kept a sensible distance though. The air between them still sizzled and sparked.

He seemed to be lost in thought though—having spoken

her name, he was simply staring at her face, not speaking—so Paige lifted a brow encouragingly. 'Yes?'

His lips tugged downwards into something like a scowl. 'You got sunburned today.'

Surprise softened her features, and disappointment swirled inside her chest. 'Yes. I was reading outside.'

He nodded, still distracted. 'I've got some lotion. I'll grab it.'

She shook her head as visions of Max lathering her body flooded her brain, making speech almost impossible.

'No, thanks, I'll be fine,' she said, hastily.

'It's just aloe vera.'

She bit into her lip, knowing she should demur, but then found her head nodding once. Their eyes met and something passed between them, a strangely powerful agreement.

His response was a gruff, 'Wait here.'

Paige stared at his retreating back, her eyes clinging to the way his jeans hugged his rear, her heart racing.

He returned a moment later, the bottle held in his hands, his eyes boring into hers. Step by step he crossed the room, until he was right in front of her, and the air crackled. His throat shifted as he swallowed, his Adam's apple jerking visibly beneath his thick black stubble.

'Would you like me to do it?'

Given what had happened between them last night, it was a loaded question.

'I'll be okay.'

His smile was lightly mocking. 'That's not what I was asking.'

Paige's eyes squeezed shut as she sucked in air, air that was tinted with Max's incredibly seductive fragrance, and her stomach somersaulted inside her body. 'I know.' A whisper—surrender.

'Do you *want* my help?'

She groaned, because the same image returned, Max's large, confident hands on her body, and she blinked up into his eyes, sinking into him, losing herself completely to a power far greater than any she'd ever known.

'I thought we agreed last night was a mistake,' she said simply.

His eyes flared. 'It probably was.'

'Probably?'

'I don't know, Paige.' His frustration was obvious. 'It shouldn't have happened, it was stupid, but it was also the best thing I've done in years and if I don't get to touch you again, to kiss you, I think I'll regret it for the rest of my life.' His eyes bored into hers, a silent question in them, and then he spoke it aloud. 'So I'm asking you, do you want my help?'

It was as though her ears were flooded with static electricity. She couldn't think or see straight but there was a beacon in the midst of it all, a truth she had to face, to grab with both hands because, just like Max, she knew she'd regret it if she didn't.

'Yes,' she whispered finally, exulting in the simplicity of that even when it felt, in some ways, as though she'd just made some kind of pact with the devil.

CHAPTER SIX

THEY REMAINED IN SILENCE, the air between them crackling. Finally, Paige nodded, and Max reached down, linking their fingers, staring at them weaved together before tugging her gently from the kitchen, down the hallway and into his office.

The space was a perfect echo of his personality, all dark wood and gleaming surfaces, masculine, strong, impressive. He closed the door and then locked it with an audible click.

Even when her own feelings were swamping the rational part of her brain, Max was switched on enough to remember that he had a daughter in the house, and that she might wander downstairs at any point.

Paige spun, pulling her hand free, but her fingers still tingled as though they were touching his and her tongue felt thick in her mouth.

As Paige watched, Max removed the top off the lotion and poured some into the palm of his hand. He stared at it for several seconds, as though he was fighting an internal battle, a war raging through him between good intentions and bad, and she wished she could say something to reassure him but the truth was Paige didn't know if this was a good idea or not. In fact, she suspected it was a very bad idea, but she still wanted to be in here, with him. And she was aching for him to touch her again.

He was hesitating and she couldn't help wondering, was that because of his late wife? He must have loved her a great deal to have been driven to years of celibacy by her death. Did he consider this to be a betrayal of her memory?

'I can do it myself,' she felt compelled to offer, nodding towards the lotion. 'If you've changed your mind.'

His eyes jerked to hers, and his jaw moved as he grimaced. 'I haven't.'

Relief surged through Paige, complex emotions forming little eddies in the room. It wasn't a time for thought and analysis though, but a time for action. She held out her arm, showing the pinkness on her skin. His gaze dropped to the limb, and then, almost against his will, he moved one hand to her wrist and held it, while with the other he began to apply the lotion, rubbing in broad circular motions. It was almost clinical, but there was nothing cold or detached about her body's response. Her knees wobbled so she swayed forward a little. His hand on her wrist dug in a little tighter but she didn't think he realised—he was holding her as if grabbing on for dear life.

They were both drowning.

She lifted her gaze, staring into his eyes, or rather, at his eyelids, because his attention was focused squarely on her arm, as though if he didn't cover every single millimetre of her skin, some great evil might befall them. Finally, he let go, as though burned, reaching for the lotion and adding some more to his hands, then took hold of her other wrist and began again. But as he reached her elbow and moved higher, his hand grew still.

'I don't want to get it on your shirt.'

She pulled her hand away, biting down on her lip, her

heart racing as she lifted her hands into the air, a challenge in her eyes, daring him to follow through on his suggestion.

With a noise that was low and throaty, he took one step closer then put his hands on her waist, swallowing, staring at her, lost, drowning, grabbing the shirt in his fists and lifting it, oh, so slowly up her sides, higher to her arms and, finally, over her head.

He groaned properly then at the sight of her in a skimpy lace and silk bra.

'You're burned here too,' he ground out, pressing a finger to her shoulder and, with one more look into her eyes, he dropped his head and pressed a kiss there, his lips searing her skin.

She trembled.

'Am I?' She bit into her lip. 'Anywhere else?'

He moved behind her, his finger trailing a line across her back, between her shoulders, then his lips followed its path, pressing kiss after kiss to her skin until goosebumps covered her body. 'Here.' Then he kissed her other shoulder, but this time it wasn't a quick, light kiss, but rather a caress, and rather than lifting his lips, he glided them higher, to the pulse point at the base of her neck, which he flicked with his tongue, his warm breath, his mouth, until she was so awash with pleasure it was almost impossible to stand.

'Max.' Her voice emerged as a tortured whisper, for surely this level of desire *was* a torture device?

His body pressed to her side and then he came to her front, his mouth parting from her body for the briefest moment before he claimed her mouth, kissing her, but not as he had at the water's edge. This was slower, a kiss of exploration, a kiss that spoke of them having all the time in the world to explore this wild, overwhelming connection.

She swayed forward, needing their bodies to be closer, to be touching, and he reached around to unclasp her bra. It might have been years since he'd slept with a woman, but he was still easily able to unfasten the garment, then slide it from her arms, letting it drop to the ground at their feet.

'Turn around,' he invited gruffly.

She did as he said, her nipples taut against the night air. The next moment, his hands were on her back—not in order to apply lotion, but rather as if from a need to touch her inch by inch, massaging her, familiarising himself with her body. His hands came around to the front, to her breasts, cupping them, and he pressed his hard body to her back, his arousal evident at her bottom so she ground backwards on autopilot as his fingers circled then squeezed her nipples until she was riding a wave of pleasure that was hot and explosive.

And Max wasn't done. One hand swirled circles over her flat stomach while the other continued to master her breasts, and his mouth kissed the back of her neck. His fingers slid into the waistband of her shorts, and then her lace thong, connecting with her feminine shape so Paige startled, the touch both unexpected and extremely welcome.

She said his name in shock though, because it had been a long time for Paige as well, and despite the way they'd been kissing and touching, she still hadn't been—couldn't have been—prepared for the overwhelming deluge of feelings.

'It's— I'm—'

He cursed beneath his breath. 'You feel so good.'

She tilted her head back on a rush of sensation as his hand moved lower, his fingers parting her sex and finding her most sensitive cluster of nerves, teasing it, tormenting it, showing his dominant superiority over that part of her too, all the while her breasts tingled from his ministrations and his kisses lit fires in her veins.

'Max,' she groaned, grinding her hips, needing more, needing so much more.

He sucked her earlobe into his mouth, wobbling it between his teeth, then dropped his mouth to her shoulder once more, sucking the skin there as he moved his fingers faster, her moist warmth building until Paige was exploding against his hand, stars filling her eyes. She stood right where she was, feet planted to the floor, as her panting slowed and breathing returned to something more like normal, but Max wasn't slowing down. He turned her in his arms, eyes hooded, almost unrecognisable for how huge his pupils were.

He pulled her by the hand, towards the armchair in the corner, which he sat down into and jerked her on top of him, so she felt his arousal between her legs and cried out because despite the pleasure she'd just experienced she needed *this*, all of this, all of him.

His name was a cry on her lips, a desperate entreaty for relief that she knew he would heed, that they both would. She rocked on her heels, moving her hips, simulating the sex she was desperate to enjoy with him, but there were far too many clothes between them, so she reached down and touched his jeans, undid the button, then the zip, her fingers shaking.

'Wait,' he commanded, finding her mouth and kissing her, his arousal so huge against her sex, his body so powerfully warm. She didn't want to wait though. Impatience was like a river about to burst its banks. He dropped his mouth to her breasts, taking one nipple inside, swirling it with his tongue then pressing his teeth to it just hard enough for Paige to cry out, with the kind of pleasure she'd never known before. It was too much. She was floundering, unsure how to process these feelings.

Sex had never been like this before.

Sex had never been anything other than what was expected of someone like her.

She'd been taken advantage of by older men, made to feel that her livelihood depended on her compliance, on her participation in something that was supposed to be special and meaningful. Oh, it wasn't as though she'd had many lovers, in fact she'd only slept with a couple of men, but she'd made out with more, been touched by even more, as though her body were a commodity that they were entitled to because of the industry in which she'd worked.

This was entirely different.

This was an equal-participation activity, both as maddened by the connection as each other and, even though nothing could come of this, it was meaningful to Paige because this was her decision. She was exercising her agency to enjoy him, to enjoy this. On one level, she knew it was wrong, but in all the ways that mattered most it was a watershed experience, a gift Paige was giving to herself, and no matter what came next, she'd always have had this moment of euphoria.

'I want you,' she said simply, blinking at him wildly as she pulled her head up, wrenching away from him so he could *see* the need in her face, could hear it in her words, could *feel* it. It felt so good to admit that! For the younger version of herself who'd never known real pleasure like this, she wanted to claim these delights and hold them to her chest. 'Please,' she added, with a wisp of a smile, hoping it hid the raw emotion he'd invoked with his talented ministrations.

He lifted a hand, cupping her cheek, holding her still.

'Paige—' His voice was deep, husky, but there was hesitation in the way he said her name and her heart squeezed, squelched.

'Don't you dare say you can't do this,' she warned, even as that fear began to grip her, turning her lava-like veins to ice.

'Amanda is the most important thing in my life,' he said through gritted teeth.

Paige didn't want to talk about his daughter right now.

'I'm not looking for a relationship.'

She ignored the tugging in the middle of her gut. Wasn't that obvious? He didn't need to spell it out. She wasn't looking for love, either. They were safe. This made sense.

'But this.' He gestured from him to her.

She shook her head, needing him to understand that they were on the same page. 'Is sex.'

'And you're okay with that?'

She nodded.

'You're okay with it only ever being this?'

Something twisted then, something she didn't want to analyse, but she nodded, giving no clue as to the slight wobble of certainty.

'I don't want a relationship either,' she promised. 'And especially not with some Australian guy.' She smiled to show him she was serious. 'I'm only here for three months. My life is over the other side of the world.'

What life? a little voice in the back of her mind demanded urgently, because Paige had been on the run for years, never staying put long enough to make connections, never risking attachment or love.

'Because for the next eight, nine, ten years, however long she needs me, Amanda is the only person I have room for. I'm not going to stuff her up the way— I'm going to do this right.'

She was impressed by his dedication, by his commitment, even when it hurt to hear it—because she'd never known that kind of parental love and sacrifice. 'I get it.'

'So if you think this is going to make you want something else, something more…'

'I don't,' she promised, wishing she could explain to him that she wasn't like other people. Her upbringing had made her physically unable to want or expect love. She would certainly not be looking to Max Stone to provide it. But how could she even begin to explain what she'd been through? Besides, it was a part of her past she didn't welcome to her present. 'Trust me. Everything's going to be okay.'

He probed her eyes a while longer and must have seen something in their depths that convinced him because a moment later he was lifting up and kissing her again, with more urgency, with such desperate, agonising longing that Paige felt herself tipping over the edge already, her nails digging into his shoulders until she was worried she might draw blood. But the way he was making her feel…it was too much.

He broke their kiss only to rip off his shirt and throw it clear across the room, and in that same motion Paige was standing, stripping out of her shorts and underpants, watching as he reached for something from his wallet—a condom—and opened the pack.

'Christ, I have no idea how old this is.'

She reached for it, studied it against the light and grinned. 'Looks fine to me.'

He didn't return her smile. The air pulsed with raging need. She brought the condom to his tip and, with fingers that were still unsteady, pressed it down, trying not to think about how huge he was.

His jeans were still on, but Paige was too impatient to wrestle them from him. Instead, she climbed back onto the seat, straddling Max and hovering just above his arousal, nervous suddenly, even though they'd just discussed this, and they both agreed this was what they wanted.

'You are so lovely.' The statement was said with a note of surprise, as if he hadn't looked at her before now, but his eyes lingered on her face, so she felt his praise deep in her bones, knew it was genuine, and it somehow seemed like the nicest thing anyone had ever said to her—she didn't think he was saying it because he wanted anything from her, he wasn't saying it pro-forma. It had been dredged from within him with utmost sincerity.

'Right back at you,' she murmured, moving closer to his arousal, needing him, already fantasising about the moment she took him in, madness overcoming her.

'Dad?'

She blinked, the voice coming from a long way away, at least the other end of the house, but Max's instincts were faster, more finely honed, so he startled, shifting quickly, somehow displacing Paige without knocking her to the ground. He was standing, chest heaving as he went to control his breathing, face drained of colour before he quickly zipped up his jeans and turned away.

'Dad?'

Still far away, but growing closer.

Paige squeezed her eyes shut, waves of feelings rocking her to the core, from embarrassment to disbelief to impatient shock.

'Just a second, honey.'

His voice was almost completely steady. Almost, but Paige heard the hint of huskiness to it and had to bite her lip to stop from reacting because even that was so sexy.

He grabbed his shirt and pulled it on, stood stock-still for a couple of seconds longer, then, looking completely like himself, strode to the door.

'Wait here,' he barked, eyes sweeping over her on the smallest exhalation, but Paige trembled in response.

'I need you to sign this form.' Amanda's disembodied voice came down the hallway but Paige didn't hear anything else. The door latched closed behind Max, giving Paige complete privacy once more.

Alone in his office, she felt the cobwebs of desire began to clear, leaving her with conflicting feelings. She knew she wouldn't have regretted sleeping with him, but maybe Amanda's interruption had been for the best?

Maybe it was a message sent by some higher power that they should think carefully about what they'd been about to do. Attraction was one thing, but how could they continue living together for the next three months if they slept together?

And would Paige be able to do her job properly?

It was obvious that Amanda needed help, that Max needed help, and Paige was determined to be the person that could render that assistance, but if she was distracted by *this*, whatever the hell 'this' was, then how could she make that work?

She dressed slowly, almost as if she was tempting fate, seeing if it would deliver him back to the office before she could finish putting her clothes on, but it didn't. Not only had Paige pulled on her clothes and finger-combed her hair before he returned, she'd also studied the photos on his wall until they were committed to memory. Mostly, they were photographs of the ocean and pearl-farming operations, beautiful snaps that had a professional quality, the flat-bottomed boats lined up at sunset, workers just silhouettes against the orange-tinged sky, thick-trunked trees that she somehow just knew belonged to the forest at his doorstep, and a picture of two young boys, so similar except for their eyes—one had eyes of ice, the other of coal, but they were both strikingly handsome with square-set jaws and determined mouths.

She lifted a finger to Max, touching his lips, her fingertip tingling, then she quickly dropped her hand from the glass front of the picture as the door clicked and he strode back into the room, those same ice-blue eyes sweeping over Paige in one motion as a muscle jerked in his jaw.

'Okay?' she prompted, skimming his face. Something tangled in her chest. Pity. A desire for this man, and also a desire to take away his worries, to ease this burden.

'Just time for one last shouting match before bed,' he said with a shake of his head, rubbing his hand over his jaw. They were worker's hands, showing that, while he was a billionaire, he still prided himself on the manual parts of running the pearl farm.

'Paige—' He looked at her, frowned, at a loss for words, evidently, and she didn't want to hear those words anyway. Paige had known the deepest of rejections, had felt it cut right through her soul, but she didn't want to hear it now, from Max.

'Would you like a tea?' she asked quickly, a soft smile showing awkwardness.

He lifted both brows. 'A tea?' he repeated, voice deep, so Paige almost groaned. Did he have any idea how incredibly handsome he was?

'Sure.' She shrugged, hoping she seemed almost like normal, when her heart was still pounding hard against her ribs. 'I always think a good cup of tea can fix anything.'

He laughed then, the reaction surprising her, and him, if

his expression was anything to go by. The sound cracked around the room like a whip, sending a little tremble down Paige's spine. It was desire—but not just for him physically. For his laugh. His smile. She pushed the thoughts away: unwelcome and treacherous.

'I hate to break it to you, but that theory seems at odds with reality.'

'We'll see,' she challenged. 'It's always worked for me.'

His eyes narrowed thoughtfully. 'Has it?'

Paige thought about that. There were plenty of times in her life when it had, in fact, failed, but it had calmed her nerves at their most frazzled and given her time to gain a little more perspective. 'It helps,' she amended ruefully.

'I'll have a coffee,' he said after a beat.

'At this hour?'

'It's a compromise.'

She smiled, relieved in the depths of her stomach that they weren't going to part ways, yet.

'But let's sit outside.' His eyes dropped to her mouth, lingered there, and Paige's heart sped up again. 'I—need some fresh air.'

The balcony that wrapped the perimeter of the house was wide enough to comfortably accommodate furniture and several different pieces had been arranged at intervals around it. There was a white wicker daybed with a perfect view of the beach, and then, a little further around the corner, two deep chairs with beige cushions, a single footrest and a rounded coffee table between them.

She chose the one with the footrest, putting her feet on it and listening to the sound of crashing waves, aware on a subliminal level of how that sound echoed the torrent of her pulse. The mood had changed, but something had been set in motion between them so Paige knew it was no longer a question of 'if' but when they slept together. Anticipation made her nerves skittle even as that certainty was somehow calming.

Max sat beside her, placing their drinks on the coffee table. Paige reached for her tea, cupping her hands around it.

'I wish you could have known what she was like.'

Paige's heart stammered. 'Your wife?'

He stared at her, confusion briefly visible in his symmetrical features, before he shook his head once. 'Amanda. Before…this.'

Paige sipped her tea, hating herself for feeling relieved, but the truth was she didn't want to talk about his late wife, nor to think about the woman. 'I can imagine.'

'She was so sweet. I mean, I don't know the faintest thing about raising kids, despite the books I read after Lauren died, but somehow, Amanda was so great anyway. Just her, I guess. And now…' He lifted his palms up, staring straight ahead. The moon formed a perfect slice of silver across the ocean, rippling as the waves churned. The fact he'd read books did something funny to her emotions. She blinked away quickly.

'She'll get through this.'

'You're sure?'

'Yeah.'

'Why?'

She sipped her tea. 'My first nannying job was in Dubai, and there was a teenage daughter in the house. She was different from Amanda, but the moods, they were similar.'

'Why Dubai?'

She toyed with the fabric of her shirt. 'I liked that it was different from what I was used to.' She wasn't so well known there, and she'd sought refuge in wearing a hijab—she'd craved anonymity, and in Dubai she'd found it. 'My first clients were an American family, so it didn't matter that I didn't speak the language. But slowly, I learned to speak some Arabic, in the time I was with them, so my next job posting was to another family in the same city, and then my next job too, and so on and so on.'

'You stayed there until now?'

She nodded.

'You must have been very young when you took your first job.'

Paige's smile was wistful. 'In fact, I was only nineteen myself.' She tilted her head to the side. 'I felt older.'

'Nineteen seems way too young to be looking after kids.'

'Maybe it gave me an advantage. I really could understand what Carrie—their daughter—was going through. She sort of looked up to me as well,' Paige admitted but with a hint of reluctance because she didn't want to tell him that, in fact, she'd been worshipped by all the children, idolised because her fame was still relatively recent and, as Americans, they'd grown up with her in films. They couldn't believe they had a real-life celebrity as their babysitter. 'So while she would have these awful moods with her parents, she connected with me right away. That helped.'

'And Amanda?'

'It's going to take some time. I guess, losing her mom the way she did, she's probably pretty good at keeping people at a distance.'

'She didn't used to.'

'People change.'

He frowned. 'Without reason?'

'Sometimes, but I'm sure there'll be a reason. Even if it's just growing older and becoming newly conscious of what's missing in her life and feeling the burden of that injustice.'

He was quiet, drinking his coffee, before he placed it on the table between them.

'What made you decide to become a nanny?'

She almost dropped her tea, so moved it to her lap, employing both hands to keep it stable.

'Opportunity,' she said, after a slightly too long pause. 'I was offered the job.'

'You didn't want to go to university?'

'I studied childhood education while I worked, via an online university. The kids I looked after were at school during the day and once I'd organised their activities and tidied their rooms, I still had a lot of time left.'

'And your own parents?' he prompted softly, as though on some level he understood that this was a difficult conversation for Paige. She kept her face averted, staring straight ahead.

'They're not in my life.'

His gaze was heavy on her face, his probing curiosity searing her, and for the first time in for ever Paige felt as though she wanted to answer the question directly.

'For any reason?'

She turned to face him slowly, sensed the chasm between them. How could someone like him understand? She opened her mouth, contemplating how to tell him, to even begin, and then shook her head. 'For about a million,' she said with a grimace that had been quite famous at one point.

He frowned, as though he was still trying to place her, and Paige hurriedly looked away. Her secrets were her own; she wasn't ready to share them. And especially not with Max. It had become important to Paige, more important than she could explain, that he saw her as she really was, not as she'd once been, not as her parents had made her. She wanted to close her eyes and pretend the rest of the world simply didn't exist, that it was just her, and Max, and this stunning tropical paradise…

CHAPTER SEVEN

BUT THE REST of the world did exist and, regardless of how absorbing she found life here with Max and Amanda, she couldn't ignore the fact that time was marching on, and her parents' book was getting closer and closer to being published.

She couldn't face it, which was precisely why she was hiding out here.

Her first instinct on reading about the upcoming 'memoir' had been to dig her head into the sand. And yet there'd been a part of her that had wanted to fight back, too. Her parents had no right to speak about her, to control the narrative of what her life had been like, to speak about her childhood and adolescence. It was yet another example of how they totally disregarded her as a person and saw Paige simply as an extension of themselves.

Even though the book was on the horizon, she felt safe here, as if Max were somehow capable of protecting her, even though he couldn't possibly. He didn't even know who she was, nor what she was up against.

And so she needed to keep hiding, to keep pretending it wasn't happening, otherwise the sadness of all this would swallow her whole. Tuning out the big wide world was an important self-preservation technique so she focused on the here and now with all her might. She would work harder, be better, invest everything into Amanda—and Max—so that the book lost some of its power to hurt her. At least, that was what she hoped.

On the drive to school the next morning, with Amanda sullen and Reg talking non-stop, Paige eventually managed to interrupt his monologue.

'Amanda, we're going to cook dinner tonight. Any requests?'

Her response was predictable. 'I don't want to.'

'It's important to help out around the house,' Paige responded. 'So? What's it to be?'

Amanda sighed as though she'd just been asked to scale a brick wall with her fingernails.

'Don't care.'

'Great. Pickled ox tongue it is.'

Amanda gasped before she could remember not to react, and Reg cackled. 'You might think that's gross, but actually my mother used to make it all the time.'

Paige flicked a conspiratorial smile at the older man. 'Last chance,' she told Amanda. 'Otherwise you'll get whatever I decide.'

'Fine. Whatever. I don't care.'

She hopped out of the car and slammed the door.

Paige sighed heavily. 'Is there a shop somewhere we can stop at?'

'Yes, ma'am.' Reg's face crinkled with amusement as he turned the car in the direction of the only grocery store in town. 'You've got your work cut out for you with that one.'

Paige watched over her shoulder as Amanda crossed the street to the school gates, shoulders hunched, arms crossed over her slender frame.

'Reg, do you have any idea what's going on with her?'

'Nah.' He shook his head. 'The missus says it's just one of

those things. That she'll come good. But it sure is a shame. She used to be one of the sunniest kids, smiled all the time.'

Paige was waiting by the gates when Amanda finished school that afternoon, and she saw the girl emerge from her classroom. As on the day before, she was alone, a group walking just behind her. One of the girls looked up, scanned the waiting parents, presumably for her mother, and looked directly at Paige, then glanced away, before her eyes travelled back again. Paige barely noticed—her attention was focused almost completely on Amanda. She did see, however, when one of the girls ran up to Amanda, grabbed her arm and leaned closer, said something and laughed, then skipped away. Amanda stared after her, face like thunder, then spun around to look at Paige, lips parted, eyes wide.

Self-conscious, Paige glanced down at her clothes, then up at Amanda, who'd resumed her trademark sullen look. But when she came close to Paige, she slowed, stared at her long and hard then crossed her arms.

'Hi.' Paige ignored her sense of misgiving. 'How was school?'

Amanda frowned at her. 'Fine.'

Paige repressed a sigh. 'Ready to help me in the kitchen when we get home?'

'I have homework.'

'Okay, after your homework, then.'

'Fine. Whatever.'

At the car, Amanda slid into the back seat and slammed the door, staring resolutely out of her window and refusing to speak the rest of the way home.

Amanda didn't resurface until Max returned home. She'd been studying in her downstairs living area and Paige had thought it best to give her some space. It was enough that she'd extracted a promise for help in the kitchen.

But with Max's return, Amanda appeared in the hallway. 'Can you both come in here?'

Paige glanced at Max, her heart speeding up. There was something in Amanda's voice that set her nerves on edge but she maintained an appearance of calm, barely looking in Max's direction. When she did, finally, slide her eyes to his, she saw the same look of confusion in his features. Nonetheless, they walked side by side into Amanda's study.

The girl stood with her hands on her hips, looking from one to the other, then pinpointing Paige with her steely blue gaze.

'Is there something you'd like to tell us, *Paige*?'

Paige's heart skipped a beat. She felt Max stiffen beside her. Everything was wonky; her breath wouldn't come properly.

'Amanda.' Max's voice held a warning.

'What, Dad? Did you know about this?'

She pressed a button on the remote control and a movie began to play, the scene instantly familiar to Paige. She squeezed her eyes shut, but didn't need to look at the screen to see it playing out in front of her eyes. She remembered everything about this movie. It was one of the last films Paige had done—a teen feature film, a romance, that had been a smash hit around the world.

She heard Max's reaction—a rough expulsion of breath.

'Turn it off.'

'She's lying to us. She's using us. This is obviously some kind of sick joke, like research or something. Why else would some famous Hollywood actress come and pretend to be a babysitter? Jeez, Dad.'

'That is *enough*.' Max's voice was quiet and controlled but Paige could hear the anger in it.

'Did you know?' Amanda demanded and Paige finally forced herself to be brave and open her eyes, to watch what felt a little like a car wreck. Amanda's face was almost wild and Max's was the opposite, perfectly controlled, but Paige saw beneath that, to the throbbing of his Adam's apple and the way his chest moved faster than normal.

'Amanda, go to your room.'

Amanda stared at her father. 'Are you kidding me? Why? What have I done wrong?'

'Go to your room, *now*.'

It wasn't the right decision. Amanda wasn't at fault—but Paige was trembling from head to toe. She knew then that she should have told Max sooner. It was stupid and irresponsible to think she could keep this secret, especially with the book coming out.

Amanda glared at both of them and then stormed out of the room. Her footsteps could be heard thumping up the stairs and around the corner. Then, there was the deafening sound of her too-loud music slamming through the house.

Max turned slowly to face Paige.

'This is why I recognised you,' he said, after a long beat of silence.

She closed her eyes and nodded. 'My name, that you'd know me as, was Aria Gray.'

His hands curving around her shoulders had her blinking up at him. She swallowed, because his face wasn't anything but gentle, and that was enough to break her heart.

'Why didn't you tell me?' There was no accusation in his voice though, just curiosity.

'Because I don't want to be her,' she said quietly. 'It was a lifetime ago. I'm not that person any more. I probably never was.' She gestured past him, to the TV. 'That person is a construct of my parents, nothing more. I ran away from all of it a long time ago.'

'Why?'

'Because I hated it,' she whispered. 'They chose that for me. They had me at casting calls from practically the minute I was born. I landed a few commercials, then a TV show, then a movie, and by the time I was Amanda's age I was famous everywhere. I couldn't walk down the street without being chased and followed, and as for normal friendships, a normal life, forget it. I hated acting—I'm actually really shy—but I was the sole breadwinner in our family. They made me understand that I couldn't let them down.'

His hands tightened momentarily on her shoulders in response to that, but he made a visible effort to relax.

'So I acted. And I performed. I travelled the world and had my photo taken and went to premieres and photoshoots and, God, Max, it was so exhausting and I hated it so much. I was so miserable.'

'What did your parents say?'

'That I had to keep going. And I couldn't. I just couldn't. I made the decision to legally emancipate myself when I was sixteen years old.'

It was such a calm way to explain the tumult of that decision. It had been one of the hardest things she'd ever done.

'My parents were furious when I left them. I mean, they had all my money tied up in a trust that I couldn't access.' This time, she couldn't keep the bitterness from her voice. 'I didn't have the heart to fight them for it—I was just so immeasurably, inexplicably glad to be free. But I went off the rails. I mean, I was a mess.' She shook her head. 'I can see now that I had a form of PTSD and was just dealing with it however I could.'

He frowned. 'Where did you live?'

'On friends' sofas,' she whispered. 'Wherever. I drank heavily. Partied too much. Anything that would kind of… numb me…to it all. And of course, the tabloids loved that.' She grimaced. 'They didn't see a girl who was broken beyond repair by her parents' choices, but rather a scandal they could exploit, and I was too stupid to realise it was in my power to change that, to stop giving them a story, to stop acting like such a fool.'

'You were still just a kid,' he growled, surprising her with how protective he sounded. But hadn't that been her first impression of him? Protective, defensive, in a way she'd never known.

She pushed away the warmth she felt in response to that protectiveness. She couldn't let him be her carer—she couldn't come to rely on him.

'In the end, it was an actress friend, who'd been cast as my mom in an early movie, that came to my rescue and made me see it all had to stop. Anna Cooper. She's the one who got me the job in Dubai, with some friends of hers, and that was the start of my life turning around.'

He stared at her without speaking, and her heart beat faster.

'Anyway, apparently the money's all gone because my parents have written a tell-all book about my childhood and my slide into delinquency,' she said with a grimace. 'It's coming out in a few days.' She bit down on her lip. 'And I know I probably should have told you all this upfront, but the thing is, it's never been an issue in any other job and I came here, I took this job, because I just wanted to…'

'Escape,' he finished the sentence for her, squeezing her arms.

She closed her eyes, nodding. 'I don't want to be that person any more, Max. I never did.' Her lips parted. 'The thought of it all starting up again…' She blinked hard, squeezing her eyes shut.

He didn't say anything; nervousness exploded. Paige whispered, 'If you want me to go, I will. I mean, I want to stay. I want to help Amanda, but if this is all too much, if you're worried that something is going to spill over into your life…'

'I'm not worried,' he said with so much strength and confidence it stopped her tears in their tracks. 'I'm angry with her, if I'm honest. She had no business exposing you like that.'

Paige shook her head. 'It's not her fault. I think someone said something at school. One of her friends. I'm sure she recognised me.'

'Even so, she should have spoken to you, or privately to me. This is what I'm talking about—I don't know who she is any more. Six months ago I would have said my daughter doesn't have an unkind bone in her body.'

Paige shook her head. 'She didn't mean anything by it. She's obviously confused.' She pressed her fingers to her temples. 'This is my fault. I should have been honest. It was naïve to think no one would recognise me. I'm so sorry. If this changes things, if you want me to leave, I will. No hard feelings.'

He swore gently. 'Listen to me.'

She scanned his eyes, waiting.

'Everyone deserves to make their own life. Of course I'm not going to fire you because your parents were selfish assholes.'

She dropped her head forward, sucking in a shaking breath, but he moved then, catching her face, holding it between his hands, lifting it towards his.

'Don't cry.' It was a command, but it was also a plea, and her heart stammered because she felt so much in that simple instruction. She felt, most of all, that he didn't *want* her to cry with every single part of himself.

She sobbed anyway and he kissed her, the kind of kiss that was drugging and overwhelming, that made her whole body shake—or maybe that was the emotion of the day, the intense, all-consuming gamut of feelings she'd run since waking up that morning. No, since the night before in his office, when they'd almost made love.

Max stood, then reached down and lifted Paige as though she weighed nothing, carrying her against his chest down the hallway, until they reached the door to his study and he shouldered it inwards. It felt like the easiest, most right thing in the world.

CHAPTER EIGHT

BEFORE LAUREN HE'D been a red-blooded male, a man in his early twenties with the world at his feet and the confidence that he could have pretty much whomever he wanted. He just had to snap his fingers and they were his.

He'd made love to women out of passion, desire, lust, always with the idea of sex being fun, not serious, never serious. Lauren had been one of those women. Meaningless and unimportant until she'd told him she was pregnant and he'd had a shockingly clarifying moment. He knew what their father's rejection had done to Luca's mother, and how Luca had never forgiven their father for his years of neglect. Max wasn't going to let any child of his be born into the world thinking they weren't fiercely loved and protected, even when that had meant marrying a woman he wasn't sure he cared for at all. But he'd shelved those worries, because he and Lauren were going to be parents and nothing mattered more than doing the right thing by the tiny lifeform they'd created.

Lauren and he hadn't really had much of a sex life.

While he'd found her attractive enough at first, the more he'd got to know her and the superficial values she held in life, the less he'd wanted her. But he'd consoled himself with the fact they could both still be good parents—she had adored Amanda—and he'd buried himself harder and harder into his work.

He'd once made love to women out of passion and need, but never like this. Never out of a complete jumble of emotions that was almost impossible to make sense of. There was lust, of course, and desire, the sort of white-hot passion that could melt a man's bones, but there was also a wish to comfort and soothe, to promise Paige with his body that everything would be okay, even when he didn't know for sure it would be. It was a gift he wanted her to have, a moment of pleasure and relief before her world cracked apart again, as surely it would when the book was released.

He kissed her until she was breathless and he undressed her as though she were some kind of precious artefact: gently, reverently, his hands running over her soft, still-sunburned skin so she pulled back from him, pressed a hand hard to his chest and said, 'You're not going to break me.'

Their eyes met and held and for no reason he could think of, he said, 'I'm not going to break you.' Maybe it was because she had been broken, he thought, and she deserved to know that he had no intention of being someone else in her life who hurt her.

Her skin was so soft and smooth. He worshipped her body, kissing her all over, tasting her, wishing they had days and days to explore each other, not only hours, as he parted her legs with his knee and moved his body over hers. 'You're sure?'

She bit down into her lip and nodded, eyes flashing with his, daring him to change his mind so he understood the same desperation he felt was pummelling her from the inside out.

'God, yes, I'm sure,' she groaned, tilting her back and lifting her hips in a desperate, hungry invitation for him.

He didn't need to be told twice.

Moving quickly, he sheathed his length then hitched himself at the entrance to her sex, eyes holding hers, watching her as he sank into her slowly, her muscles squeezing around his length so he swore into the room between clenched teeth because she felt so inexplicably good, so damned tight and wet that he had to hold himself up on his arms and focus or he was half worried he'd lose it already.

'I haven't done this in a long time,' he reminded her grimly, cursing that he hadn't foreseen this and taken matters into his own hands this morning to relieve some of the pressure that had been building inside him since Paige Cooper had first walked into his life.

'So you've said,' she murmured, rocking her hips then latching her ankles behind his back, pulling him all the way in so he swore, dropped down, his heavy, hard body on top of her small, soft one, his voice a caress against her ear as he spoke words that were probably unintelligible—he had no concept of what he was saying, only that a spell was building around them and with each movement of his body, each answering shift of hers, the world was taking on a whole new shape. He pulsed with sensation, with the need to release, but there was determination too, a need for her to find her own release before he gave into his. With the willpower he was famed for, Max held on, watching Paige, feeling her body's responses, her convulsing, her tightening around his length and her muscles' responses as she fell apart in his arms, crying his name over and over in a way that was more beautiful than anything he'd ever heard.

He cursed inwardly, thanking every star in the heavens that he'd managed to hold on, moving once she'd quietened down, moving until her muted cries grew faster again and this time, when she exploded, he was right there with her, breath fast, chest moving rapidly, body shaking with the force of his release, of his pleasure, of his unmitigated euphoria.

Paige had needed to shower and have a quiet cup of tea before she felt as though she could face Amanda, but she knew then that she couldn't put it off any longer. The music was still blaring so Paige gave only a cursory knock—which wouldn't have been audible anyway—before opening the door.

Amanda was lying on the bed, staring at the ceiling, and, while she was no longer crying, her little face was tear-stained and blotchy.

At Paige's entrance, she turned her head, bit down on her lip but didn't look away.

'Hi.' Paige lifted a hand in the air.

Amanda sat up before grudgingly reaching for an iPad and pressing pause on the playlist.

'I suppose you have some questions,' Paige prompted gently, coming to sit on the edge of the bed, but far enough away from Amanda not to seem as though she was trying too hard.

Amanda shook her head.

'Are you sure? Because if I was you, I'd be curious. I'd want to know why someone who'd been really famous once upon a time chose to be someone else now, why they chose to keep that secret.'

Silence.

And then, 'Why did you?'

'Well, the thing is, that whole movie-star thing really wasn't what it was cracked up to be. In fact, I hated it. So as soon as I was old enough, I quit and started a new life.'

'But you use a different name. It's like you're lying about who you are all the time.'

'It's complicated, Amanda. I didn't choose to be famous. That was a decision my parents made for me. When I was old enough to choose, I realised I wanted to just be a normal person, and that meant having a new name and not talking about my old life. I changed my name legally, so it's not really a lie.'

'But you came here and you expected us to live with you and open up to you—'

Paige was impressed by the girl's maturity. 'You feel betrayed,' she said gently.

Amanda's eyes flew to Paige's. She saw confirmation in their depths.

'Believe it or not, one of the things I love most about my job is that I get to focus on other people. I'd rather think about you than me.'

'I'm boring.'

'Not to me.'

Amanda rolled her eyes. 'Come on. I Googled you. You were, like, really, really famous.'

'Yes, I was. And do you know what that meant? I spent most of my life feeling incredibly solitary. I didn't have any real friends. I wasn't close to my parents. I was completely alone and miserable. So now, what I care about most is working with kids who maybe need a friend, who might be going through a difficult time a bit like I did.'

'I'm *not* famous,' she said, which wasn't entirely true. While Max had done a great job of keeping Amanda out of the public eye, the Stone family were tabloid fodder when major life events took place.

'But you are struggling with your friends, right?'

Amanda's face became stony, and she looked away. Paige didn't want to push it.

'I'm here if you want to talk, any time, Amanda.'

She stood up, moved towards the door. 'Are you still okay to help me with dinner?'

When she looked over her shoulder, Amanda's little face had crumpled. 'Do you actually want me to?'

Paige's heart felt as if it might break for the poor, vulnerable girl. 'Yep, for sure.' She kept her voice light.

Amanda nodded. Then, as Paige slipped from the room, Amanda called out, 'Paige? I'm sorry for...that. I thought they were laughing at me, because I didn't know, and they'd all recognised you yesterday. I felt stupid, and I was mad. I should have just asked you.'

Paige hovered in the doorframe. 'Probably, but you were upset, as you said. Besides, I'm the one who's sorry. Even though it doesn't really impact my job, I still should have explained. You were right before: I want you to open up to me. I'd like us to be friends. And that's a two-way street. So from now on, let's have a rule: we'll be honest with each other, and ask each other anything. Okay?'

Amanda's relief was palpable. So too was Paige's. 'I'll see you downstairs in, say, a half-hour?'

Amanda nodded. 'Thanks, Paige.'

It was the most normal conversation she'd had with her young charge and Paige couldn't help grinning as she left the room. It felt as though she'd had a breakthrough with Max, and a breakthrough with Amanda, and her worst fears had happened—they knew the truth of who she was—and the world hadn't ended.

Paige had lost count of the number of times she'd made this dinner. When she'd first moved to Dubai and been charged with three kids under fourteen, she'd needed to find a way to entertain them that they all enjoyed. Cooking had been it. However, as Paige had had next to no cooking experience, she'd had to rely on a 'beginner's cookbook' she'd bought online. This had been one of the recipes, and a firm favourite for the kids.

It was easy enough.

Marinate the chicken while the rice cooked, then start preparing the vegetables and chicken. The whole dinner took less than thirty minutes to cook.

Usually.

But now, she was distracted.

How could she not be?

Max wasn't in the room, but that was even worse, because she couldn't get what they'd done out of her head. He hadn't been awkward about it—anything but. He'd been kind. Gentle. But he'd left his study almost immediately after they'd finished, saying he needed to check something at the farm, and that had been the end of it. He'd seemed distant. Distracted.

She sighed softly.

Could she blame him?

He hadn't had sex since his wife's death. There had to be a heap of emotional baggage to go along with what they'd just done. So he was taking time to process it. Regretting it? Wishing he hadn't done it? She hated the thought of that.

'What now?' Amanda asked, clearly doing her best to be helpful.

'Now…' Paige smiled encouragingly '…we check the rice.'

'The timer went off already.'

'Yep, once the timer buzzes and we turn off the heat, the rice needs to sit a few minutes. Now, we fluff it with a fork.'

Amanda let out a tiny giggle—it was music to Paige's ears. 'Fluff it?'

'Sure. Here. Give it a try.' She handed a piece of cutlery

to the girl, then stepped back, waiting for her to approach the pan.

'Um, how do I "fluff" rice?'

'Exactly like it sounds,' Paige explained. 'Take off the lid, and lightly move the rice around until it's separated. Just watch for the steam as you remove the lid.'

Amanda did as Paige had instructed, flicking a glance at Paige. 'Like this?'

'Perfect. You're a natural.'

Amanda rolled her eyes but her demeanour was sweet. 'Like making rice is hard.'

'Perhaps not, but fluffing it well is an artform,' Paige teased. 'Okay, time to cook the chicken.'

They worked mostly in silence after that, but Amanda's face was the most relaxed Paige had seen since arriving. In fact, she even looked, to Paige's attentive eyes, as though she was enjoying herself. In the back of her mind, Paige began to collate some other recipes they could try, easy things that someone Amanda's age would enjoy making—and eating—and for the first time since arriving in Australia, Paige allowed herself to relax, just a little. She felt that she'd won a crucial battle with Amanda tonight, and turned a corner with Max, too.

The book was coming out soon, yes, and anxiety about that hovered on the edges of her mind all the time, but there was something about this house and family that made the rest of the world, and all her worries, feel so very far away.

He didn't know what he'd expected when he came home but it wasn't this. Max had needed space, to process what had happened firstly with Amanda and then with Paige, but he'd come home knowing he'd need to roll up his sleeves and deal with his daughter and her behaviour.

Only instead of finding the house in sullen silence, he saw Paige and Amanda were in the kitchen cooking, side by side, and while they weren't talking non-stop, they were making companionable remarks to each other. Amanda was even smiling.

He stood unobserved with a shoulder against the wall, silently watching, his heart twisting painfully in his chest. Because it had been so long since he'd seen Amanda at ease? No. That wasn't it.

It was seeing them together. It was the first time Max had witnessed Amanda and Paige and the bottom was falling out of his world because they looked so good and right together, it was like walking into one of those houses of mirrors at an amusement park—a thousand different images flooded his brain, including a future filled with moments like this.

What if he got Paige to stay?

What if she wasn't here for just three months, but for ever? What if he could give Amanda a proper family?

His stomach churned because he thought he'd been enough, that by prioritising Amanda the way he had, by moving out here away from the trappings of his former life, by keeping her home with him rather than sending her to boarding school, he'd provided her with all that she could need. He hadn't realised that a gap had been forming in their lives, that the two of them were rattling around like pinballs in this big, empty house. Until now.

And just like one of those haunted houses, the visions shattered and tore away from him with psychedelic speed.

He couldn't ask Paige to stay longer. Even if they hadn't slept together, it would have been too complicated, but, given what had happened between them this afternoon, their relationship had to remain strictly business from now on.

And if he needed any further reminder of why that mattered so much, seeing his daughter and Paige locked in a scene of such happy domesticity reminded him squarely of why those boundaries mattered.

He'd told Paige when she arrived that this was temporary, and that he didn't want Amanda getting hurt. Well, fine, but if he let Paige become a part of the family for the next few months then wasn't hurt inevitable?

His glance flicked to the horizon, as if seeking signs of the storm he felt brewing, but it was clear, all the way to the edge of the ocean.

He frowned, turning his attention back to the kitchen right as Paige glanced up and their eyes met so the air sparked between them and he had to shove a hand in his pocket to anchor himself to reality and his realisation that he needed to make sure nothing more happened between them.

'Hi,' she half whispered, then cleared her throat and blinked quickly, as if to return her voice to normal. But he'd heard the husky sweetness in her tone and it was doing strange, looping things to his insides.

He turned his attention to Amanda. This was all about her, after all. He had to stop thinking about Paige, even when that seemed almost impossible. 'It smells so good in here, honey. Did you cook dinner?'

Amanda's eyes showed wariness, as though she was expecting him to reprimand her for what had happened earlier. And Max would talk to her about it, but not now. 'Yeah. Well, mainly it was Paige, but I helped.'

'You were great,' Paige said. 'Remember, the rice?'

A flicker of a smile teased Amanda's lips and Paige's eyes flew to Max's to see if he'd noticed. Of course he had. He hadn't seen his daughter smile properly for months.

'What are we having?' Now it was his own voice that

was gruffer than usual, tinged by the tightening emotion in his gut.

'Umm, Paige?'

'You know what we're having,' Paige encouraged, busying herself with filling water glasses.

'Oh. Um…these chicken-wing things, and veggies, but they actually smell quite good because Paige cooks them in butter and garlic.' She moved across to the rice with a little flourish of her hands. 'And fancy rice.'

'Fancy rice, huh?'

'Well, not really.' Another flicker of a smile. 'But just… rice I did something fancy to.'

'I see. Well.' Max patted his flat stomach but stopped when he saw Paige's eyes drop to the gesture and his body reacted instantly, remembering how she'd dragged her tongue down his wall of abdominals, tasting his skin, and his gut squeezed involuntarily. 'I'm starving.' His eyes clashed with Paige's and the air exploded with electrical energy.

'Great.' Her voice wobbled. 'Let's eat.' Her cheeks were a little pink as she dished out their food and placed the meals on the counter. She was obviously avoiding him, taking care not to look at Max, not to stand too close to him. It was as though they were two magnetic poles but with the same charge. If he moved one way, she went the other. Maybe she'd come to the same conclusion he had? That Amanda had to take precedence.

Over dinner, he expanded his repertoire of questions, buoyed by the glimmer of happiness Amanda had shown, but also to fill the crackling silence. Paige also interjected, asking questions that were generic, impersonal, about the history of the house, the property, the farm, but they were both speaking to Amanda, as if encouraging her to open up, and to Max's surprise, it was working.

But while Amanda and Paige seemed relaxed and at ease, for Max, every minute that passed, the opposite could be said. He felt his own nerves stretching to breaking point. The more peaceful things seemed on the surface, the stormier his insides became. He couldn't help imagining what it would be like if this was normal for them, if Paige, or maybe even some other woman, was permanently a part of their lives. If Lauren hadn't died. Except Lauren would never have made things feel like this. Lauren was too volatile and selfish, and family dinners were definitely not her forte.

And another woman?

He didn't really want to think about that right now.

No, when he imagined this dinner being replicated again and again, it was Paige who populated his thoughts. Damn it.

Beneath the table, his fingers tightened around his knee.

'You should show Paige the attic,' Amanda said, mouth full of rice. Max resisted the temptation to remind her to wait to speak until she was finished eating.

The attic. Something exploded inside him—a wave of desire so strong it took his breath away and terrified him at the same time. Yes, terrified him. Max Stone, who would have said a week ago he wasn't afraid of anything. But the idea of being alone with Paige again when all these feelings were frothing inside him making it hard to know what was real and right any more, he needed space, not time *alone* with her in the dark confines of the old attic. When he spoke, his voice was sharp with irritation. 'I'm sure Paige doesn't want to see it.'

Paige's eyes flew to his, hurt obvious in their depths. Great. He kept his face impassive, reached for his water and took a sip.

'Another time, perhaps.' Paige's response was aimed at Amanda, her smile slightly wobbly but given for the benefit of Max's daughter.

'Oh, but it's super-cool.' Amanda seemed to have temporarily forgotten her sullen nature altogether but Max wasn't even capable of glorying in that right now. 'It actually used to be servants' rooms, so it's big, runs the whole way across the house, and there are skylights so you get the best view of the stars up there. I used to love playing in it when I was a kid.'

That was interesting. Since when had Amanda stopped thinking of herself as a kid?

Paige was looking squarely at Amanda. 'But you don't now?'

'Nah.' She glanced away, focusing on the wall across from her.

'Well, maybe *you* could show me on the weekend?' And despite himself and his fierce rejection of Amanda's suggestion that he take Paige to the attic, something like annoyance slammed into Max. He'd shut down the idea but at Paige's easy acceptance, he wanted to fight for this. He wanted to take her up there even when he knew he couldn't because of what might happen.

This was a damned mess. He'd been right earlier: he needed space to sort his own head out before he could deal with Paige again.

Amanda shrugged, not willing to commit to the plan. 'I don't really like to go up there any more.'

'I see.' He felt Paige's gaze slide to his, but he determinedly kept his gaze focused across the room.

'Dad?'

'Yes?' He could no longer avoid the conversation. He looked right at Amanda.

'It's okay, Amanda.' Paige offered the young girl a smile.

'You'll show Paige the attic, won't you?'

Finally, he looked at Paige, because he had no choice, and something in his soul ignited. Her lips parted, his gaze dropped briefly and he felt as though he were losing a part of himself. He was terrified by how much he wanted her and how much he'd been thinking of her, he was, if he was honest, terrified of what he'd felt when they'd made love. He'd been trying to rationalise it away as overwhelming because of his celibacy but with one single glance something rolled in his chest that made a mockery of all those very sensible explanations.

He was falling from a great height; disaster was unavoidable.

'Dad?' Amanda's voice was sharp.

The ground was rushing up at him; crashing was inevitable. 'Yes.' The word was louder than he'd meant. He cleared his throat, shrugged as if he weren't making some kind of a deal with the devil. 'If Paige wants to see it, sure.'

'You don't have to do this,' Paige muttered as they ascended the final, narrow staircase towards the now infamous attic.

'It's fine. Let's just get it over with.'

What had she been expecting? Roses? An invitation on a date? What was wrong with her? Paige was usually the one avoiding commitment like the plague. Why was she upset by the way he was distancing himself from her when she didn't even want more from him?

Paige blinked quickly, hating that her emotions were so close to the surface, hating the tears that threatened to spill over. But everything had felt so good before dinner. She'd been reflecting on how great it was to have achieved so much with Amanda, to have had such a breakthrough, and as for Max… Her heart stitched painfully. What they'd shared had been…life changing. Not because she expected more from him, but because in that moment, when she'd been feeling lower than low, when her past had rushed up to her and threatened to swallow her whole, he'd found the perfect way to draw her to the present and to remind her of who she was, and it had been a beautiful gift she'd wanted to cherish for ever.

She'd expected him to have some issues with it, because of his late wife, but she hadn't been prepared for him to show up at dinner and treat her like some kind of pariah.

'After you,' he said at the top of the stairs, pushing an old timber door inward. It creaked a little, the noise spooky. It was not well lit—a single light bulb dangled from a long white cord in the middle of the room. Paige hesitated a moment before crossing the threshold, her arm brushing Max's as she went, so she was grateful it was too dim for him to see the goosebumps that lifted over her skin.

She could see why Amanda had insisted she come up here. She was distracted enough by the beauty of the space to remark, 'Oh, wow. It's amazing.'

She stepped deeper into the room and it felt as though she were slipping back through time. Despite the fact the house hadn't operated as a hotel for decades, several single beds, wrought iron with brass knobs, were lined up along the wall, reminding Paige of an old-fashioned orphanage. The room though was huge—Amanda had been right, it clearly spanned the whole house, but there were no internal walls. All the furniture was old-fashioned: a leather armchair, a big, wide desk, a wardrobe with a mirror—this one put Paige in mind of *The Chronicles of Narnia*. It was like something out of a dream.

'I can feel them,' she said, lifting her fingers to her lips.

'Who?' Max was close, just a step behind her. She turned quickly, blinked, then it was Paige who took a step away, because the temptation to reach out and touch him was too great and she was worried she wouldn't be able to control herself—and he clearly didn't want anything to do with her, despite what they'd shared only hours earlier.

'Them,' she said unevenly, clearing her throat. 'The people who used to live here.'

His smile pulled pinpricks at her heart because it was so unexpected. 'A hundred or so years ago?'

'Sure, why not?' She moved deeper into the room, glad for the reprieve of space, running a finger over a dusty beam. 'I wonder what their lives were like.'

'Stinking hot, I'd imagine.'

She shot him an arch look. 'Can't you play along, just for a moment?'

'I see a heap of old junk that should have been got rid of years ago.'

That offended every cell in Paige's body. 'You can't be serious?'

'It's just furniture.'

'No, it's so much more.' She shook her head. 'It's the physical manifestation of times gone by. It's beds that were slept in by people with dreams and hopes, who'd lie here at night and look through the skylights and say their prayers for whatever wishes were in their hearts. It's lives lived and woven into the fabric of time. It's history, Max,' she said, breathlessly. 'Can't you feel—?'

'No.' The single word was harsher than it needed to be, hissed between his teeth, and Paige realised belatedly that in her desire to convince him of this magic, she'd moved towards him, close enough to reach out and touch, again. That hadn't been her intention. She'd just wanted him to see…

'It's just furniture,' he said again, as if to push the conversation firmly to the side. Pragmatic and unfeeling. Except he wasn't either of those things. On the surface, perhaps, but Paige had glimpsed more, she'd seen deeper.

'Max—' She didn't know what she'd been going to say and never found out because at that moment the light bulb dangling in the middle of the room went out, plunging them into complete darkness, and the ghosts of those people were suddenly all around them. 'Oh, my God,' she gasped, moving unconsciously closer to Max, needing to feel him for a different reason now.

She heard his rough exhalation, and the strong, muscled arm that clamped around her back was supposed to be reassuring but it made her body tingle as awareness jolted through her.

The stars were incredible from in here. Large, old skylights, circular in shape, showed the heavens as a blanket of lights—not enough to illuminate the room but striking for their vividness; every single one of Paige's senses was on high alert.

'What happened?' She gasped, clinging to his shirtfront as if for dear life.

'The bulb blew. It's old. No one ever comes up here.'

'It's dark.' Such an inane comment, but awareness of Max had tipped her over so she was barely conscious of anything but him. How could she think clearly enough to formulate a rational statement?

'Yes.' His voice had changed. The gruffness had given way to something else. Something throaty and deep, his breath audible. 'You're safe.'

From ghosts? The bogeyman? Maybe. But whatever

was swirling between them had Paige on edge. Max wasn't safe; what she wanted from him wasn't, either. It was all complicated and scary. 'Am I?'

Silence fell, and in the absence of noise Paige heard her own body's escalating rhythms, the rapid thundering of her pulse, the frantic storming of her heart, her lungs, pushing air out faster than they could draw it in, the air seeming to squeal inside her ears.

His hand at her back was vice-like; maybe he was afraid too?

Max? Afraid? She dismissed the thought instantly. He was always in control. Even that afternoon, when they'd made love, his body, having been deprived for so long of a woman's touch, had still been able to contain itself, despite his warnings.

There was no way he would fear the darkness of the attic.

Something else though, maybe?

His breath was warm on her temple; the only hint she had that he'd moved closer, that he was looking down at her.

'What happened this afternoon,' he said quietly, and his fingers stroked her back, moving higher up her spine, then lower, until Paige was trembling all over.

'Don't say it was a mistake,' she murmured, because she couldn't bear to hear that.

'No.' The word was wrenched from him, the concession one he struggled to give. 'Not a mistake.'

Her heart fluttered.

'But it can't happen again.'

His hand lifted her shirt a bit, so his fingers grazed her bare skin.

'It can't.' More forcefully, the words almost choked by his throat.

'Are you telling me, or yourself?' she whispered, tilting her face up, body pressed to his by the way he was touching her, moving her forwards.

His voice was a groan. 'Primarily me, apparently.'

'Tell me why.'

'You know the answer. We both do. It's…complicated. There's Amanda. My life—it doesn't include room for you.'

She blinked, shocked by how much that hurt when she'd met this man only days ago, when he'd already been clear about this.

'For anyone,' he clarified. 'I've been married once; I hated it.'

Curiosity sparked inside Paige—she had presumed his marriage to have been happy—but other emotions were taking more of her runtime. She felt the need to point out how far ahead of himself he was getting. 'Do you think I want to marry you because we had sex?'

She heard his rough laugh, just a short, sharp sound. Maybe it wasn't a laugh? Maybe it was surprise that she'd spoken so directly? But really, was there any point in not calling a spade a spade?

'It's easy to get carried away. To think sex might lead to something more. Not necessarily marriage, but a relationship. Seeing you in the kitchen with Amanda…'

Ah. Something about that made sense. Even she'd felt the niceness of that, the similarity to being a normal family. But for Paige, that was part of the job. Everywhere she went, she slipped into the routines and occupied a space that made her family-adjacent. She was used to it, but for Max it must have been confronting. It had just been the two of them for a long time—was he worried about where the lines would be? How to make sure Paige didn't forget herself? Yes, that had to be it!

Taking a deep breath, and steeling herself to be calm, she explained carefully, 'We have a relationship now. You're my boss. I work for you.'

'That's different.'

'It doesn't have to be.' She didn't know what she was saying, only she could see a clear path through this, a thread of logic she could grab hold of, and then everything would be okay. 'We're both on the same page. You don't want a relationship…all your energy is reserved for Amanda. Well, I don't want a relationship either. I mean, not a serious relationship. I like…spending time with you.'

And she really did, she realised. In the midst of the mess that was her personal life, something about Max had become a talisman, a beacon of calm—safety seemed to radiate from his core goodness. 'I've liked getting to know you. But I—' She dug deep into her heart, remembering her awful past, and something about his proximity and just *who* he was gave her courage and comfort. 'I don't think I'll ever be able to get seriously involved with anyone.'

'Oh?' It was a quiet noise of encouragement into the dark.

'Are you kidding? I legally divorced my mom and dad. I had to face the fact at sixteen years of age that my own parents saw me as an income stream and nothing else.' She shook her head angrily. 'The guys I dated after that, they weren't much better. I was their way to get exposure, maybe some introductions to Hollywood heavyweights, it was never about me.' She sucked in a breath, furrowing her brow as she tried to get to the bottom of what she was feeling, what she needed to tell him. 'And now my parents are selling me out, yet again. I'm just a commodity, not a person, not their child, they don't love me.'

'Paige—'

'No,' she interrupted whatever he'd been about to say. 'It's okay. It took a long time to just accept the bald truth of that fact. They don't love me. And if my own parents don't love me, why would anyone else?'

'Stop.' He groaned, catching her face in his hands, holding her steady. 'Don't say that.'

'Why not? I'm happier alone; truly, I am. I can enjoy getting to know you, sleeping with you, without it changing how I *feel* and what I want in life.'

'Which is to be alone for ever?'

'Sure, why not? Is that any different from you?'

'I have Amanda.'

'And I have the kids I look after.'

'You've just told me that your relationships are all skin-deep.'

She tilted her chin, frustrated that he was criticising her approach to life. What was wrong with it? 'So?'

It was too dark to see his face, and he was silent, so she didn't know what he was thinking, and she hated that.

'What about the woman who helped you? The actress?'

Paige thought of Anna Cooper, her features not shifting. 'I'm very grateful to her.'

'But you don't love her.'

'She's a very kind woman—'

He sighed, the breath fanning her forehead. Paige felt as though he was going to keep arguing this point and she really didn't want to discuss her life's philosophy vis-à-vis relationships. 'I understand that most people don't live like I do. I even understand that for most people, their goal in life seems to be to meet their perfect mate and give all of themselves to that one other person, that their happiness is derived from those connections. But that will never be me. Whenever I think of getting close to someone, really close, I mean relying on them and making them a big part of my life, I feel as though I'm suffocating.'

Even now, she felt the pinpricks of panic lighting her eyelids. 'It's just who I am.' She held onto that, a beacon she needed. Being solitary was her choice, it was her power. 'So if you're worried that sleeping together is going to make me, I don't know, fall madly, head-over-heels in love with you then you can forget it. I'm just not wired that way. I can keep my work with Amanda completely separate from…this.'

Somehow, in the midst of all the madness and confusion, she'd found the magic key to unlock the door to what she desperately wanted. 'Max, being with you makes me feel good. Something between us just…works. We don't need to overthink this. We both know it's temporary but that doesn't mean it's not also incredibly beautiful and…'

'Right,' he said on a groan of surrender, and then, holding her face as though she were the most precious thing in the world, he dropped his head and kissed her, and despite everything Paige had just said, it was her heart that rejoiced the loudest, leaping through her body like a firework, exploding so she couldn't help but be aware of the way it was practically abusing her ribcage.

But Paige wasn't worried. She knew her heart wasn't ever really going to be a problem. She'd locked it up nice and tight years ago and that was one key she had no intention of rediscovering.

CHAPTER NINE

WHEN PAIGE RETURNED from dropping Amanda at school the following morning, Max was waiting for her, and as she stepped from the car her stomach gave a lurch, then dropped all the way down to her toes.

He was so incredibly beautiful, she wanted to remember him like this for ever. But that was a thought Paige pushed aside abruptly.

When she left this place, she'd put Max out of her mind. She'd move on. Never get attached—it was her guiding missive. Leave before she could be asked to leave.

'Got any plans for the day?'

Paige shook her head slowly and a warm breeze lifted from the beach and carried her hair against her cheek so she brushed it away.

'Now you do.' He strode down the steps. 'Come with me.'

Her heart, her untouchable heart, raced.

'Where?'

He closed the distance between them. 'You'll see.'

'A surprise?'

His eyes were as vibrant as the ocean beyond the house, his nod was just a shift of his head.

Evidently, their conversation last night had convinced him that there was no risk of Paige falling for him, because he'd let go of any inhibitions and she liked that, because she'd been honest with him. She enjoyed spending time together. She found him exhilarating. Yes, that was the perfect word. He was unlike anyone she'd ever known. Intelligent, charismatic, charming, handsome but also good, his moral fibre impressive and admirable. Just the way he loved Amanda and made her his top priority showed Paige what a great guy he was—and also the polar opposite to her own father.

'I like surprises,' she said, then qualified it with a wrinkling of her nose. 'Some surprises.' The memoir that was about to hit shelves was a surprise she could have lived without.

'Great. Let's go.'

Paige had known Australia was a vast and beautiful place but she couldn't have conceptualised quite how expansive and stunning until she was in the air in a helicopter being piloted by Max, hovering high above this land of stunning nature and stark contrasts. The ocean was mesmerising for its colour changes and vastness. Near the coastline, it was turquoise, almost transparent, so she could see a pod of dolphins in the warm, shallow waters of the oyster farm. Paige held her breath as he brought them in low enough to observe the details on their gunmetal-grey bodies, emerging from the water then diving down again. She couldn't help smiling.

Max piloted them further out over the ocean and the colour change was dramatic—here it was a dark, earthy blue, no less beautiful, but somehow menacing. The white caps of the waves frothed towards the shore as Paige watched. Back over the land, she delighted in the lush green rainforest, the sound of the birds imprinted on her mind now so, even up here, she could remember those sounds as if they were in her ears again now.

But the rainforest and dramatic cliffs and waterfalls were all near the ocean. After another ten or so minutes, they were back over the desert, bright red, strikingly beautiful from this height, particularly when contrasted with the azure blue of the sky. Even better, the helicopter had ice-cold air conditioning so, while Paige could see the heat hazing off the ground, she couldn't feel it as she had that first day, when she'd felt as though her skin were going to sear from her body.

'Incredible,' she murmured, to herself, but, courtesy of the headphones they wore, Max heard and turned to her, grinning.

'Every tourist should fly over the country like this.'

She liked that he considered her a tourist. It was yet another reminder of how temporary her time here was.

'Hungry?'

Paige was surprised to realise it was lunch time. She had no concept of how far they were from home. 'Yeah. I'll need to get back for Amanda—'

He nodded. 'Plenty of time.'

With expert control, Max brought the helicopter lower, and through the swirls of dust Paige could just make out a collection of a few buildings, small and rickety, made of timber and tin.

'Where are we?'

'This used to be the old town,' he said, landing them on the ground to the left of a two-storey building with a rickety-looking veranda. 'The drought closed most of the farms around here down. The town is limping along, but there aren't many people out this way any more.'

'What's this place?'

'The pub.'

'How can such a small town have a pub?'

'It's important to the remaining locals.'

'Sure, but it's hard to see how it could cover its costs. Isn't that why most of these places get shut down?'

He nodded once. 'It's important to keep places like this though. Not just for the locals,' he conceded, 'but because it's a part of the history of the area. This pub used to do a roaring trade, then the highway moved, and it was all but forgotten.'

'It's charming,' she said, glancing up at him as a thought occurred to her and she just *knew* her gut feeling was right. 'Max, do you *own* the pub?'

He looked at her for several beats, shrugged his shoulders, then turned to the building. 'It's part of the place's history. Come have a look.'

The pub was cool and dark and just stepping inside she knew her suspicions were correct, because while the fit-out retained the charm of the pub's history, it was also immaculate and clearly no expense had been spared.

The ceiling was ornate pressed metal, the floor was wide, dark timber boards, and the artwork on the wall comprised stunning landscapes of the outback—originals that she guessed hadn't come cheap. Max led Paige to a table near the back—there were only two other patrons, both sitting at the bar. No sooner had they sat down than the waitress appeared brandishing a couple of menus, with an extensive selection of food—further evidence that the kitchen was bankrolled by someone who didn't rely on the place turning a profit.

'What's good?' Paige asked with a small smile.

'Everything.'

She heard the pride in his voice and her insides leaped. 'That's high praise for a country pub.'

'Trust me.'

And because everything between them felt just a little *too* right, because they were a little too in sync, she wanted to remind him that she didn't *trust* anyone, but it was enough just to remind herself.

She turned her attention to the menu, selecting a garlic prawn dish. When the waitress arrived, Max ordered a bottle of white wine, and his own meal, a rather more substantial-sounding 'surf and turf'.

The waitress was friendly with Max, in a way that Paige couldn't pretend she didn't notice, and couldn't pretend she didn't *feel* a hint of envy about. But that was normal. On a purely primal level, they were lovers, and, just like in the animal kingdom, she temporarily felt she'd staked some kind of claim to him. It didn't mean anything beyond that—she just didn't want another woman making eyes at Max while they were having lunch.

But given that he'd been celibate for the past six years, she probably didn't need to imagine him suddenly leaping over the bar and making love to the other woman. If that was going to happen, he'd have the decency to wait until Paige left, she was pretty sure.

Having been intimate with Max, she found it hard to imagine him living without sex. He was so passionate, so powerful, so…skilled…in that department. To have denied himself that pleasure was bad enough, but to have denied other women seemed almost criminal. That same little blade of envy pressed into Paige as she thought of his wife and wondered about their marriage. He must have loved the other woman a great deal. Except…hadn't he said he'd hated being married?

Curiosity burst through her, irrepressible and urgent. 'What was your wife like?' Paige asked, before she could think better of it.

If Max was surprised, he didn't show it. He lifted his gaze to Paige's face, let his eyes linger there a moment, his lips tugging downward as he lost himself in his thoughts. 'Volatile.'

It was the last thing she'd expected him to say.

'Very beautiful,' he amended, his voice softening, so that jealousy dug in a little deeper.

'How did you meet?'

He tugged a hand through his hair. 'We were part of the same social circle. She was friends with my friends. I don't actually remember the first time we met, I just became aware of knowing her one day.'

'Not love at first sight, then?'

The waitress appeared with an ice-cold bottle of Riesling and two glasses. Max poured the wine, and Paige sipped it just because she wanted something to do with her hands.

'You and I have our cynicism in common. I don't believe in love at first sight any more than you do.'

'Why do you think I'm cynical?' she prompted.

He lifted his brows. 'Our conversation last night?'

'Knowing that I don't believe in love for myself personally is different from saying I don't believe in it for other people. I think love is out there, and that some people, maybe even lots of people, get struck by that mythical lightning strike. Just not me.'

'You're a little young to speak in such absolutes.'

She shook her head. 'I'm an expert on this one subject: myself. I know who I am and what I want from life. It's not that.'

'Lightning doesn't always listen to what we want,' he pointed out, rocking the base of his wine glass against the polished tabletop, eyes locked to hers so she had the strangest feeling he was picking her apart and studying her, piece by piece, even the parts Paige didn't fully understand about herself.

'So what was it like?' she asked. 'I presume you loved her very much.'

'Why do you say that?'

'Because you were married.' Paige floundered a little, realising that one thing didn't necessarily equate to the other. 'And because you haven't—you've been—'

He almost looked to be enjoying her discomfort because he leaned closer across the table, and their legs brushed so Paige shifted a bit, her insides quivering with recognition at the contact.

'Celibate?' he prompted in a stage whisper, so Paige quickly looked around and ascertained they were out of earshot.

'Yes.'

'I'm not embarrassed by that, Paige. It's not for lack of opportunity.'

Heat flooded her cheeks. 'Okay, Mr Ego. No need to go into what a desirable bachelor you are.'

His eyes crinkled at the corners with a suppressed smile. 'I only mean that I have made a choice and I have no issues with it.'

'And this? You and me?'

'Lightning,' he responded, then leaned closer, beneath the table his palm grazed her knee and goosebumps danced across her skin. 'Of a purely sexual kind.'

Her heart fluttered, her stomach tightened, but in the back of her mind there was something else, something sharp and a little uncomfortable.

'I suppose it was the same with Lauren,' he said, frowning, and that uncomfortable feeling grew bigger. 'She was very beautiful and quite…intriguing at first. She was—fun. Always the centre of the party, laughing, dancing, carefree, quite free-spirited. I suppose I wanted her,' he said, sipping his wine, lost in reflection. 'Because everyone else did.' His frown deepened. 'Back then, I always had to win at everything.' The final statement was muttered, an indictment against himself. 'It's how I was raised.'

'I guess a lot of people in your position have that mindset. Most of the successful directors and financiers I got to know were similarly driven.'

He was quiet, considering that.

'So you wanted Lauren and…?'

'And we got together. It was a short relationship. We dated for a couple of months, but a lot of that was spent with me travelling. We weren't exclusive.'

Paige leaned closer, fascinated.

'Do you know anything about my brother?'

'I know you have one,' Paige said with a lift of her shoulders.

'He's a few months younger than me. Our father had an affair with his mother—she was a cleaner at his hotel in Rome.'

Paige blinked.

'He claims he didn't know about Luca, that she never told him, so until Luca was twelve, we never met. Then his mother passed away, and in the will instructions were left that he was to be sent to my father, with a copy of his birth certificate. After the requisite genetic testing, Luca came to live with us. My mother left the same week.'

It was all said so matter-of-factly, but Paige's heart, which in fact had not been rendered completely offline, gave a thud of pity. 'How absolutely awful, for everyone.'

Beneath the table, she laced her fingers through Max's. 'You must have resented him at first.'

'Naturally. I went from being an only child to losing my mother and suddenly having a brother, a brother who was almost the same age and who was of great interest to my father. He pitted us against one another and my anger over what his arrival had done to my family meant I was, initially, more than willing to fight Luca. To try to beat him at everything, all the time.'

'To need to win,' she repeated gently.

He nodded, fingers tracing the bottom of his wine glass distractedly. The waitress appeared with garlic bread and some olives, placing the little platter between them on the tabletop and disappearing again. Another couple of people came through the door; Paige turned to look at them, blinking. She'd almost forgotten where they were.

'Eventually, we stopped competing. We became friends and finally, brothers. We were a team, too, united against our dad.'

'What was he like?'

Max's hand tightened momentarily on the stem of the wine glass then released, but with visible effort. 'An acquired taste.'

Paige's smile was a flash on her face. 'Oh?'

'I spent my teenage years hating him—with Luca. But as I got older and things got a little more complicated, I saw how nuanced life can be. I hate so many of the things he did, the decisions he made, the way he was with Luc and me, but at the same time, nobody's perfect. I didn't want to spend the rest of my life hating him.'

'So you forgave him?'

'It's not quite so clear-cut. I just…came to enjoy the parts of our relationship that worked. He was good at what he did professionally. I respected him for how he grew the business, and for how he let me step into his role when he realised I could do it better.'

Paige dipped her head to hide a smile at that. It was an honest admission that from anyone else might have smacked of arrogance but from Max was just accurate.

'But the thing with Luc, that's complicated. He found it a lot harder to move on with Dad.'

'Why, do you think?'

'He saw his mother suffer. She raised him alone, money was tight, she was shunned by her very traditional family, had to move to Sicily to get any kind of support. And then he was thrust into the lap of luxury and made to think of himself not as a Cavallaro but as a Stone. He was bitter about it for a long time.'

'And now?'

'They reconciled, shortly before Dad died. It brought the old man a lot of peace.'

Someone at the bar laughed loudly and it pierced the solemn air that had surrounded them.

Paige sat a little straighter, took a drink of her wine, then reached for an olive. It was plump and juicy, and she savoured the flavour, until she became aware of the way Max was staring at her lips. His hand on her thigh moved higher and, unconsciously, she shifted further forward in her seat, bringing them closer together.

'So...' he picked up his train of thought anew '...when Lauren told me she was pregnant with my baby, I wasn't going to let her raise Amanda without me. Marriage made sense to me. I wanted to be in my child's life all the time, not just sometimes.'

Paige had almost completely forgotten what had started his conversation. 'And did she want to get married?'

'Yes. She didn't hesitate.'

Paige frowned. 'Did you know—?' But she stopped herself in time, realising how insensitive the question she'd been about to ask might appear.

'I didn't know Amanda was mine for sure,' Max said quietly. 'Not until she was born and she opened her eyes, so like my own, and I felt this instant, powerful connection. I loved her. I knew I'd made the right decision. She was mine, and while Lauren and I weren't in love, we were going to raise her together. Lauren loved her too. She was a good mother. Better than my own, at least,' he said with a gruff laugh. 'Better than yours, too, by the sound of it.'

Paige stroked the back of his hand without responding. She didn't need to.

'I didn't do any testing. I didn't need to.'

'No,' Paige agreed, but she couldn't help admiring him for his commitment.

'In every way, I wanted to be the opposite to my father. I had a front-row seat to how his choices had made our family implode, had destroyed, in many ways, Luca's mother's life, and Luca's too. From the moment Lauren told me about Amanda, I was her father. It's as simple as that.'

It was impossible not to feel something like love for the sentiment he was expressing. It was exactly what she wished someone had felt for her. What had always been missing in her life. An ache throbbed in the back of her throat and she blinked away, hating the quick sting of tears in her eyes.

'Paige?' His voice was deep and husky, probing. She turned back to him slowly, her smile ambivalent, apologetic.

'I just never experienced that kind of love,' she said wistfully. 'I can't imagine what it must be like for Amanda to know that she has you.'

He was quiet, considered that. 'I'm the last person she seems to want to be around right now.'

Paige lifted her shoulders. 'Being a good dad isn't always about having the answers, it's about knowing how to get them. Your instincts were bang on: Amanda needs more right now. She needs a fresh perspective, and you're giving her that. Recognising that you have some shortcomings, that you can't fix everything, makes you brave and responsible. You're not letting her down.'

He hadn't said anything like it, but somehow, Paige just knew he needed to hear that. Perhaps it was a relic of the man Max had once been, the man who'd always needed to win.

Their meals arrived and they ate in between bursts of companionable conversation about the area, Max's family history here, and how much he loved this part of the world. He explained how it was his great-great-grandfather who'd moved to the north of Australia and opened a pearl-farming operation, that he'd been both lucky and canny, finding enormous pearls within his first five years of operation, some of which had been sold to the royal family for coronation jewels, and which quickly garnered a reputation as some of the most prestigious pearls in the world. From there, the operation had grown and successive generations had invested into other industries, had expanded their luxury holdings, so the Stone family was worth billions before being a billionaire was even a thing. But always, Wattle Bay and nearby Mamili had been special to them, because here it had all begun.

He painted such a picture and Paige was so pleasantly full of delicious prawns and lovely wine that she found herself relaxing back in the seat, listening and letting herself be pulled away by the richness of his history.

'I always wanted to live here. After Lauren died, I knew

I needed to go back to basics. Lauren had loved the finer things in life, the fast pace, the luxury and glamour of Sydney, and our frequent trips overseas—whenever I suggested moving to Wattle Bay, she refused, told me I could come but not with her and not with our daughter.'

Paige gasped.

Max continued, 'She died because she went to some concert, got loaded backstage with the band, then let some equally drunk guy get behind the wheel of her ridiculous sports car. He wrapped the car around a pole. And suddenly I realised: my daughter can't grow up with any of this stuff. I don't want her going to schools with other rich kids, thinking it's normal to have an army of servants in the house, like I used to live, like Lauren lived. I didn't want her being chauffeur-driven in a Mercedes from one birthday party to the next, doing drugs at fifteen, in rehab by seventeen. It's as though Lauren's death forced me to grapple with the scaffolding of the world I was providing for Amanda. She was only five, so it wasn't too hard to strip away those luxuries, to bring her here, to the middle of nowhere, a home where she has to make her own bed and clear the table, where very few of those creature comforts infiltrate our world.'

'You don't take her away with you, if you travel for work?' Paige asked over the now cleared table. 'I presume your job requires you to leave the property?'

'Yes,' he agreed. 'Sometimes she comes with me, but most of the time, Amanda stays home, with Reg and his wife, Cass. They're great with her.'

'You don't think they could help, with her current moods?'

'They've raised five kids of their own,' he said fondly. 'They babysit their million grandkids in their off hours. I didn't particularly want to saddle them with my issues.'

'I've seen Reg with her. He's great. I'm sure he'd have been happy to help.'

'I needed more. I wanted proper support. Twenty-four-seven, help on tap. Hence, you're here.'

'Yes,' she agreed, nodding slowly. That was why she was here, and it was important not to forget that, even when they were inching closer and closer together, legs entwined beneath the table, heads close together, as though they were the only people in the pub. 'And you didn't consider a more permanent solution? Like hiring a nanny for the long term?'

He stiffened and Paige shook her head, worried he'd misinterpret. 'I don't mean that I want to stay,' she hastened to add, ignoring the awful pain in the centre of her heart at his quick and complete rejection of that idea.

He practically grunted his response. 'I was raised by nannies. An army of them. It's no way to live.'

She bowed her head forward. 'I thought I was the poster child for dysfunctional upbringings.'

'If it's any consolation, I think that's a prize you still get to keep.'

She blinked up at him and saw sympathy in his amazing eyes. Her fingers tingled with a need to touch him. She leaned closer, then let her hand lift, to his face, to his lips, tracing the outline as if committing it to memory.

'Would you like to see the dessert menu?' The waitress appeared, flicking a curious glance from one to the other.

Paige startled, surprised to find they were still in the middle of the pub.

'Paige?' Max's eyes were hungry, but not for dessert, and it was a feeling that was reverberating inside Paige like a flag in a cyclone.

'I think we should go,' she said, eyes locked to his.

'I'm delighted to hear it. Put lunch on my tab, Clara.' He stood then reached for Paige, half pulling her out of her chair in his haste to exit the dining room.

Control was slipping away, inexorably and completely, as he pushed Paige's skirt up her body and dragged down her pants. He'd barely been able to wait until the helicopter door was closed and he'd never been so grateful that the chopper was a decent size *and* that it had darkly tinted windows. Confident they were screened off from anyone out there, and not much able to care beyond giving privacy a cursory thought, he pulled Paige down on top of him, as he had that first night in his office when his control had been dangling by a thread. Even then, he'd been powerless to fight this.

Lightning.

It had struck him again and again, always with Paige.

It had never been like this with Lauren. He didn't know why he'd said that it was. Maybe because it seemed wise to add in that kind of detail, some hint of self-preservation and guardedness? Or maybe because he'd actually believed it in that moment, but as Paige fumbled and finally undid his button and zip and released his rock-hard erection from his jeans, pausing only to take the condom from his wallet and sheathe him before lowering herself over his length with a loud, wrenching cry, he knew it had never been like this with anyone.

This was true lightning.

Life-changing, if you allowed it to be, but neither of them would. So instead, they'd both just sit back and enjoy the ride, as many times as they possibly could before Paige's contract was up and she left.

CHAPTER TEN

AN EASY RHYTHM established itself. Amanda was Paige's sole focus whenever she was home from school and awake, and, to Paige's relief, Amanda continued to let Paige into her life, relaxing into conversations, even suggesting some shared activities like watching a movie together. But once Amanda was in bed and fast asleep, Paige was all Max's, and he was all hers. They used a guest room, far from the family's bedrooms, because it was imperative that Amanda should never have any possible hint of what was happening between the two of them.

It also seemed right to separate what they were doing from their normal lives. This was something they'd carved out that existed in its own space, away from the rest of their worlds.

In that room, Paige wasn't Paige and Max wasn't Max, they were just two people who found they came most to life when they were in each other's arms, bodies bonded, for those few hours each night before taking themselves back to their beds to wake up the next morning and resume the rhythm.

Strange, though, how after a week of this Paige felt simultaneously the most and least satisfied she'd ever been. On the one hand, sex with Max was fulfilling and incredible, each time they came together somehow *more* wondrous than the last. She simply couldn't fathom how it could keep getting better.

But on the other hand, when it came time to say goodbye, she felt frustrated. A yearning was beginning to build inside Paige for the most ludicrous thing—particularly given the level of intimacy they'd shared.

What she really wanted though was to wake up beside him.

She wanted to see him sleep, to watch him wake, to be kissed awake by him—all impossible dreams, made just out of reach by the precarious nature of their situation and their overriding responsibility to do the right thing by Amanda.

And so it was that in the kitchen each morning they were back to their dance of the magnetic poles, skating around each other, maintaining a very safe distance at all times. They knew that if they happened to accidentally brush up against one another, sparks would fly that surely even Amanda wouldn't be able to miss.

It was almost a relief to leave each morning with Reg and Amanda, just so Paige could take some time to breathe, to unwind, before coming home and being alone with Max.

Their routine had even managed to push thoughts of her parents' book from Paige's mind—almost completely. There was still the odd moment when it burst into her brain, the knowledge that it was now published, on shelves, being read by people, and she would feel a visceral pain radiate through her chest, so she would clutch at her breast and breathe deeply until it passed and she remembered that she was here, that she was safe, far from the influence of the people who'd given her life and some of life's toughest lessons.

Here, there was just Max.

At first, they'd spent the days out. Doing things. Swimming. Exploring the oyster farm, so that Max could teach her about something that was so new to Paige. She'd known that pearls came from oyster shells, but hadn't understood quite what a laborious and careful process harvesting them was, particularly when done humanely, and, watching Max talk about it, she couldn't help but perceive his passion for the art of it.

But as the days went by, and the pressure between them built, eventually they reached a point where it was harder and harder to leave the house. Yes, the farm was fascinating and compelling, but it involved seeing other people and being out in public and neither relished that. Not when they could be alone.

The moment Paige returned from the school run, and the front door was closed, Max was there, pressing her against it and kissing her, his hands roaming her body as though they hadn't seen each other for years and years, as though a drought had been building and this, finally, were the storm come to quench the land. In reality, it had only been hours, and it shouldn't have been physically possible to want and need like this but, oh, how they did! She yearned for him on every level, and evidently he felt the same, because there was no restraint in their lovemaking. They were each as desperate as the other.

They often didn't make it upstairs to a bedroom. His office was closer, or there was the floor in the hallway. It didn't matter. So long as they found their way back to each other, the location didn't come into it.

Each day passed far too quickly. Paige had set an alarm on her phone, just so she didn't let time get away from her and forget to collect Amanda—a very real risk given the level of distraction Max presented.

Ten days after their new routine had begun, on a startlingly hot and humid afternoon, Paige went with Reg to collect Amanda, glowing from the inside out, pleasure bubbling inside her as anticipation built already, for later that night.

But when Amanda got in the car, slamming the door behind her, and burst into tears, every single thought of Max and romance fled from Paige's head.

'What's happened?' Paige asked, but Amanda sat there silently, staring out of the window, arms crossed, tears leaking from her eyes and rolling slowly down her cheeks. It felt like a torturously slow drive home but finally Reg pulled the car into the drive and Amanda bolted out the moment he came to a stop, running up the steps and inside without a backwards glance.

'I— Thank you,' Paige murmured, face pale as she stepped from the car and walked towards the house, tossing over possibilities in her mind, trying to imagine what could possibly have happened.

Max stood in the door to his office, and even then, when their eyes met, Paige felt a crackle of electric energy fire through her blood. She ignored it.

'Amanda—'

'I saw. Why?'

Paige shook her head. 'I don't know.'

He sighed heavily. 'I'll go talk to her.'

Paige put out her hand. 'I'll go.' She squeezed his hand with her own. 'Let me try. I just have a feeling this is something I can help with. Do you mind?'

He looked uncertain but, after a few moments, nodded. When she went to pull away though, he flipped his hand, easily capturing hers in his. 'She can be fierce when she's in these moods. Don't let her get to you.'

Paige's heart skipped a beat. 'Max Stone, are you actually being protective of me?'

Something shifted in his eyes—surprise? And then guardedness, as he lifted one shoulder half defensively. 'Just a warning.'

'Consider me warned,' she said gently. Again, she tried to move away but, instead of letting go, he pulled her closer and pressed the lightest of kisses to the tip of her nose.

After everything they'd shared, all their intimacies, it was this kiss that had the power to take her breath away and make her toes and fingers tingle, to steal her breath, all her breath, and give her knees the shakes.

'Good luck.' He pulled back then, putting physical space between them but also changing his stature completely so he was somehow stronger, more imposing, less familiar to her.

Paige simply smiled, careful not to show any of her thoughts. 'Fingers crossed.'

Much later that night, having eaten a quiet dinner alone with Amanda in the downstairs play area, and shared a real, meaningful conversation with her about what had been going on in Amanda's life, Paige finally understood, and knew she needed to explain to Max.

'She's being teased,' Paige said gently, curled up on the daybed on the veranda, so close to Max she was practically in his lap. It was late. Amanda had been asleep for over an hour, and Max and Paige were in their favourite place, outside, staring up at the starlit sky accompanied by the orchestra of night birds and the rolling, crashing waves of the ocean. Every sense came alive inside Paige out here; being this close to Max supercharged it all.

'Teased?' He responded quickly, loudly, his body tensing in a way Paige felt. 'What the actual hell? By whom?'

'Just some girls at school,' Paige murmured. 'It's not

uncommon at this age. I've emailed her teacher and headmistress. I'm going to meet with them to discuss it, but it sounds reasonably benign—'

'Benign, my ass. You've seen her moods. Are you telling me that's because some awful girls are taking their own self-esteem issues out on Amanda?'

Paige pressed a hand to his chest. 'I know you're upset, but, believe it or not, this is not as bad as it sounds.'

He scowled at her, and his defensiveness made Paige's chest feel as if a thousand tonnes of cement were being pushed against it. On the one hand, she loved that this was his reaction, but she couldn't help thinking again of the absences she'd felt in her own life, how, when she was a teenager, she'd desperately needed protecting. And there'd been no one.

'How exactly is it not so bad?' he drawled, and while she knew his anger wasn't aimed at her, it still hurt. They were a team, fighting through this together.

'Conflict in life is inevitable.'

'Is this conflict? Or is she being bullied?'

Paige stroked his chest, changing her description as a concession to his point. 'Unpleasantness is a part of life. We all have to learn to deal with cruel people, unfair situations, and the more we do it with the support and guidance of trusted adults, the better we become at managing those situations independently. Think of yourself—and me—as her training wheels. We're here to help Amanda learn how to stand up for herself, to find her voice, and to draw her own boundaries of what is and isn't acceptable. By going through this now, the next time something like this happens—and it will, because that's life—she'll be better able to cope.'

He ground his teeth together. 'Who the hell are these kids?'

'A couple of girls in her grade, and a few in the grade above. I think two of them are sisters,' she said. 'I couldn't quite keep up, but I'll get a clearer picture once I've met with her teacher and headmistress—which I'll be doing tomorrow.'

'Like hell you will.'

'Max—'

'Paige, with respect, Amanda is your job. She's my daughter. Obviously I should be the one to sort this out.'

Paige flinched. While his statement was accurate, it was also cruel, and it cut right down to the middle of her chest. Had she lost sight of her role here? Of the fact she was the hired help? Dispensable. Disposable. Just like always. Unconsciously, she pulled away a little, putting some physical distance between them to echo the emotional wedge he'd thrust into the space.

'That's exactly why you shouldn't.' Her voice was hoarse. She cleared her throat, ignoring her pain, knowing she could analyse and explore it later. 'You're too emotionally involved. Try to remember, the other girls who are in this are also just getting their training wheels, learning how to interact. The situation doesn't need hot-headed grown-ups racing down there pointing fingers. It's a learning experience. In the first instance, the girls should be encouraged to do better. If they don't, if this keeps happening, then you might want to consider upping the ante.'

'I can't believe this. I will pull her out of the school and—'

'And what?' Paige asked with genuine curiosity. 'Where would you send her?'

He hesitated.

'There are kids who make bad choices at every school. The only thing you can control is how Amanda manages herself, by teaching her resilience and perspective. Don't overreact.'

'What the hell are they teasing her about, anyway? There's never been a better kid, for Christ's sake.'

Paige dipped her head forward to hide her smile, but it was a watery smile, because again and again he demonstrated his love for his daughter, his total love, and the contrast with how Paige had been raised never failed to hit her right between the eyes.

'Well…' She hesitated, aware that the next statement would seem like a criticism. 'Actually, it really started off with swimming lessons,' Paige said softly.

'That was a couple of months ago.'

She nodded. 'Apparently Amanda was the only girl who didn't have a two-piece.'

'A two-piece? You mean a bikini?' He stared at Paige incredulously.

'Amanda says she got her bathers when she was much younger.'

'Right. Reg and Cass gave them to her.' He looked genuinely baffled. 'But she never said she wanted anything else. They still fit.'

Paige nodded sympathetically. 'Yes, they do, but they're bright pink with a neon yellow frill.'

'What's wrong with that?'

Paige put a hand on his knee, and avoided getting into an explanation of how young the bathers seemed to the other girls. 'And then, one of the girls came back after the holidays wearing a trainer bra, and all the other girls followed suit.'

'A trainer bra? They're kids!'

'Kids,' she said, 'are growing up faster and faster all the time. For this generation, that's normal.'

His Adam's apple shifted visibly as he swallowed.

'Paige was too embarrassed to ask you. For the bikini, or the bra.'

'Too embarrassed?' he repeated, then swore, dragging a hand through his hair and carefully dislodging Paige so he could stand, pacing to the edge of the veranda and bracing his hands around the railing. He cursed again. 'What the hell have I been doing wrong, Paige?' He turned to face her, his eyes haunted, and she knew he wasn't really seeing her, but was rather replaying every parenting moment of the last few years.

'Nothing,' Paige was quick to insist. She stood, moving towards him, wrapping her arms around his waist and pressing herself against him so she could feel the solid, if faster than normal, beating of his heart. 'This is *normal.* Girls—and boys, but more often girls—are jostling for social dominance. It's awful and hard to watch but it's *normal.* And short of pulling Amanda out of school altogether and completely curating her life for her—which is a fast track to failure because she'll emerge as an adult with no coping skills—you really can't do anything except what you're doing. And what you're doing so, so well, Max. I mean that. You love her. You clearly love her, so much, and she knows it. Nothing, nothing, nothing is going to build her up better than understanding that, no matter what happens at school, she can come home to you, that everything will be okay because you're here.'

He tilted his face away, a muscle jerking in the base of his jaw, emotion radiating off him. Tears filmed Paige's eyes. 'You're a really great dad.' The strength of her feelings was a sinkhole, threatening to pull her in. She needed levity, something to help lighten the mood. 'And I'm not just saying that because you're amazing in bed.'

He turned back to her, eyes heavy when they met

Paige's, but then he was smiling, and she smiled back, a melancholy smile laced with all the emotions that were rioting through her, that she hoped he wasn't able to see.

'Thank you.' He paused, lifting a hand and stroking her hair. Tingles spread through Paige like wildfire. His voice grew gravelled. 'On both counts.'

Paige pressed her head to his chest, listening to his heart. His hand stroked her hair, but it was his next words that made Paige feel a thousand and one things.

'I'm sorry no one ever loved you like that, Paige. I'm sorry your parents let you down so badly.'

Her heart stammered. She closed her eyes, hoping to push away the strange feeling that was stealing through her: that he was giving her something she'd always needed, a form of salvation that shouldn't have been his to offer. 'It's fine.'

'It's not fine. Hearing you talk about them, what you've told me, what they did to you—you deserved so much better. I think it's a miracle that you're such a patient, kind and loving person.'

But Paige wasn't loving. He was wrong. It often took all of her concentration to ensure she didn't slip up, that she didn't accidentally let herself love. For while she cared a great deal about her clients, and loved looking after children, she was always careful not to let love enter the equation.

'Thank you,' she said, quietly, because there was no sense reminding him of that now. She took the praise and buried it in a special part of her brain, for the very few memories she possessed that she liked to revisit, time and again.

'I just didn't want her to be like Lauren,' he said with a shake of his head, staring at the sand beneath his feet, phone to his ear.

'I know, man.' As always, Luca's voice was comforting, because Luca *knew* what Max was up against. He'd been there for the absolute disaster that had been their marriage. He'd seen Lauren's excesses, the destruction, he'd heard Max's worries about it even then.

'This was an epic ball-drop though. I mean, how did I not realise she always wears the same goddamned bathers? And she probably only even has that pair because Reg and Cass realised what she was missing and stepped in to help.'

'She has bathers. She has clothes. A roof over her head. And you're way more present in her life than Carrick was in ours.'

Guilt washed over Max. It hadn't been his fault, but whenever they compared their childhoods, he felt bad for how neglected Luca had been. Not that coming to live with their father had been any better.

'Besides, this is an easy fix.'

'Yeah?'

'Take her shopping,' Luca said with a quiet laugh. 'Not just shopping. Take her to Sydney. Hell, take her overseas. In fact, I've got a great idea.'

'Oh, yeah? I'm all ears,' Max muttered, in disbelief that he hadn't tweaked as to what might have been going on.

'Singapore has the best boutiques—at least, according to Mia.' Affection softened Luca's voice when he referred to his wife, clearly the love of Luca's life. 'I've got to go there this weekend to check on one of my developments. Come meet me. I'll bring Mia and the kids. They'd love to see you both. And you can spoil Amanda. Send her back to school with the kind of stuff those other girls will go crazy for.'

'I'm not going to make her think she has to earn their

approval,' Max responded quickly. 'Amanda's great. She's just lacking a few of the essentials.'

'Sure, but if you've overlooked those, then imagine what else she probably needs. She's almost a teenager, Max. It's not just about what's practical. She must want some clothes that are actually, you know, fashionable.'

'Sydney has good shops.' But at the same time, a chance to see Luca, Mia and the kids was hard to resist.

Max hesitated. Despite his misgivings that any kind of shopping spree now could be seen as a validation of the bullies' attitudes, his brother was right. Max had been getting Reg and Cass to organise clothes for Paige for almost as long as he'd been living out this way. And while she always had T-shirts and shorts, maybe she had reached an age and stage where she wanted dresses. Heaven help him, shoes with little heels? Handbags? He felt sweat break out on his brow as he stared down the barrel of raising an actual teenager, all on his own.

Something heavy lodged in the back of his mind, a feeling he couldn't quite make sense of. But when he thought about raising Amanda, weirdly, Paige was somehow threaded into that idea, as though she might be able to offer an alternative, more lasting support. Just as she had that night after they'd slept together, when he'd looked at Paige and his daughter cooking together and felt a weird sense of having come home.

But he wasn't about to outsource the parenting of his child, nor to start to rely on anyone else when it came to raising Amanda. Paige was amazing. A great addition to their lives, but she was temporary. He had to continue to navigate this mostly on his own.

'Okay. We'll come to you.' He frowned, thinking instantly of Paige, and what it would mean to travel with her, of how the life they'd forged at each other's sides would have to be put on hold for the next few days.

'You'll stay in the apartment with us?'

Max immediately dismissed that idea. Luca's luxury apartment was in a prime Singapore location with stunning views and Max generally stayed with Luca when he was in town, but it lacked privacy. In a hotel room—a large hotel penthouse—he could at least still get time alone with Paige when Amanda went to bed, just as they did here. Staying in the same apartment as Luca, Mia and their children, he'd feel as though it was impossible to slip away, and there was no way Mia would miss the signs of what was going on between him and Paige, and then there'd be a thousand questions and he was afraid he didn't have any answers. When he thought about what he was doing, the truth was, he simply didn't know.

'No.' He sought an excuse quickly. 'If I'm going to spoil her, I'm going to completely spoil her, just for one weekend—I'll book a suite at the Ashworth. I'll text you details once we take off. See you soon, Luca.'

He disconnected the call with a new-found sense of purpose.

Max, a man of action, was simply relieved that there was *something* he could do to make his daughter's life better, and to atone for having failed to realise that her needs were changing as she grew up.

But he could—and would—fix that.

And getting to share Singapore with Paige? a little voice in his head taunted.

Max grinned.

Better and better.

CHAPTER ELEVEN

IT HAD BEEN a stupid idea, Max thought with a scowl, at the end of a long day spent being close to Paige but unable to touch her. And, worse, she was annoyed at him. He didn't know why, but suspected she thought this whole idea was stupid too. Maybe she had a foresight he lacked, or maybe his initial instinct had been correct—that he was somehow teaching Amanda to bend to bullies.

He sure as hell didn't enjoy being crammed into his private jet—which had never felt small before, but with Paige and Amanda playing cards across the aisle, Paige's sleeve dropping down over her shoulder as she laughed so he ached to reach across and fix it, to brush his fingers over her bare flesh, to reach for her chin and tilt her face to his, to kiss her petal-soft lips. But he hadn't. He'd sat in his chair, like a block of ice, working, reading, staring straight ahead and willing away the hours into Singapore.

It was a seven-hour flight, so when Amanda fell asleep he'd had some hope that Paige might shift across to sit with him, or, better yet, suggest they move to a private cabin, but Paige drifted off almost as soon as Amanda had, leaving Max awake, alone, trying to concentrate but finding that near impossible with Paige across the aisle and so beautiful in sleep.

He realised he'd never seen her like this.

Sleeping.

Lips parted slightly, lashes so dark against her pale skin, hair pulled over one shoulder so again, his fingers ached to reach over and brush through it. Her shirt stayed loose, dropped down on one side.

His mouth went dry and his body tightened, every muscle on alert, hopeful, wishing…

He consoled himself with the knowledge they'd touch down soon, that the presidential suite he'd booked at the prestigious harbourfront hotel would offer more than enough space and privacy for him and Paige to be together.

Except it hadn't turned out that way.

Paige had settled Amanda into her room—after the flight and waking up for the drive into the city, Amanda was disorientated and a little upset, so it took Paige longer to get her settled, and then she'd evidently fallen asleep in Amanda's room, leaving Max with nothing to do but go to his own room and hope Paige woke at some point and came to him…

Only, she didn't.

The next day was spent shopping for Paige and Amanda, and in meetings with Luca. They inspected Luca's development, as well as the flagship Stone store in Singapore, and for some reason Max found it almost impossible not to talk to Luca about Paige.

Not about their relationship, just *about* her. About her life, her smile, her hair, how good she was for Amanda, how much of a difference she'd made to their lives. He found he wanted to talk about the small things, but instead, he was silent.

They ate dinner as a family.

Luca and Mia, their kids, and Amanda and Max.

No Paige. 'There's no need to include me,' she'd whispered to him, eyes flashing, so the first wave of misgivings began to form in his gut as he realised she was potentially avoiding him on purpose, rather than just owing to the circumstances of their trip.

By the time he and Amanda came home, he'd reached the end of his rope.

He missed her.

Not just physically, but all of her. He missed sitting on the veranda listening to the ocean and talking to her. He missed hearing about her day, listening to her speak about the kids she'd raised and her experiences in Dubai, and sometimes, when she was feeling particularly brave, her parents. He just *missed her*.

It should have served as a warning to end things, because at some point Paige would be gone for good and he'd have to get on with normal life, as it had been before.

And he would, he reassured himself quickly, determined not to worry about something he wouldn't allow to become a problem.

Besides, by the time Paige had to leave, he'd have worked her out of his system. It was just the newness of this. The connecting with someone after a period of such isolation and celibacy. Of course that was drugging and hypnotic. It wasn't really about Paige at all, so much as how pleasant it was to have another adult in his life to share things with.

Temporarily.

Only right now, that other adult was doing her level best to avoid him, and he was fed up with it.

Max Stone was not a man to be ignored.

Growing up, Paige had been surrounded by luxury, from the hotels she'd stayed at on location to the Hills home her parents had bought. But this was a whole other level. From the private jet to the limousine that had brought them through the stunning, modern city of Singapore and to this old-fashioned hotel on the harbour, to the presidential suite that was brimming with grandeur and classic elegance. It was also enormous, boasting four huge bedrooms, each with their own palatial bathroom, a ten-person dining table in the intimidatingly formal dining room, a small home cinema, a state-of-the-art kitchen and plush lounge room. There were several balconies, each boasting glorious views of the city in one direction and the water the other, so every angle held a feast for the eyes.

It was a level of decadence that Paige might have enjoyed if it weren't for her frustration with Max.

She knew what he was doing, and why. This was a knee-jerk reaction to what had happened with Amanda at school, and she supposed it was understandable that he'd respond this way. He could afford to, and there was no harm that could come from it. Probably. At least, not to Amanda.

But for Paige, it was the absolute opposite of what she'd wanted.

She'd taken the assignment in the far-flung Australian outback to get away from this sort of built-up civilisation. She'd wanted to be as removed as possible from the tabloids and TV shows, from the possibility of being recognised, of seeing herself on a book cover.

And instead, he'd brought her into the lion's den.

Which he had every right to do.

When she'd accepted this job, she hadn't specified an aversion to travel. This had been reasonably foreseeable, in fact, given Max's situation. She'd often accompanied families on holiday. And until now, that hadn't been such a troublesome concept. But Paige wanted, desperately, to hide out. To hide away.

And on the farm, in his tree house, she'd come to feel safe.

With just Max and Amanda forming the walls of her world, she'd felt in control of who she was, of how she was perceived.

This trip put her right out there again. Max probably hadn't even noticed but Paige had been horribly aware of lingering stares, of people looking at her today, wondering where they'd seen her, just as Max had. She felt more exposed than she'd been in years, all because of Max.

It was a blessing that no one had actually come up to her and asked if she was Aria Gray, but that didn't mean some enterprising person hadn't used their phone to snap a picture, which they'd on-sell to a tabloid paper, and the media frenzy would begin again, but worse, because she'd been with Max and Amanda and the possibility of their being linked would add so much fuel to the fire. All Paige wanted was a quiet life—and she would never have that if she was in a job that would involve this kind of trip.

She curled her fingers around the railing, breathing in the humid, tropical air, wishing with all that she was that she was back in Australia, or, really, anywhere other than this.

Misgiving swirled inside her and she couldn't quite put her finger on *why* she should be so annoyed with Max. True, he'd thrown her into a situation she'd specifically wished to avoid, but this was still Paige's job. He hadn't asked her to do anything outside the bounds of normal nannying work. He had simply been acting in what he perceived to be Amanda's best interests.

And not Paige's.

Realisation dawned and Paige made a little noise of surprise.

He had booked this trip without considering Paige. She'd told him about her life, her parents, the book, why she'd taken a job on the edges of the earth, and he'd booked this trip anyway.

He hadn't thought about how this might affect her.

And why should he have?

They were just sleeping together. They'd both been abundantly clear on that score. Why should he factor in Paige's needs at all? Let alone allow her needs to influence his plans? That would speak to a more significant relationship, to his actually *caring* about her; and that wasn't what their relationship was.

She swallowed past a wretched lump in her throat, surprised at how deep that wound went, at how his actions had been able to cut her deeply.

Worry began to fray the edges of her mind.

Worry because her whole philosophy in life was predicated on emotional detachment, on having the ability to control her connections to people and walk away whenever she needed to.

What if that was in jeopardy now?

She'd become good at caring for children without letting them claw too deep inside her heart. She clearly delineated what she did—as a job—and while she gave herself to it one hundred per cent, she never forgot her place, never forgot that she'd be moving on.

Something about Amanda was different though.

She was sweet, and hurt, and vulnerable, and Paige had needed to work hard to really tighten a bond with her, to earn Amanda's trust. But it was more than that.

When Paige looked at Amanda, she saw Max as well. His eyes, his stubborn temperament, his strength. She saw so many of the traits that were also in Max and those traits made her feel… She searched for the right word, shaking her head, exasperated when she couldn't properly untangle her emotions. Only she knew she did *feel* something, and that alone was anathema to her approach to life.

If she didn't care about Max, his lack of consideration of Paige's feelings wouldn't have rankled so much. But she did care, so it did hurt like hell.

With a soft groan, she spun to move inside, right as Max appeared at the wide French doors, stepping out onto the small balcony. His expression was impossible to misinterpret, his features locked in a mask that showed irritation and impatience, his eyes holding a warning. Paige, in the midst of desperately trying to fathom her own reactions, wished he would disappear again. It was all too much—the sense of overwhelm was huge.

'You're home?'

'We've been home twenty minutes. Amanda's asleep.'

Paige blinked. 'I didn't hear you come in.'

'Obviously.'

'Why didn't you come and get me? I would have liked to see Amanda. To say goodnight to her.'

'To take refuge in your duties to her, you mean? To hide from me again?'

Paige felt as though she'd been shocked with live voltage. 'I didn't—I don't know what you're talking about.'

'Come on, Paige. It's just the two of us now. Be honest with me. Why are you avoiding me?'

'I'm just doing my job,' she pointed out, the ground beneath her unsteady, because his accusation was justified and she didn't think it would be possible to explain what she was feeling without revealing something important—to herself, and him. She needed space to work out what was going on, damn it.

'You were doing your job back in Australia too,' he pointed out huskily, 'but you were also available to me.'

'Available to you?' she repeated, his choice of phrasing rubbing her completely the wrong way.

Something shifted in his eyes. Doubt? Uncertainty? Remorse? But it disappeared again quickly, the emotion replaced with arrogant certainty. 'We were both available to each other,' he conceded, arms crossed over his chest. 'What's changed?'

She turned away from him, staring out at the view, the beauty of the setting at odds with the turmoil inside her.

Realisations were coming at Paige like a runaway train and she couldn't move out of its path. Her head was spinning. She wanted to curl up under a rock, to run away and hide.

'I don't know what you're talking about,' she muttered.

'Oh, yeah?'

She did her best to feign innocence. 'Have I done something wrong with Amanda?'

'This isn't about—God, this isn't a job evaluation, Paige. I'm not talking about Amanda. I'm talking about us.'

Us. The train was screeching closer, the lights blinding, the clarity so close Paige could almost reach out and grab it, comprehension of her deepest feelings within grasp. But whenever she felt as if she was coming to understand herself, something shifted, morphed, so she no longer knew what she was feeling.

But the word 'us' sparked danger in her blood. She wasn't a part of an 'us', she never had been and she didn't ever intend to be.

'I think we've made a mistake,' she said slowly, but with firm resolve. 'Amanda has to be our priority.'

'She *is* our priority. I'm not criticising the way you are with her.'

Paige swallowed past a throat that seemed lined with

razor blades. Everything was wrong. Flashes of their time together blinded Paige, bursting into her consciousness.

She'd been so confident—arrogant—assured that she could control this, and all the while something about Max had weaved deep into her soul. And Amanda had done exactly the same thing, in a way no other child Paige had been charged with the responsibility of had managed.

Despite her best intentions, something about this pair had been too impossible to resist and she'd come to really care for them. To rely on them. To want them in her life.

So much so that the thought of leaving in a little over two months' time made her heart turn to ice.

It was one too many departures.

One too many goodbyes.

A single tear rolled down her cheek and she was so grateful her back was turned, that she was staring, troubled, out at the bay, rather than facing Max and this disaster head-on.

'For God's sake, Paige. Have I done something to hurt you?' There was desperation in his plea, as though hurting her would be the worst thing in the world.

She closed her eyes on a wave of unmitigated sadness. He really had no idea. And why should he? Nothing in his behaviour had been at fault. He had every right to book this trip, to expect his child's nanny to accompany him. He had every damned right.

The problem wasn't Max, it was Paige. She'd started to want more from him than he'd ever offered, to want the same protectiveness he gave Amanda to extend around Paige too. In the middle of the mess that was her personal life, she'd wanted Max to wrap his broad arms around her, to care for her, to show her that she could actually trust someone else with her heart, and even her life. She'd wanted him to realise the risks and discomfort to Paige, in joining him on this trip, and to factor that into his plans. To think about her, not as a nanny, or someone he was sleeping with, but as a woman he truly cared about.

He'd failed her, and he didn't even realise it, because her expectations were so wildly out of step with the reality of their dynamic. He'd failed her by not being what she needed—and she hated that she needed anything from him at all. He hadn't done anything wrong, and yet he'd hurt her.

Paige had come to Australia to run away from her old life, and now she wanted to run away from what she'd found in Australia: her own fallibility.

Her heart was vulnerable.

She was capable of loving, of wanting to be loved. It had just taken the right person—people—to make her see that.

'Damn it.' He was right behind her, his hands on her arms, turning her to face him, his eyes raking over her face, desperate to see, to understand, to know what had upset her, but Paige couldn't answer him, because all the answers were flying at her thick and fast and it was an answer she could never give him anyway, because she'd broken faith: she'd promised him she could be trusted, that everything would be fine, and, in the end, she'd lied.

Because despite what she'd told him, Paige loved Max.

Looking up into his eyes now, she saw it as clear as day. Every kiss, every moment, every conversation that had bared her soul to him and vice versa, Paige had been falling unknowingly in love.

It shocked and terrified her.

She lifted a hand to her lips, pressing it there, her eyes smarting from the tears she was desperately trying to hold in check.

'Paige?' But he was angry now, frustrated with not being

able to understand. 'Has something happened? Is there something more going on? Is it the book?'

She shook her head quickly. 'It was the book. Sort of. I was—I was—'

'You were what?'

He groaned, and he was so close to her, so achingly close, that everything seemed both complicated and simple at the same time.

'Just—forget about it,' she whispered, lifting up onto her tiptoes and kissing him. It was a kiss that obliterated thought and sense and all the parameters of the world as Paige had perceived them because she *felt* love. She felt it radiate through her body, permeate her soul, fundamentally change who she was. She was losing herself, just as she'd always been terrified of, but she didn't know if she minded, she only knew she couldn't stop. Not then. She couldn't walk away from him. From this.

It was all her worst fears come to bear but surrendering now was also the most sublime form of completion she'd ever, ever known.

It didn't sound, on paper, like something that should have bothered him, but the next morning, with Paige back to ignoring him, Max couldn't shake the feeling she'd used sex to avoid having a heavier conversation. That rather than explain to him why she was upset, she'd pushed their chemistry to the fore, and he'd let her. Hell, he'd needed her. He'd been driven mindless with missing her, wanting her. They'd made love and it had been so perfect, different, somehow, from before, perhaps because of whatever was going on with her. Or maybe it was because he'd had to reckon with how much he loved being with Paige when she'd become unavailable to him; her absence had made him grapple with how used to her he'd become. When she'd pulled away, he hadn't enjoyed it.

But they had more than two months left before her contract ended and, far from resenting the necessity of a nanny, he was praying his thanks to every god that existed for the fact she'd be with them for so long.

They would fly back to Australia the following day, and everything would go back to normal. It was the thought he comforted himself with throughout the day, whenever he'd look at Paige and she'd determinedly avoid making eye contact with him.

Everything would be normal again soon. He didn't want to analyse why that thought reassured him so much…

Paige's fingers shook as she sent the email, and the moment it whooshed out of the computer and into the ether her stomach dropped to her toes and she angsted over whether she'd just made a colossal mistake.

She was running away again.

She was scared, and she was leaving, because she didn't know how to stay and fight. Because she couldn't. She couldn't fight for a future with Max. He'd told her it wasn't possible, and while she might have *hoped* he'd changed his mind, as she had, she couldn't bear to think of what his rejection would feel like. Another rejection, but this one so much worse than any other. It would be the straw that broke the camel's back—or at least, broke Paige.

And so she would leave.

It would hurt like hell at first, but once she managed to put some distance between herself and this place, from Max and Amanda, and even bloody Reg, Paige would start to feel more like herself. She just needed, desperately, to get away.

CHAPTER TWELVE

MAX STARED AT his computer screen with the sensation the bottom had just fallen out of his world.

Dear Mr Stone,

I regret to inform you that for personal reasons Ms Cooper will no longer be able to continue with her contract. While such occurrences are rare, from time to time we do find our staff members' situations change for reasons beyond our control. Please accept my most sincere apologies for this. Ms Cooper has advised that her last day will be in one week.

I have attached the profiles of three different nannies who would be available immediately to replace Ms Cooper.

Please advise which staff member you would like to engage when you've had a chance to review their CVs, and if I can help with anything in the meantime, please do not hesitate to be in touch.

Best wishes

Nicholas Tankard, CEO

'What the actual hell?' he snapped into the air of his study, flicking his laptop down and scraping back his chair, staring at the door for about three seconds before prowling over to it and pulling it open as if the thing had done him some great personal wrong.

What the actual hell?

The house was silent except for the sound of his rough breathing.

He stormed from room to room, throwing open the doors, his mood worsening with each room he looked into and found empty.

At the back door of the house, he stared out, frowning mutinously at the darkening sky, the heat of the day sticky and oppressive, but he barely noticed any of those things. He was focused on Paige with a singular intensity.

He took the old timber stairs—rarely used—onto the lawn at the rear of the house, stalking past an enormous, ancient frangipani tree, a threadbare blanket of the tree's first flowers starting to brown at the edges. Max trampled them without noticing.

On the edges of the lawn was the rainforest, and a throwaway comment Paige had made a few days before Singapore reverberated through his mind. *'I'd love to explore it. I'll have to, before I go.'* At the time, he'd dismissed it, because of *course* there'd be time for that. He hadn't realised that she'd already been planning an early departure.

He ground his teeth, step quickening, sky darkening behind him. By the time he reached the edge of the rainforest, the first of the big, fat raindrops had begun to fall and the petrichor was instantly familiar to Max, who'd grown up with these sorts of tropical storms.

'Paige?' he shouted, anger tangling with worry now as he mentally catalogued the number of things that could go wrong in the rainforest for someone lacking experience. From snakes to spiders to leeches to slippery rocks, lantana, dangerous edges, fallen branches. 'Paige?' His voice ripped through the moss-covered tree trunks as he went deeper and deeper, his gut churning for a thousand reasons, none of them good.

She woke as if from a long, long sleep, eyes heavy, head fuzzy, and the first thing she noticed was that the light was so magical—almost green—and then, she heard it again. Her name, loud yet muffled. Standing, she moved to the edge of the attic where a small window showed a bird's eye view of this tropical paradise. Her heart twisted because she wouldn't be here for much longer to appreciate this stunning vista. She would always remember this place though; it was here that she'd realised something about herself she'd thought impossible. She wasn't so utterly destroyed that she couldn't love.

It scared her but, on another level, it also gave her hope.

Maybe, maybe this meant her future would be different from the grim one she'd always anticipated.

Except…how?

She'd felt love here, but it was love for Max and Amanda, for this place. Despite what Max had said, Paige didn't believe lightning would strike twice.

This alone was it.

When she left, her heart would remain behind.

Always.

'Paige?'

There was something in his voice, something awfully, blood-curdlingly panicked, so she was running before she realised it, out of the attic door and down the old narrow stairs, to the next level of this magical house, then down the next stairs, and the next, then out of the front door, onto the lawn, where she paused, panting, hands on hips as she waited, listening—where was he? Rain fell, heavy, and out to sea a blade of lightning sliced through the thick, leaden sky. A moment later, thunder rolled, so loud it vibrated in the pit of Paige's stomach.

And then, another sound—his voice, and from out here she could distinguish its direction: the rainforest.

She ran to the edges. Worry slicked her palms with sweat; at the barrier of the rainforest, it was much darker and cooler. The canopy was so thick it effectively blotted out almost all of the light, and the trunks were covered in lichen and moss and strange, green vines that almost looked to be strangling some of the thicker trees—she'd seen these in the photograph in Max's office.

She stepped across the threshold and amongst the trunks, peering into the forest.

His voice came again.

'What is it? Max?' she called, lifting her hand to her eyes to block the falling rain. Strangely though, the same roof of leaves that prevented light also slowed the rain, so only the odd drop got through.

Silence.

Worry built in her gut.

Where was he? She moved in deeper, but it was so dark, and the path had craggy rocks everywhere. 'Where are you?'

She stood still, listening, but all she heard in response was the call of a whip bird, and the splatter of raindrops—more now, as the weight on the leaves gave them a downward tilt.

'Jesus Christ, Paige, where were you?' He came almost out of nowhere, like a spirit conjured by this magical jungle of a place. But it wasn't a spirit, it was Max, her Max.

She closed her eyes, bracing herself for reality: he wasn't hers and never would be.

'What's wrong? What's the matter?'

'You don't ever come in here alone—do you understand that? This is not a safe place.'

She stared at him, confused, but there was so much emotion in his face, his eyes, the tightness around his lips, that she struggled to know how to respond. 'I only came in here because you were calling for me,' she said, eventually, shivering without knowing why. Despite the rain, it wasn't cold. The air was thick with humidity.

'What's happened?' she asked, wrapping her arms around her chest.

His eyes bored through her soul, lancing her with their intensity; Paige's shivering intensified.

'Would you care to explain this?' He reached into his back pocket and withdrew his phone, his hand slightly unsteady as he paused, scanning the screen before holding it up for her to see.

Her heart dropped to her toes. Paige had asked her boss to let *her* tell Max and Amanda. Evidently keeping the client happy was more important than looking after his staff.

'I can explain,' she whispered, lifting a hand to his chest, pressing it there, almost falling to her knees at how close she was to his rapidly beating heart, at her desperation for that heart to beat for her.

'Can you?' he demanded, stepping away from her, so Paige's hand dropped into the air between them. 'Give it a shot, then.'

She swallowed, brows drawing together, at a loss for words because, actually, *could* she explain? How could she tell him that she'd fallen in love with him?

She stared up at Max, mouth gaping, then shook her head. 'I have to go.'

His eyes flashed with so much anger that she almost did a double take. This version of Max was completely foreign to her. She'd never seen him physically reverberating with emotion before. A glimmer of hope lifted inside her, because if he was this angry, maybe it meant he did actually care?

Or maybe it meant his ego was smarting, she thought. Or that he was irritated at her reneging on their contract. Those options were far more likely.

She tried to remember what she'd planned to tell him, back when she'd put this plan in motion. A sanitised version of her thoughts that made it all so calm and rational.

'With everything going on in my personal life right now,' she began, haltingly, 'with the book, I just need to take some time to myself. I'm sure you can understand—'

'You want space?' He dragged a hand through his hair. 'Fine. Have your space. But stay here. You can still work for me. Be with Amanda. You and I don't have to continue our personal relationship.'

She closed her eyes, pain lashing her, because he said that so immediately and with such ease, as if he could simply flick a switch and shut down what they were doing. For Paige, there was just no way. If they were living in this house together, she'd be overwhelmed by her need for him, by her love for him. She'd want things that weren't, and never would be, possible.

'It's not that easy,' she whispered, the words almost completely drowned out by the forest.

'To hell it isn't. You're making it complicated.'

She gaped. 'How, exactly?'

'You said you came here to hide out. To get away from

that damned book. So what's changed?' he demanded, crossing his arms over his chest and staring down at her. The sound of falling rain was like the quickening of a drum, perfectly echoing the fast pace of her heart.

'Where are you going to go next, Paige? Antarctica?'

She flinched. He was so angry!

'Amanda needs you,' he said with quiet disgust, so her heart turned to ice. Amanda needed her. That was true, but it was also hurtful, because Paige wanted to be needed by Max too.

'I know,' she whispered, pressing a hand to her chest. *I need her too.* 'But she has you. She's doing better now. She'll be okay.'

'You tell yourself that if it's what you need to believe, but the truth is you're running away for your own selfish needs and, in the process, you're letting down a little girl who relies on you.'

She gasped and staggered backwards, one step, so angry, so hurt, so desperately, achingly sore. 'How dare you?'

'How dare *I*?' He glared at her. 'You're kidding, right?'

They stared at each other across the chasm of their emotions, the air pulsing with hurt, betrayal and a million unspoken words.

'You are incredible,' he said, shaking his head. 'I can't believe I ever thought—' The words stopped. He frowned, silenced, mid-sentence.

'You thought what?' Everything hinged on his response. Anticipation stretched, desperate, intense, in the very centre of her chest. The noises of the forest took on an almost deafening quality—crickets, rain, whip birds, a stream.

'That you were the answer to our prayers.' He spun around and stalked out of the forest, but at the edge, he stopped, hands on hips, staring a little way in, evidently waiting for Paige, who could barely think over the cacophony of her rushing blood.

'What does that even mean?' she shouted, making her legs work, moving towards him. 'The answer to what prayers?'

'You were so good with her. So good for her. I thought—I thought you were a miracle-worker, but you're just as selfish as her mother.'

Paige sucked in a sharp breath, her fingertips itching and then, before she could realise what she was doing, before she could stop herself, her hand lifted and struck his cheek, the slap loud even against the backdrop of the storm. Rain fell, drenching them, and they stared at each other, both shocked by what she'd done. His cheek changed colour, dark pink, and Paige's hand stung. She pulled back, disgusted by herself, by what she'd allow herself to become, but she couldn't apologise. She was too hurt, too angry.

'You don't know anything about me,' she said quietly to herself, as a defensive mechanism, self-protective, because she didn't want his charge to be true. She was putting herself first, though. Above him, and above Amanda, but only because she knew that if she didn't, the loss would be impossible to bear. She would wither away if she didn't go now.

'I hate you,' she said, surprised how satisfying that felt to say, when the truth was she loved him. Even then, in the midst of this, she loved him in a life-altering way, but she also hated him for what he was saying and for how he was reacting.

'I think that's mutual.'

Paige's gut churned. Her words had been thrown out carelessly, seeking satisfaction, but Max's? His, she believed.

She turned to face him, glad that it was pouring with rain, that she was saturated, glad because her tears were disguised by the raindrops. Only they weren't disguised, not really. Her eyes were a perfect mirror to her sadness and shock, showing anyone who would look at her just how she was feeling.

Max though didn't soften.

'Pack your things. Reg will take you to the airstrip.'

She stared at him.

'What?' The word was dredged up from deep inside her chest.

'You heard me. Go,' he shouted, pointing to the house.

She shook her head, lifting a hand to her lips to silence the sobs. 'I want to stay the week. I want to break this to Amanda. To say goodbye properly. To cook with her again, and explain—'

'Do not stand there and act as if you give a flying—anything about her. She's my daughter, and I'll look after her, just like I always have.' His features were like iron. She sobbed audibly now. 'Go!' he said again, voice rich with command and fury.

With her heart in shreds, Paige did exactly that, spinning on her heel and running back to the house, running so fast her feet kicked mud up against her legs, running, crying, utterly destroyed.

He shouted a curse word into the forest, closing his eyes as the last ten minutes replayed in his mind like some kind of horror movie. He'd set something in motion by coming out here when he was so angry, but he was still too angry to see that there was any alternative, to contemplate how to fix this. All he wanted was for Paige to go so he could concentrate on getting the hell on with his life. Without her.

* * *

The storm cleared in time for Paige's flight to take off, as if the same hand of fate that had brought her here to Max was also paving the way for her to leave, perhaps realising that their magnetic poles really didn't mix after all.

She stared out of the window of the light aeroplane at all of the things she'd come to love in her time here, at the scorched, orange desert now rendered dark brown by the rain, at the almost ethereal trees, dried out on the side of the dirt-track roads, no leaves, no life, and she felt a strange sympathy for them, a kinship, because she was sure that if there was a way to peer inside her soul, that was exactly what it would look like right now.

Withered, empty, lifeless.

'What do you mean, she had to go?' Amanda's face showed confusion.

Max wanted this day to be over.

He wanted to wash his hands of it completely.

Paige was still in the air of the house. If he closed his eyes he could smell her, see her. He half expected her to come walking through a doorway at any point, her beautiful smile, her sparkling eyes… His gut tightened.

She was gone. He'd made sure of that.

And what alternative had there been?

Let her stay until it suited her to leave?

Just roll over and have it all on her terms?

No.

It was just him and Amanda, like always. The two of them. He wasn't sure why he'd let himself start to see Paige as part of their team, but at some point, he had. It was a mistake.

She was a temporary fixture in their lives and whether

she stayed three weeks or three months, it didn't matter to him.

He repeated that to himself silently, sure that eventually it would ring true.

'Dad? You're kidding, right?'

'No, honey.'

'Dad?'

Amanda pushed her chair back, staring at him with teary blue eyes. His gut rolled, and rather than admitting how much he understood Amanda's feelings, he felt his anger surge. Paige had done this. She was supposed to fix things and instead she'd come and messed it all up even worse.

'I don't want her to go. I wanted her to stay.'

'She was never going to stay for ever, you know that. Paige just came to help out a bit.'

'And she was helping,' Amanda cried. 'I liked her. I loved her. She was so fun, and kind, and when I hugged her, I just felt—like everything was okay again. How could you do this?'

He felt as if he'd been punched. Not just because of the accusation but because of the way she'd perfectly articulated her feelings for Paige, and the way they somehow resonated with his own.

'It was her decision.'

'She would *never* leave without saying goodbye to me. I know her.'

He grimaced. His daughter was right; her faith in Paige was worthy. Paige had wanted to stay, to do this better, properly, maybe in a way that would have avoided Amanda experiencing this pain, but he'd forced her to leave earlier. For his own sake.

Who exactly was the selfish one?

He ground his teeth.

'There is no sense discussing this further.' His words were unnecessarily abrupt. He stood, moving into the kitchen and bracing his palms against the counter. 'She's gone. We'll be fine without her. Fine.'

'I don't want—'

He didn't want either, but it hadn't been his choice.

'Go to your room, Amanda.' The response was sharper than he'd intended. 'You must have homework to do.'

She shoved her chair into the table, stalked to the door. 'I hate you!'

He closed his eyes, despair a fog that was seeping into his cells. He was two for two, then, in both the most important conversations of his day. Just bloody brilliant.

'I knew she wouldn't leave without saying goodbye,' Amanda shouted victoriously, ten minutes later, stalking back into the kitchen and slamming a piece of paper down in front of him.

Max was standing exactly where he had been when Amanda left the room.

It took him a moment to focus his attention on the page.

Dearest Amanda,

Darling girl, it breaks my heart to leave you; I'm so sorry.

I came to Wattle Bay thinking I was just accepting another job, that you would just be another child, but you're not. You are so special, Amanda, and you are so very special to me. I have adored spending time with you, and I'll always be grateful for how you opened up to me. You are so brave.

I'm sorry to leave you. Please know that while I

won't physically be here, my heart remains in this magical, amazing place. I might be on the other side of the world, but you will be in my thoughts always.

Any time you want to speak to me, you can call.

With all my love,

Paige X

She'd included a phone number at the bottom of the letter.

There were also a couple of smudge marks to the ink. Tears?

Max found it hard to breathe. And then it occurred to him that if she'd left a note for Amanda, maybe, just maybe, she'd left a similar message for Max? Something to explain…to tell him… 'Where did you get this?'

'She left it on my desk.'

He stalked out of the kitchen without another word, down the corridor to his study, into his office, where he wrenched open the door, looked around and then slumped his shoulders.

There was no note for him, but what would such a letter say, in any event?

They'd spoken all the words, out in the forest, and those words had been brutal and eviscerating. From him.

'You're just as selfish as her mother.'

Was it any wonder Paige hadn't left a lovely little goodbye note in here for Max?

He groaned, pressed his palm to his forehead and tried to settle the feeling that he'd set the world spinning in completely the wrong direction.

Amanda had left the note on the bench and gone back to her room so when Max returned to the kitchen, he lifted it and reread it, more slowly this time. Certain sentences required him to read them a few times over.

It breaks my heart to leave you.

She'd promised her heart wouldn't break. That her heart didn't get involved when she was on a job. Did she mean what she'd written to Amanda? Or was she just trying to soften the blow to a vulnerable kid?

You are so brave.

He couldn't say why, but those words lodged in his brain, making something shift, something change, so he found it hard to think of that sentence without feeling a thousand and one things for Paige.

Please know that while I won't physically be here, my heart remains in this magical, amazing place.

He read that sentence many times.

Was that true?

It was like staring into murky water. He couldn't see a damned thing and didn't even know what he was looking for, but he knew he wanted the water to clear; he wanted to understand.

He drove himself half crazy that night, memorising the letter and listening to it in his mind, hearing it as though Paige were reading it, and as he fell asleep he imagined that the letter had been written to him, and not Amanda. It was a stupid, indulgent form of torture and he should have known better.

CHAPTER THIRTEEN

PAIGE HAD ENOUGH savings to take some time off. Not a lot, and she couldn't live luxuriously, but she could buy herself a bit of breathing room, rack up her credit card a little if necessary. She could take a break.

And that was exactly what she needed—something to stave off the constant sense of weariness. Only, in not working, Paige lacked occupation and purpose and, rather than having a reason to get out of bed each morning and face the long, lonely day, she found herself dithering, the days blending into each other, all as pointless as the next, everything lacking importance and urgency.

At least Sydney was a beautiful place to wait out her heartbreak—she could acknowledge freely that, yes, her heart was indeed splitting apart. Leaving Max and Amanda had been much, much harder than leaving her parents, than facing their betrayal. That had taken years and she'd had so many examples to look at to justify why she had to get out.

With Max, everything had been so perfect, except for how she'd fallen in love with him.

But then, there'd been that last day, and the way he'd acted, and the things he'd said, and she couldn't remember that fight without feeling as if she was going to fall over. It had been so awful. For his face to contort with anger and that anger to be directed at her!

Ten days after leaving the farm, she had no idea if she'd ever be able to put him from her mind, if she'd ever wake up without wanting to reach for him, without wanting to run to the kitchen to wait for him to appear. Without wanting to hug Amanda and cook dinner with her. Without feeling she'd briefly belonged to a family, even if that was just a fantasy in her head and heart. It had been the closest thing to a family she'd ever known.

Paige didn't realise she was crying until the tears splashed onto the backs of her hands, clasped in her lap. She stared at them, not surprised, not reacting, not bothering to wipe away the tears. They were par for the course these days. They would pass, just like the storm on that last day in Wattle Bay. But the feeling of loss would always be a part of Paige. At least it was something to hold onto, a reminder that yes, one time, she had loved, so deeply, she had known for certain that she was changed.

She'd been brought back to life—no matter how painful it was.

He hated himself for it, but in the end he bought her parents' damned tell-all book. He bought it because, after two weeks of missing Paige like a limb, he was desperate for *anything* remotely connected to her, and too proud to use the number she'd left Amanda and just call her.

Besides, what would he say? What had changed since she left? Nothing.

She'd run away. He didn't know why, but she'd left. He couldn't have changed her mind: he'd tried. Okay, admittedly not very well, but he'd made it obvious he wanted her to stay. She'd wanted to leave, more than she'd been willing to listen, and so he'd made her leave.

But just remembering the way her shoulders had sagged and her face had fallen when he'd shouted at her to go made shame swirl through him.

With a glass of earthy red wine on the table and Amanda asleep for the night, he began the gruesome job of reading the book written by her parents. Page by page, story by story, year by year of young Paige's life, he read about the woman he'd come to know, and it was like having the gaps of his understanding filled in. Not by the stories in the book. He wasn't sure they were accurate, nor was he sure they had any merit in the telling, but in the way her parents wrote about her, in what *wasn't* on the page, he came to understand more about Paige than he had before.

He came to understand what she'd been through, what it must have been like to be raised—no, not raised, so much as exploited—by people like this. People who were still trying to exploit her. In their stories, cynically told to paint Paige in the least flattering light possible, he saw through that, all the way to the heart of a warrior, of a girl who'd been rendered so vulnerable by her life's circumstances, but who'd fought back. How she'd fought back! That she was so strong and wise and capable was completely beyond belief. That she was capable of love, as she professed to love Amanda?

Remarkable.

He read the book through the night, until the dawn light filtered through the kitchen and the day awakened, fresh and golden, right as a different kind of awakening moved through Max. A fresh perspective.

An understanding, finally.

Now as he replayed their time together, and particularly

that last day, his comprehension was less certain, his own anger far less justifiable. His selfish stupidity completely unforgivable. But that didn't mean he was above asking for forgiveness.

If he knew anything now, it was that miracles were possible—you just had to be smart enough not to screw them up.

Paige didn't move when the knock came at the door.

She didn't know anyone in Sydney, and she didn't want any room service or any other kind of interruption. She wanted the world to go away.

She shifted on the sofa, lifting her feet up and pressing her chin to her knees, watching the daytime television without really seeing what was on. Some medical drama with far too much angst for Paige to enjoy it, but then again, she was hardly paying attention. It was just background noise as she tried to thaw out from the numbing of all her feelings and senses.

The knock came again, more imperative and demanding, an open-palmed punch almost. She flinched, turned the TV down.

'Go away, please,' she called out. Then muttered, under her breath, 'I'm not interested.'

'I need to talk to you, Paige.'

She froze, her heart in her throat, as the voice she'd been hearing in her dreams flooded her mind, made the hairs on the back of her neck stand on end, made everything hum as if with electricity.

It *couldn't* be Max.

She was imagining it.

It was her mind, playing tricks on her. She stood only because she needed confirmation of her insanity—maybe a hospital was a better place for her? She needed to know just how bad things were for her to conjure him up like this.

At the door, she hesitated just long enough to pull her hair over one shoulder—she couldn't remember the last time she'd washed it but thanked God she'd had a shower that morning and actually put on a fresh outfit.

Not that he was really here, she told herself sternly, wrenching in the door and expecting to see clear air.

But instead, she was confronted by the sight of Max, the same but different. Facial hair was longer, face was pale, eyes had a smudge of darkness beneath them. He looked as exhausted as she felt.

'Max?' Was it really him?

'I need to talk to you.'

She blinked at him, frowning, not understanding. In a monumental effort, she summoned every protective mechanism she'd built in her lifetime, wrapping herself in a shield, quickly trying to fortify her heart and soul. 'What? Why? Is it about Amanda?'

'No. Not directly.' His Adam's apple jerked as he swallowed. 'Can I come in?'

She shook her head instinctively. Memories were too intense, too strong. The power he wielded to hurt her was terrifying.

'Please.' He put a hand on the edge of the door frame, looking past her, a hint of desperation in his face. 'Just give me a few minutes.'

She shook her head again. Apart from anything, the tiny apartment she'd rented for the next few weeks was a mess, courtesy of the complete lack of a care she'd been capable of giving since flying into the city.

'You can't come in,' she said throatily. 'But there's a cafe around the corner. We can go and grab a coffee.'

He breathed out slowly. 'Great. That will be great. Thank you.'

So polite! Such a startling contrast to the day on the edge of the forest. She spun away from him blindly, moving back into the apartment, tears sheening her eyes. Her emotions were rioting all over the place.

'I'll just get my keys,' she mumbled.

'I'm sorry, what did you say?' Damn it, he'd followed her, he was right behind her, and the door swung softly closed, leaving them alone in the small, unimpressive space. His eyes flicked across the room, sizing it up in a few short seconds, then returned to Paige's face.

'Paige…' His voice was so gravelled and hoarse. 'Why did you leave us?'

It wasn't fair for him to be here! Not after two weeks. 'I can't—' She sucked in a breath, trying to calm her nerves. 'I can't talk about this here.' She needed the safety of others, of crowds, of strangers.

A muscle jerked in his jaw. He moved closer and she stiffened, terrified that he'd touch her and she'd combust. That her self-restraint and pride would fly out of the window.

'Don't.' She held up a hand, closed her eyes. 'Please don't.' She shook her head. 'How did you find me?'

'The agency.'

She lifted her brows, eyes pinging open. 'They're not supposed to give out our addresses.'

'I told them you'd left something personal I needed to get back to you.'

'You lied?' She shook her head. 'Why?'

'I don't consider it to be a lie. Paige, I want you to come home.'

Home.

The word was like a dagger to her heart. She spun away from him, staggering into the living room, sitting down because she wasn't sure she could stay standing.

'Listen to me.' He came to crouch in front of her. 'Listen to me, all of me, everything I say, before you react. Do you promise?'

She didn't think he was in any position to be asking her to promise anything, but she nodded because she wanted to hear whatever he'd come to say, and she needed some time to strengthen her nerves before she asked him to leave. *Go.* She shuddered as she remembered the way he'd ordered her out of his life. Her chin tilted defiantly as she did everything she could to stay strong against him, against his closeness.

So she nodded, and then, when he frowned, she wondered if he'd really expected her to agree, because he seemed momentarily lost, distracted, his eyes simply clinging to her face as if he'd never seen her before. She wore no make-up, she'd barely slept. Self-consciously, she wiped her cheeks and that seemed to pull him from his reverie.

'I miss you.'

She sobbed, tilting her face away. This was just too cruel.

'I miss you, every second of every minute of every hour of every day. I wake up looking for you, wanting you, needing you, looking forward to spending time with you, to being with you, to showing you places and things and experiencing them through your eyes, and then, when I realise you're gone, it's like losing you all over again, it's like reliving that awful fight we had, it's like walking through my very worst nightmare. When you came to the farm, I thought you'd be a temporary employee, someone who'd slot into our lives and then leave again without any difficulty. I couldn't *wait* for you to go, before you'd arrived, because I viewed the hiring of a nanny as a necessary evil. I didn't want to repeat the mistakes of my father. But you were nothing like I imagined. Nothing like I could have prepared for. You're not like anyone I've ever met.'

Another sob. She blinked away.

'Did you leave because you were scared of how much you were coming to care for us, Paige?'

Her tortured, aching heart. It was too broken. She didn't have the strength to lie, and so she lifted her head in a half-nod, her eyes boring into his, daring him to hurt her with that information.

'Because you were falling in love with me after all?'

Her throat hurt from the effort of not crying.

'Please stop this.'

He put a hand on her knee though, a gentle, sensitive hand, and her insides trembled.

'I read your parents' book.'

'What?' It was a plaintive whisper. Tears streamed down her cheeks. 'Why?'

'Because I missed you,' he said honestly. 'I was so desperate for anything of you, anything. I couldn't just call you after the way I'd spoken to you, I didn't even have a photo of you. So I bought the book and I read it last night.'

She closed her eyes. 'I don't want to hear about it. I've been avoiding the whole thing, you know that.'

'I do.' His other hand shifted to her cheek, gentle and caring. 'Paige, what you went through with those people…'

She jerked away from him, standing, trembling, moving to the small, grimy window that looked out onto a multi-storey car park. 'I don't need to hear this,' she said with a valiant attempt at strength. 'I lived it once.'

'I know. And you told me. You told me how awful they

were and how you had to divorce them and I didn't get it. It wasn't until I read the book that I really understood what your childhood was like, and what an incredible, unique, brave, giving person you are. That for you to have come through that, to have emerged with such strength and dignity, to have had the courage to write the life for yourself that *you* wanted, that you have had the ability to love at all, after that, I was blown away. You fell in love with Amanda. I know you did, because she showed me the letter.' He was silent. 'I think you fell in love with me too. I think you fell in love with me and you were so scared that I wouldn't love you back, that you left. Am I right?'

She closed her eyes, hating that he'd worked this out, hating how stupid she must seem to him. He was being so nice about it all, but Paige was mortified.

'So what?' she asked, spinning around and staring at him, hardly seeing through her tears. 'What good does it do to come here and have this conversation? Are you so desperate to understand that you'd really make me admit this to you now?'

'Can you really not see?'

She *couldn't* see. Not literally or metaphorically.

'Paige, you are the only lightning I've ever felt in my life. I have never known anything like this. You think that didn't scare me to hell too? I was so scared I didn't even admit the truth to myself until a few hours ago. But God, Paige, I love you. You have taught me the true meaning of love, you have been the answer to questions I didn't even know I had. You are a piece of me that has been missing all my life. That day in the forest, I was so angry I was almost out of my body. Even as we were arguing, I was shouting at myself to shut up and calm down, to stop ruining everything, but I couldn't, because I was standing on the precipice of the greatest loss of my life and I couldn't bear to lose you, Paige. I can't bear to lose you again.'

'I don't believe this,' she sobbed, but a different sob now, one of confusion and wonder. Was he being serious?

'Really?' He held his palms wide. 'Look at me. Just look. I have come here with more desperate longing and hope than any man has ever felt.'

'What do you want?' she whispered, still cautious.

'You were brave enough to fall in love with me. What I want to know is are you brave enough to live in that love? To let it be a part of you, your daily life, every day, for the rest of our lives?'

She gasped, shaking her head, because it was way too much. Way more than she could ever have hoped for. That he loved her was one thing, but that he wanted to marry her? Was that what he meant?

'Yes, damn it,' he said on a tortured groan, and Paige realised she'd spoken the question aloud. 'I want to marry you. I want to marry you two weeks ago, I want to marry you ten years ago. You are the missing part of me and now that I see that, I never want to miss you again. You're my family, Paige, our family. Amanda and I both miss you. We want you to come home. To *our* home, where you belong, where you'll always, always belong. Please.'

His voice was so rich with emotions, too many emotions for Paige to doubt his sincerity. She felt it radiating through her, seeping into her pores first, then her blood, and, finally, her heart, leaving no room for worry.

She nodded once and it was enough. Max strode the short distance across the room and lifted her up, arms wrapped around her middle, kissing her through salty tears, holding her tight to his body, holding her right where he intended for her to be for the rest of their days.

EPILOGUE

SUNSETS OVER THE beach were one of Paige's favourite things. It was strange, she supposed, that the ending of the day could make her think of new beginnings but it did, for dawn was an implicit promise in the going down of the sun. Or perhaps it was that here, in Australia, the colours were different from anything else she'd known before.

Two years after her parents' book was published, Paige could honestly say she barely thought of them. There were times when she was reflecting on her own family—married to Max, and a much-loved stepmother to Amanda—when Paige wished she had a better parenting model to base her own decisions on, but in those moments Max would simply remind Paige to follow her instincts. Her instincts, he told her, were always good.

And perhaps they were.

It had been instinctive to come to Australia. To be brave and let herself love Max even when that terrified her. To return here with him, quite simply, to come home.

And it was home: this tree house on the edge of the continent, with the ocean lapping at the cliffs beneath them. Two years after that awful time in her life, Paige could honestly say she'd never been happier.

Amanda met Paige's eyes in the mirror and grinned. At thirteen, Amanda was a beautiful, funny, smart and confident teen. While she had the occasional emotional outburst, it was abundantly clear that having Paige in her life had been good for the girl. They loved one another very much, and Amanda's friendship issues had settled down too, so sleepovers in the attic of their house had become a regular occurrence for Amanda and her friends.

'Are you ready?' Paige asked.

'Oh, yes.'

'You're sure this isn't too much?' Paige gestured to Amanda's outfit.

Amanda's grin widened. 'Don't lose your nerve now.'

Paige laughed. 'Okay, okay. Well, let's do this quickly, before your aunt and uncle arrive.'

Though they were happily ensconced in their life in Sicily, Mia and Luca were regular visitors to Australia, and their children had become a staple for Paige, Amanda and Max. Neither Mia nor Paige had ever had a sister, and yet they'd become that to one another, almost immediately.

Paige had given herself over to the idea of loving without limits—once she'd started, she'd found she couldn't stop, anyway—and in exchange, she'd received an abundance of love. From Luca, Mia, and their beautiful children—now her nieces and nephews. Her heart was full. While in an ideal world it would be the parents who loved and doted on a person, there was no guarantee this would be the case, and Paige, unable to change her past, simply accepted with gratitude the happiness of her present.

Downstairs, Max was putting the finishing touches on dinner. The sun was low on the horizon, bathing the kitchen in a golden light. Nerves filled Paige's tummy with butterflies, but when Max turned and smiled at her, they dissipated. Everything was okay. Better than okay.

'Max,' she said, reaching for an ice-cold glass of water

and taking a sip. 'I bought a new shirt for Amanda. I… hope you like it.'

A frown briefly flickered on his face. 'If you bought it, I'm sure I will.'

'I hope so.'

He arched a brow then turned as Amanda entered the kitchen. The shirt itself was oversized and a crisp white, so Max shrugged. 'It's nice.'

Paige nodded thoughtfully, nervous once more. 'Why don't you spin around, honey?'

Amanda's grin was pure cheek as she did what Paige suggested, so the back of the shirt came into view.

Big Sister—Coming Soon.

Max read the words without comprehending and then, a moment later, turned to Paige, jaw dropping. 'Does that—is that just the design of the shirt?' His voice was hoarse, thickened by emotion.

Paige shook her head.

'You mean—we're having a baby?' He looked from Paige to Amanda, a thousand emotions rushing through him. The last time he'd found out he was going to be a parent, it had been an incredibly conflicted time. He'd loved the idea of Amanda from the start, and had known he'd do anything and everything to protect her, but being tied to Lauren was not something he'd relished. Whereas, the idea of their family welcoming another baby, a baby that he and Paige had made together out of the deepest form of love…

'Say something,' Paige demanded, tilting her head back, so he was jolted into action, wrapping her into a big hug, holding her tight, his eyes meeting Amanda's over Paige's head. Their daughter was smiling, looking at them from a couple of metres away, and though Paige couldn't see Amanda, she held out her hand, reaching for her, so

Amanda joined them in the hug, their family, the most precious people in his world.

He was so happy he could hardly bear it.

Much later, after the Cavallaros had left and Amanda was in bed upstairs, Paige settled herself on Max's lap, out on the veranda, a beatific smile on her face.

'You, my darling wife, are an excellent secret-keeper. How long have you known?'

'Only a week,' she said, snuggling in close to him.

He let out a low whistle. 'A week!'

'I know. I wanted to tell you, it was so hard not to, but then I accidentally let it slip to Amanda and she came up with this idea—how could I say no?'

He shook his head, arms wrapped around his wife. 'You couldn't, and I'm glad. It feels right that she was a part of announcing it, not just to me but to Luc and Mia too.'

'That's exactly how I felt. I wanted Amanda to know that this is our news, not just yours and mine, but hers too. I never want her to feel excluded.'

He kissed the top of Paige's head. 'You are so thoughtful. Have I told you today how much I love you?'

She laughed, because these were words Max spoke often. 'Nope,' she lied, because she loved hearing it.

'Ah.' He grinned. 'How remiss of me. Then let me tell you, my darling, beautiful Mrs Stone, that you are my everything, and always will be.' He pressed a hand to her flat stomach. 'I cannot wait to meet the baby we have made together.'

Wait he did though, another seven months, and then, on a balmy, starlit night, at a hospital in the nearest city, in a fast and smooth delivery, Paige propelled their son from her body, clutching the little boy with his shock of dark hair to her chest. Love exploded through her—she felt it when she looked at Max, Amanda, and now their baby, the beautiful little boy that they named Everett, meaning strong, because he was every bit as strong as his parents.

Another baby followed within the next eighteen months, and, with their family complete, they found themselves spending most holidays and birthdays with the Cavallaros, whether in Italy or Australia, or Singapore, or France, or wherever the wind blew them. Paige no longer felt she had to hide from her past, from the fame that had been thrust upon her. It was a part of her history, her life, but it did not define her: she was her own woman, and her life was hers to curate and create, to fill with the people she loved, who loved her back fiercely, determinedly, and always would.

* * * * *

MILLS & BOON®

Coming next month

ACCIDENTALLY WEARING THE ARGENTINIAN'S RING
Maya Blake

Abstractedly, Mareka registered that they'd cleared the building, that they were out in the square with a handful of people milling around them.

But she couldn't break the traction of Cayetano's stare. His heavenly masculine scent was in her nose. The powerful thud of his heartbeat danced beneath her fingers, his breathing a touch erratic again after his gaze dropped to linger on her mouth, his own lips parted to reveal a hint of even white teeth.

And just like that she was once again thrown to that night in Abruzzo when this foolish crush had taken a deeper hold. When the only thing she'd yearned for, more than anything else in existence, was to kiss Cayetano Figueroa. Who cared that she'd sworn to be rid of this madness a mere…half an hour ago?

Half an hour ago…while she'd been choosing the engagement ring he intended to give to another woman.

Her eyes started to widen. He sucked in a sharp breath.

A camera flash went off, dancing off the diamond ring she'd forgotten to take off and illuminating their expressions for a nanosecond before immortalizing it in life-altering pixels.

Continue reading
ACCIDENTALLY WEARING THE ARGENTINIAN'S RING
Maya Blake

Available next month
millsandboon.co.uk